The Last Bookshop

First published 2021 by
FREMANTLE PRESS

First edition reprinted 2021.
This edition first published 2024.

Fremantle Press Inc. trading as Fremantle Press
PO Box 158, North Fremantle, Western Australia, 6159
fremantlepress.com.au

Cover images from iStock Photos / istockphoto.com
Designed by Hazel Lam.
Printed and bound by IPG.

 A catalogue record for this
book is available from the
National Library of Australia

ISBN 9781760993443 (paperback)
ISBN 9781925816310 (ebook)

Fremantle Press is supported by the State Government through the
Department of Local Government, Sport and Cultural Industries.

Publication of this title was assisted by the Commonwealth
Government through Creative Australia, its arts funding and
advisory body.

Fremantle Press respectfully acknowledges the Whadjuk people
of the Noongar nation as the Traditional Owners and Custodians
of the land where we work in Walyalup.

The Last Bookshop

EMMA YOUNG

 FREMANTLE PRESS

Emma Young has always traded in words. Armed with a BA in English Literature, she became a bookseller. When the customers finally wore her out, she retrained as a journalist. She is now a digital reporter for *WAtoday*, with work regularly appearing in sister publications *The Age* and *The Sydney Morning Herald*. Her eight wins at the WA Media Awards include the 2018 Matt Price Award for Best Columnist. After turning thirty, she burst with belated urgency into novel-writing and has since been selected for the Katharine Susannah Prichard Writers' Centre First Edition Retreat and the Four Centres Emerging Writers Program. In 2019, *The Last Bookshop* was shortlisted for the inaugural Fogarty Literary Award.

For Mum and Dad, who encouraged a bookworm

ONE

It was already five past nine, but the shop was dark. Sebastian was late.

'Damn you, Seb,' Cait said aloud, unlocking the doors and propping them open with the stone Snugglepot and Cuddlepie statues she'd bought from a Gumtree seller some years back. They were stupidly heavy and sadly battered – Cuddlepie's nose had been bashed off somewhere along the line – but Cait was still delighted with the purchase. 'I know they're not exactly beating the doors down on a Saturday, but I can't afford to be missing out on passing trade while he's getting his act together,' she told Snugglepot.

She flicked on the lights and started hauling out the first of the two front trolleys. Made by the same carpenter who had made the rest of the shop's fittings, each had four wheeled legs supporting a large, shallow wooden tray at waist height. Cait had filled them with rows of books standing face-forward, leaning back like slanted dominoes, for display outside. She had hand-picked every title. Impulse buys, little joke and gift books: 1001 songs to listen to in love, another 1001 for breakups, 101 countries to visit when you finally manage to get off your arse and stop wasting money on impulse buys. Et cetera. But also novels and nonfiction, teasers to hint at the vast range of stock inside.

The trolley's weight pulled it swiftly down the ramp, Cait struggling to hang on to it and not let it career across the road to the cafe opposite. The street looked sad and stained in the morning light, stripped of both its night wildlife and weekday rat-race. It was too early for most of Perth's sleepy centre to be open on a Saturday. The cafe was pretty much it. But it was doing a roaring trade, thanks to the brightly coloured cyclists who packed it like exotic birds, their bikes parked in a big drift on the footpath. They yelled genially at each other, holding conversations over the crash of plates and the screaming coffee grinder. Cait went in for the second trolley. Now she'd been hauling them in and out for years, they were rickety and their wheels were stiff. They were the only fitting that hadn't really worked for her. She thought about getting rid of them every morning when she put them out, and every night when she brought them in.

'Pain in the arse,' she told Cuddlepie now, as she butted the second into place beside the first. But just because she was grumbling about them didn't mean she would actually ditch them. Cait disliked change, especially in her shop. Her daily fantasy about setting the trolleys on fire and sending them flaming down the street was just another part of a gloriously reliable routine.

She went back in, pushed the big casement windows facing the street wide open and hefted the *Open* sign out onto the pavement. The steel A-frame was as heavy as the trolleys but she'd picked it on the advice of Phil Crabbe, the chemist who'd been her next-door neighbour before Gucci shouldered him out. 'This street is almost as windy as the Terrace,' Phil had told her. 'It's because of all the tall buildings. And not enough trees to slow the wind down. You need a good heavy sign like mine.' And he'd written down the name of his signmaker for her. The sign bore the shop's name, Book Fiend, at the top in the same angular Gothic script that was painted on the facade above the doors. Below it was chalkboard. She had no time today to find a new quote, so she left yesterday's chalked on it: *A book must be the axe for the frozen sea within us – Kafka.* Bit esoteric, maybe, but what the hell; there were plenty of pretentious gits up this end of town to appreciate it. And it was her shop, after all. She looked fondly back at it, its windows flung outward like beckoning arms.

Her first order of business when she'd opened had been to make the shop welcoming, and she figured she'd nailed it. Behind the front windows, the first third of floor space was open plan, full of display islands radiating outwards from the central front table: her pride and joy. The back two-thirds contained library-style stacks for the second-hand stuff. That had been another must, selling second-hand alongside new. It allowed for the kind of serendipity she just couldn't get in choosing stock from catalogues alone. And it gave her customers that sense of infinite possibility, that thrill of treasures lying maybe just around the next dusty corner, or perhaps the one after that. You only ever got that in a second-hand bookstore.

Among the stacks were scattered armchairs: mismatched, squashy things with lamps hanging obligingly over them and tiny wooden coffee tables beside them, functioning as rest stops for browsers and also for Cait to put things on while she was stocking shelves. She never had enough hands. Though by now she did have a ninja-like ability to sense when a book was about to fall off a shelf, and to catch it on its way down. Annoyingly, this skill did not carry over into any other environment. She'd need to think of another party trick, should she ever again have the misfortune to find herself at a party.

Surrounding it all, lining the walls, were floor-to-ceiling shelves, whitewashed and crammed with the new stock, all crisp and shiny and sweet-smelling. They might not have the chancy mystery of the preloved, but then, the old ones could never bring this sense of pure, white-paged, black-inked newness, the latest releases stacked ten deep, their very abundance suggesting they must be the next big thing. The upper levels around the walls were reached with rolling ladders mounted on tracks so Cait and her customers could push them wherever necessary. It was essentially the dream library Cait would never be able to afford at home, made flesh in a Hay Street shopfront.

Today, Cait's own flesh was hot. Already. The air-con had been struggling lately, not helped by Cait insisting on leaving the windows open. She should ask Seb to climb up and have a look at the filters. Where the hell was he, anyway? She went to sort out the till, wiping the trolley dust from her hands onto her jeans. She'd jettisoned her usual top-to-toe blacks in honour of the weekend. Today it was blue jeans, once-white tennis shoes and a loud red singlet that clashed violently with her hair, a mane of wiry copper usually twisted into a knot for practical purposes, but today let run riot in a what-the-hell mess. That was the nice thing about the mobile clients. Old people tended to think you beautiful just because you were young and able-bodied. And around them, it was easier to appreciate that yourself. There was plenty Cait loved about Book Fiend's location, but the place did little for the self-esteem, being awash each day with coiffed young office ladies whose YouTube-enabled hairdos, held in place by invisible means, were as finely crafted as the tall takeaway lattes they clutched as they stalked about the shop on their lunchbreaks. The daily parade of the well-dressed never failed to make her feel as though she should make more of an effort, but thankfully the feeling was usually fleeting and today, entirely absent.

Cait was about to focus on the till when finally Seb galloped up, trailing satchel, earphones and ropy dreadlocks. Seb's stovepipe body in black skinny jeans, topped by its shock of long dreads, always put Cait in mind of a young and vigorously growing palm tree. She put on her sternest face.

'Sorry! Sorry-sorry-sorry, Cait,' he said, leaping behind the counter and stowing his tangle of stuff with one hearty shove. 'Slept in.'

'Must've been nice,' Cait said. 'I, on the other hand, got up early to make sure I had plenty of time to come in here and pick out the books for the mobile clients while you opened. Which I didn't have time for last night, because after a dead-quiet day, the Friday night crowd decided to come in and trash the place, and I was too busy keeping it tidy for you so you didn't come in to a disaster zone.' She felt it appropriate, as owner and boss, to be a bit strict with Seb sometimes. But, God, he had that puppy dog routine down pat.

'Give me your most horrible jobs as punishment,' Seb said, lifting his chin as though prepared to accept justice nobly. 'Go on. Name it. Thy will be done.'

'Well, get on with counting that, and I'll go pick the books, and then we'll talk.' She left him counting coins and went into the stacks. She was now a bit pushed for time, but at least she already had some ideas. A day of mobile clients could sometimes be worth as much or more than a day's takings in the shop, and the shop was not doing so well right now that she could afford to let the quality of her selections slip. And, while she needed to keep the mobile clients happy for financial reasons, it was about more than money; it was a matter of pride to her to get it right, and not come back with a reject pile.

First, June, who had been laid up with the flu. She had downplayed it on the phone, but she must have been quite ill because it took nothing short of an earthquake to keep June off her feet. She had probably long since run out of books to read – June was completely incapable of lying down and doing nothing – so she would need a big haul. Cait could head straight towards her first choice.

Last time, she'd brought June the entire Chronicles of Narnia series. It had come out in an irresistible new special edition, all seven books in one volume, and the sheer beauty of the fat, gold-stamped hardcover had lured Cait not just to give it to June but to re-read the series herself. She hadn't read it since she was a kid, when she'd fallen headlong into that warm, lively evocation of English childhood – the truest escapism an Australian child could get – combined with the fantastic realism of the world C.S. Lewis created, in which unforgettable good guys and bad guys had spellbinding adventures in the land beyond the wardrobe. The wintry evil of the White Witch, the mighty reassurance of Aslan, the sweetness of the incorruptible Lucy: these were some of the most alluring and enduring characters Cait had ever encountered.

Revisiting Narnia as an adult, she'd realised it wasn't just the adventures and the characters that had captured her. There were darker themes here, and they'd completely passed her childhood self by, on a conscious level at least, but now she saw the reach for greater truths that had resonated so deeply.

This new appreciation had sparked a curiosity that prompted

Cait to next read a biography of Lewis, whose body of writing had gone way beyond his children's works, covering theology and criticism and academia, and had immense influence on the world. She'd loved the biography nearly as much as the Narnia books, and would lay money on it that June would feel the same way, so she was bringing a copy today. And, in a beautiful example of the synchronicity that was one of the best parts of her job, only yesterday had come in three colourful little matching paperbacks, with vintage covers and brittle spines: Lewis's first three novels, all sci-fi, possibly even out of print. She hadn't had time to google it, but she'd never come across them before. It gave her a little pang not to put them straight on the front table, but she had to at least offer them to June first.

She grabbed them from where she'd secreted them out the back. Right, that did it for old stuff. She needed something a bit shinier to balance it out. She skirted round to the walls, the floorboards under the threadbare carpet creaking beneath her feet, and scanned the literary fiction. The opening notes of Led Zeppelin started coming through the speakers, at an appropriately subdued volume. The first album – one of Seb's shop go-tos. She pulled out Yann Martel's *The High Mountains of Portugal* from the new releases and added *Amnesia* by Peter Carey. June was behind in her Careys. She paused at the Ds. More Don DeLillo? It would be a risk. The man was widely accepted as a genius, but his books often lay somewhere between postmodern and downright surreal. June had liked *White Noise*, and so last time Cait had brought her *Underworld*, an absolute doorstopper. Maybe she'd wait and see how June went with that before bringing his new one. Following the wall back, she picked up something on a whim. Umberto Eco's *On Literature*. A mix of philosophy and literary criticism. Dense, no doubt, but a beautiful hardcover, and maybe June would like a stab at it, given Eco's death had been in the news. She checked the time on her phone and saw she'd have to be quick about getting Max and Dorothy's stuff. She put down June's pile, which was getting heavy, and went over to the general and crime fiction. Max had recently worked his way through the Dark Tower series as well as *Mr Mercedes*, so more Stephen King probably wouldn't go astray. She pulled out *Finders Keepers*, the sequel to *Mr Mercedes*, and *Doctor Sleep*, the follow-up to *The Shining*. Wait, had Max read *The Shining*? She grabbed that too, just in case, and some Joe Hill for good measure. Now, she needed straight crime. She picked up the new Poirot mystery by Sophie Hannah. That should rattle him. She grinned to herself. Then she did a quick lap of the second-hand stacks and saw a well-worn *LA Confidential*. Well, if he hadn't read that already, he certainly should. OK, Max done. Thankfully, she had already had an idea for Dorothy, and it only took a minute to gather the final pile. She dumped it all into a box Seb had waiting for her at the till.

'Reporting for duty, ma'am. Don't hold back.'

'Well, since you're asking for punishment, I think the air-con filters need clearing. And there are six boxes of comics out the back that came in yesterday. You could sort those and ring the guy and let him know how much credit we'll give. If he's cool with it, process them and put them out. Mmm, what else?' She cast her gaze around. 'Just cleaning, I guess. The dust is back up to eyeball level.'

'Can't let the bunnies breed,' he said. 'Want a hand out to the car with that?'

'Nah. It's not that much. No nursing home today, just June and Max and Dotty Dorothy.' It was impossible to keep up the stern tone. She couldn't stay mad at Seb, despite his elevation of tardiness into something approaching an art form. 'Make me some money today, all right? It's been quiet all week.'

Seb saluted. 'Charm officially turned on. Say hi to June for me. Oh! That reminds me.' He dashed off into the stacks towards the sci-fi. Seb was nuts about sci-fi. Early in his employment he had amused himself on a quiet day by micro-classifying the large and chaotic section into sub-genres: dystopian, climate change, space opera and cyberpunk. He had earnestly explained to Cait that cyberpunk had itself spawned numerous sub-genres: steampunk, biopunk, nanopunk, postcyberpunk, atompunk, clockpunk, dieselpunk ... even splatterpunk, a gory, horror-like sci-fi.

'Like Clive Barker?' Cait had asked. 'I've got him in Horror.'

'Well, you could do that, too,' Seb had replied, with an air of humouring her. She hadn't had the heart to tell him there was no way those shelf divisions were staying, resolving to let them dissolve back into chaos on their own. But Cait couldn't deny he'd proved there was a strong market for well-chosen sci-fi and fantasy. She now let him do the stock orders for those himself.

He re-emerged from his domain now with a book in hand. 'Tell her she should try this.' Cait looked at it doubtfully. *Ender's Game.* A classic by a master of the genre, but it was still genre, and technically a kids' book at that. June was less gentle with Seb than Cait was. Her refusals of all the titles he tried to recommend were decidedly unvarnished. But the perennially good-natured Seb saw this as a challenge, and from the messages the pair now passed back and forth through Cait, Seb's persistence and June's rejection were only endearing them to each other.

'You've got no chance,' she said. Seb put it in the box as if he hadn't heard her. 'All right, I'll suggest it, but you're a glutton for punishment.'

'Have a good day,' he replied, with a sunny smile.

It was early enough that she'd been able to park right outside at the kerb without paying or fighting for a space. Sluggish takings aside, there were definitely positives to living in a city still fifteen years off reaching the size of Melbourne, or so they said.

The sun, already hostile, lit up the dings and scrapes on her car. These scars, and that other embattled traveller, Arthur Dent from *The Hitchhiker's Guide to the Galaxy*, had inspired its nickname: Dent. She dumped her box on the passenger seat and started the engine. The cracked old vinyl on the steering wheel was hot to the touch. Damn it: almost nine-thirty already.

TWO

Partly due to her disinclination to break routine by being late, partly out of a guilty love of speeding, Cait flogged Dent at 110 up the freeway to June's, an old, bush-fringed house in Perth's sprawling outer northern suburbs.

Her parents had hired June as nanny when Cait was less than a year old. Cait's dad, Ken, worked FIFO and her mother, Tania, had returned to working long hours as soon as possible after Cait's birth so they could pay off their Maylands townhouse, so it was June who was most present throughout both Cait's toddlerhood and the afternoons of her school days. June passed her love of books on to Cait, introducing her to classics of children's literature and enduring with infinite patience her Baby-Sitters Club phase, her Saddle Club phase and her insistence on reading possibly every English novel ever written about young, pony-owning girls. Cait had read many of these aloud to June while this real-life babysitter did the ironing, fondly believing she was saving June from boredom, which she may have been. Then June would move into the kitchen and Cait would melt away to a corner of the couch, curl up and keep reading alone. There she would lose all consciousness of the real world and only look up, in vague surprise, as June would finally tire of calling her and arrive in the lounge, hands on hips, to tell her dinner was ready.

June's demonstration to a smart and introspective child that books could be a way of life, more than just ten minutes at bedtime, had been if anything a little too successful. Cait found both June and the characters in her books easier to understand, generally speaking, than the girls at her school. Their giggly, sometimes catty conversations, and the games and brief crazes that seized their break times, both bored and baffled her. The boys were equally mystifying in their predilection for intimidating sports that involved running round the oval, throwing balls, catching them and sometimes – most terrifyingly of all – hitting the balls with bats. By Year Three, she was spending most breaks either in the school library or cross-legged on the playground's concreted edge with a book, remaining engrossed until the bell rang. Eventually a well-meaning teacher intervened, telling Cait she wasn't allowed to read at lunchtimes anymore, that she needed to 'socialise'. Cait had not agreed, but eventually she had learned to fit in just enough to avoid unwanted interventions like these. She found solace and understanding in her friendship with June, which lasted long past her childhood and her parents' divorce. Eventually, when Cait had opened Book Fiend, the roles of her childhood were reversed: it was now June whiling away afternoons in Cait's domain, reading and poking around, while Cait got on with work and tidied up behind her.

As Cait left the arterial road and entered the fifty kilometre per hour zone, she barely noticed her surroundings, so familiar was she with the drive. But it was undeniably a long one, and June's increasing difficulty in making it as she passed eighty had partly been what motivated Cait to start the mobile service. The idea had come from her friend Sylvia Rose, who had worked at Dymocks with Cait before returning to university to qualify as a librarian. She now worked in the state library, but still visited Book Fiend to browse undisturbed and trade stories from the trenches.

Inspired by Sylvia's description of the library's home delivery service, Cait had taken the concept and run with her own version, testing it on June then contacting nursing homes and putting a running notice in the community newspapers' free diary sections to capture elderly people who lived independently. Soon she had more than enough clients to fill the time available for the service, and it had the added bonus of keeping her visits with June regular. The discussions that began over the ironing board in Cait's childhood, then moved to June's back patio, then to the Book Fiend counter, had finally circled back to the patio. But they retained the flavour of childhood routine: June always had a tea tray ready for Cait, with biscuits or scones, and their preferred brand of Irish breakfast.

Cait arrived at June's late, but June had an apparently supernatural ability to time things for her arrival. The old lady was in the kitchen, pouring boiling water into a teapot. Steam rose in the sunlight streaming through the window. Fat, golden-brown biscuits sat on a saucer, jam glistening in a little depression the size of a thumbprint atop each one.

'June, you absolutely should not have. I keep telling you not to take this kind of trouble!'

'Yes, you'd think by now you'd have learned I'm not paying attention,' June said, passing Cait the tray and grabbing her walker. She led the way to the patio. 'I'm not too busy to bake.

I've got nothing else to do and it's the least I can do to feed you. Seeing as visiting me makes it six days you're working, and earning bugger-all money for it.'

'Client days aren't so much work. More like a Mad Hatter's tea party, going around eating teas I didn't order and talking to people who pay no attention.' Cait put the tray down on the patio table and went back inside for her book box. She chose not to argue June's point about having nothing to do but bake, though it was patently untrue: even at eighty-four, June still sped between activities from dawn till dusk like a sharp-tongued wind-up toy. She also ignored the comment about her earning bugger-all money, which was true, though she didn't know how June knew it. Maybe June was reading all the news on her beloved iPad about the pitiful state of the bookselling industry, not to mention retail in general; retailers were collapsing across Perth like houses of cards. Or maybe June was judging by the state of Cait's clothes, whose rattiness revealed quite as much about her income as they did about her personality. It was very hard to hide anything from June.

Returning with the box, Cait heard June chuckling, evidently delighted at the image of herself as the Mad Hatter. Nothing brought colour to June's cheeks like a sparring partner. 'Mad, is it? You be careful, my girl, or no jam fancies for you next time.'

Cait sat down with the books and picked up a 'fancy'. It was fresh and warm and soft and crumbly, oozing apricot jam. 'You wouldn't deprive me of your jam fancies,' she said around her mouthful. 'You just said so. How are you, anyway? Over the flu?'

'All right now. But I've been going crazy with boredom while I've been laid up. And now the place is a mess. The roses out the front have needed beheading for two weeks; the whole garden looks atrocious. The neighbours are probably already plotting to have me committed. Cart me off to the old folks' home, buy me out and subdivide.'

'Atrocious might be a strong word,' Cait said, looking at the garden before her with its flawless lawn and riotous bougainvillea. The lawn never went brown like every other in the city, thanks to June's constant vigilance, her complete disregard for Water Corp reticulation days and her obsessive use of a supplementary portable sprinkler, which was even now rotating nearby, hissing gently. Cait poured the tea, taking pleasure in the delicate china set. Like nothing she had ever owned, or ever would, most likely. 'I take it you've finished the last lot of books, then, if you've been so bored?'

'Lord, yes, I'm all out and I have been for a week. I got so desperate I almost – almost, mind you – switched on the TV. So you've arrived at the critical moment, and you'd better have a good big haul.'

'I took the liberty of going overboard.' Cait clinked her teacup carefully back onto its saucer, and picked up the first book.

'Good girl,' said June, pushing aside her tea and stretching out both hands.

Cait withheld the book. 'First, tell me about Narnia. Did you like it?'

'Oh! I haven't told you. I think that was my third go at it, but, yes, it did take me right back to my childhood. Having said that, those stories are timeless, aren't they? I declare, they waste the best stuff on children, when it's the rest of us who really need the magic.'

'Oh, I totally agree. But they go far beyond fantasy, right? Not to mention they're way more sophisticated than what you'd expect from kids' books. Like, this is now classic literature.'

'Yes. They are layered. With every new read, it's like ...' June paused, 'You see more.'

'I know! All that stuff about religion and war? I definitely didn't notice that stuff as a kid. I just don't think anything like this has ever been done again – not in a children's series. Not even Harry Potter ... though I don't mean to be disloyal.'

'I still won't go so far as to read those, no matter how many times you suggest it. But I do agree that Narnia was an inspired choice. Happy? Now give!'

'All right. I just wanted to make sure I was on the right track with this.' She handed over *C.S. Lewis: A Life*.

'Ooh, yes! I'd love to find out more about him. Well, he was religious, that much is bleeding obvious.'

'He was, but the rest might surprise you,' Cait said, taking another biscuit. 'Like, did you know he started out an atheist? A *raging* atheist. And he was close with Tolkien.'

'J.R.R.?'

'Of course J.R.R. It was actually Tolkien who got him to convert to Christianity. In a drunken four a.m. conversation no less, when they were young. And then, it was Lewis who convinced Tolkien to carry on with *The Lord of the Rings* just when he hit a tough patch and had pretty much given up. Just think, the world might never have got Narnia or *The Lord of the Rings* if not for two encounters between friends. One night of drinking and arguing for Lewis. And another day of encouragement for Tolkien. How's that for a backstory?'

'You're telling me all the good bits. No point in reading it now.'

'I promise you I'm not. It's an awesome read. Now, drumroll.' Cait bent back down to the box. 'Here's my trump card. These were Lewis's first ever novels. I haven't read them, but aren't they gorgeous? And you will notice that I am offering you this vintage set instead of overcharging for them on my front table. Watch the spines, they're brittle.'

'Well, I don't normally go for space books, as you well know … and you forget that what you call a vintage cover isn't as exciting for a vintage *reader* … But I have to admit, you've got me intrigued.' June added them to her yes pile and took a sip of her tea. Then she got up and started to move, slowly and sideways like an elderly crab, towards the lawn, intent on repositioning the sprinkler. 'Good lord, I'm going to have to start using that frame more.'

'I can move that for you.' Cait started up from her chair.

'Get away with you,' June said, flapping a dismissive hand. She inched over to the sprinkler, moved it a couple of metres over, then made her way safely back to the deck, where Cait was unloading the rest of her stash.

June's eyes widened at the height of the stack of books Cait thunked down on the table. She leant forward and scanned the titles. 'I did say I wanted a haul, but you know I'm an old woman, don't you, Cait? I'll be six feet under before I finish these.'

'Don't be ridiculous. You'll be ringing me up next month, asking to reschedule because you've just decided to fly to Singapore and go to the casino.'

'Now that you mention it, it has been a while since I got over there. I've barely even made it to bingo lately,' June said thoughtfully, with the unmistakeable air of someone making a mental note to buy plane tickets to Singapore.

'Do I take it you want the lot, then?'

'Yes, go on. And pour us another cuppa, because I want to know something else.'

'What?' Cait said, pouring, and then taking a third biscuit.

'What I want to know is, how's the love life going?'

Cait choked a little, spraying crumbs on the immaculate decking.

'What do you mean, how's the love life? What love life? And since when have you wanted to know?'

'Lord, Cait, since now!'

Cait tried to think of how best to answer this question in a way that did not sound pathetic. She couldn't. 'Well, there is no love life.'

'Why's that?'

'I don't know!'

'Well, are you happy?'

'Of course! I've got Macduff, I've got the shop –'

'I'm not talking about your cat, Cait. Or your job. Or your other clients for that matter. You're a thirty-three-year-old woman. I want to know if you've got anyone to take to bed.'

'Well,' said Cait. 'As it happens, I took a man to bed just the other night.'

'That's more like it. Who was this man?'

'Well, his name was Jack.' Cait smiled innocently. 'Jack Reacher.'

'Cait, a man in a book doesn't count.'

'Damn, I didn't know you'd heard of him. It's not really your cup of tea. More of a Max kind of series. Are you sure he doesn't count? He's pretty hot.'

'Cait! I'm having a serious conversation with you, my girl. It's very early for you to be resigned to spinsterhood.'

'I'm not "resigned to spinsterhood". I'm just busy. Where on earth would I meet a guy? I hate going out and, like you said, I'm always at work. I've got enough to worry about trying to keep the business afloat. My job and my cat are actually plenty, thank you.'

'But what about someone to talk to, to be with? You haven't

had a parent live in the same state as you for, what, eight years? And I know you're not seeing your girlfriends from school. Do you remember what I told you when you were eight and everyone was trying to encourage you to get your nose out of your books long enough to make some friends?'

Cait groaned. She remembered it well. Her rebellious eight-year-old self arriving home, flinging her weighty schoolbag to the floor by the ironing board and announcing to a startled June that she felt like Harriet the Spy when they took away her notebook. June had paused in ironing Tania's work shirt, looked straight at Cait and reminded her what Harriet's nanny, Ole Golly, had advised Harriet. First, to apologise; and then, to lie. In Cait's case, June had said, this meant to pretend: stay true to herself inside, but cut the other girls some slack, take an interest and join in, even it felt a little forced, and perhaps in the process find they were not so bad after all. Cait had pointed out she did not have to act with June. Or when she was reading. June, slipping the freshly ironed shirt onto a hanger, had agreed, but told her to try it anyway. And Cait had learned to 'socialise': enough, anyway, to see her through school. But it didn't mean she had to enjoy it.

Cait contemplated a fourth biscuit, decided against it, and took a sip of tea instead. 'I hang out with Sylvia, sometimes,' she volunteered.

'Sometimes, eh? When was the last time?'

'Well … I've been busy. And anyway, I've got you to talk to!'

'And what if you didn't?'

'What do you mean, what if I didn't? You're here, aren't you?'

'Nothing. Listen, you won't be this beautiful and smooth-skinned forever. What about that Sebastian?'

'*Sebastian*? What about him?'

'Well, he's a nice young man. Is he good-looking? Apart from the dreadlocks. You've told me about the dreadlocks.'

'I suppose,' said Cait. She focused on chasing biscuit crumbs around the saucer with a fingertip. 'In a – well, in a *lanky* kind of way. But June, Sebastian's just a friend. Plus, he's my employee.'

'Well, that hardly matters, does it?'

'June.' The amusement with which Cait had first greeted June's intervention was turning to exasperation. 'I appreciate the concern, but I am perfectly happy as I am and, what's more, I will not be falling in love with Seb. Case closed.' She suddenly remembered, with gratitude, the copy of *Ender's Game*. 'Speaking of Seb, he wanted me to give you this.' June took it, flipped it, read the opening lines of the blurb then dropped the book like a hot potato.

'Tell him he's dreaming,' June said. 'And I won't pester you anymore for the moment, but just think about what I've said, all right?'

'All right,' said Cait. Anything to stop June trying to set her up with Seb, for goodness' sake.

'Is that the lot, then?'

'Yes. I thought about bringing you another DeLillo. But I thought I'd wait and see what you thought of the last one.'

'Good instincts. That *Underworld* was just too much. What was it, eight hundred pages? Even I haven't got time for that. I gave up halfway through.'

'It was a little dense,' Cait said, thankful to be back on solid conversational ground. 'Still, you can't deny he's brilliant.'

'No, I can't. Poetry in motion. But at eight hundred pages you don't get a whole lot of "motion". Let me give it back to you for the shop and you can sell it on to some whippersnapper whose mind still has some elasticity.'

They finished their tea and moved together back into the cool of the house, where June went over and retrieved the weighty tome from the groaning bookshelf. 'There you go. And don't forget to send me the bill for the new lot,' June said. 'Want some fancies to take home?'

'It's OK. They'd be sitting in the car for hours,' Cait said, and gave June a hug and a kiss goodbye. June stood on the porch, waving, her other hand steady on her walker, as Cait backed out of the driveway.

Now she was late for Max's. She again risked 110 on the freeway. Since when was it so urgent that she got herself a 'love life'? Her life was entirely comfortable the way it was, wasn't it? She hadn't written off love, not exactly, but she sucked at makeup and dressing up and small talk and flirting and basically everything you needed to be good at to have even a chance at snagging a one-night stand, let alone a boyfriend. Talking to her clients, her customers and her cat was the only kind of social interaction she was good at. No, far better to stick to the plan, focus on the job at hand, and forget June and her – frankly maddening – interference.

It was a split second after she saw red and blue lights flashing in her rear-view mirror that she realised she should have slowed to eighty. A kilometre back.

≪

Cait got to Max's three demerits down and smarting at the prospect of a fine that would certainly wipe out the profits of her labours today. It was all June's fault. She'd been distracted and rattled after June blindsided her with all that crap about love, she thought, walking up the front steps. Max, a widower, lived on a leafy street in West Perth and had been a regular in the shop before his rickety knee finally gave out and put an end to what had been his twice-weekly constitutional. He had no car and though he still occasionally took the bus to the shop, Cait could tell losing his walks had demoralised him. He had become more and more grumpy over the past year, and relied on her periodic visits to feed his rampant addiction to crime novels. Meanwhile, Cait relied on Max to feed her rampant addiction to his special spiced potatoes, so each was happy with the arrangement. On top of this, June's taste in books had never expanded to share Cait's predilection for what the industry rather snootily termed 'genre fiction', and the chance to pick over the latest new releases made a visit to Max a pleasure for more reasons than just his cooking.

The sweet and spicy smell that hit her when she poked her head around the door was instantly enough to start saliva going in her mouth, and to soothe her jangled nerves. Her heart rate, which had spiked at seeing the cop car signalling her to pull over, was only just returning to normal.

'In the kitchen,' Max called. Cait inhaled deeply as she perched on a stool at the kitchen bench, luxuriating in the smell. Max had his back to her and was stirring a pan of spices snapping and popping in hot oil. An apron topped his usual uniform: a spotless polo tucked into ironed slacks, positively screaming 'retired accountant', which was precisely what Max was. Somehow he had avoided even the hint of a belly despite his culinary skills.

Max drained steaming water from a pot of cubed white potatoes and set them aside while he added oil and butter to the sizzling spice paste. He swirled the pan, then added the potatoes, tossing them until they had a fragrant, spicy, buttery coating. He then put another, smaller pan on the heat beside it and cracked two eggs into it. 'Now,' he said, turning as though suddenly able to focus on her, 'how are you? Merry Christmas? Happy New Year?'

'Yep, all good. I took a week off after the Boxing Day sales. Went to Melbourne, to see Mum. Seb covered for me. How about you?'

'Yeah, not bad. Went to my daughter's place for lunch and watched my grandchildren running around like headless chooks, seizing presents and screaming. The best part was coming home and tucking into that new Strike you brought me last time. Saved it as a Christmas present to myself.' He glanced back at the stove. 'Eggs are done.' He scattered green onions over the potato mix and added chilli and salt. He took two shallow bowls from a cupboard, spooning a mound of potato into each, then sliding an egg neatly on top. The yolks quivered enticingly.

'Forgive me for not including the fried curry leaves this time,' he said, handing her a bowl and fork. 'I ran out.'

'That's cool, Max. You know how I feel about garnishes,' Cait said. She watched Max blowing on a forkful of potatoes. The action made him raise his eyebrows, deepening the orderly network of wrinkles on his face. Not for the first time, Cait reflected privately that these, combined with Max's rosy cheeks and round blue eyes, gave him a more than passing resemblance to an ageing Noddy.

'I take it you liked the Strike then?' Booksellers everywhere were watching with glee the progress of the crime series from Robert Galbraith, J.K. Rowling's pen-name for her post–Harry Potter crime series. Cash cows like Rowling were few and far between.

'Very much. You read it yet?'

'No! So no spoilers.'

'All right. Well, suffice to say there's some solid character development. I normally don't go in for the characters' love lives, but I've got to admit this one is tantalising.'

'Right,' said Cait. She had no desire to talk any more about love, and they fell silent while they ate.

'Done?'

'Yep,' Cait said, looking down at her spotless bowl. 'That was really good, Max.'

They repaired to the living room. Max was delighted with his new pile of Stephen King and intrigued by the Joe Hill, but pulled up short at the *LA Confidential*. 'This is ancient.'

'I know, but it just came in. I read it myself recently and I thought it was outstanding.'

'Even if I've already seen the movie?'

'*Especially* if you've seen the movie. They're nothing alike.'

'All right, I'll give it a go. Now, what in God's name is this? The new Agatha Christie by Sophie Hannah? Who's that when she's at home?'

'I know it's unorthodox, but I'm very curious about this. Lots of customers ask about it and I don't know whether to recommend it. So I'm consulting you as the expert.' Max looked slightly mollified. 'Hannah's a solid crime writer from what I can tell, and a Poirot nut; apparently, she got the family's blessing to resurrect him.'

'All right. Are you sure this is enough to keep me going?' said Max, who, like all thriller tragics, was hard-pressed to make a book last long.

'Yep. You'll find *LA Confidential* takes you a while. It's very challenging. Very complex.'

'All right,' Max said, looking at the tattered paperback with increased interest. He received her swift kiss on the cheek with a preoccupied air and Cait smiled to herself as she clattered down the front steps, knowing he was considering which book to open first.

The heat outside was intense, and Cait chugged her entire bottle of water, now tepid, on resettling in Dent. Air-conditioner blasting with limited effect, she got back on the freeway, this time heading south of the city, and this time scrupulously obeying the speed limit.

There was no denying the mobile service could make for a tiring day, especially on the ones that also included a nursing home visit, but the pay-off was the mental stimulation. See? Who needed to wade into the horrific-sounding world of Tinder profiles and late-night groping at tired clubs that had all changed hands multiple times since she knew them at nineteen? After high school, her small group of friends had largely and lightly dispersed, like chaff in the wind. No uni degree meant no new social circle to slip into. And once you had left a social life, it seemed harder and harder to invite yourself back in. Small talk and late nights seemed to her onerous requirements; barriers, really.

Take today, for instance. Today, she'd had beautiful meals, talk and laughter with people she knew and liked, and she was going to get home in plenty of time to feed the cat, wind down and get a good night's sleep. And putting aside June's uncharacteristically awkward questions earlier, the oldies didn't seem to think her weird. They were generally happy to do most of the talking. And her connections with them and with Seb – and her intermittent texts with Sylvia, though they were each too busy to catch up very often – meant if she ever did feel a stab of loneliness, it was so seldom she could easily ignore it until it passed. Yes, she was fine. Her priorities were right. And as long as she had June, she would never be truly lonely.

Cait turned off the freeway, east towards the hills of Roleystone, and the roar of the bitumen beneath Dent's wheels decreased in volume. The suburbs gave way to industrial estates, then housing estates paved bald and baking, then slowly to paddocks where cows grazed by roadside fences and the odd horse enjoyed the odd patch of shade. She'd been in the car half an hour by the time the road narrowed and began to climb into the hills, flanked by the massive trunks of eucalypts. The temperature in the car dropped beneath their shade and once she was respectably far from the suburbs she succumbed to temptation and floored the accelerator as the deserted road led her to a peak, then dropped steeply into a valley.

She eventually slowed so as not to miss the turn-off to Dorothy's driveway. This ran for nearly another half-kilometre, gravel crunching beneath Dent's tyres and scrub scraping its flanks. It felt like driving into another world, though she knew other properties actually stood quite close. Forcing her way through the thick vegetation, she wondered if Dorothy had a bushfire plan.

She parked in the shade of an enormous tree covered in huge, red flowers, and opened the car door to another blast of heat. The clicking of cicadas was loud in the stillness. Cait mounted the porch steps with her now much lighter box, and knocked. Within seconds, Dorothy's elaborate beehive swam into view behind the stippled orange glass panels, and Cait heard her working arthritically at the bolt. The heavy door swung inward to reveal the tiny woman, all of ninety-two but still resplendent in denim-look stretch pants and waistcoat over a floral blouse. Dorothy's platform mules clacked on the gleaming flagstones as she ushered Cait inside and immediately vanished. The potatoes and all the driving had made Cait sluggish and she lagged behind, savouring the coolness of the hallway air settling on her damp skin. She arrived in the kitchen to see Dorothy's bedenimed behind sticking out of the fridge.

'What would you like, duckie? Tea? Diet Coke? I could rip open a packet of biscuits?'

'No, that's OK,' Cait said hastily. She had once watched Dorothy raise and lower the same biscuit to and from her mouth for the duration of an entire visit without ever actually stopping talking long enough to finish it.

'Oh, you must have something. What about a Coke? With a slice of lemon? Take the can too; you can pour the rest in when you're finished,' she said, pushing a glass and an icy can into Cait's hands. 'You must be parched. How are you? Come and sit. Just move that, that's right. It's lovely to see you! You look lovely. Cool as a cucumber. How do you young people manage it? Now, what have you got for me?'

'Well,' began Cait. She was used to Dorothy asking questions without requiring answers. She didn't take it personally. Dorothy always seemed genuinely delighted to see Cait, whose theory was that the old lady had developed the habit of ceaseless verbalising because of many years operating her dog grooming salon. After all, animals never talked back. Cait herself talked to Macduff like he was a human being while home alone. She suddenly wondered if she was going to end up as unaware of herself rattling on as Dorothy was. She pictured herself as a lonely old lady, still working in her nineties because she had nothing else to do. Then she shut the thought down. Man, June really had gotten under her skin.

Dorothy had already helped herself to the books. 'Charlotte Wood ... that rings a bell. Don't they have beautiful covers? I do think these people with e-readers are missing out, don't you?'

'I thought you might like a project,' Cait said. 'These were all on the Stella Prize shortlist, just announced. It's –'

'Stella Prize – now I definitely have heard of that one. Let's have a look. I am sure I've read a Charlotte Wood before. Got to be twenty years ago. I can't for the life of me remember what it was called. I do remember it was a rather nasty-feeling book, very good, but sort of creepy, if you know what I mean?'

'I –'

'Hmmm … No, too long ago to remember. How's that cool drink? Nice and cold?'

The Coke, like Cait, was sweating. The living room was warmer than the hall. 'I –'

'Goodness me, what a sordid-sounding topic,' Dorothy went on blithely, reading the blurb. The book was about a group of women being held captive in the outback. Dorothy's description of 'good, but creepy' was probably not far off the mark.

'Well, I thought you might like to read everything on the shortlist and sort of pick the winner, and see if it's the same one that's announced,' Cait broke in, speaking quickly to get a full sentence out.

'What a lovely idea. I do wonder what that other one of hers was. I've probably got it round here somewhere.' She looked vaguely around at the cluttered room, in which bookcases were doing double duty as display cabinets, with musical memorabilia placed in front of the book spines. Dorothy's son was a concert pianist, who always seemed to be touring, and of whom Dorothy was fiercely proud. Most of the house's available surfaces were given over to his pictures, albums and posters. 'Well, I'll have a poke around for it later. Maybe do some dusting after my next client. I've always got so much dust.'

'Yes, the shop –'

'Oh, I'm sure you can sympathise with my dust problems! It must be a hard slog, that bookshop!'

'Well, it can be –'

'Never mind, you're young, you've got the energy to stick with what you love. Just like my Charles,' said Dorothy, gazing fondly at the nearest photo of Charles, who was no looker.

'How is –'

'Oh, he's good, duckie. He's in Europe, in very high demand. But he rings me every week,' Dorothy said. Cait speculated, rather unkindly, as to whether Charles simply recorded himself repeating 'Yes, Mum', and set it to play through these phone calls, while he went off and played scales or had himself a quiet tot of single malt.

Eventually, Dorothy talked herself out and stood up. 'I'm terribly sorry to kick you out so unceremoniously, duckie, but I've got an Afghan coming and it's sure to be pandemonium.' Cait tried to imagine ancient, five-foot-nothing Dorothy wrangling an Afghan hound, and found her imagination wanting. 'Thanks ever so much, duckie; drive safely, now. Got everything? Until next time, then. Right you are. All right. Bye-bye …'

Safely back in Dent, the interior cooling as the sun slipped lower in the sky, Cait and her empty box sagged beside one another. 'Phew,' Cait said, and turned the key. The thought of her empty house right now seemed not only acceptable, but downright attractive.

THREE

Cait let herself into the shop fifteen minutes ahead of opening time and looked around to see immediately that Seb's tidy was a bit rough around the edges. The tidy was the shop's major daily must-do task; rain or shine, the place had to be recovered from the last onslaught and made ready for the next. She hoped the general disarray was a signal Seb had been busy at the till, but this proved overly optimistic when she looked at the weekend totals. Cait fixed a few of the more glaring messes, enjoying the peace, moving unhurriedly as streams of businesspeople rushed past the closed windows. They looked harried already, minds on their overflowing inboxes. She wondered how they dealt with being stuck at a desk all day. The sight of them never failed to make her feel lucky to be her own boss. She filled the float for the day, counting out the fifties, the twenties, tens and fives. She emptied each pile of coins from its little plastic bag onto the counter in a jingling rush, then counted them, whizzing them two by two off the edge into her cupped hand. She was out of gold, so smashed open cardboard tubes of one- and two-dollar coins on the counter's edge, enjoying the moment they broke open and the coins thudded out. There was a tactile pleasure to handling real money. She straightened the signs adorning her cash register. The first read, *Books must pass from person to person in order to stay alive*, a quote from Margaret Atwood. The second said, *NO CHANGE without purchase! SORRY!!!*

A man banged on the window, peering through cupped hands for signs of life inside. She pointed to the sign right next to his face showing that she opened at eight on weekdays. He looked at his watch and scowled, no doubt thinking it was so close to eight that she might as well let him in.

Sorry, buddy. The fifteen minutes before opening and the fifteen after closing were some of the most jealously guarded moments of her day. She loved that the act of opening up let in the breeze, the street noise and, of course, the people, with their endless curious and funny needs, sometimes baffling, sometimes touching. But this crashing symphony of sensory input made the peace and still air of the shop when it was closed something to savour. It felt different when it was just her in here with the books, watching over her in friendly, silent ranks. She was long past opening early for anyone, no matter how alarmingly they scowled at her.

'Not my fault you forgot your daughter's birthday,' she mumbled to herself. The counter was too far from the front windows for the man to see her lips move, but he clearly realised she was not budging and backed off.

The word 'birthday' triggered a thought. She looked at the calendar tacked to the wall behind the counter. March fourteenth – five years to the day since Book Fiend had opened for the first time. There was one thing she had to say for her years in retail: it sure had toughened her up. Her smile still looked sweet, but it in fact overlaid several layers of steel, honed by years of haggling and refusing to open early.

Cait had worked in retail ten years before opening Book Fiend. Thanks to June, she had grown up into someone quite unable to walk past a bookshop without veering automatically inside and disappearing, the same way her mother had done with jewellery shops. It had seemed to Cait as a child that the workers in these bookshops must be the happiest people on earth to spend their days in such a place, and so she had early on conceived a desire to join them. After finishing school, she defied her parents' pleas for her to apply to university and applied to all the bookshops she could find, but the jobs were competitive. While she waited for an opening, she worked in other stores: Rebel Sport, pretending to be sporty; Valleygirl, pretending to be girly; and finally, Roger David, faking flirty. She'd never played any of these roles very convincingly, but thankfully the bar was not set particularly high. It was with enormous relief that she finally got a job on the shop floor at the big city Dymocks. Working the sections she'd always ignored as a reader and a shopper opened her eyes to the sheer bigness of the world, the variety of its preoccupations: cars and collecting, westerns, military history, genealogy. Vampire fiction. Werewolf fiction. And the rabbit hole only went deeper. Romance, for example, turned out to be an umbrella term for a range of preferences so diverse that, like warring siblings, they would never get along at the same Christmas dinner: crime romance, rural romance, paranormal romance, historical, Regency. Even medical and scientific. And erotica, which turned out not to be romance at all: any person asking for romance was, Cait soon learned, offended if shown erotica.

She ended up at Dymocks for around seven years. She was manager after four. Doing the ordering, she learned what sold, the core stock Perth people liked. How many *Catcher in the Rye*s you needed to keep on the shelf at any given time, how many of *Shantaram*, how many *Tuesdays with Morrie*. She rode the waves of Oprah's Book Club titles as they went from hot cakes to stale. But the major thing working in other people's shops taught her was how much she disliked following orders, always doing things someone else's way. And eventually she took the plunge. She got a bank loan for the kind of bespoke fit-out she'd always dreamed of – the banks had been loosening their purse strings in happy anticipation of the next mining boom – and signed a lease at one of the most prominent spots on Hay Street.

She discreetly let the sales reps know she'd soon go it alone. They came to see her at home, with their latest catalogues and 'top one hundred' lists. She went through with a highlighter and picked out what she wanted. Her favourite rep, Melinda Magalotti, known to the entire industry as 'Mags', had been particularly supportive. The Random House rep, who boasted a killer wardrobe full of strictly op-shopped vintage gear and whose hearty laugh frequently dissolved into a smoker's cough, had dismissed Cait's every crisis of confidence with, 'Babe, you'll smash it!' Finally, she handed in her notice at Dymocks. She'd wondered how her boss, who was really a lovely old bloke when all was said and done, would react, but she need not have worried. He was happy for her, and was totally unbothered at the prospect of a competitor opening not ten minutes' walk away. 'A city can never have too many bookshops, Cait,' he told her. 'When it's too few – now, that's when a bookseller should worry.'

It was a heady few months between getting the keys to opening the doors for the first time. She got most of her stock on a sale-or-return basis, minimising her risk. She bought a hundred thousand dollars' worth. It felt incredible; a dream shopping spree. Inside her newly leased building, piles of boxes waited everywhere while the fittings were installed, then painted. More arrived daily and were stacked atop the rest. The business of unpacking them all, receiving them onto the computer system, then shelving them, had been enormous. Cait slaved from sun-up until well past sundown each night. June turned up a few times, ostensibly to help, but in reality to wander about and get in the way, poking into boxes, getting lost in reading all the blurbs and making piles of things for Cait to 'hang on to' for her. And every time Cait began to think that she must be just about ready, another ten grand's worth would arrive from Penguin and the whole process started again.

But the local buzz, everyone's friendly curiosity about the new bookshop, spurred her on. She had crunched the numbers and figured the astronomical high-street rents would be worth it for the foot traffic alone, and it did seem that even before she'd opened, she couldn't poke her head out the front door without being stopped by someone eager to know when she would be opening. The Lims, who had owned the newsagent next door before Prada moved in, and Phil the chemist had been full of encouragement and helpful suggestions, such as giving her the contact details of the glazier they had on call for the inevitable break-ins. Meth-heads, they told her. 'But don't worry – they won't touch your stock, they only want cash.' And more than once Phil had brought Cait a coffee as she worked into the night, shelving and arranging with the happy fervour of someone completely absorbed in a task.

The result was just as envisioned: the walls like the fantasy library in a grand old country house, like *Beauty and the Beast*, or an Austen novel. She remembered the opening day like it was yesterday. The journalist from the local paper – not the state daily, just the city one – had arrived with her photographer. Cait had invited her at June's insistence. 'Power of the press,' she said, and Cait bowed to her judgement. Best to get all the publicity possible. She didn't want to be one of the sixty percent of small businesses that capsized within three years, or whatever that horrible statistic was that her mother had insisted on quoting to her down the phone.

Erica the journalist had prominent teeth, long, shiny brown hair, long, shiny brown legs and expertly winged eyeliner. She interviewed Cait with bewildering rapidity then left. Cobie Strange, a young Perth crime author, had then arrived – thankfully with a bunch of book-loving friends and family in tow – for a signing to celebrate the launch of her debut. It had become a blockbuster, and Cobie, who had hit it off with Cait instantly, would over the intervening years return to Book Fiend to sign her second blockbuster, then, recently, her third. A Hollywood film version of the debut had recently been announced. But all Cait had known on that long-ago opening day was that Cobie had brought the crowd she needed. And by the time Cait had hauled her trolleys back inside on that first evening, she was exhausted but exhilarated.

Erica's article had appeared in the *Perth City Gazette* and brought a rush of customers. Some began to appear regularly and Cait grew familiar with their faces and quirks. She learned that a bookshop was regarded as a sort of unofficial city information booth that invited a diverse range of inquiries: 'Do you know where I can buy sheet sets?'; 'Do you know where the post office is?'; 'Can you point me towards the Indonesian consulate?' And even when people understood that a bookshop did in fact sell books, some of their queries were real face-palmers. 'Do you have any … you know, like docos, but in books? What do you even call that?'

'Non-fiction?'

'No, I mean true stories.'

Book Fiend did not go out of business within three years, in spite of her mother's dire predictions, but others did. In a single year both Angus & Robertson, then Borders, closed their doors in Perth. Then, sometime later, Cait read in the *Gazette* that Dymocks, her former employer, and the CBD's last chain bookstore, was closing after twenty-five years in business. Some smaller specialty stores hung on within the city limits – a motoring bookshop, a map shop, a tiny sci-fi cave – but Book Fiend was now the last general-purpose bookshop standing. Not to mention one of the last independent businesses remaining on her increasingly exclusive strip. Cait had felt no pleasure seeing her competition vanquished by the digital economy; it was lonely, trying to make a go of things, knowing so many others had failed.

The federal small business minister had made some spectacularly unwelcome comments about how he believed bricks-and-mortar bookshops would cease to exist within five years. The industry had gone into uproar and the politician had hastily backtracked, saying he was merely highlighting that they would need to adjust to the digital marketplace 'very quickly'.

Cait took heed. Her new casual staffer, Sebastian, hired after she'd been open a year, turned out fortuitously to be an underemployed web designer, who was happy to create an online shop for her. And the mobile service proved successful, as well as satisfying. The balance of the bank loan shrank slowly but steadily. While it didn't recover to pre-digital days, the industry stabilised and adapted. Indie bookshops priding themselves on personality and service survived where the bigger chains had faltered, and the second wave of WA's mining boom bolstered retail in general. The lingering smells of new paint and new print at Book Fiend faded, replaced by the smell of old books and dust; of 'silverfish and ancient inkiness', as Cait had once read it described by Robert Dessaix. Cait, who at Dymocks had had the luxury of a cleaner on staff, had never appreciated before running her own shop just how dirty a cavern filled floor to ceiling with small objects could become. After a couple of years of ruining work clothes, she finally clued up and ordered a set of new black aprons, starched and crisp, with *Book Fiend* embroidered across the chest in white lettering, to match her signage. She had considered taking on another staffer, but some instinct – perhaps her consciousness, courtesy of her parents, that every boom was followed by a bust – had bade her wait, and now, in 2016, she was glad she had. Only two years after the peak of the boom, commodity prices had tanked, unemployment had spiked and people were saving their cash rather than blowing it on consumer goods.

She lifted one of the aprons, now soft and faded, over her head, and tied it around her waist. It helped hide the minuscule holes she'd noticed this morning in her work T-shirt, a threadbare V-neck in regulation weekday black. Damn it; she needed to buy more. But the next loan repayment was due. Clothes would have to wait.

The morning passed peacefully. Mags came in, bearing glossy new catalogues and, as always, a flurry of industry gossip. Cait sold new kids' books to parents seeking to distract crying children. She sold a second-hand *Gone Girl* to an impoverished-looking backpacker. She sold William S. Burroughs and *Twilight*, and a Goosebumps novel to a rather doubtful lady who wanted something for her young niece, but had no idea what kind of person her niece was or what she liked to read. She found a copy of *Me Before You* requested by a woman of about her own age. The woman's face fell when Cait handed it to her. 'Oh, it's *long*, isn't it? I think I'll just wait until the movie comes out. Thanks anyway.' She left the book sitting on the counter. But there was another customer right behind her, smiling hopefully. This woman wanted a book. They all started that way. 'I'm looking for a book ...' This woman wanted one called *Falling Pine Trees*. She was pretty sure it was called that, anyway. This stumped both Cait and her database. She thought hard for a moment, hating to turn the woman away. Then in a flash of inspiration, she said, 'Oh! Do you mean *Snow Falling on Cedars*?'

Yes! That was exactly it. Cait sold her a copy, smiling. This was the simple, lovely reliability of the shop, each customer a new opportunity to make someone happy.

Or not. The next customer was a friendly young man who asked for change for the bus and, when Cait refused, turned abruptly into a much less friendly young man in a Jekyll-to-Hyde–style transformation.

Her feathers somewhat ruffled, Cait was pleased to see that the next face to materialise was a familiar one. 'Oh, hi, Mr Cowper. How are you today?' She raised her voice a little, though she tried to keep speaking naturally. Mr Cowper was becoming increasingly hard of hearing but did not seem aware of it, and she guessed he would rather avoid that awareness. Many older people, she had noticed in her years of doing the mobile service, were in denial about their hearing loss.

'I'm well, thank you, Miss Cait. I just thought I would check whether you had got any of these in since yesterday.' Mr Cowper was a historical and nautical fiction buff. His favourites were Bernard Cornwell, C.S. Forester and Patrick O'Brian and he refused to read newcomers. He kept track of each series he was reading with lists handwritten in beautiful old-fashioned script, and would spend months and sometimes years looking for a particular title second-hand. Mr Cowper liked the thrill of the chase, the unexpected and serendipitous find, and considered giving up and ordering a title something of a last resort. He pulled out one of his lists now, fingers curled over the bit of paper made soft and delicate with rewritings and refoldings and crossings-out. He gazed at it, then at Cait. His eyes had gazed for so many years they now appeared colourless. His hair was so thin it was almost invisible. He looked like a great old craggy bird of prey, feathers falling out, no longer beautiful, but still on the hunt. He held out the list. Cait knew nothing had come in this morning that was on it – she knew it pretty much by heart – but she peered obligingly at it anyway.

'Sorry, Mr Cowper, I don't think so. I'll make sure I give you a call if I see one of these, though – you know I'm already keeping an eye out.'

'Of course, of course. I'll just have a little browse, anyway, while I'm here. Make sure I don't miss anything.' He made no move. Mr Cowper would inevitably stay talking, quiet and unhurried, as long as he was allowed, until she gently ushered him on. Sometimes Cait would have to invent a 'job' to do out the back, in order to escape and get on with things. True to form, he stood and passed the time of day there at the till for a good five minutes before another customer came along and he shuffled off to check the stacks. All in all, an ordinary morning.

The store filled, as always, during the lunch hours, as workers sought to prolong their breaks by browsing. Cait led them deep into the aisles to find what they asked for, dashing back to the counter every time she heard the ding of the little bell she left there to alert her to someone waiting to pay. She loved the sheer busyness of the lunch rush, whirling with a smile from one person to the next, connecting with the nice ones and managing the grumpy ones, relishing the sense of heightened efficiency, and somehow of importance, that came with having many tasks to do at once and yet still doing them well.

It was nearly two before things died down. The last of the crowd to leave was a man in a suit who stopped at the counter.

'Have you got *Good to Great* by Jim Collins?' he asked, drumming his fingernails on the counter, body turned towards the doors, already poised to exit. Cait did a quick computer search. 'No, sorry. I don't keep a lot of business books in stock. I can order it for you, though – it's in stock over east, so it would be about a week. It's forty-nine ninety-nine, hardcover.'

'Really? Fifty dollars? Look, don't worry. I can get it cheaper online.' He was halfway through the door before he stopped and turned back. 'I just had a thought,' he said. 'Do you want to donate a prize for a raffle I'm organising? It's for my son's footy team. We want to support local businesses.'

Cait refused, as politely as she could. Dickhead, she thought. How about you support local business and buy a book? She had more trouble than usual in letting go of her irritation, until she realised: lunch. She needed lunch.

Cait's lunches usually consisted of things like raw vegetables, boiled eggs and crackers. Anything that could be eaten in bits, standing up and on the go. There was no point in anything that needed to be eaten hot, because invariably she would be interrupted and return to a stone-cold meal. Before getting out her Tupperware, she did a lap of the store, doing a mini tidy to mitigate the destruction the lunch rush had left. Then, rounding the end of the last aisle into the back corner of the shop, she almost walked into someone.

FOUR

'Oh! Sorry. Didn't see you there. Do you need a hand with anything?'

Usually people reacted to this question either by immediately launching into their spiel about what they needed, or by saying 'Just browsing', so Cait was taken aback by the man's jump and his look of shifty embarrassment. Hazel eyes lifted to meet hers for a split second, widened a moment, then quickly dropped to the floor. 'No, thanks, just browsing,' he mumbled, and turned away, but not before Cait spied the source of his embarrassment in his hand. *It's Not You: 27 (Wrong) Reasons You're Single.* Keeping a straight face, she backed away, saying over her shoulder, 'No worries – I'll be by the counter.'

The second-hand Self-help – Relationships section was always crammed. There was a high stock turnover. It was full of titles like *Kissing Frogs*, and *Our Love is Too Good to Feel So Bad,* and that perennial favourite, *Why Men Don't Listen and Women Can't Read Maps.* Most of the books were various shades of pink, and their spines stood out in the gloom of the corner. This guy had looked highly out of place in front of that girly backdrop. She wondered what exactly he was looking for, and sneaked a glance backwards, under cover of ducking below the counter to take out her lunch. He was hunched protectively over the book so she couldn't see his face, but she thought he had been about her age. He was tall and in office clothes. He had square shoulders and a trim waist and thick, shiny brown hair, lopped only just short enough to be office-appropriate. He didn't strike her as someone who would need any help landing a girlfriend. She skulked behind her counter, eating her carrot sticks, watching surreptitiously. She saw him gaze around at the till a couple of times, too casually, as though deep in thought, and betted he had hoped to wait until she was distracted before slinking out. But she stayed put behind the counter, where he'd have to pass her. He lingered a while longer, flashing glances, then with an air of sudden decision he headed to the counter. 'Just that, thanks,' he said in a would-be nonchalant tone, handing over a second-hand *Getting the Love You Want* and looking her defiantly in the eye.

She took pity. 'I reckon you're better off with this than the one you had before,' she said. 'This has stayed in print for so long, it must be all right.'

His face broke into a smile. His eyes looked suddenly, brilliantly green. 'Thanks,' he said. 'I don't have a clue.' About books or getting the love he wanted, he did not specify.

Cait smiled back. 'Want a bag?'

'Very much so,' he said, and she bagged the book for him.

'Have a nice day.'

'You too,' he said, and strode out, tucking his safely disguised purchase under his arm. Cait crunched another carrot stick, smiling.

That afternoon Cait unpacked a big delivery, refreshed the displays and resisted the urge to put aside a stack of new stuff to take home. She attempted to explain the finer points of recommended retail pricing to a young man who demanded to know why two books were different prices when they had 'the same amount of pages'. She had just got rid of him and bent back over her display when the next person walked up. A woman in her late forties, carrying a large and heavy-looking box. Cait groaned inwardly. Somehow she was getting to be able to tell a dud pile just by the look of the box. 'Want some books?' the woman said, as they all did.

Cait straightened and wiped her hands on her jeans. 'Sure,' she said, pointing the woman towards the counter and heading there herself. 'You want credit for these?' She began to pull books out of the box in handfuls.

'I was hoping for cash,' the woman said. They were always hoping for cash. She never gave it. And she had to be increasingly selective about what she took. Second-hand books seemed to multiply in an almost supernatural way, as if someone came in and chucked water on them and fed them after midnight while she was at home sleeping, like in that old movie *Gremlins*. And they required extensive sprucing up to be sale-ready. So she only took those in mint condition. Except for the unicorns. *Shantaram*, for instance. An epic novel about a bank robber who'd fled to Bombay, *Shantaram* could shamble in as creased and dog-eared as the backpacker bearing it, and spend no more than five minutes among much smarter neighbours on the front table before a shopper pounced on it and whisked it back to the counter. Barely a day went by without someone asking for it. So Cait had to at least check everything offered – sometimes, just sometimes, these boxes contained windfalls.

Equally, they sometimes contained surprises of the non-book variety. She had once pulled a ladies' vibrator, thankfully still new and in its packaging, from a box dropped off for a quote. She had decided not to mention it when she rang to offer a price. But the cardboard carton that sat before her now yielded no surprises. She remembered George Orwell writing that books gave off more and nastier dust than any other objects, and that the top of a book was where every fly preferred to die. This box was proof of both rules, and a third: any long-forgotten box of books represented to silverfish a luxurious Airbnb. Avoiding the insects dead and alive, Cait looked over the titles. Too many hardcovers. The titles would have been fine, if paperback – mostly general and crime fiction, some Di Morrissey, some Wilbur Smith, some Matthew Reilly. But hardcovers took up too much space and were almost impossible to sell. No-one wanted to carry around a giant book these days. And even the paperbacks here weren't in the best nick. Mostly literary fiction. She had multiples of some of them already. She had plenty of Donna Tartt, Barbara Kingsolver. Oh, God, here was another copy of *The Third Brother*. Would this book never die? *The English Patient* – now, that would sell. She looked through all the titles, in case a *Shantaram* or a Terry Pratchett popped out. Nothing doing. She could sell maybe a third of it. The rest would have to be divided between the op shop round the corner, the two-dollar box and the bin. She did a rapid mental calculation. 'I can give you twenty dollars in store credit,' she said, pulling her credit pad towards her in a businesslike fashion and bracing for the inevitable.

'Twenty dollars in *credit*?' the woman said. 'There's fifty books in there. Or more. I want cash. You must be able to give fifty in cash at least.'

'I'm so sorry. I'm only able to give cash for new releases, in quite large quantities, and those have to be in almost-perfect condition.'

What Cait meant was that if she gave fifty bucks cash for every box of crap that came across her desk she would end up in the poorhouse. Despite her choice of far more diplomatic terms, the woman positively quivered with annoyance, as though the water in every cell in her body was coming to the boil. But she contented herself with disgruntled muttering as she flounced off to spend her twenty.

Cait never budged on her quotes, no matter how upset people got. They were free to reject them and take the books away again. But they invariably gave in and accepted her offers. She thought it was partly that they wanted her to lift the burden from them, both physically and mentally; they wanted to turn away from the store feeling lighter. But they must also know their only other option around here was the Good Sammy's or the bin. Some people gave in with good grace, some did not. This lady got over her disappointment while browsing the shelves, and returned to the counter with a couple of newish chick lit paperbacks in perfect condition. She handed over four dollars to cover the difference happily enough, and wished Cait a nice afternoon, which Cait returned. Bygones were bygones.

She put away the stock that had come off the refreshed displays and moved on to cleaning. She dusted, vacuumed and Spray n' Wiped. She pulled discarded takeaway coffee cups and balled-up shopping lists from the most unlikely nooks and crannies. It was so quiet that she started the evening tidy early. The trade was always so slow now, outside the lunch hour. Even the Christmas period, usually berserk, had not produced the reliable river of cash that generally subsidised the rest of the year. It was only the adult colouring-in book craze that had got sales over the line in December. She knew she was not the only bookseller in the country experiencing flat sales, but perhaps she needed to make a bigger effort. Plan some author events? She hadn't done any since the storm of them that had surrounded the summer festival season. She tried to brainstorm some ideas, but she couldn't focus on what event she should hold. She just felt the same sense of distraction, of nagging dissatisfaction, that had hummed along in the bottom of her consciousness for a couple of days now. What was the matter with her? Maybe it was just too hot. Maybe when the weather changed, she'd feel better.

⋘

The weather didn't change for the next fortnight, and neither did the niggling sense that some kind of equilibrium had shifted, leaving Cait slightly off-balance. The hazel-eyed guy came on several more occasions during lunchtimes, while she was occupied with the endless tide of people looking for the usual suspects, the bread and butter of her trade: Robert Ludlum, Fiona McIntosh, Danielle Steel. Endless copies of *The Girl on the Train*, which Cait had read out of curiosity, but couldn't see what the fuss was about. Requests for 'that gardening book they talked about on that show last night; it was green, with a tree on it.' And, always, the book they couldn't quite remember the name of, but it had this picture on the front … a girl in a hat. She had a sort of flowing dress on. Did Cait know it? Sometimes, amazingly, she did.

She never saw the hazel-eyed guy enter, but caught glimpses of him skulking in the Self-help – Relationships corner with a pile of books at his elbow. When the lunch rush began to clear out, so would he. She kept her distance. She told herself that this was because he clearly didn't want help and ignored the little voice that told her she was only afraid of saying something awkward. She had forgotten how to talk to men. Wait, that was bullshit. She'd never known how to talk to men. She would only say something horrendously inappropriate and scare him away. But there was nothing stopping her indulging in idle speculation as she gave him a wide berth during post-lunch tidies, then retreated behind the counter to process new piles of second-hand stock. She fanned each book out to find the boarding passes, shopping lists and love letters inevitably left inside after being used as bookmarks. She inhaled the familiar smells, one after another. The paper dust that rose into the air in clouds as she sanded back yellowed page edges. The Windex she used to remove grime. The eucalyptus oil that removed sticker residue and discolouration. Then she priced and she shelved, and all the while, she covertly watched her mystery shopper.

He was definitely around her age, definitely presentable. His clothes looked way more expensive than hers. It made his predilection for self-help even more intriguing. Thirty-something hot guys in pricey businesswear were hardly the target market for Australia's multimillion-dollar self-help industry.

After he'd left, she would tidy the section, attempting to deduce which books he'd been looking at. Maybe he needed to advise an unlucky friend. No, even she wouldn't believe that. No-one would gift-shop in a self-help section. Besides, if he was gift-shopping in an unfamiliar genre, he would be asking for her help.

Maybe he was going through an agonising breakup. But tormented lovers were supposed to be hollow-cheeked, wild-eyed and unwashed, like Heathcliff. Not neatly pressed and nicely muscled and smelling of some kind of delicious man-cologne that she always caught the faintest trace of as he left. His hair was a little dishevelled, true, but it kind of suited him.

Cait suddenly realised that in the lull between customers, she'd been sitting and staring into the corner where he was browsing. Now someone stood before her, waiting for her to look up. She leapt to her feet, toppling the stool she'd been perched on. She rescued it before it hit the floor and turned, belatedly arranging her face in a smile. It was one of her regulars, a man on the tail end of middle age who always bought something, but never missed a chance to complain. 'Sorry about that – off with the fairies,' she gabbled, taking his books and scanning them. 'Quiet moment.'

'I can see that,' he said. 'Now, you would have some more people in here if you didn't charge so much. See this one! Twenty-four dollars for this little slip of a book! Surely you can take something off that for me.'

'Sorry, sir,' she said, looking at it and mingling just the right amount of regret into her smile. 'This is a new one, and that gives me even less wiggle room than on my second-hand stock. Would you like to take it today anyway?'

'Twenty-four dollars!' he insisted, keeping a firm grip on his other two books. 'It's ridiculous what you're charging for these books! The profit must be astronomical!'

'I can assure you it's not, sir,' she said, gamely maintaining the rueful smile. 'I make pretty slender margins on my stock, and the rents in this part of the city are extremely high. There's no big company behind me. It's just me, and I assure you, I'm not rolling in it. It's just what books cost these days, I'm afraid. But they're worth it, right?' Her smile became encouraging. Come on, you grumpy old bastard. Meet me halfway.

'Yeah, well,' he said, taking out his wallet and handing over the other books, and she drew a silent, deep breath as she rang them up. Heaven grant me patience, she thought.

'Forty-eight dollars today,' she said apologetically. He paid. 'Have a nice day!'

She looked up to focus on the next person in line and saw with a little start that the eyes on hers were those of her corner-dwelling mystery shopper.

'Nice guy, hey?'

'He's not too bad.' A pause. She willed herself to say something else. 'He just likes to have his say. At least he ends up buying stuff in the end.' Right. That was enough. Stop while the going was good. 'Just this one?'

'Yep,' he said, and she glanced at it as she rang it up. *No More Mr Nice Guy: A Proven Plan for Getting What You Want in Love, Sex, and Life.* Goodness. Watch out, world.

'Nineteen ninety-five,' she said. She changed his fifty and bagged the book. 'Thanks. See ya.'

'See ya.'

Ha! A successful exchange, entirely without disaster. Why was he having so much trouble finding a girlfriend? Maybe he was a controlling psycho, or a jealous type. Or a workaholic. A mean drunk? Maybe he was just socially awkward, like her. Anyway, he had to be an idiot for thinking self-help books actually helped people. But he didn't seem like an idiot. And he had a nice smile. A really nice smile, actually.

She shook herself. What would she know? She hadn't managed anything but a handful of atrocious dates over the past few years. They all turned out either nice but unsexy, or sexy but arseholes. Some were both unsexy and arseholes. And all types seemed put off by her punishing schedule, completely uninterested in what she did for a living and utterly incapable of talking about what they were reading, because it was generally nothing. At least Mr Mystery Shopper was reading books instead of just googling *HuffPost* dating advice at his desk. Maybe he, like her, was a perfectly nice, normal person who just had better things to do than practise flirting. After all, there was nothing wrong with focusing on work and getting ahead. Not that this week's sales put her particularly far ahead.

FIVE

Mystery Shopper upped the ante with two books on his next visit, less than a week later. One, a second-hand *What's Love Got to Do with It?: The Evolution of Human Mating*; the other she'd thought looked interesting herself: Aziz Ansari's *Modern Romance*. He seemed to have gotten over his embarrassment. His smile was genuine. It definitely *was* a nice smile. Was he flirting with her? Testing out his new techniques? Well, if he wanted a decent shot at practising on an undefended shop assistant, he should stop coming in at lunchtime when she was busy, she thought as she rang them up. Well, she might not be able to flirt, but she felt pretty safe to give her opinions on the stock.

'This looks good,' she offered, holding up the Ansari. 'You should let me know what you think.'

'Will do,' he said. He flashed her that smile again as he turned to leave, and her stomach flipped. She turned her attention to the next man, a guy in his forties in the kids' section. He looked hot and harassed in his sharp suit.

'Can I help you with anything?'

'I need a book for my newborn nephew,' he said.

Cait thought a moment, looking around. 'How about a Mother Goose collection? It's one of those classics that never goes out of style.'

The man looked dubious. 'He's a boy. Will he like that?'

Cait was fleetingly stupefied, then rallied. 'Well, he's got a mother, hasn't he?'

'I guess,' the man said. He headed to the counter with the Mother Goose and paid, but shied away when she held the slender book out for him to take.

'I need a bag. I can't take it like that. How would I look carrying this around the office?' he said sharply.

Like a nice man who just bought a book for his baby nephew, Cait thought. 'Of course,' she said, fishing one out. 'Enjoy the rest of your day.' He strode out without returning the pleasantry, and a girl loomed in his place. 'Change a ten?' she said.

'Sorry, I can't,' Cait said, pointing to her sign.

'Fuck you!' the girl yelled, and lurched out. Cait shrugged and picked up her duster.

The next time Mystery Shopper surfaced was only days after his previous visit. It was later in the afternoon this time, and the heat was fading from the air. Cait slipped unobtrusively between the few people lingering on the shop floor, tidying around them as they browsed. They all ignored each other companionably, like sheep grazing in a field. The ceiling fans ticked overhead. The music became audible. When the shop was busy Cait often either couldn't hear it or tuned it out because of its familiarity. On now was a favourite, an old Crowded House album. She sometimes thought she should probably choose some new music, but her customers seemed to love the old stuff, too. She frequently heard them singing along, under their breath. And now she had heard these albums so many times they formed a soothing soundtrack to her days. She tidied her way to the back and bent to pick up a paperback of an eye-watering turquoise that had fallen to the floor. Emblazoned on the cover was the title *Why You're Not Married ... Yet* and a black-and-white illustration of a curvy brunette, left hand parked sassily on hip to display a giant ring. The diamond had little jagged spikes of light drawn around it, presumably to indicate its staggering lustre. The brunette gazed accusingly at Cait. The tagline below her jutting hipbone read, *This is not a book about finding a man. This book is about* you.

She didn't even remember seeing this one come in. Must have been in a pile of second-hand stuff she'd bought and processed in a trance. With idle curiosity, like an office worker succumbing to one more bit of clickbait after lunch, Cait opened it.

Like all the highest quality reading material, the book opened with a true-or-false quiz and, reading the questions, she began to smile.

For each 'true' answer, the reader earned a point. The more points they got, the more they were deemed in need of the author's help. Points were awarded for having multiple godchildren – one point per child; for gossip magazine subscriptions; for showing up unannounced at a man's place of work; for owning self-help books; and for having read *Twilight*: three points for having completed the book, seven for buying advance tickets for the movie, twenty-three for camping out in line for the movie. Points were also awarded for having names picked out for your future children, and bonus points if those names happened to be Bella or Edward.

Tickled by the *Twilight*-bashing, Cait sat on the squashy little couch pushed against the back wall and kept flipping. Wow, she really must have been in some kind of daze to both take in and process this book without once flipping through to check its interior: the inner sections were liberally covered in shocking pink highlighter. Cait let margin notes slide for something like *The Handmaid's Tale* that was both a common school text and a bestseller, but bulk highlighting like this was usually a flat-out no. It was kind of endearing, though, how seriously the book's previous owner had taken the author, Tracy's, advice.

Tracy said being nice to people was not demeaning and was in fact the key to a successful marriage. She said many single women were not particularly nice, especially to men, because they did not think they should have to be. Even more commonly, they thought they were nice but really, they weren't. Therefore, a dead giveaway that you were a bitch was if you were sure you weren't. The diligent reader had highlighted this, as though it might be on a future exam. Another way of figuring out if you were a bitch, Tracy wrote, was to ask three close friends if there was any chance you might be seen this way. If in return you received a long, wary gaze, you had your answer.

Cait actually snorted with laughter at this, and that was precisely the moment she heard a male voice say, 'Got a good one, have you?'

Cait looked up and nearly dropped the book.

SIX

Cait's stomach swooped as Mystery Shopper looked down at her, with a crooked, quizzical smile. 'Oh!' she said. 'No –'

She made to get up, but before she could, he had actually sat beside her on the couch. It was not a big couch. She had to get up. She made an attempt, but the strength had somehow gone from her knees. She smelled shampoo. Crowded House chose this moment to finish the affable 'It's Only Natural' and begin the far more sensuous-sounding 'Fall at Your Feet'.

'I would have thought a bookstore owner wouldn't be into highlighting her books,' Mystery Shopper said, leaning even closer to look at the highlighted page, while Cait struggled to get a hold of herself.

'Oh – it's not mine,' she said wildly. 'It's stock. I just picked it up while I was tidying because it looked so terrible.' Damn it, why couldn't he have surprised her with *The Iliad* or *The Canterbury Tales*? Even a Germaine Greer? 'I just noticed that its first owner had highlighted it. Comprehensively.' She showed him. 'It made me curious. But it's actually pretty funny.'

'Funny that they took it so seriously, or the book itself is funny?'

'Both.'

'Give us a look,' he said, and she handed it over. She felt terribly shaky all of a sudden. What was wrong with her? Was she overheated? Dehydrated? Her heart was thumping. It felt like it must be obvious from the outside that her whole system had gone into freefall, but he hadn't noticed, apparently. He was thumbing through the pages, seeming quite at home beside her on the tiny couch as she flicked a nervous glance ahead to check she wasn't wanted at the till. She jumped when she heard him chuckle, and looked back down at the highlighted passage he was holding out for her to see. 'Look, here's some idiot-proof advice for knowing what to do in any situation,' he said. 'Basically, an urge is a signal of temporary insanity and so should never be acted on. The stronger the urge, the more insane you would be to act on it.'

Cait laughed, and felt the tightness in her stomach muscles relent somewhat.

'I totally know what she means,' he said, looking her straight in the eye. There was green in the hazel again. He was flirting with her. She hadn't imagined it. Oh, God! She wasn't ready. To cover her confusion, she dropped her eyes back to the book and pointed. 'Look, she's highlighted another bit lower down,' she said hastily. 'Listen to this: the insanity is probably childhood-related.'

He laughed. 'Ain't that the truth.' Then he stuck out his hand, which on this couch required turning further towards her. Their knees touched lightly. 'I'm James, by the way. James Gardner.'

'Cait Copper. Short for Caitlyn,' she said, shaking the offered hand. Was her hand damp? It had to be. And dirty from processing. There was a short silence, then a loud double ding from her bell.

'Excuse me,' a voice called from the counter. 'Can I get a little service here, please?' Cait dropped James's hand and leapt to her feet, knocking the book to the floor. She dashed to the counter and by the time she reached it, she could feel that her entire face had flushed: an even more unflattering look on a redhead than it was on other people. 'I'm so sorry about that,' she said to the person waiting, cringing further when she saw it was her regular haggler. 'I got distracted by something.'

'I could see that,' he said as she scanned his books. He spoke with his usual sharpness, but when she looked up, she saw he was smiling slightly. She didn't think she had ever seen him smile. And – wonder of wonders! – he was holding out a fifty-dollar bill without any protest about the prices, or even pausing to hear the total. She gave him his change and he turned to leave, but at the last moment gave a half-turn back.

'Keep him keen, won't you,' he advised. 'Young men these days are too cocky. We had to work for a woman in my day.' Cait spluttered a little and she actually heard him chuckle to himself as he walked out the door. Mystery Shopper – James – sauntered up in his wake, still holding the girly turquoise book. 'What was that about?' he inquired, leaning an elbow on the counter and looking at her still-pink face.

'Oh, just one of my regulars, giving me grief,' she said, striving for a casual tone. 'Did you find any more pearls of wisdom?'

'Well,' he said, opening the book to the contents page and running a finger down the chapter titles, 'I learned which category my problems might fall into. I'm either going to be a shallow bitch slut, a self-hating liar or worse.'

'What could be worse?'

'I could be acting like a dude.'

'Right. And *that's* why you're not married yet?'

'Seems that way. But she doesn't scold the whole time,' he said, flipping the book open again to a place marked by his thumb. 'She says if I want to bring love into my life, I have to be an open person. I have to turn up a pink light in my heart and shine it everywhere. Men will flock to me, she says,' James concluded, shutting the book. 'But women and children too, so that's a plus.' He looked at her. 'Is it working?'

'What, the little E.T. light in your heart? You turned it on already?'

He held her gaze. 'It's now or never, right?'

Cait laughed awkwardly. Why would her cheeks not return to their normal temperature? 'You want me to flock to you? Sounds undignified.'

'Yeah, nah; just come out to dinner with me.'

'We don't even know each other.' Why had she said that? He would think she didn't want to. Stupid! Ask me again, she thought.

'We can get to know each other. In a public place and all that. I'm not some random. I've been coming here for ages and I'm reading these stupid books about how to date and the whole time I'm thinking, the girl who works here is beautiful and nice and obviously smart. Just ask her out. So, on the admittedly dubious advice of Tracy, I'm asking you out.'

Cait remembered telling June she was perfectly happy on her own and had to focus on her business right now. She considered the almost-certainty that a date would result in being stuck for hours with yet another being who might as well be from another planet, for all they had in common. Even if it went well, there would be mind games over what happened next.

'Don't leave me hanging, just say yes.'

'OK. Well, yes,' said Cait, surprising herself. 'But only if you stop badmouthing Tracy. Maybe there's more to her than meets the eye.'

'Let's hope so,' he said, indicating the frivolous cover. 'What do I owe you?'

'Just take it,' Cait told him. 'It's covered in highlighter; I can't sell it like that. I can't think why I took it in.'

'Fate,' he said. 'Gift accepted. I'll buy dinner. And I'll study this further beforehand.'

They swapped numbers and he was barely out the door when the phone rang. Simultaneously, another customer appeared before her, book and wallet in hand. 'Good morning, Book Fiend. Please hold?' Cait answered politely, giving the guy waiting a 'just a second' smile at the same time.

'No, I won't hold!' shrieked a female voice, and the line went dead. Cait put the phone down and took a Game of Thrones brick from her next customer.

'Didn't want to wait, huh?' he said.

'Nope,' she said. 'Not to worry. That'll be twenty-two ninety-five.'

⁕

The goals for this date, Cait had told herself earlier that Saturday evening, were simple. One – look good; two – don't make a dick of yourself; three – prove to June and yourself that you're still a functioning member of society. But she was already stuck at number one, as the growing pile of clothes on the floor made abundantly clear.

Mac was watching from a safe distance, on the bed, and for all that he was only a cat, he had a pitying look on his face. Cait had bought him five years ago, telling herself every self-respecting bookseller needed a cat. She'd been in a Shakespeare phase at the time and had called him Macduff, after the avenging hero of *Macbeth*. June had thought it altogether too much name for a fluffy ginger kitten, but Cait had insisted that he would grow into it, and she had been right. He was now an imposing beast, closer to a small lion than a big cat.

'Don't look like that,' she told him. 'You should be excited for me. How long has it been since I went on a date?' Mac merely looked at her. She tried to decide if the sunshine-yellow, knee-length dress she had not worn since she was twenty-five still looked OK. 'Too fluoro. I should just get rid of this.' She wriggled out of the synthetic dress and chucked it on the floor with the rest of the reject pile. Why hadn't she done this earlier in the week? She should have known that she wouldn't have time to agonise over this tonight after rushing home from visits to June, Max, one of her nursing homes and finally Dorothy, whose arguments regarding why *Hope Farm* should win the Stella had been compelling but lengthy. Cait had had to inch out the door backwards, apologising all the way, and had taken the drive out through the hills faster than even she would normally like. Now, as she and the cat together gazed into her ravaged wardrobe, she considered for approximately the twentieth time the alternative: just calling James and cancelling. Then she had an idea.

She went into the study and pulled out the carton of clothes her mother had donated to her when she moved. Cait had never got around to sorting through it. Maybe now was the time. She opened the carton and began to pull things out. Most of it looked kind of restrictive. The kind of stuff that would make you look good, but that you would be forever tugging at and adjusting. She stopped at a skirt in a long, soft grey cotton. Now, this looked comfortable. Cait pulled it on and was instantly convinced. It was floor-length and narrow, tight around the hips and upper thighs then falling straight to the floor. The shape was sexy, but the fabric was casual enough that it didn't seem too dressy. Encouraged, she went back to the box and dug through it for tops. She tried a red one, with layers of hanging fabric, but it made her look strangely top-heavy, and it clashed with her hair. Usually acceptable, but not tonight. Then she tried one that looked black, but glittered gold when she moved, thanks to a shiny thread somehow woven into the fabric. She debated, looking into the mirror. Mac made a sudden choking noise. 'I agree,' she said, and yanked it off. She wasn't the glittery type. She went back into the box and withdrew something tiny. A dark blue, very crumpled scrap. 'How about this, Mac? Shall I wear this hanky?' She smoothed the top flat on the bed to ease out the creases. It turned out to be a silk singlet with thin, flat straps, perfectly plain but for a strip of cotton lace edging the bustline. She got into it and turned to the mirror. Her mum had taste, she couldn't deny that. It was very simple, but hot, in an almost-underwear-but-not-quite sort of way. The silk clung and skimmed in all the right places. Didn't it? Oh God, she needed validation before she wore this in public. She reached for her phone, made an excessively lengthy and complex business of taking a full-length selfie by propping the phone precariously on the bureau – how did Instagram teens do this? – and sent it to Sylvia Rose.

> Hey, sorry we still haven't caught up but meanwhile ... is this OK for a date?

> OMG. YOU? A DATE? WHO WITH? Mystery Shopper?!

> I'll tell you later! Got to go. Just tell me if outfit's OK?

> On point. You look smashing. Expect full report later!

Right. It would do. But it was way too creased to wear like this. 'And now there's ironing, Mac,' she said to the cat. 'You see? It's a slippery slope.' Macduff underlined his boredom with the entire process by getting up, stretching then heading over to the bedside table and swiping the little jade elephant who stood there onto the floor.

Cait liked elephants. Whenever she travelled anywhere, she liked to visit museums best, then art galleries, though she stuck to the old collections. She didn't get the contemporary stuff. She always looked in the gift shop for elephants, though she didn't really know why. She had never seen one, apart from a dim memory of the one at the zoo when she was a kid. She just liked the thought of them. They seemed so solid and calm and immoveable. Until she got them home, that is, and they became playthings for Mac. He peered down at the elephant on the floor now in apparent surprise, as though he couldn't imagine how it had gotten down there. Cait looked longingly into the wardrobe at her comfy Converse sneakers, then reached into a dark corner to retrieve her only pair of shoes without laces and rubber soles: a pair of black kitten heels. She brushed off the dust, abstractedly using the first dusting implement she saw, which happened to be the doona cover, and instantly regretted this when she saw the black mark she'd made. She retrieved the elephant from the floor before she could stand on it. The jade was a particularly painful one to stand on.

Cait ironed the top, showered, shaved her legs for the first time in rather a long time, did a blow-dry, which with her quantity of hair took forever, and a rudimentary makeup job. 'Right,' she said to Macduff. 'What's the time?' She checked her phone. 'Shit!' She had forgotten how long all this personal grooming stuff took. She couldn't really afford an Uber, but it was so late she had no choice.

It seemed to take forever to arrive, and once it got to the CBD they got mired in congestion that was fiendishly unusual for Perth, where bad traffic was pretty much exclusively confined to weekday rush hours and the customary freeway bottlenecks. But at least the Uber took her relatively close to the doors of the bar. It was disconcerting walking in high heels, especially with the addition of a skirt that suddenly made her feel like someone had bandaged her legs together. What had been sexy in her bedroom seemed suddenly ridiculous. She briefly considered just getting back in the Uber, but when she turned around it had already gone. She hopped up the kerb, nearly fell over, swore, and hiked the lower half of the skirt up to her knees, holding it bunched in her hand as she made her way to the entrance.

SEVEN

The bar was plush and crowded and dim. Thankfully the skirt had not objected to being scrunched and fell nicely back into place as she started to descend the carpeted stairs, trying to look around for her date without looking like she was looking around for her date. Cait had intended to be early precisely to avoid this scenario, of gazing around like a person getting stood up, while the early party got to bask in a dark corner deciding when to show themselves and put the hapless one out of their misery. She was not quite panting, but she knew she was flushed. She was horribly late. Just as she was starting to think that he must have left – if he had ever turned up in the first place – a hand waved from a corner and she saw his face. God, he was handsome. A hard word to use seriously, connoting Disney heroes and Ken dolls, but in his case appropriate. She wondered for the hundredth time what he saw in a skinny, freckled redhead who was usually covered in smudges of dust. She walked over, taking tiny steps because of the skirt and hoping this did not look silly. 'Hi,' she said, sitting down opposite him in the booth and smiling.

'Hi,' he replied, smiling back. He already had a beer. He was wearing a button-up shirt, no tie. It was different to his office shirts, though she couldn't put her finger on exactly how it was different. 'Can I get you a cocktail?'

'Thanks,' she said, taking the menu. It was actually a hardback folder, unexpectedly heavy. 'Sorry I'm late.'

He made a dismissive gesture, as if to suggest he had all the time in the world, and she flipped open the folder, glad to have an immediate task. But this was more of a book than a menu. The cocktail list went for pages and each one cost twenty dollars or more. They all looked amazing. There were too many. Her heart was banging treacherously. Aware she was taking forever, she closed the book. 'Just a glass of white wine, please,' she said, raising her voice to be heard above the noise of the crowd, and of Doris Day, singing 'Perhaps, Perhaps, Perhaps'.

'Sure?' he was staring at her. Had she wrecked her hair in the run from the Uber to the door? Why was this city so windy? She restrained herself from putting a hand up to check, felt her blush deepen and nodded. He got up and she let out the breath she hadn't realised she'd been holding. No wonder she didn't date. This was way too nerve-racking. What the hell was she going to say to him? What was she doing here?

When James returned, the noise in the bar helped dispel their awkward politeness, forcing them to sit close and talk loudly. The wine helped too. Cait didn't normally get much of a chance to drink, so quickly arrived at a pleasant buzz. James turned out to be easier to talk to than she had thought, especially by the time they were into their second drinks. They were both only children, both lived alone. While she had Macduff, he had a goldfish named Maclary, after *Hairy Maclary from Donaldson's Dairy*, which he said had been his favourite book as a kid. They laughed at the similar sounds yet wildly dissimilar origins of their pets' names. 'Shows what mental level I'm at, compared to you,' he said, but she didn't think he sounded lacking in the brains department. He was a property agent in an office around the corner from Book Fiend, and he was managing the commercial leases for an entire city arcade, along with a lot of other properties. She didn't have the foggiest idea of what might be involved in such a job, let alone much of an interest, but for the sake of manners she asked the name of the company and recognised it as the same one that she dealt with for her own lease. She playfully asked for a discount. He asked if dinner would do.

'Where?' she asked, and he told her he'd already booked at the restaurant above the bar. Cait had never heard of it, but decided this was probably in its favour. Fancy city venues were not her area of expertise. Sure enough, the restaurant was the fanciest one she had been to since she was a teenager going out with her parents. Thank God she'd gone for the heels and not the Converse. James gave his name to a maître d', who led them to a table beside the windows. The maître d' pulled out Cait's chair for her and she sat down, the bare skin of her shoulder brushing against the velvety fabric of floor-length, blood-red curtains on her right. He then floated a white linen napkin down onto her lap and vanished. Another waiter arrived within seconds. 'Some water for the table? What kind would you like?' Cait was momentarily confused. Water was water, right?

'Sparkling, please,' James said smoothly. He picked up the wine list. It wasn't an actual folder this time, but it still looked intimidating to Cait. It didn't appear to intimidate him, though. He ordered a bottle after only a brief look and the waiter withdrew, footsteps noiseless against the carpet.

Cait, thanks to the two glasses she'd already had, was feeling bold. 'So, how's Tracy's book turning out?' she said. 'Have you worked out why you're not married yet? I mean, I've done a preliminary inspection and you seem all right to me.'

He laughed, but still looked faintly embarrassed. 'I actually am reading it. It's pretty funny. It's aimed squarely at women, obviously, but there's food for thought there.'

'Like what?'

'Well, her basic premise is that you've got to recognise your own issues and work on yourself before you can expect any decent human being to be interested in you. Which does make sense.'

'Do you really have so many urgent issues? You're hardly an old bachelor.'

'Well, I'm a bit of a workaholic. I know that.'

'How come? Like, have you always been one?'

'Really just for the past few years. I've been trying to get ahead at work. I want to be able to look after my mum ... She was pretty old when she had me and she's already retired, but she's still got a mortgage and she's not in great shape. My dad died five years ago, from lung cancer.'

'Oh, I'm sorry,' Cait said, awkwardly.

'Yeah, no big fanfare over my thirtieth that year. I spent it in the hospital with Dad. Anyway, he didn't leave much behind, money-wise, and I guess I wanted to make sure I'm far enough ahead to cover anything Mum might need. Medical bills, or a nursing home. You just never know what's coming, you know?'

'That's mature,' said Cait, who could relate to his work ethic but not its purpose. Her own parents were able-bodied, relatively young and living their own lives. Her obligations didn't go much beyond the occasional phone call and visiting one or the other at New Year. And June was very self-sufficient, always had been.

'I guess. After I turned thirty I stopped mucking around, stopped going on Contiki tours and all that. I just knuckled down and worked. Bought my apartment, nice car, furniture. Helped Mum downsize, got her all set up in her new place. But it's like all my friends suddenly turned thirty and had switches inside them go, "Ping! Better go find a wife and get her pregnant!"'

Cait laughed. 'Your switch didn't go off?'

'Maybe it did and I just didn't hear it. I was busy, what with Dad, and with looking after Mum. Unfortunately, I never twigged that I only had to do one thing to make Mum happy and it wasn't earning heaps of money to ensure her future comfort.'

The waiter returned and set down a basket of evidently complimentary bread. 'Would you like to taste the wine?' he asked, and Cait was about to tell him just to pour it when James said, 'Yes, please.' Cait stared covertly as James swirled and looked and tasted. She had never actually seen anyone taste wine before accepting it in a restaurant. 'Go ahead,' he told the waiter, who poured the glasses while they hastily attended to their menus, so far ignored. They ordered, and he vanished again. Cait, childishly excited by free bread, loaded a hunk of it with butter. It was still warm. Maybe they baked it here. There was even salt to put on the butter, sitting in a dish that was really a chunk of wood with the flakes nestled, like something precious, in a shallow indentation.

Perhaps more wine on top of what she'd already drunk was not the most sensible option. It was very nice wine, though. A little more wouldn't hurt. She was always being sensible. And wine certainly made talking easier.

'What do you mean, you only have to do one thing to make your mum happy?' she asked, realising belatedly that she had talked with her mouth full. James looked at her pointedly and she wondered for an awful moment if he was disgusted with her table manners. She gulped the bread down, where it promptly and painfully lodged itself somewhere in the middle of her chest. Then she understood what he had meant. 'Oh,' she said. 'I'm a sacrificial lamb, hey? An offering to the Mum god? Have you got a horse and cart waiting outside to take me to the church on time?'

'No!' he said, stretching out his hand in a forestalling gesture, as though she might actually get up and flee, like Julia Roberts as a runaway bride. Now, that was where sneakers would have come in handy. 'That's not what I meant. I mean, yes, she wants me to get married. But I think she maybe would be happy to just see me going out more and working less. Living, you know? She and my dad worked hard all their lives and they never got to enjoy it. They talked a bit after his diagnosis about how they should go away together and just have a good time, but the treatment had to start straightaway, and after it he was in no fit state to do anything but lie down and slowly die.'

'I'm sorry,' Cait said, again, wishing she had something better to say.

'It's OK,' he said, smiling at her. 'I just wanted to explain why Mum wants me to be going out more and having fun. She thinks I'm a catch, obviously, being my mother and all. She's been ramping up the pressure, telling me I have to make an effort, telling me about all the coffee catch-ups she's having with the mums of my high school friends, who are of course all telling her about how their kids are all married now.'

'Of course.'

'Yep. All people I don't see much of, needless to say.' He took a sip of wine. 'They just occasionally invite me to dinner parties where I'm one of two single people, and the other single person has obviously been invited because they think I'll like her. And the couples spend the whole party nagging each other, or fighting over who's telling a story wrong, or over who's going to check on the baby.'

Cait laughed. The bread had finally gone down.

'I've always been hopeless at asking women out. I figured it's time I started putting myself out there. But it turns out the dating world has changed big-time. Now there are apps!'

'Oh, I know,' Cait said. The thought of writing her own blurb on a dating app made her blood run cold.

'I got on Tinder and the first girl I talked to on it asked me to send a dick pic. A dick pic! So that was a wash. Clubs are a wash. All my wingmen are married and by the time the other punters have finished their pre-drinks and arrived out, I'm ready to go home to bed. I guess I felt a bit lost.'

'Hence the books?'

'Hence the books. Suppose I'm a bit of a sad case.'

'If you're a sad case, then so am I. I can't remember my last date, it was so long ago. I work all the time too. I want to get into my escape pod every time someone so much as mentions Tinder. I totally relate to feeling like you get better life advice from books than from an android. And that's probably why we're both alone,' she concluded. 'At least you're making an effort. Even if it's just because your mum told you to. And, hey, I'm happy to be your practice girl.'

'Oh, no,' he said, looking at her with such sudden intensity she could have sworn she felt her skin prickle. Then he dropped his gaze and swirled his wine around in its glass, seeming to hesitate. She heard the murmur of the other diners nearby, and the ding of a bell in the kitchen. She reached for her own wine glass and missed. Hoping he hadn't noticed, she reached for it again and took a sip. A treacherous drop dribbled down the outside of the bowl, down the stem and onto the white linen napkin on her lap. She thanked her lucky stars he had taken her cue from downstairs and ordered white. 'If anything, I was thinking I'd need to practise to ask you out,' he finally said. 'But the other day I just felt comfortable with you. You didn't feel like a girl.'

'Well. Thanks, I think,' Cait said, trying for wry amusement, another blush rising.

'What I mean is, you just felt like a person.'

There seemed to be nowhere her eyes could go to escape his gaze, except into her lap.

'Mushroom soup,' announced the waiter, materialising with unnerving suddenness beside them, as though he was paid to foil awkward moments as well as deliver food. He placed a large, shallow bowl before Cait. An earthy fragrance rose from it.

'And the *boeuf bourguignon*,' he said, with a French accent ostentatious in its perfection, placing the dish in front of James. 'May I get you anything else?' he turned to ask Cait, who tried not to laugh at James mouthing '*bef booginyon*', nose in air, behind his back.

'No, thanks, we're fine,' she said, keeping a straight face until he'd refilled their glasses and stalked away. They both laughed, and James picked up his fork, surveying his dish. 'Enough about me. What about you?' he said. 'How much are you disappointing your own parents?'

'Moderately,' Cait said. 'They consider working in a shop something you do as a teenager, not as an adult. Never mind that I actually own this shop. But I don't have to deal with them much. Just the odd phone call mostly. Sometimes Mum flies me over for New Year – they both moved over east after the divorce. Dad to Queensland, pretty much straightaway, and Mum went to Melbourne a few years later.'

'When did they get divorced?'

Give him the short version, Cait told herself. 'Years ago. More than ten years ago. My dad works in the mines and Mum's an occupational therapist, though she's more of a paper-pusher these days. Between his swings and her shifts, they barely saw each other.' She thought about Ken's final drunk drive home that had ended up capsizing both his new Triton ute and his marriage, and her mother's long subsequent depression, which had in the end ensured that Cait had largely stopped depending on either parent for much in the way of support or nurturing. Yep, definitely keep it to the short version. Cait busied herself stirring in the dollop of cream that floated on the glossy surface of her soup.

'Tough subject?'

'Not really. It was all a long time ago.'

'Why'd you open a bookshop?' he said, evidently deciding that a safer topic was in order.

Cait had not been asked this question in years, since she'd initially had to justify herself to her parents. 'I guess ...' she began, and had a sip of wine to buy some time. He waited, looking at her. He had such lovely eyes. Right now they looked pure hazel, no green. She saw no judgement in them, only attentiveness. You don't need to defend yourself, she thought. He wants to understand you. 'I guess it started with June. She was my nanny growing up, but more like a grandmother, really. We talked about books constantly. I felt like the authors I read as a kid understood me better than people in real life. Books talked about stuff I was interested in. I never knew what to say to the other kids at school.'

'Well, I don't know. You seem pretty good with people to

me. You handle so many people who seem like total dickheads. And look how sweet you are to that annoying old bloke who comes in and asks you for exactly the same thing every day. You'll chat away to him no problem.'

Cait felt a little leaping sensation. So she was not the only one who had been watching the other.

'Well, working in retail has kind of taught me how to interact with people. And it's always talking about books. And Mr Cowper's all right. It's meeting new people, or talking to big groups of people at parties, that's the hard part. I'm fine once I know the person.'

'I'll take that as a challenge,' he said, his gaze direct. 'Still, from shy kid to shop owner seems like a big leap. Didn't you want to do something less people-focused?'

Cait thought. 'Well, I knew I wanted to work with books. After school, everyone trooped off to uni like lemmings. I couldn't imagine myself at uni, so I was treading water for a bit.'

James loaded his fork with beef and added some of his side dish, a velvety-looking mash flecked with fragments of some green herb. 'You could have been a librarian,' he said, then added, 'This is great. How's yours?'

'It's really good,' Cait said, and took another spoonful. It was. Dark, rich and silky in texture. Max would have approved. 'I thought about being a librarian, but then I found out you needed a degree. I thought about going into publishing, but I wanted to stay in Perth, near June, and the publishing industry is tiny in WA, and I just ... I couldn't see a way in. I thought about being a sales rep for one of the distributors, but you need to be a smooth-talker for that. So I went into retail. I worked at Dymocks for years, but I always wanted to go out on my own. I thought that shop was a bit impersonal. I wanted to make a place for myself, but where other people liked to come, too.'

'Well, you've done that,' James said, and she beamed at him.

'My parents thought I was insane,' she said. She remembered the phone call with Tania very well. Her mother had said she was making a mistake. Cait had told Tania she was no-one to be giving life advice. She had later regretted this comment and apologised for it, but it had opened a rift that was hard to mend through irregular phone calls and even more irregular visits. 'The only person who didn't think I was crazy was June. I guess she found it easier to swallow because she didn't come from a time where it was so inevitable people go to uni.'

'I can see that,' James said. 'It's true a lot more people go to uni now than they did a few decades back. I remember when I did my undergrad, it seemed like half the students didn't have any particular reason to be there, it was just that uni was what they automatically did after school.'

'Yes,' Cait said eagerly. 'It wasn't so much uni I had a problem with. It was just this assumption that it was the only thing to do. I thought, why the hell is this the automatic choice, when it's got nothing to do with the only thing I could conceivably be good at?' She paused for another spoonful of soup. 'The only thing is, it leaves me with no fallback. If the shop fails, I'm qualified for precisely zilch.'

'You seem to be doing all right. It's a pretty big accomplishment in this climate to be running any profitable small business at all, let alone a bookstore. Especially since it looks like you're doing it pretty much single-handedly.'

'Well, I've got my weekend guy, Seb. And I don't know that I'm doing all that well. It's always a struggle. It was OK during the boom, but it's pretty dismal now. People just don't seem to be spending, and I'm still paying boom-time rent.'

'When did you sign your lease?'

'Almost five years ago.'

'Ah, that explains it.'

'Yeah, maybe I should have gone for a shorter one and renegotiated, but I didn't know back then the way things would go.'

'No-one planned for the bad times,' James said. 'Not even the government. So don't feel too bad.'

'True. Like you said, at least I'm still going, and there have been so many shops close around me.'

'There will probably be more, too.'

'No, don't tell me that. Why?'

'Well, like you said, people aren't spending in 2016 like they were in 2011. They've got lower disposable incomes than they did during the boom. Your rent is the same, and your weekend guy isn't getting any cheaper. None of your operating costs are getting any lower. And in my properties, most of the businesses that close are just closing; they're not choosing to relocate. So that suggests that it's not just rents, but that the businesses themselves are unviable.' James buttered a final piece of bread and used it to mop up the gravy remaining in his dish. 'They might have been profitable in the boom, but not anymore. There are actually fewer people in the CBD to be buying stuff.'

'What do you mean?' Cait said, and finished her soup.

'Well, there are ten thousand fewer office workers in the CBD now than there were in boom time. All the hotels are half empty. And they have a lot of choice. Shopping centres are growing and people are buying a lot of stuff online' – 'Tell me about it,' Cait muttered – 'so, I would say even when the economy improves, small retailers will keep closing.'

'Well, that's a downer. I guess I'll hold off on getting finance for that Mercedes.'

James laughed as the waiter approached, cleared their plates and proffered the dessert menu.

'No, thanks,' said Cait, who felt very full, mostly of wine, but James took one.

'There's never any harm in looking,' he said, with a rather roguish smile, and scanned it. 'Sure I can't tempt you? Mousse? Dark chocolate tart? Or a dessert wine?'

'No, really, I couldn't. You have something, though,' she said, not wanting to suggest she was in a hurry. 'If you want.'

'No, I'm full too,' James said. They sat for a moment, savouring the last of the wine, then James called for the bill and paid, despite her protestations. Cait didn't know how to negotiate the next part of the evening. Should she thank him and leave? Or were they supposed to leave together and then she could call a cab from the street? She didn't really want the night to end just yet, but after their conversation she was hardly going to suggest they go out to some club. Clubs probably weren't open yet anyway. Another bar, maybe? But she had really had enough to drink. And she had zero idea of how she would word an invitation back to her place. No, that whole scenario was too intimidating and complicated. Oh God, she was OK at conversation while it was flowing, but then it eddied around these points of transaction. How to keep it running, smoothly, into the next activity?

Thankfully, James once again proved more graceful at it than she. 'Hey, how about we head along the river for a bit, walk off this wine?'

When they got outside, the air had cooled noticeably. 'I think summer's finally over,' James said.

'And not a moment too soon.'

The Saturday night crowds thinned as they crossed the Terrace, then dispersed altogether as they crossed the Esplanade to the river. The scent of mown grass drifted up from beneath their feet. Cait tried not to struggle too obviously in her heels. They had fallen into an easy silence by the time they reached the footpath and turned to walk along it. She could hear the water lapping placidly at the retaining wall. It was actually nice, talking to James, Cait thought. For that matter, it was equally nice being quiet with him. No-one was demanding anything of her: no service, no decisions. In fact, she hadn't had to make a decision for herself all evening. She shivered. The wind was building, whipping her hair around, and making the silk top feel more impractical by the minute. He was definitely looking at her again, she could feel it. For want of any better way to react, she stopped and turned to face the river as though admiring the view. The flat, dark water stretched and disappeared into a long blackness, becoming visible again as it reflected the lights along the footpath of the far shore. The lights were very evenly spaced, like pearls strung at intervals along a necklace.

'Cold?' he asked, also turning to face the water.

'A bit,' she said, and he took off his jacket, shushing her as she started to demur.

'Come on, you must be freezing,' he said, draping it over her shoulders in a sideways movement. 'I'm wearing long sleeves, anyway.'

'Sensible. I should have done the same.'

'I'm glad you didn't.'

She stilled at his tone, and he reached across her chest to pull the collar closer around her neck, then tugged harder on its far side, turning her towards him. That leaping feeling shot through her stomach again, like she'd gone too high on the swings: exhilarating and scary all at once. She automatically tried to duck her head to keep her eyes on the safe territory of the ground, but her hair, trapped in the jacket collar, impeded the movement. 'Looks good on you,' he murmured. He leaned closer. Just as her breath caught and she was certain he was going to kiss her, his hands reached behind her and lifted the trapped hair from beneath the jacket. His fingers grazed the back of her neck, feather-light. 'We'd better call it a night before you get any colder, hey?'

She drew in a deep breath, and hoped he didn't hear its unevenness as she let it out, turning away from the lapping water, back across the grass to the lights, the Saturday-night-drunk teens and the rattling, fluorescent train station. She'd already blown her Uber budget getting into the city. She felt absurdly disappointed that he hadn't kissed her, and as they entered the station she came to a decision. Bugger it, everyone had their issues. Surely she could manage a relationship on top of her own. Functioning human being and all that. If it turned out he wanted to see her again, she would say yes.

It was when her train drew in and they'd said goodnight, and she'd given back his jacket and started to turn away, that he grabbed her bare shoulders and turned her towards him and kissed her. His lips were hot, his fingers cold on her skin. Then the bell dinged and a cool female voice warned the doors were closing and he thrust her back from him and through the doors into the carriage. As their eyes locked through the closing glass panels, his lips curved into a grin, a recklessly happy grin she could not help but return.

EIGHT

The sun shone brightly but without heat in the early winter sky. The air was fresh and bracing, and Cait was going through her routines in a state of delicious abstraction. The shop felt like a hazy background to the real action taking place in a small, electrified zone between her body and the computer, her conversation with her boyfriend of precisely two months – not that she was counting, of course. Cait had begun half a dozen tasks since midday, but every 'ping' announcing an arriving message sent her wheeling back towards the counter. She stood bent with elbows propped before the keyboard, heedless of the stool before her, savouring the words appearing in the chat window, a small, secret smile playing on her lips as she contemplated her responses.

Book Fiend, meanwhile, looked like a bomb had hit it. The last box from the Penguin drop-off sat half unpacked on the floor behind her, where she had tripped over it twice already. A history display lay three-quarters finished on one of the front islands. A stack of new second-hand stock lay sanded and Windexed but still unpriced on the counter, and when she dashed to discover what lay behind this latest ping, Cait hastily stuffed her Spray n' Wipe and filthy Chux into a gap in the shelves in Parenting and promptly forgot about them as another messaging storm commenced.

> Hey! Has it been long enough since I messaged you to message you again?

> Well, I'm feeling exceptionally unmotivated this morning, so you can't make me any less productive. And a whole half-hour has passed, after all.

> My urge to taste you again hasn't passed.

Cait felt her breath catch. What to say?

> :~~~~))))) ... (That's me smiling a lot)

> 8=====D

Cait was busy trying to figure out what this picture meant when another message arrived.

> That's a penis.

She laughed aloud.

> Even your virtual penis is a terrible distraction.

Then she received another assortment of symbols creating an image even she needed no assistance deciphering.

> I'm trying to be a professional here, James! I've done zero work today! What have you done to my motivation?

> I'm keeping your motivation in my bedroom for personal use, silly.

They continued in this vein until Cait was interrupted by a customer, a balding middle-aged man brandishing a copy of Peter H. Wilson's book about the Holy Roman Empire, marking another hole in her unfinished history display. 'This one's got no price on it. It must be free!' he said, evidently feeling he was the first person ever to make this joke. Cait, too full of private joy to be impatient with anyone, gave him a chuckle before telling him the price. He bought the book, and the outside world shrank again as she returned to her messages.

> Warwick just asked if I could help Rachel ... made about 20 calls for her, did some minor paperwork. Time is back to limping.

> I am over today too. Just got the old 'this has no price on it, it must be free' chestnut again. Don't worry, I laughed like it was the first time I'd heard it today.

> I wish I was there, watching you work your charm. I'm counting down to when I see you again. Speaking of which ...

> Tonight?

> Alas! I already told my mother I would see her for dinner. Tomorrow night?

> Late night shopping, remember?

> Noooo! I guess Saturday ☹

> Saturday night at that. I have visits during the day. June, Max, Dorothy AND nursing homes.

> Wow, full day.

> It's not always all at once but it's also been a while since I've seen June. She went to Singapore for shopping and the casino. And thanks to a recent DISTRACTION we shall not name, I am well overdue for Dorothy and the nursing homes.

> Guilty as charged. I guess we have been glued at the hip.

I know. Can you believe we have only been going out two months?

Must say it's a nasty empty feeling knowing I can't touch you for another 48 hours plus.

If only there were several more of me to go around. Even if it meant my soul was irreparably damaged, Voldemort-style.

Can I be your Horcrux? Potter-style ... I could be your giant snake and eat all the people who piss you off.

I think I like your human form best.

The phone rang. 'Hello, Book Fiend. Cait speaking.'

'Oh, hi. I'm looking for a book, but I can't remember what it's called, or who wrote it.'

'OK, well, what was it about?'

'It's about a girl who travels into the magical realms through these energy paths. Everyone is fighting for control of the land and I believe she meets Satan, who's possibly her father?'

'Right,' Cait said, trying not to laugh. 'I'm not sure I know that one. Have you tried googling it?'

'Yeah, I can't find it anywhere.'

'Sorry I can't be of more help. If you remember anything more about it, feel free to give me a call back.'

James hadn't messaged back yet. Cait took advantage of the lull to call Dorothy, who wasn't content with just arranging a time for the weekend's visit, and wanted to settle in and chat. Cait disentangled herself by promising they could talk further on Saturday. Next, she rang Max, who informed her he had finally finished *LA Confidential*.

'Took you long enough!'

'Well, I've been on grandchild duty a lot lately, so I didn't get the chance to start it until a few weeks ago. Then I found it very dense, like you said. But a bloody ripper in the end.'

'Wasn't it? Didn't I tell you the movie was different?'

'A pale shadow,' Max agreed. 'Positively anaemic.'

Max asked for more Sophie Hannah, and once she got off the phone, their visit confirmed for Saturday, Cait thought she'd better go and hunt one out before she forgot. She grabbed *Kind of Cruel* plus a Janet Evanovich thriller, about the bounty hunter Stephanie Plum. Max claimed the series was too 'fluffy and female' to be a favourite, but Cait knew he secretly couldn't get enough of them. She headed back to the counter, almost tripping for a third time over the Penguin box, and added the books to Max's stack. Why wasn't James messaging back? No, must stop obsessing over the chat and do work. Now, what was it she'd been doing? She stared at the cluttered mess behind the counter, trying to focus. Then she noticed a stack of mail overdue for opening by several days already, and pulled it towards her. She opened three letters before there was another ping.

> Sorry about that. I was called upon to do some actual work for a minute there. Anyway ... I like your human form too. I miss it. Tempted to cancel on Mum tonight.

> As much as I want to see you, you shouldn't do that. You're too good a son.

> I know, I know ...

> Tell you what. If you're being a model son tonight, I will be a model daughter. I'll ring my mum. I'm well overdue for a duty call.

> I bet she would love to hear you describing it that way.

> Well, she's just hard work is all.
>
> I know what you mean, trust me. Maybe soon you can double your parental workload and come meet my mum.
>
> Wow :-)
>
> I'm just saying. I like going places with you and looking at your face. I like walking hand in hand and making out in my car. I like everything about you.

Cait took a deep breath. She could not prevent herself grinning like an idiot as she wrote back.

> I like looking at you too ... and marvelling that what I see is really mine.
>
> We should celebrate on Saturday. Go on a romantic date. I'll get you drunk and take advantage of you.
>
> OK, it's a date! Now I really have to do some work.
>
> Cool. I'd better get some work done too. Rachel is being her usual unreliable self ... Counting down till Saturday.
>
> Talk later?
>
> Talk later.

Cait took a deep breath and tried to control the smile that appeared to have become cemented onto her face. Her cheek muscles were actually starting to hurt. But she had to clean up quickly. Still smiling, she priced the second-hand pile and aimed each title into its section with a level of care equal to that of a tipsy darts player. She snatched the new releases remaining in the Penguin box, chucked them into their sections too, flattened the box and jammed it into the overflowing recycling bin out the back. She grabbed a few second-hand history titles and rammed them unceremoniously into the gaps in the display. She could tidy it all up in the final lap. Oops, there were people at the till. She dashed back, passing her cleaning gear in Parenting. When the hell did she leave that there? She stuffed the cloth and spray bottle into her apron pocket and careened back behind the counter like a baseball player sliding into home. Her half-opened mail was still covering the countertop, forcing the customer to hold their pile of books in their arms. She shoved it to the side, under a pile of paperwork to be sorted through. She must remember to deal with that later. She turned a hundred-watt beam onto the customer, whose frown softened as they smiled back. 'Sorry about that,' she said. 'I did have a bell under there somewhere. Now, what have you got for me?'

NINE

The days were getting too cold to sit outside, so Cait took the tea tray from June's kitchen into the living room, where they sat curling their fingers around their warm teacups.

'Well, out with it!' June said, with a Cheshire-cat grin.

'What?' Cait protested, though her own lips were already forming a sheepish smile.

'You're positively incandescent,' June said. 'The rest of us are scaly and shrivelled as women can only be in the middle of winter, but you are pink-cheeked and bushy-tailed. Your heart is glowing on your sleeve. Things getting serious with your young man James, then?'

'Oh, *really*, June,' Cait said. Her cheeks were certainly pink now if they hadn't been before. Then she relented. There was never any hiding anything from June. 'How do you know?'

'I don't need to know. I have only to look and there is love written all over your face. I've never seen it on your face before, mind you, only others', but love is love.'

'Love is a bit of a strong word! We've only been going out for a few months. It's nothing serious, June,' she protested as the old lady cackled with delight, spilling her tea.

'Good golly, nothing serious … Listen to her!' June gloated, taking the napkin Cait handed her and soaking up the puddle of Irish breakfast. 'A few months are enough to know. What does he do for work? I never asked you.'

'Oh, he works in an office in the city, near my work,' Cait said. 'Property management company. It's the same one that has my lease, but he manages different areas, I think. I'm not too clear on what he actually specifically does every day. Lots of paperwork, I think.'

'Paperwork, she thinks,' said June. 'Probably too busy between the sheets to come up for air and talk. Mind you, it's shaping up to be so cold this winter, that's probably not a bad idea.'

'*June,*' Cait said. Her tone was scandalised, but June was uncomfortably close to the truth, as usual. Oh, she and James did talk. They talked about everything. But they talked about themselves, each other. They didn't talk about work or politics or the news, or even all that much about books, because James tended pretty much exclusively towards non-fiction, despite her having made a few attempts to lure him into widening his tastes. Anyway, she didn't particularly want to come out from between the sheets and get some air, as June put it. James's sheets were perfect for burying yourself in. He was the cleanest bachelor she'd ever met. He didn't even throw rubbish on the floor of his car, unlike Cait and everyone else she had ever known. James opened champagne bottles with discreet, celebratory pops. James killed cockroaches calmly and efficiently. James had his appointments entered on a Google calendar that chimed reminders at appropriate times. James sent meals back to the kitchen if they were disappointing, albeit very politely. James parallel-parked with precision. He had a 'portfolio' of 'index funds', whatever the hell they were.

No doubt his tax returns were up to date. James turned up when he said he would. He needed none of the solicitude she gave her clients. In short, James had his shit together. When she was with him she felt a sense of security, of being looked after.

'All right,' June said, taking pity on Cait for her tongue-tied silence. 'So he shuffles papers, makes a living. And what kind of family does he come from?'

Cait described James's mother, whom she had met a fortnight ago, bringing out all the details of the family she knew for June to pick over and comment on, not resenting this process in the least. June's probing was shot through with the kind of excitement and curiosity Cait was craving. She'd caught up with Sylvia a few weeks ago, and gossiping with Sylv had been good, though altogether too brief, but Seb was the only other friend around her age she saw regularly. Though he had met James several times, Seb did not seem keen to ask questions about him. Maybe it was a man thing. And her ring of high-school girlfriends, starry with PhDs, government jobs and European holidays, had drifted so far from her she felt it would soon entirely disperse into the heavens, leaving her in the same place: contentedly earthbound. Every time she had seen them in recent years, they had seemed to have less and less to talk about, and the last get-together had been more than a year ago.

June was a gratifyingly good listener, and asked all the questions Seb had not. Cait went on until she saw with a start that June was drooping visibly over her empty teacup.

'I'm sorry, June, I've talked your ear off,' she said. 'How have you been? What's happening with you?' She poured June a fresh cup and stuffed a biscuit into her own mouth to shut it up. Coconut sweetness dissolved on her tongue. It was more like a Bounty chocolate bar than a biscuit, but without the chocolate, and with bigger, rougher chunks of coconut. 'These are great, June.'

'Good. And don't worry, I'm interested,' June said. 'There's nothing half so enthralling going on with me. You'll have to bring James along one day. Maybe we can go and have a coffee. A sit-down coffee, mind you. Every time I go to the shops to get my bits and pieces, the number of people I see going around with takeaway cups glued to their hands is ludicrous. We never walked around like that when I was young. We sat and drank our coffee, and then, once we were finished, we went about our business.'

'I know, our modern culture is hopelessly depraved. So, did you read the Helen Garner essays?'

'I did. By God, that woman can write. I thoroughly enjoyed them all. Even the few I'd read before. Particularly the one about how when women get old they turn invisible. She's got that one right. Anyway, what else have you got for me?'

Cait presented her picks: the first of Elena Ferrante's Neapolitan Novels and *Barkskins* by Annie Proulx.

'Good lord, it's always the doorstops with you, isn't it?' June said, taking the 700-page Proulx and pretending to almost drop it onto the floor. 'Oh, I see, this Ferrante person. I've heard a lot about these. Four of them, aren't there?'

'Yes, I'm a bit late to start you on them. I kept disregarding them. I was thinking the fuss about them would die down but I'm selling more than ever now even though the last one came out ages ago.'

'Have you read any?'

'Just this one. I found it a bit slow going,' confessed Cait. 'I'd be keen to hear what you think.'

'I'll consider myself warned, then. Speaking of slow going, I've been very tardy with the Lewis biography, but I've finally finished it.'

'Ooh, what'd you think?'

'The stuff about the friendship with Tolkien was excellent … fancy how this big famous writing club grew from two men drinking beer together.'

'Yes! Meeting on Monday mornings "for a glass"! Can you believe it?'

'It did sound an excellent way to spend a Monday. I wonder what was going on with him and Mrs Moore. I mean, I know he promised his friend he'd look after her if Paddy didn't survive the war, but I'm sure poor old Paddy didn't mean his friend should move in with his mother for the rest of her life in whatever mysterious arrangement that was. Obviously it wasn't exactly a mother–son relationship.'

'Well, obviously not. But they clearly loved each other, and I guess he'd hope that was all that mattered in the end.'

'True. The poor man, having to hide that from his father.'

'Yeah, he had a pretty hard life.'

'Hard death too. A sad end, wasn't it? Dying all alone like that, wife dead, son at school, the rest of the world watching JFK dying on TV, all the journalists distracted. Not much fanfare for such a writer. And far too young. Mind you, the medicine back then was pretty dodgy. The contraptions they rigged up for his prostate! Fair made my toes curl.'

'That was awful, wasn't it?' Cait said. The archaic treatments had put the famous writer through much indignity and unnecessary suffering. Her own toes had curled at the descriptions.

'Poor bugger didn't stand a chance. I hope when I go it's gentler.'

'June, don't forget, you're going to live forever.'

June frowned. 'Anyway, a fascinating read. Much better than those space books were. A bit of a chore, those! Far too much Christian stuff. I shouldn't have read them first, or I'd have picked up the biography sooner.'

'Yes, I remember you saying they weren't all that enjoyable.'

'I gave up halfway through the third one. Oh, will you listen to that.' For rain had abruptly begun to thunder on the roof.

'Bugger,' Cait said. 'I've got Max and Dorothy now. The freeway's going to be awful.'

'Well, you drive carefully. No speeding,' June said, pulling herself up with the aid of the walker.

'Who, me?' Cait kissed June and put her hood over her head for the dash out to where nature was giving Dent a much-needed wash. She saw out of the corner of her eye that the roses out the front had not yet had the savage pruning June religiously delivered in the first week of July. That was odd. But the thought was soon crowded out by a more immediate consideration: what she would wear for her three-month anniversary date that night.

<hr />

The shop was a nurturing refuge from what the media, and everyone else, was proclaiming an unusually cold and dreary winter. Book Fiend's windows glinted invitingly to frozen passers-by, the lamps, worn carpets and armchairs contrasting favourably for once with the glassy stares of Prada and Gucci on either side. These remained chilly and aloof, seeming to repel all but the most privileged visitors. Cait, lit from within by thoughts of James, failed to be depressed by the weather, rugging up and working with a joyous energy that seemed to infect her customers. She beguiled them with artful displays of the cosiest winter armchair reading she could find, grouping piles of new crime and romance and biography temptingly on every coffee table. She set up displays of erotica, with little signs suggesting customers 'warm up with some steamy reads this winter'. She accompanied her refusals to give change with such radiant smiles that the applicants, charmed, acquiesced without complaint. Some lingered and bought books they had not intended to buy. Even her regular haggler seemed not to have the heart to give her grief about her pricing and, apart from the odd mutter about how something was half the price on Amazon, parted with his cash relatively peaceably. Even incidents that normally would have enraged Cait amused her. Like a family, browsing one day, whose son spotted a book in the stacks. 'I've been looking everywhere for this!' he said, grabbing it and beginning to read the back.

'Fantastic. Let's get it,' his mother said.

The daughter leaned across and whispered loudly, 'Just get it on Book Depository.'

'Why?' her mother asked.

'Because you save on postage.'

'Why do we need to save on postage?'

Why indeed, Cait thought, privately grinning.

It was late on a very dim Friday that she got a fresh delivery of mail and settled at the desk to go through it, along with the damp and wrinkly stack of older mail that had been building up at her elbows. She had been so busy and so full of energy she hadn't felt like hunkering down to do something so prosaic, and the pile now verged on unmanageable. There were the usual catalogues and junk, which she threw out, and the latest few issues of the *Gazette*. She threw out the older ones and put the newest in one of her reading nooks for customers. There were flyers from local businesses, teenage babysitters and odd-job-doers, which she pinned to her community noticeboard, taking down a few older items to fit them on. There was the latest issue of *Books+Publishing*, protected from the weather in its immaculate plastic sheath, which she put aside to savour later – maybe tonight before closing, if it was quiet. Then there was a slim, businessy envelope from Lease Freedom. This made her smile and think of James, and the night out they had planned for tomorrow. She opened and read it, expecting to see a notification about the lease. Same terms, maybe a bit of an increase in line with CPI. Then she stopped and went back to the beginning, and read it again. Her eyes widened. She got a funny feeling in her chest.

'Hi,' said a friendly voice in front of her. She started and looked up. A guy was standing there. He held a copy of *How to Win Friends and Influence People*. A nice, clean second-hand copy she'd marked up at fourteen dollars because it was a classic, and always sold quickly. The guy had hair past his shoulders and loose cotton clothes that seemed too light for this weather. He had an easy smile and carried a cotton string shopping bag with the strap slung across his chest. 'Hi,' she said, smiling back automatically, then she took the book, checked the price and let him tap his Visa. Hippie types didn't usually like to be given plastic bags, so she held the book back out to him when the card machine beeped its OK. 'Thanks,' she said.

He stared at her. 'Aren't you going to give me a bag?' he asked, dropping the casual tone and sounding positively hostile.

'Oh! Sure,' Cait said, hastily grabbing one and slipping the book inside. 'Here you go.'

'Thanks,' he said coldly, and stalked out, string bag flapping. Cait stared after him for a second. If that was how he planned to go about winning friends and influencing people, he had his work cut out for him. She looked back down.

Dear Ms Copper,

We are following up on our notice last month of the rental increase for the commercial property referenced above. A copy of this earlier communication is enclosed for your convenience.

In addition to this reminder regarding the rental increase, we wish to remind you that your lease will expire on 1 September and to provide additional information that may assist in your decision of whether to apply for renewal.

A surge in demand for such properties has resulted in a waiting list of competitively advantaged international brands, already established on the east coast, seeking appropriate locations to enter the Perth market.

You have been an exemplary tenant whose care of the property and prompt payments thus far have been appreciated.

Should you wish not to renew your lease, but plan to relocate, we extend this invitation to join our relocation assistance program to obtain support in finding an appropriate property.

Please do not hesitate to contact our Tenant Liaison Team with any questions. I look forward to your prompt response.

Cait looked at the enclosed letter, a copy of an original notice of a rental increase. Yes, it was dated well over a month ago. She could have sworn she had never seen it before. She skimmed it.

Please note that, given the substantial increase, ninety days' notice has been given.

It had been ninety days then. Now it was considerably less.

Cait felt suddenly, deeply cold, her fingers frozen around the letters. She realised she was crumpling them and put them down on the counter. She was sure she had never seen this notice. She would remember. What had she been doing on 3 June? Between the sheets with James, no doubt, as June would put it. Why hadn't she been more careful with the mail? What a stupid, vacant, in-love fool not to keep on top of things. But she was sure she hadn't got the first letter. She looked through the older mail and saw nothing else from Lease Freedom. Had she put all the mail in the right place? Missed something, thrown something out accidentally? Maybe it was a postal error. Australia Post was getting slower and slower. A fellow victim of the digital age, she thought bleakly. The sweet voice of Stevie Nicks continued, pure and changeless, through the speakers.

'Well, hello there, Miss Cait.'

Mr Cowper was standing right in front of her, clutching a book. She had not seen him come in. Maybe she had been with a customer and he'd proceeded directly to the stacks. She thought, not for the first time, that Mr Cowper had a positive talent for turning up just at the wrong moment. 'Oh, hello, Mr Cowper,' she said, forcing strength into her voice. 'Have you found something you like?'

Mr Cowper handed her the book. Patrick O'Brian's *The Far Side of the World*. 'Found the next one, first try,' he told her proudly. Cait nodded and smiled vaguely. She tried to hold it together as he kept talking, though she barely heard him. Something about the book having been made into a movie. Something about him having trouble with his hip. She put a sympathetic look on her face and nodded, and kept nodding, hoping she was smiling in the right places, while her mind reverberated.

There was no way she could absorb a thirty percent increase by just cutting a few corners. Especially with what was now substantially less than ninety days' notice. September was just over a month away. But she couldn't relocate. This location was her store's lifeblood. In a suburban mall, she knew from the research she had done before opening Book Fiend, any benefits from the high foot traffic would be cancelled out by the astronomical rents they charged for guaranteeing that traffic. And the people passing by wouldn't be *her* people. She knew her market like the back of her hand. Rich businesspeople too busy to bargain over their gifts. Highly educated ladies wanting suggestions for their highly educated book clubs. Hipsters, seeking beat poets and whichever philosophers were in fashion. Nietzsche, for example, was out. It was all Seneca and Stoicism now. Loyal locals like Mr Cowper, who considered her an institution, who kept her in business when all the other bookstores nearby had closed, one by one. Even the chains, with their no doubt 'competitively advantaged' business models. In a suburban mall, she'd be out of business in six months.

TEN

Cait closed the shop early for the first time in five years. There had been no-one through since Mr Cowper left. It was bitterly cold, and the post-work crowd had got what they needed and split. The Friday-night revellers were subdued and rugged up. Nobody was weaving drunkenly about the pavement, convincing themselves that only impulse buying could fill the void left by another weekday just like the last one, and the one before that. Despite knowing she was leaving Seb with a mess for the morning, she didn't do the tidy. She had to think. She dragged the trolleys up the entry ramp with fingers so cold they hurt, and left them there in disarray. She scribbled Seb a note of apology, saying she felt sick and could he please do the tidy after he opened? She left no other tasks. She put on her coat and scarf, stuffed the letters into her bag, locked the doors, put her hands in her pockets, tucked her chin and set off, mind whirling.

That letter sounded as if a lot of tenants were getting major increases. More than major, she told herself – unaffordable. She didn't like the tone of the letter. It was like the powers that be at Lease Freedom already knew she wouldn't be able to afford this kind of rent and wanted to boot her out for someone who could. Some store with more hard, glassy surfaces that never got dusty, with more eight-hundred-dollar pairs of sunnies and one-hundred-dollar pots of lip balm. They already had a program to relocate the retailers getting booted out; there must have been a few, then. She suddenly thought of the Lims. They had run the newsagency and convenience store next door for twenty years before giving way, quite suddenly, to Prada. She had thought at the time it was odd to move so suddenly after that shop had remained there unchanged for so long. She had thought they would eventually retire and sell the business, not close it down. It was because of them moving that she had to be organised with bringing her lunches, because they had been the last place to sell anything resembling groceries anywhere near here. Crabbe's chemist had gone not long after the Lims. Phil had told her his rent had gone up, but she somehow hadn't quite realised he might have faced anything like this. Rent hikes were always just a phrase that you heard about, and shrugged and figured it was a fact of life, that they would be reasonable, incremental. Now she realised the Lims and Phil Crabbe might have faced twenty or thirty percent increases. Then there had been the music store down the road, a niche establishment like Book Fiend, quirky and independent. That had not shut down, but had moved to a much smaller place in the suburbs, only a few weeks ago. She had noted it with a twinge of sadness but not paid much attention beyond that. It was probably reported on in one of those *Gazette*s she had just chucked out.

She was parking Dent before she realised she did not remember the journey home. It was typical of how little attention she'd paid to anything recently, she told herself. You'd have to be blind not to notice the influx of high-end boutiques, but should she have noticed what they were replacing? Should she have been more connected to her little community of business owners, the network of locals threaded between all those lustrous new stores like tiny blood vessels? Should she have been part of an association, or something? Started a conversation with one of her neighbours, maybe? Should she have recognised the 'surge in demand' the letter had referred to as it was happening before her eyes? She should have read the newspaper more often instead of relying on June to pick over the news of the day with her on their visits. But June had seemed a bit run-down on her last visit. Cait didn't tend to talk about current events with Seb. Or with Max, who made everything sound somewhere between grim and apocalyptic. And she had still not caught up properly with Sylvia.

The fact was, Cait had been absorbed in James. His face, his hair, his magnetic skin. His flirty texts filling her days and his bed warming her nights. Their conspiratorial jokes rapidly forming for them a private world, a giddying distraction from her shop and her responsibilities. She felt sick.

The house was cold and dark. She flicked on lights, removed her jacket and scarf and hung them on their hook. Macduff barrelled down the stairs. She swept him up and held him against her chest, craving warmth and comfort. He wriggled loose and demanded food. She fed him and went upstairs and got into bed, where Mac presently joined her, having made short work of his dinner.

Panic banged against her insides. James read the papers. James worked for Lease Freedom. Why hadn't he alerted her? He must know about the general situation. Maybe he even knew about her particular situation and hadn't brought it up. Why? Don't panic, she told herself. Tomorrow, you will ask James about it, and you will figure out a way to save money. Quickly. She held Mac close. His breath smelled like cat food.

She forced herself to focus on the sound, and the feeling, of his motor-like purring against her collarbones.

≪≪≪

Saturday. Delicious freedom. No work, and for once it wasn't a mobile client week. Only dinner with James, tonight. She stretched, dislodging Macduff, who had at some point squirmed from her clutches and settled beside her in the curve of her waist. Then she remembered the letter and felt an uneasy coiling in her upper belly. She took a deep breath and let it out. Nothing is going to happen to you today, she told herself. Or tomorrow. You do have some time to think about this. No amount of thinking is going to help, said a mean little voice in her head. You're going to need a fairy godmother. She told it to shut up and lay there for a few more minutes, trying to breathe deeply, until the feeling in her stomach subsided, though it didn't go away. Mac, who had been chewing a miniature dreadlock on his fluffy foreleg since being woken, got up and humped his back in a giant stretch before climbing on top of her and gazing straight into her face. He bumped his nose forcefully into hers. 'All right,' she said, giving his head one rough stroke and sitting up, tumbling him off. He dashed out. Cait followed him downstairs and made coffee, a tide of thoughts roiling in the back of her mind, rising as if against an enormous dam. The dam couldn't just let one thought through, to be examined separately from the rest. It was just an amorphous mass of rising anxiety. She got the letter out of her bag and re-read it. 'What the hell am I going to do?' she asked the cat. 'I can't increase prices. I'm already more expensive than online, not to mention Kmart and damned Target. I'm already on bare bones. What costs could I eliminate? I mean, I need a substantial saving, not fifty bucks here and there.'

Already keyed up, she jumped when an arriving text made her phone buzz violently against the counter. Seb.

> Just got your note. You all right?

She remembered that she had told him she was sick.

> Fine now. Sorry about the tidy.

> Don't be stupid, it's fine, just making sure you're OK. Do you need anything? I could come round.

> No, that's OK, seriously.

> OK. Well, let me know.

She put the phone down. Tears threatened. Lovely Seb. Nothing ever seemed to bother him. What would she do without him? It was then that a highly unwelcome realisation arrived, a realisation she pushed carefully to the back of her mind, until she felt ready to deal with it.

She tried to distract herself with reading, but she couldn't make herself focus. She needed something dumber. She turned on the TV and stayed in front of it all day, in a nest of blankets filled with the comforting heat of her own body and that of Mac, who was delighted with this rare stability in Cait as a couch-mate, and kept her company virtually all day. Cait peeled herself off the couch in the early evening, having finally found out why everyone was so excited about *Game of Thrones*, and went to get ready for dinner. At least she'd be able to participate in a *Game of Thrones* debrief for the first time.

But in truth, the thought of any kind of conversation felt abstract, like it was something she might only be able to do in another reality. Not this one, which had been rudely shattered, exposed as a reality balanced upon a set of assumptions that she now saw to be as false and fragile as every other fucking thing in life.

'Except you,' she said aloud to Macduff, who had followed her upstairs and now sat in the bathroom doorway. He absorbed this recognition with an air of calm entitlement and she stepped over his head to get into the shower. After she got out, he hopped onto the bath mat and stuck his head into the stall to lick the water droplets off the floor. She found this habit cute but kind of weird, and sometimes she stopped him doing it and sometimes she didn't. Tonight, she didn't.

⚜

Cait was, as usual, the second one to arrive. James sprang up and wrapped his arms around her, pinning her hands to where she had been starting with her coat buttons, and kissed her before releasing her and letting her continue with the coat. He made her smile, despite herself, and she realised it was the first moment of pleasure she had felt since yesterday afternoon, when she'd first ripped open that letter. How happy she had been, how complacent, before that moment.

The restaurant, a newly opened place at the very end of the Vic Park strip, was cosy, with dim booths and white napkins and a long, dark bar lined with black stools. Gleaming glassware reflected points of candlelight. James had already ordered wine and filled her glass. Cait let herself feel comforted, as though reality had slipped back into place, its disruption just a bad dream. They talked about their days. James told her about his visit to his mother. Cait filled him in on her *Game of Thrones* progress, and he refrained from giving spoilers. The food, share plate style, was meagre and expensive, but good. They focused mainly on the choosing, divvying and eating of it without a lull. Their plates were being cleared by the time Cait could bring herself to tell James about the letter.

'I got some kind of bad news,' she said, when the waiter

departed. James looked appropriately concerned, and she retrieved the letter from her bag so he could read it. 'And no, I don't remember seeing a first notice,' she forestalled him when he looked up.

'Are you sure?' he said. Cait felt a flash of irritation and had opened her mouth to retort when he held up his hands in a placatory gesture. 'OK. I'm only saying, these processes are pretty routine. I'm sure there was a notice.'

'I'm not saying there wasn't. The notice doesn't matter. Having a few more weeks to think about it wouldn't have made a difference in whether or not I can pay it.'

'I'm guessing from the way you're talking that you can't,' James said, folding the letter and returning it to her. She stuffed it back in her bag with unnecessary force.

She opened her mouth to say no, but the word didn't come out. In fact, no sound came out. It felt as though something was lodged in her throat. She took a sip of wine and another breath, and tried again. 'No,' she said. Saying this aloud made it feel inescapable. The letter would not be content with being crushed angrily into a bag forever. It would have to be answered. More conversations like this would have to be had, and quickly. Any grace period the first notice might have afforded her had been removed.

'I'm sorry,' James said, reaching out and taking her hand with a look of penetrating sympathy that threatened to collapse the imaginary steel scaffolding she'd erected inside herself to keep her dry-eyed and upright. 'I know you're at home there. It's a shame that it's such a good spot that everyone wants in. I know there's been a lot of activity in that area. I didn't know they'd specifically targeted your location. But ... listen, I could help you move. Find a good new spot.'

'It's not that simple. I've got a hundred-thousand-dollar fit-out. It was bespoke, it was for that space. My customers have been going there for years. A lot of them are elderly, or office workers. They're not going to hop in their cars and drive all over the city hunting for the new venue. The suburbs don't have the foot traffic I need.'

'Even the strips? I could ask around. Find you a good deal.'

'Like where?'

'I don't know. Here in Vic Park, Mount Lawley, Leederville ... no, wait. I just read online this week that the bookstore on the Leederville strip was closing. That's probably not a good sign.'

'You think?'

James sighed.

'You're the one who's supposed to know the market. You tell me what the situation is.'

He paused. He looked as though he was trying to choose his words carefully.

'It's true there's stuff closing on a lot of these strips. Strips tend to take off by offering punters independent shops, ones they can't find at the Galleria or at Carousel or wherever. The strips mature and they become desirable locations, so the rents go up. Then the independents get priced out by the chains. We've seen it on Beaufort and Bay View and Rokeby Road. And now we're seeing it in Leederville.'

'Great,' Cait said.

'National operators can pay higher rents,' James said. 'Especially luxury stores. They can generally pay up to twenty percent of their sales on rent. That's a way more comfortable margin than categories like yours. You're probably closer to ten percent. A supermarket would be closer to five.'

'You've lost me.'

'Well, a Prada turning over a million in sales each year can afford to pay two hundred grand in rent, but a small retailer like you, if you were earning the same amount, can only afford to pay a hundred grand, because you have different overheads and profit margins. A supermarket would be more like fifty.'

'And I'm not making a million a year,' Cait said. 'Obviously. Why can't they just stick to shopping centres?'

'The chain stores like the strips, because they're still cheaper than the shopping centres. And they've got personality.' A waiter approached, bearing the dessert menu, but Cait did not want to go through their ritual of getting the menu because there was 'no harm in looking'. She waved him away.

'But those strips you talked about, where small businesses have been squeezed out, they're still full, right? And it's not all luxury stores filling the gaps when they shut.'

'Yeah, but if you look more closely, you'll see they're filling with food and beverage tenants. Takeaway, cafes, small bars – all that stuff is doing well.'

'I thought you said consumers weren't spending money now the boom is over. How can cafes and bars be doing so well?'

'Well, I think that's consumer psychology. People will always spend money on eating out and coffee. And of course, cafes aren't competing against online shopping.'

'Of course,' said Cait, trying not to sound bitter. She remembered June bitching about young people walking around glued to their coffee cups. He was right. People might have stopped buying stuff from shops, but they never seemed to stop spending on coffee and beer.

'Why can't the rents drop, if our economy's doing so badly?' she asked.

'They have, in a lot of places. Just not the CBD's fanciest strip. And big chains aren't based here, so they're not struggling financially, and to them, Perth is still cheap,' James said. She thought that his sympathetic look had changed into a condescending, pitying one. As though he were about to tell a child there was no Santa, but half thought that child should have worked it out already. 'Moving might be a risk, but I don't see what choice you have, really,' he said.

'I'm just going to have to make some changes,' Cait said, trying to sound confident and hard-nosed. 'Restructure. Businesses do it all the time.'

'*Big* businesses do it all the time,' James said. 'I'm not sure what structures you've got to play with. It's not like you've got a team of people to lay off and surplus assets to sell. Well, unless you've been keeping those assets a secret.' He gave his usual charming smile, but Cait didn't feel like being charmed. She swigged the last of her wine.

'I have one person to lay off,' she said. 'I've got to tell Seb pretty much straightaway. I'll have to do Saturdays myself, and maybe I'll just close Sundays. They're dead at the moment anyway. Not paying casual penalty rates should give me breathing space. Time to think about how to find more savings.' She took a deep breath, aware that, having said it, there was no going back. She couldn't pretend to herself any longer that she wouldn't have to talk to Seb. Seb, who had been with her for years. Seb, who, despite his habitual lateness, was a good employee. And a friend, who hung out with her and joked with her whenever they saw each other or talked on the phone. Who wasn't a client or fifty years older than her. She had James now, of course. But James appeared unaware of what this decision would cost her in non-financial terms.

'Well,' he said. 'You have to go there to open up for him half the time anyway. And I'm sure you've been overpaying him.'

'I pay him the award plus the penalty rates I'm obliged to,' Cait said. 'I know what I'm doing.'

'Well, you could have fooled me,' James said. As she stared at him, momentarily speechless, he continued. 'It seems like you've got no-one else giving you any sensible opinion, so I will. Have you thought about what you're saying here? Working six days a week, six *long* days, just so you don't have to move? You've already got a pretty sad social life,' he said, smiling to show he meant no harm, crashing on, despite the look on her face. 'I mean, we really only get to see each other a couple of times a week because you're always tired or working. I thought we were getting a bit more serious here. I want to see you more, not less. It already seems like every second Saturday you're off to see one of those old people you deliver to. I mean, even that's a huge time commitment, for the amount of money you must make from it.'

'This *is* my social life. They're my friends,' Cait said stiffly, knowing how pathetic this sounded, wanting to cry, wanting the conversation to end. 'I see them because I want to. *Seb* is my friend. He's been with me practically forever.'

There was a short silence, in which an ugly look settled over James's handsome face. 'Forgive me. I thought I was the one who was with you,' he said.

'You know that's not what I meant.' But James did not respond, and after a tense pause he got up to pay the bill without looking at Cait. She watched the casual way he whipped out his card without pausing to check the details on the bill, more aware than ever of his comfortable finances, and how precarious her life must seem, how emotional her decisions, compared to his sensible existence with its credit cards and its shining office, its pitiless executives swooping like buzzards on every unexploited corner of the city.

'Well, it sounds like you've made your mind up,' James said, in a kinder tone than he had used before, as Cait got up and they buttoned themselves into their coats. 'I support you, all right? I guess you can try to manage it. Even though in practical terms I feel obliged to say that I think you might be sticking your head in the sand.'

'OK,' Cait said gratefully, reaching for the olive branch, slender as it was. 'Thanks. Let's not talk about this anymore. I've been thinking about it nonstop. Do you want to go for a walk on the river?'

'It's too cold. Let's go back to my place.'

Back at James's, instead of falling straight into bed as they would have done a few months ago, they settled with more wine in front of the TV. They were working their way through old episodes of *Boston Legal*. James loved courtroom dramas. *Law and Order*, *The Good Wife*, that sort of thing. The episode was about to start when James hit pause and turned to her.

'My dad was in small business,' he announced, in an abrupt sort of way that sounded as though he'd been struggling to decide whether to say this and had now made up his mind to. Cait looked at him, waiting for more. 'Electronics repair. He never made much money, he worked long hours, and he left us with bugger-all … not that I blame him for it. But again, he was a victim of change. Small businesses are inherently risky – they're vulnerable. That's why I like working for a big business, even if it's a bit …' he stopped, considering, 'a bit impersonal. It's a good life. I have superannuation and meal breaks and overtime. I have paid holidays and sick days. I have certainty.'

'Yes, but I have freedom,' Cait said.

'Freedom's not everything, that's all I'm trying to say.'

It is to me, she thought, but she kept that to herself. She was touched by James's admissions, this glimpse into a past he didn't talk much about, and she finally relaxed into the warmth of his body beside hers. They watched Denny Crane destroy his lawyerly opponents with a sense of harmony restored. Half-watching James's enormous TV, Cait let her mind drift and hover in an uneasy limbo somewhere between the real world and the screen. Eventually, they fell asleep together on the couch. They woke, stiff and freezing, around midnight, and moved into the bedroom. James fell asleep again almost instantly, but Cait was now wide awake, her thoughts racing. She managed to get into a doze again eventually, but only after making her mind up. She had to do it in the morning.

ELEVEN

James, half-roused once again by Cate's fidgeting, threw an arm heavily across her in an instinctive attempt to soothe. It didn't, but it did pin her down. Cait fought the urge to turn over yet again and stretch her limbs in search of the magic position that would send her back to sleep. To do any more tossing would wake him properly and she didn't want to wreck James's sleep-in too. She tried to lie still and wait patiently until a more respectable time to get up. She watched the walls lighten and the objects in the room become visible: James's gym bag, some files he had clearly brought home from work, and her own clothes, lying in a puddle on the floor, where she'd dumped them after moving from the couch last night. She knew clothes on the floor annoyed the hell out of James, but what he didn't see this morning wouldn't hurt him. By seven-thirty her back was screaming with stiffness and she could no longer suppress the urge to move. James seemed to have gone properly back to sleep. She pulled out from under his arm and rolled off the edge of the bed as lightly as possible. Her clothes were cold to the touch. She shivered as she shook the worst of the creases from them and pulled them on. Her mouth felt red-wine-rancid. She hadn't brushed her teeth before falling asleep. She went into the ensuite and used James's fancy sonic toothbrush. Its sound normally sliced through the house like a circular saw, so she used it with the power off. Thankfully James was still asleep when she finished. Normally, she would have relished waking slowly with him. Lingering in bed, only finally rising from the tangle of bedding to seek out a leisurely Sunday brunch. But today she bent and kissed him swiftly, not wishing to bring him far enough out of sleep to register that she was leaving and start asking difficult questions, just enough to prevent him waking later alone and being confused by her absence.

'Bye,' she whispered, and he rolled over, freeing an arm and putting it around her, hooking her down to his chest, so that her hair fell around him. It made a little cave, just the two of them inside.

'Where you going?' he said. 'Stay.' His own breath was full of wine and sleep. In the earliest days of their relationship, even his worst breath would have smelled good to her, and she couldn't honestly say this was still the case. But still, he was warm and smooth and his arm was strong. She wanted to stay, to crawl into the hollow of his body and pull the blanket over her head.

'Can't, not today,' she said, pulling away. 'Things to do.' She didn't want to say where she was going, not after last night. She remembered again the look on his face, saying 'I thought I was the one who was with you'. She'd never felt like she had to account for her movements before, but she'd also never thought of James as someone insecure enough to be jealous of Seb. Why must people persist in thinking there was something going on between her and Seb? If this was what functioning human relationships were like, they sure were complicated.

James rolled over, turning his back. She pulled up the blanket and tucked it around him as she rose. She put on her shoes in the living room and went into the kitchen for a glass of water before heading out. 'Bye, Maclary,' she whispered to the goldfish, who lingered at the side of his bowl to watch her go, silently mouthing a farewell in his own mysterious fishy language.

Cait ran through the shocking cold to her car. James's car, a solid, silver-grey sedan, made Dent look even more disreputable beside it in the pale, wintry sunlight. But her heater worked, that was the main thing, and she ran it until the frost disappeared from the windows and windshield. It was only just eight when she got to Mount Lawley. She hesitated out the front of Number Fifty, as everyone called Seb's place, realising suddenly that it would be a miracle if Seb or any of his scaly housemates were even awake. Seb's Sunday shift wouldn't start for hours yet. Like the rest of the city shops, Book Fiend only opened at a luxurious eleven a.m. on Sundays. She dithered in the car until the cold drove her to the front door. As she waited for a response to her knock, she belatedly thought it might have been a nice idea to bring Seb breakfast. She debated giving the household time to stir by nicking off to the Maccas drive-through. But no sooner had the thought surfaced than the door was opened by an enormous man, over six feet tall, with a wiry cloud of hair sticking up about another foot. He was naked save a pair of boxers. He peered down at her, scratching his chest and giving every impression of having been called from the bowels of the earth to answer the door.

'Hey … Tom,' she said, mentally crossing her fingers that she had the right name. She saw no comprehension dawn, but soldiered on. 'It's Cait. I think we've met. From Seb's work?'

'Right,' he said, brow furrowed. 'Hey.'

'Is Seb home? Sorry, I know it's early for a Sunday but I need a chat.'

'Yeah,' he mumbled, turning and leaving her to follow him inside. He made an indeterminate gesture towards the living room and went down the dim corridor as she hovered in the entryway. 'SEB,' he shouted. He banged on Seb's bedroom door. 'GIRL HERE TO SEE YA.' He banged again, several more times. Cait winced. 'SEB.' As a final point, he opened Seb's door and let it drift open, signalling to the occupant of the darkened interior that there could be no doubt it was indeed this Seb being summoned. He then vanished into the bedroom opposite, and Cait, realising she probably shouldn't be standing right outside Seb's door when he emerged, darted to the living room.

She perched on the couch, fidgeting. The living room had a blokey smell and the floor was a mass of cables travelling to and from various consoles and screens arranged around its edges. A bookcase held not just books, but also Seb's enormous collection of obsolete or nearly obsolete technology: homemade mixtapes on cassette, CDs, videotapes, DVDs. She'd once asked him why he kept all this stuff, figuring that such a tech-savvy person should surely keep all their media digitally.

'It's a reminder,' he had said.

'Of what?'

'Impermanence.'

She'd been here before, but only for the house parties she could never avoid, since Seb always saw right through her lame excuses. She didn't know why he kept insisting she came. She had felt out of place at these events, but never so ill at ease as she felt now. She got up and crossed to the bookcase, unable to resist an age-old habit of examining people's bookshelves, even though she had seen this one before. The books were mostly sci-fi and fantasy: Arthur C. Clarke, Ursula Le Guin, Orson Scott Card. Some of Margaret Atwood's futuristic stuff. And a couple of surprises: Richard Dawkins, Christopher Hitchens. She looked at the CDs. The same stuff he played in the shop – Led Zeppelin, Grateful Dead, the Doors – and some she hadn't heard of. The Glitch Mob. Infected Mushroom. She started to feel like she was snooping and returned to the couch. This was a mistake. She should have given him a call later on, invited him out for a coffee, not blundered onto his home turf during his Sunday sleep-in. She cursed her own selfishness in being unable to put this off, consumed only with her own desire to get the thing over and done with. She was just getting up, half relieved he had not appeared and ready to sneak back out the front door with no harm done, when he appeared in the entryway, squinting, and said, 'Cait?'

Seb was in a pair of sweatpants, dragging a hoodie over a bare chest. Cait averted her eyes, trying not to stare, as he struggled to get the neck over his hair. Eventually his head reappeared and the dreads sprang once more in every possible direction, as well as some seemingly impossible directions. Shit, why did she feel so awkward? Well, she usually saw him clothed, for a start. Who would have thought Seb was hiding such excellent abs underneath all those band T-shirts?

'Fancy a walk?' she said.

He looked at her as if she were insane. 'It's good to see you, man, but no walking.'

'OK,' she said. 'Sorry. I know it's early. I wanted to chat.'

He scratched his entire head indiscriminately with both hands, making his hair even bigger, and said, 'Come in the kitchen.'

She followed him to the kitchen, which was thankfully cleaner than the living room, and sat meekly while he ground beans, then made coffee using an immense espresso machine. The flat white he placed in front of her looked professional. She saw the coffee in his own cup was black and realised, with a little pang, that he knew her well enough to know without asking that she preferred the flat white.

'Nice machine,' Cait said.

'It's the most expensive thing I own, besides my computer.' Seb stood and looked around a little vaguely. 'I don't have any, like, muffins or anything.'

'That's OK,' she said, and patted the seat next to her. He sat down. She wished herself miles away. She'd never sacked anyone before, not even when she was at Dymocks. 'Sorry,' she said again. 'I just wanted –'

'To talk?' he said, mustering a grin and beginning to look a little more awake. 'It's cool, crazy lady. No problemo. I forgive you for crashing into my home in the dead of night.' He frowned. 'Is it one of your wrinkly mates? Not June?'

'No, no. Nothing like that,' Cait said. She took a sip of her coffee. It was sweet and aromatic. 'It's just –' And now, mortification flooding her just a moment too late, she did what she had not done by herself, not done with Macduff or with James, not done in any of those logical and appropriate times and places. No, in front of her employee, one she was about to fire for no fault of his own, she burst into tears. She positively howled.

TWELVE

Seb looked so perfectly horrified by her tears that if Cait was not so overcome with shame and misery, she would have found it funny. He sat frozen to the spot for a minute, then dragged his chair a foot closer to give her what was less a hug than a sort of tentative sideways shoulder-squeeze. After a moment's further observation of the various fluids Cait was now producing, he went and pulled a few tissues from a box. En route back to where she sat, he halted, about-turned and went back for the whole box, which he placed in front of her. He then resumed his seat and simply waited for her to finish. She was grateful that, whether through tact or simple awkwardness, he was not staring, or attempting further conversation or comfort. Cait would have found any of these reactions even more embarrassing. She noticed for the first time his sphinx-like ability to sit completely still. Other people would jiggle a leg or pick their nails, but Seb simply sat motionless, occasionally sipping his coffee until it was gone. He waved away her apologies as she finally got control of herself. Then she spoke, forcing herself to look at him.

'Seb, they've put up the rent on the shop. I was expecting a bit of an increase when it came time to re-sign the lease, but they've jacked it way beyond what I ever expected. Way beyond what I can cover. I need to cut costs, big-time.' She stopped and took a deep, shuddering breath. 'Seb, I am so, so sorry, but I … I have to let you go. I've been thinking about this ever since I got the notice and I just can't see any way that the shop has a shot at surviving, not unless I take on your shifts myself.' She saw him take a breath to speak, and interrupted. 'No, wait, there's more. I can't give you any notice. Like, it has to be immediate. They gave me a grace period, but I somehow missed the notice, and it's only about five or six weeks until I have to make the first new payment.' She stopped and drew breath. She dared not look at his face again. How to say this? 'Seb, I can't tell you how great it's been to have you with me. I mean, with the business. And as a friend, of course.' God, she was stammering. 'I really wish I wasn't here saying this to you right now,' she finished lamely, and finally ran out of words. There was an agonising silence. Would he be upset? Or angry? She had never seen Seb angry, but she didn't want to start now.

'So,' he said, finally. 'No work today, huh?'

'I guess that's what I'm saying,' Cait said miserably. She finally forced herself to look at him, and could hardly believe it when she saw a smile split his face. 'Is that all?' he asked. 'Jesus, I thought somebody must have died.'

Cait felt a wave of relief. 'You're not upset?' Her instinct was to hide her damp and swollen face in her wad of tissue rags, but instead she made herself keep looking into his brown eyes, searching for signs of distress. She didn't find any. Instead she saw warmth, and something else. Concern? Well, whatever it was, she sure didn't deserve it.

Seb swivelled his empty mug on the table and sighed. 'I'm upset for you. It sounds like you've got some tough times ahead. But you just worry about that. Don't worry about me.'

'Really?'

'Look, of course it's not ideal. This has been an awesome job for me. Not just because it's always fit in around freelance jobs and everything. It's just been good, you know? You and me get on so well, and the shop feels – well, it feels like home now.' She nodded mutely. Seb was perhaps the person who best understood her attachment to Book Fiend's four walls, its cobwebbed corners and peaceful aisles. 'I knew it wouldn't last forever. I mean, it might be ending a bit sooner than we would have liked, but I'll get something else. I always do. If you give me a decent reference, that is.' He grinned at her, inviting her to cheer up.

'Course I will,' Cait said. 'If you come and visit sometimes. I mean, if you want.'

'Course I will,' he echoed. 'Not today, but. I've just scored the day off.' He held out his hand in comradely fashion and she shook it with a trembling laugh that came out perilously close to a sob. She refused a fresh coffee, eager to end this interview and get to the shop. She would put up the *Closed* sign and start in Seb's place next week. She could not face it today. She just wanted to be at home, shower and change, lick her wounds in private. They both rather lamely assured each other that they would catch up soon. Cait hastened out the door, but turned back at the last moment, surprising them both by giving Seb a hug both clumsy and fierce. He was so tall she was really hugging his middle, and his lanky frame felt unexpectedly solid, instantly reminding her of her earlier inadvertent perving. At the moment she started to pull away, embarrassed by her own impulsiveness, she felt him recover from his surprise. His arms went around her, then tightened. So she let herself stay there a second longer, awkward yet comforted.

'It's not the end of the world,' he said into her hair.

Maybe not, she thought on the way back to Dent. But it sure feels like it. And this was only a small step on the way to what right now felt like an impossible goal. How was she going to come up with the rest of the cash?

⋘

Cait titled it in her head: Operation Work Saturdays, Save Cash, Keep It Together, Keep Everyone Happy. This would have worked perfectly well if people weren't so damn hard to keep happy.

'I just hate reading books sometimes, you know? Because most of the books I read, I don't like.'

This mind-boggling statement was delivered loudly and with a breathtaking lack of irony by a teenager to her friend. The pair, waiting behind the customer she was serving, looked about sixteen and were in virtually identical outfits of short-shorts and striped cotton shirts, in defiance of the freezing rain outside. Cait had a second to wonder which ill-fated book the teen had chosen this time when the phone rang. 'Hello, Book Fiend. Please hold?' she asked the receiver.

'Have I got any choice?' a savage voice said.

'Not at the moment, sorry – won't be long, thanks for your patience!' she trilled, putting down the receiver to finish the transactions in front of her. The leggy teen bought a truly awful-looking vampire book, part of a series that had clearly spun off one of the better and more well-known series before it.

Cait picked up the phone. 'So sorry about the wait. What can I do for you?' she said.

'I'm looking for Peter Mayle,' said the woman without preamble. 'That's M-A-Y-L-E,' she added, with an air of this being the hundredth time she had repeated the spelling that day.

'Yes, I know the one. Just a moment, I'll have a look for you.'

'Do you even know who he is?'

'Yes, he writes travel narratives? That Peter Mayle?'

'Oh. Yes,' the woman said, in a tone of deep suspicion.

Cait had two Mayles, but the woman desired neither and hung up, hell-bent on phoning the next luckless bookseller on her list. What was *with* these people, who appeared to blame whoever they encountered next in the world for everything that was so obviously going wrong in their lives? Why was it never OK for Cait to take out her problems on them?

Literally the second she decided she needed a rest and flumped onto her stool, a smiling Asian man appeared before her. Mid-thirties, smooth-skinned, dazzling white teeth, dazzling white polo. 'Hi there. I've been meaning to get back into some reading,' he said. 'Can you recommend something?' Ah, a bookseller's dream: someone who just wanted you to tell them what big, fat pile of books to buy. She lapped the store with him, cheering up as she quizzed him on his tastes and took him to the relevant sections, where she pointed out a few titles she'd just written recommendations for, and the best new releases in his favourite genres. He seemed keen, picking things up and examining them, carrying around a pile, and she felt sure he'd buy at least a couple. But in the end, after she'd left him alone for ten minutes to finish his browsing, he just put the stack he'd collected down on one of her display tables and left without looking at her or saying thanks. Cait returned grumpily to her stool. She plastered a smile back on when she heard a fresh set of footsteps, but it widened to a real smile as she saw James, bringing in his own disarming grin, the scent of fresh air, and laden carrier bags. 'I thought

I'd cheer you up on your first Saturday in captivity,' he said, leaning over the counter and hooking a finger into her apron pocket. He pulled her close and kissed her. She breathed him in, savouring the scent of him, touched by this unexpected appearance.

'I needed it. What's all this?' she said.

'Just a few bits and pieces,' he said. He took her by the hand and led her to the back of the shop, near the little couch that she now thought of as 'their' couch. He commandeered one of the little coffee tables and unpacked the bags. He had brought a pile of gourmet deli stuff – olives and crackers and cheese. Then, looking about with exaggerated discretion, he pulled two bottles of beer from his pockets with a flourish. They were slick with condensation. 'How's that?' he said, plainly proud of himself, and sat down to open them with a bottle opener also pulled from his pocket.

'You're amazing,' she said, hugging him. 'But I thought you were putting up shelves for your mum today.' Cait had been supposed to go along with him and spend quality time with his mother while he did so before she had found herself working. She had not been looking forward to it anyway. James's mother was very absorbed in her own problems, and clearly didn't think this skinny, redheaded shop-girl a viable candidate for the bride she hankered after for her good-looking, successful son.

'I'm halfway through it,' he said. 'I'll go back after this. I just missed you. Wanted to see how you were doing. Why did you say you needed cheering up?'

'Oh, I've just had some real doozies this morning,' she said. 'One guy, I asked him if he needed help, and he said, "It's OK, I'm just making notes of books to get for my Kindle."'

'Ouch.'

'I suppose it could have been worse. Once I had a man ask if he could actually borrow a pen and paper so he could make notes of books to get online.'

'Oh, you poor baby,' James leaned over and kissed her. The beer tasted good on his lips. 'It sucks that you have to be cooped up in this joint on a Saturday.'

'It's not so bad. Book Fiend is pretty cosy on days like this,' she said, backtracking like someone perfectly happy to criticise a family member themselves, but turning to defend them in response to any external slight. And it was true, she realised. The rain drummed on the roof, the lamps glowed and the iPod cruised softly through a playlist as familiar, and about as fashionable, as a pair of old slippers: Joplin, Clapton, Dylan. And apart from the odd few that had got her disgruntled, the browsers were in general more casual than weekday shoppers, which was nice. The odd soaked pedestrian scooted gratefully inside, stuck a dripping umbrella in the pail at the door and looked around, settling visibly, like a ruffled hen reaching the henhouse after escaping a playful dog. Though their first motivation had been shelter, they inevitably began to peck around, waiting for the rain to stop. Lulled by the atmosphere, they picked up a book or two and eventually bought one. It was a season for reading.

James and Cait munched their way through their makeshift picnic, James bitching amiably about his mother, before they were interrupted by a lady who wanted to be reminded who had won the Stella Prize and did she have a second-hand copy of whatever it was. Cait apologised, telling her the book was hot property at the moment and it was unlikely to last long on the shelf if she did happen to get a used one. But she did have a new copy. The lady reluctantly handed over her twenty-five dollars and requested a plastic bag, which she then tucked into a pristine pocket of her capacious handbag. Cait had almost gotten back to James when she was flagged down by a couple in Young Adult.

'Excuse me,' the woman said in a harried-sounding voice. 'Could you recommend something for a teenager who doesn't like reading?' She did not explain why she was gifting a book to someone who disliked reading.

'One second!' said Cait.

'Why are all these books about vampires?' the woman added loudly to her partner, who shrugged.

'Sorry,' Cait said to James.

He was already sweeping the remains of their meal back into the bags. He necked the rest of both their beers. 'It's OK,' he said. 'Do what you gotta do. See you tonight.' He smiled.

'Oh … listen. I'm so worn out, I'm dead on my feet. And I've got Max booked in early tomorrow. Could we take a raincheck? I'll make it up to you.'

James's cheerful look vanished. 'Max, is it? Yeah, all right. Don't worry about it. Call me when you get an opening in your schedule.'

'Baby, I'm sorry –'

'Don't worry about it.'

He strode off. The surprise lunch date had been so sweet and intimate, and Cait had somehow managed to wreck it as quickly and easily as he had created it. She stood for a moment looking after him. Then she headed down the aisle to give a brief history lesson on The Takeover of the Vampire in Adolescent Literature: Annoying, but Temporary. It was a lecture she had delivered many times before.

That afternoon, Cait rang James and wheedled her way back into his good books, saying she wasn't that tired after all. That he was important to her, that the thought of missing their customary Saturday night dinner date was making her so miserable that her weariness paled by comparison. This wasn't quite true. The thought of a night at home alone, with a book and no words to speak to anyone but Mac, was almost irresistible. Even the cat was getting neglected, and he was by far the easiest relationship she had. But she couldn't bear the guilt of not only cancelling the day with James's mother but then cancelling their date as well. The memory of the look on his face, like she'd slapped him … She couldn't bear the thought of him being mad at her, on top of everything else. She then rang Max and confirmed their Sunday appointment, having already previously explained that she couldn't come Saturdays any longer. He told her she needn't come if she was too busy, but she overrode this breezily, telling Max she expected a decent meal out of it at any rate.

THIRTEEN

Cait arrived at Max's the following morning feeling somewhat sleep-deprived, as well as guilty for again getting up and fleeing before James awoke. She was starting to wonder whether the lazy Sunday routine they had fallen into, of breakfasts out, or nursing their hangovers with takeaways and TV binges, was in the past before she had really had a chance to appreciate it. The rest of Perth remained drowsy; she street-parked easily at Max's, where a rich, buttery aroma immediately distracted her from her self-pity. He'd evidently taken Cait at her word regarding food. His tiny kitchen was oven-warmed and a quiche stood on the table, bubbles of cheese puffing on its surface.

'Ooh, what's this?' she said by way of greeting, and bent to inhale the smell.

'Onion and blue cheese,' Max said in a self-satisfied sort of voice. 'Get away from it, it's got to cool and set.' He looked at her critically. 'You look tired. I told you not to come if it was too much.'

'And miss this? Yeah, right. Also I wanted to see what you thought of the last lot. And I've got some good new stuff for you.'

'Let's have it then,' Max said. 'Please tell me you've got the new Strike.'

'Not out yet.'

'Still!'

'Give her a chance,' Cait said. 'It's not been a year. Max, is that an *iPad*?'

Max's dislike of technology had always remained firm. She couldn't quite believe the shiny tablet charging on a side table, even though she saw it with her own eyes.

'I'm on Facebook now,' he said, fixing her with a stony stare that dared her to laugh. 'My daughter got it for me. Said I needed to rejoin the world. As if *this* is the world.' He gestured at the gadget, then the window. '*That's* the world, out there, and I'm stuck inside on a bung knee.'

'It's not great walking weather anyway, Max,' Cait said, glancing out the window at the leafless plane trees and sullen, spattering rain. 'Want me to show you how to like the Book Fiend page?'

'Already done,' he said smugly. 'I've been talking on there with your other hopeless cases. That June woman is speedy on the keyboard. No appreciation for crime, though.'

'*Max!*' Cait said in delight. Wonders would never cease. 'Show me your skills!'

'I'm not playing on the bloody computer when I've got a guest. That's what your generation does. Not to mention the grandkids. You'd think the urge was now implanted at birth. All right, that quiche should be ready.'

The quiche was gooey and rib-sticking. Max delivered his verdicts on the books from Cait's last visit. After they pushed away their plates, Max pored over his new haul. More Sophie Hannah – the new Poirot wasn't out yet, so Cait had brought one of her others – and a couple of new releases. *The Dry*, a promising thriller debut from Jane Harper, an Australian author, and *End of Watch*, the next book in the Mr Mercedes series.

'Let me know when you're done with that lot and I'll come back,' Cait said. 'You could even message me online, now you've joined us in the twenty-first century.' This was blatant hypocrisy on her part, given she used social media strictly on sufferance, for business purposes, at Seb's insistence.

'All right. Thanks for coming and making an old man's morning on your day off. You're a good girl.'

Cait normally responded to his thanks with a joke along the lines of it all being for his cooking, but was touched by his words. It was as close as he'd got to admitting loneliness. 'It's no worries, Max. I love coming to see you.' She kissed his cheek. 'Catch you soon.'

'OK. Don't work too hard.'

Her heavy heart suddenly lightened at the idea that she had brightened his day. And it had been easy, really. It was simply a matter of turning up with a boxful of books she knew would delight him, to share food and conversation that was all reassuringly routine and satisfying. Max, at least, did not change. Apart from the Facebook! That was definitely an evolution. She grinned as she reached the car. Maybe she could take inspiration from the knowledge that Max had mastered this new and utterly unfamiliar skill. If Max, one of the oldest and grumpiest people she knew, could adapt to a changing world, then so could she.

But positivity became harder to maintain as winter dragged into its final month. Cait signed the new lease, but was aware that the saving made by sacking Seb would only somewhat offset the imminent increase in rent. Cait didn't want to slow down on loan repayments when they were so close to an end, so she 'paid' herself less. And though she loved Book Fiend, though she had little interest in wealth over and above getting by, the combination of a pay cut with working an extra day was galling. Not to mention the prospect of her ever making any super contributions was dwindling quickly. Her usual fortnight off in January was equally unlikely without Seb to step in. She had given up half her Sundays to fit in her mobile clients. And what if she got sick, or something went wrong with the shop or its fittings? The air-con would pack up one of these days. The carpet really needed a clean. And eventually the whole place would need a spruce-up. She had planned this for when she finished paying off the loan. Some months back she had felt pleasure, even excitement, at the thought of some renovations, perhaps alongside a fifth-anniversary celebration: a birthday event for regulars, or a special promotion. Now these had become more thoughts to avoid, like the aggrieved way James was too-obviously avoiding mentioning her plummeting free time and energy levels. She was struggling to keep up with the evening tidies as she grew more fatigued, arriving late at James's only to sink to the couch and fall asleep, glass of wine in hand. For the past fortnight they hadn't even seen each other in daylight. He had acted understanding, but she knew he thought her stubborn and irrational for not even considering moving Book Fiend. He was still urging it. Perhaps he was hurt at her lack of faith in his ability to help find her a new place. The trouble was, he had no personal attachment to the shop himself. His job focused on the impermanent financial arrangements between tenants and leased buildings. He didn't much understand attachment to objects, or places, at all. His own unit was one hundred percent IKEA issue: grey and white with Venetian blinds, floating floorboards, white walls, LED downlights; much tidier than her own place, but kind of lacking in personality.

Comfort was, instead, coming from quite an unexpected corner. It had soon become obvious that Seb was more attached to the shop than Cait had fully realised. He had found work with ease, as he had predicted, in a city cafe ten minutes' walk away, but it shut earlier than Book Fiend and Seb had taken to turning up for half an hour most afternoons to browse and shoot the breeze, though Cait sternly refused his offers to help with the tidy. She felt it wouldn't be right.

But he hadn't turned up today, and Cait had done the tidy without the pleasant diversion of his conversation. She'd straightened out all the displays, then worked systematically around the shelves from the outside in, butting each line of spines in until they were straight and flush with the edges of each shelf. She was nearly done, but it had taken a long time tonight, given near-constant interruptions.

'Do you have any Lickety Split?' asked a very thin girl in a hot-pink tank top. Cait's brain laboured, then clicked.

'Oh, do you mean Lemony Snicket?'

'That's what I said,' the girl replied, and Cait showed her the books. She bought the first one and Cait went on with the tidy. Her tiredness and the mechanical motion had placed her in a kind of reverie, which was suddenly interrupted by a movement caught out the corner of her eye. The bedraggled man in a beanie and tattered track pants was not browsing, as she had earlier assumed. He was in fact following Cait around her tidy, methodically pushing in the newly straightened spines, in random clumps, to the backs of the shelves. Cait, seeing this, then swivelling to survey the trail of destruction in his wake, realised he had ruined the effect that had tonight taken almost two hours to produce. He must have been at it for some time; she'd been too foggy to notice.

She dashed over. 'What are you doing?' she demanded. He turned in surprise and they locked eyes. His had the skittish, unfocused look that usually spelt trouble, the kind of look that usually caused other people to cross the street rather than risk an interaction. She suddenly became aware they were the only ones in the store and probably invisible from the street outside, which was already dark and emptying rapidly as commuters drained from the city.

'I mean,' she said, a bit more politely, but unable to keep the strain from her voice. 'You cannot do that. Please do not do that. In fact, I'm going to need you to leave, please; I'm closing.'

To her relief, the man scuttled away without a word, probably to pass the freezing night in the shadow of the town hall, leaving her among her ruined shelves. She resisted pity and held onto her sense of violation. What was wrong with people? Why this urge to destroy, to cause trouble, to continually disturb others who were only trying to get on with their lives and do their jobs? Well, bugger it, she would fix it in the morning. She dragged in the trolleys, locked the doors and went out the back to where Dent awaited. She resisted the urge to bow her head against the wind that plucked at her clothes, but instead lifted her eyes and looked carefully around her to make sure the man had not followed her into the laneway. Driving home, she pondered her money issues yet again and decided she really had no alternative but to bite the bullet, reopen the shop on Sundays and reclaim that day's meagre custom. Mobile clients could move to evenings. Not Fridays. She needed the late-night shoppers, though she could probably do without the meth-heads. Earlier in the week, maybe? Whatever. She could make this work.

'There is no way in hell you can make this work.'

Cait remained silent before James's incredulous look. Not a good start to date night.

'This is stupid, Cait. You can't operate a business of this size entirely on your own, seven days a week, without help. Even working six days, you're exhausted. Anyone can see that.' He paused. 'Except possibly you.'

'I'm not an idiot. I'm an adult. I don't want you parenting me. I managed fine before I ever met you.' Cait instantly regretted saying this, and James fell silent, as if to underline how nasty she had sounded. She took a deep breath and told herself not to let this turn into a fight. 'Listen, why don't we say I'll try this for a month and see how the bottom line looks, if it's enough to cover the rent. I've got a bit of energy left. A month won't kill me … Hey, let's go out. Let's go somewhere nice and cosy with cheap food and cheap wine so I don't feel bad about you paying.'

James looked as though he were about to argue, then visibly changed his mind. His keys jangled as he grabbed them off his spotless countertop. She felt limp with relief. She couldn't take another argument. They got into his sedan, the car that effortlessly balanced good-looking and responsible. Rather like James himself, she thought with a sudden rush of affection, and pulled him to her and kissed him.

'What was that for?' he asked, looking pleased, and all at once thoroughly distracted from their dinner mission.

'Just love you,' she said, and kissed him again.

More than once over the month that followed, Cait questioned her own assertion that working a month of Sundays would not kill her. Perth was renowned for its sunny, mild winters – winters so lovely that elsewhere in the world they might masquerade as spring. But this winter was different. She could not ever remember one so long and dreary. It dragged into September, with temperatures at the start of that month so low even the book-insulated shop could not feel anything other than draughty and unwelcoming, like a hug from a bony and unpleasant relative. The chill seemed to have sunk into her bones.

Cait postponed her mobile client visits. Finally, Saturday night date nights fell by the wayside. She was not sleeping well, and the Sunday sleep-in became too vital to spend in a bed not her own. She didn't invite James over, because her place was fast becoming a pigsty. Instead he turned up at lunchtimes, often bringing lunch for Cait, which she deeply appreciated. She was beginning to tire of the peanut butter and celery sticks that were all the meal prep she could be bothered with these days. Could you get scurvy from eating nothing but peanut butter and celery? She must remember to google it. But her health was the last thing she had to worry about. The magic was haemorrhaging out of her relationship almost as fast as the savings from her bank account. She had long since worn out her mother's nice clothes. James hadn't seen her out of her work gear in weeks. They hadn't had sex in about that long, either. The couple of times she'd turned up at his house, missing him so much she just needed to see him, they'd clung to each other but she'd then done her special new party trick of passing out on the couch almost immediately.

James refrained from giving further opinions on Cait's situation. This was good. She didn't, frankly, want to hear his opinions. She didn't want anyone's unwelcome, responsible, sensible suggestions about cutting back or letting go. She wanted unwavering support. James, sensing this, gave it, or at least faked it, and pretended not to notice her unwashed hair and general abstraction.

Her saving grace was Seb, who continued to lope in most afternoons and listen as she unloaded whatever anecdotes she needed to about the more difficult customers. Were they nastier lately? Or was she not looking after them so well? Or was it the weather, making everyone grumpy? Everyone except Seb, who remained sanguine and good-natured. He somehow turned her rants into jokes, working to make her smile, leaving her calm by the time she left in the evenings and enabling her to avoid bitching too much to James. She did not mention the frequency of his visits to James, sensing that this information would not be welcome.

Instead, she maintained a brittle cheerfulness, insisting she was not that tired, and hiding the feverish back-of-the-napkin sums she was doing to prove to herself the business was going to make it past this setback. It was on the Monday that followed the final Sunday of her month-long trial that she realised, categorically, unavoidably, unequivocally, that there was absolutely no way in hell she was going to make this rental payment.

FOURTEEN

Cait stood and looked down at the sums she'd jotted on the scratchpad by the till. All of a sudden, she no longer felt the stiffness of her back or the way her fingers, clutching the pen, were stinging and dry with cold. The realisation she was not going to make the rent sent her into a daze that felt close to catatonia. She was wearing thermals to the shop, and still couldn't tell whether she was more numb on the inside or the outside. The place was almost deserted, customers perhaps sensing that it might be nicer to just stay home with their toasty reverse-cycle air-con and browse the virtual shelves of Amazon instead. Indeed, her next customer – one of her only customers that especially quiet afternoon – asked to order an out-of-stock title, then when she told him the price, loudly told her Amazon's quoted price was forty percent cheaper. Cait did not demand if he'd factored in shipping costs to Australia. Usually, she would have entered into a spirited account of how Amazon treated its workers, and how bricks-and-mortar retailers had higher overheads, and what Amazon was doing to the global publishing industry and therefore to struggling authors. But today she lacked the fire to do anything but humbly accept that, yes, it was cheaper online. With a ghost of her former smile, she told the customer he was paying for her superior service. He snorted and left, and she couldn't say she blamed him.

An hour after him, a woman came in, relieving the monotony.

'I'm looking for a book,' she said. 'I can't remember what it's called, or what it's about, but I'm pretty sure it's got a blue cover. Do you have that one?'

'Well,' Cait said, leading her over to the new release fiction, 'let's have a look.'

'Everyone's reading it,' the woman said helpfully. 'I think it could have the word "water" in it.' They surveyed the shelves together.

'Do you remember anything else about it?' Cait said.

'I still think it's blue, but now that I think about it I'm not so sure about the word "water" actually being in the title.'

Two more people that day asked for the mysterious title with the blue cover. Nobody bought anything. Mags came in, resplendent in thigh-high brown boots, fake fur and winged eyeliner, but even she showed little inclination to stop and shoot the breeze once she'd gone through the new releases. 'Unseasonable, isn't it?' Cait said.

'More like bloody unreasonable,' Mags said, and took her leave.

By four o'clock, Cait had had a gutful. The sky was so deeply overcast and the wind chill so vicious she could not imagine anyone who stepped out of their office deciding to linger for a spot of shopping. She considered texting Sylvia and seeing if she wanted to have a drink after work, but the thought of talking to anyone about her life right now was unappealing, like dragging out your dirty laundry at the dry cleaner's and pointing out the stains. So she did a cursory tidy and dragged the trolleys inside. Rugged up as she was in a bulky, stiff coat, hat and scarf, it was a task to lock and bolt the doors. Her fingers were half numb, and the shoulders and sleeves of her coat were made tighter by the multiple other layers underneath them, restricting her movement. The instant she stepped out from under cover, the blackened heavens opened. In moments, it grew dark as night and rain emptied itself unceremoniously onto Cait's head as if from a bucket. '*Fuck!*' she said aloud, with an entirely disproportionate flood of rage. She ran to Dent and turned on the heater, which began blasting cold air. Suddenly feeling strangled, she pulled off the wet hat and scarf and undid her coat. Then she sat in silence for a minute, waiting for the air to start heating, watching the rain cocoon the car in water, as though she were inside a giant, world-sized car wash. She wished for a moment she could just stay there forever, idling. But she made herself keep going. She pulled out of the tiny rear parking lot and headed for home. She permitted herself to speed, despite the other rain-maddened drivers increasing the chances of a crash. At this moment, she felt as though she would not care if someone did crash into her. She asked herself what she planned to do about this situation. She told herself it was time for plan B, which she had been desperately hoping to avoid.

The lonely Macduff leapt into her arms and pushed his nose into hers. 'Hey, Duffer,' she muttered into his neck, and held him so tightly that he struggled free. Power balance thus restored, he waited for her to collapse on the couch, clambered onto her lap, circled twice and settled.

'A customer asked me today if I had the Black Caviar *autobiography*,' she told him. Mac looked disdainful. 'I know. I had to resist the almost overwhelming temptation to ask when racehorses learned to write.'

She sat there a moment longer. Right. No point putting this off. She got out her phone and called James.

'Do you know what I should do about maybe asking for an extension on the rent?' she asked. She'd steered very clear of this subject for as long as possible. She generally tried to pretend he wasn't working for the same firm that had put her in this position, the firm that held sway over her livelihood.

'Just ring and ask for retail leasing,' he said, with equal embarrassment. 'They'll have some kind of option, there always is. But they might want to talk more about it, seeing as it's only recently you re-signed at the new rent. They'll want to make sure you're good for it.'

'OK,' Cait said, striving to sound cheerful. 'Thanks.' She wondered if she was good for it. Was she good for any of this? She already longed to be off the phone. 'Well, I'm going to go to bed. Talk to you tomorrow?'

'OK.'

'Love you,' she said.

'Love you too. And, baby –'

'Yeah?'

'Good luck.'

<hr>

It was eleven a.m. by the time Cait screwed up her courage to make the call to retail leasing. She knew the lunch rush was approaching and she didn't want this call hanging over her head until the afternoon. But the phone call was less horrible than expected. The woman she spoke with was friendly and behaved as though receiving a request for an extension was perfectly routine. She asked Cait a series of only faintly embarrassing questions and told her the director of the retail department would have to look at the request, but that Cait should hear back in a day or two.

'Thank you,' Cait said, with relief.

'Not a problem. Have a nice day.'

Cait dared to hope this would be all right after all. That afternoon, buoyed by having made the dreaded phone call, she decided to ring June and ask if she could come at night. Until she knew about the rent, she'd have to continue opening Sundays. She was hesitant to change her mobile clients' routines, but they weren't busy people, after all, and she knew they'd welcome her whenever she could make it. Still, she had put off letting them know, reluctant to signal her changed working hours and fend off questions. But she couldn't delay the visits any longer, or they'd start to call and ask where she was. Dorothy, in particular, was even less controllable on the phone than she was in person. Cait pictured herself as a skeleton holding a telephone, having withered and died while Dorothy chattered animatedly down the line.

June's phone rang and rang. Cait waited, knowing June might be in the garden or on the couch and it would take her time to get going. But even so, she was about to hang up when June finally answered, sounding out of breath. Cait proposed to bring forward their weekend visit to that evening and June assented readily. No, she wasn't busy. But she didn't have anything in the oven. Cait assured her it did not matter. They settled on a time Cait hoped would allow her long enough to get out of the city in rush hour. Cait saw from the corner of her eye a middle-aged customer approach with a pile of teen vampire novels and a tortured expression. She farewelled June and hung up hastily.

The days were getting longer. It was not yet dark when she left. The sky was clear and the air perhaps not quite as frosty as it had been of late. The drive on the packed freeway, then through the suburbs and finally through June's more rural suburb took far longer than it used to on weekends, though, and night had fallen by the time she arrived. But June's windows were lit, and as Cait knocked she felt the weariness of the day fade, replaced by the simple pleasure of anticipating a visit with an old friend after too long an absence.

At first glance, framed in the doorway, June looked the same as usual, gripping her walker, curls nicely set. But she also looked different. Shockingly different. Thinner. And somehow greyer, though she had on a cheerful fluffy yellow cardigan. The knowledge thundered into Cait's head, fully formed, that something was terribly wrong with June. But she was now staring in silent dismay and she collected herself. 'June,' she began, and stopped, hearing her voice sound high and weak, a sort of horrified plea.

'Don't stand out there gawping,' June said, in such a reassuringly brisk tone that Cait was startled into stepping over the threshold. She hugged June.

'Sorry. Hi,' she said against June's shoulder, feeling with renewed shock how bony the old lady suddenly felt. 'Sorry. I didn't expect – you don't look well, June! What's the matter! Have you got the flu?'

'Come and sit down and have a cup of tea,' June said, steering her by the elbow into the living room and sidestepping her questions so neatly that Cait was swamped by fresh, sick terror. She knew June did not have the flu. June got colds and flus every winter, just like everyone else, and never looked like this. June sat down, very slowly, beside the tea tray and poured the tea. It was steaming and smelled fresh. June had an uncanny knack of knowing the moment Cait would arrive and having everything in perfect readiness. This had always impressed Cait, since June could not possibly know to the minute when Cait had left the city, or what the traffic was like, and yet her tea was always strong, never over-brewed. Biscuits warm but never burnt, and perfectly chewy. Except now, with a sense of sudden displacement, as though she had actually wandered into Dorothy's house by mistake, Cait noticed the biscuits on the tray were plain digestives from a packet, though prettily arranged on a saucer with a paper doily. In years, she didn't think she'd ever set foot into June's house without the smell of fresh baked goods greeting her. Stop freaking out, she told herself. No-one bakes on a Tuesday night at dinnertime. And she's probably just not got her face on. You're both out of routine. You've come at a stupid time. She's tired.

She watched as June set down the teapot and picked up the milk jug, offering it to Cait. She took it mechanically and milked their teas – the merest drop for June and slightly more for herself.

'I've got cancer, Cait,' June said. She picked up her cup and looked directly at Cait, peering at her with the usual alertness that reminded Cait of a bird waiting for crumbs to be dropped before it would hop closer.

'What?' Cait said stupidly. She felt an urge to delay this conversation, even while it was happening, but she could not think of anything to say that would make June stop talking.

'Pancreatic cancer.' June softened her tone ever so slightly, but was still proceeding with an almost indecent haste. Must she? 'I've been told I haven't got long.'

'Until what?' Bewilderment swirled about her. June looked at her with a combination of patience and pity.

'It's advanced, Cait. I'm old. I've got a few months, perhaps.'

'What, to *live*?' Cait said. Obviously this conversation was now happening and there was nothing she could do about it, short of running from the house with her hands over her ears. She doubted June would take kindly to this. But it was tempting.

FIFTEEN

'Yes, Cait, to live.' June sipped her tea. Cait picked hers up too, to give herself something to do. She suddenly felt very tired. Even her hands, holding the tea, felt tired. She felt her back ache, her neck. A band of pain tightened around her forehead. She sipped her tea. Perfect. Not weak, bitter or lukewarm. Cait stared into the cup, willing herself to keep it together. June disliked scenes. Their mutual discomfort with expressing emotions overtly was partly why they had always got on so well, and why they had remained close. That and the books, of course. Always, there had been the books.

'Well, don't bloody sugar-coat it, will you,' said Cait. June merely looked at her in the old way she had when Cait had foot-stamped about things as a child. June had always simply waited, her expression telling Cait she'd better grow up, and fast.

'How do you feel?' Cait asked her, finally. It seemed a dumb question, but she had to say something.

'Tired,' June said. 'Sick. Useless. I can't cook or clean much at the moment. I've got a group sending people to help and they're all useless too. My garden is neglected, and I don't like that.' She paused, looking into space, and sipped her tea. Then her eyes found Cait's and held them. 'I was taken aback, Cait. I thought I had plenty of good years left. But that's life, isn't it? And I've had a good one. I'm glad it's going to happen quickly – I don't want to spend years losing my mind in a nursing home or being a burden on anyone – so if I'm going to die, I'd rather just get it over with.' She gave a dry chuckle. It was somewhat humourless, but Cait welcomed the sound. She wondered if June had really received the news with this kind of equanimity. 'Taken aback' could mean anything. She wished she had been with June when she received this diagnosis. 'How long have you known?'

'About a month,' June said. 'I've had a bit of time to think.'

'Oh,' Cait said. She watched steam curl up from her teacup. 'Have you told Mum?'

'Yes. She promised to wait to talk to you until I had had a chance.'

'Oh,' Cait said again.

'I'm sorry if I did the wrong thing, not telling you straightaway,' said June. 'Just because I'm old, doesn't mean I know what I'm doing all the time. You were so happy, with James. I've not seen you so excited for years, not since you opened the shop. I didn't want to wreck it.'

'You wouldn't – I mean – it's OK,' Cait said. If she had known time left with June was so precious, she would have been here every week over the past month, talking with her and spending time with her. A worm of anger began to twist inside her, but she shut it carefully away for later examination. June did not deserve her anger. June was dying. June was dying. She tested the sound of the phrase in her head. It was unreal.

She set her tea down on the tray and got up, moving to the other side of the couch to be next to June's little two-seater sofa. June, too, put her cup down, looking rather apprehensively at her. Cait sat down on the sofa beside June and leaned over to give her a sideways hug. She clutched the old lady hard. If it gave June discomfort, she did not show it, but returned Cait's embrace, one hand gripping Cait's forearm where it encircled her, the other patting her hand. She rested her cheek on Cait's for a moment, a surprisingly intimate gesture for June. Her cheek felt very dry and very soft, like a bit of tissue paper that had spent a lifetime being wrapped and re-wrapped around a precious object brought out only for special occasions, ending up smooth and translucent.

They stayed there like that for several long moments, until the hard knot in Cait's chest began to get harder and the tears began to threaten. She let go and moved back to her own sofa, picking up her tea. It had grown cold quickly in the tiny cup, and she downed the rest without tasting it while June told her the details. The chemotherapy she had declined. The Silver Chain care she had accepted, which would increase over time as she got sicker. How she was doing right now, which was largely fine, though she lacked energy. The hospital she would hold off on for as long as possible. Cait, knowing June's hatred for hospitals, did not push it, and allowed June to change the subject. 'Well, then, what have you got for me?' she said. She gestured towards the book box Cait had set on the floor.

'Are you sure you want that now? We don't have to. I mean, I don't have to leave it, if you're – well, if you're not well enough to read.'

'I'll stop reading when I'm dead, my girl, and not a moment sooner,' said June, with a trace of her usual tartness. 'In fact, with all the jobs these Silver Chain women are stopping me doing round the house, it looks like reading's all I'm allowed. They did prune my roses, though, so that's something. Probably only because I complained so much.'

Cait manufactured a smile, and took up the box to open it as June watched, a gesture she had repeated in this home, on this sofa, so often it had a familiarity all of its own. She wrenched her mind away from this fact and pulled out the first book, *Here I Am*, by Jonathan Safran Foer. She watched June's eyes light up, as they always did, when she got it right. And the conversation that followed was so satisfying, so routine in itself that Cait was able to hold herself separate from the news echoing in her mind. They reminisced about how much they had loved Foer's *Extremely Loud and Incredibly Close*. They agreed they couldn't see what everyone got so excited about in the first Neapolitan novel. June reported that the Annie Proulx was heavy going and she was still at it. She was much more excited about the new Ann Patchett: hot off the press, Cait told her, released and received at the shop that very day. Had June not looked so drawn it would have been easy for Cait to convince herself that there had been some kind of mistake.

They hugged with their usual quick conviviality when it was time to say goodbye, and Cait, her heart aching with increasing insistence, longed to slip away. But June had more to say.

'You're looking a bit unwell yourself,' June said bluntly, holding her by the shoulders and peering into her face, the bird-like look back. 'Working too hard.'

'It's fine,' Cait said. 'Seriously! I just needed to commit more time to the shop for a while, like I told you on the phone.'

'I bet there's plenty else in your life requiring commitment you've put on the backburner while you work yourself silly,' June continued. Her grip on Cait's shoulders was feathery, but her gaze was unwavering. 'And I'm not talking about visiting old people. Take it from me. There are more important things in life. And they don't wait forever.'

Cait dropped her eyes. She felt as though June was shining a searchlight into the back of her mind. She didn't know what to say.

'All right then,' June said, releasing her. 'Come again soon, but don't hurry. I'm being very well looked after and I'm in no danger of falling off the perch for a while yet.'

'OK. I'll see you soon,' Cait said, stepping back, already turning her face away. She suddenly wanted nothing more than to be out in the night air, alone on the freeway in Dent, not hearing more bad news, not getting any advice, no matter how well meant. She escaped into the cold. When she sat down in Dent she took a long, steadying breath and started the car immediately in case June thought she was bawling out here and came out to check. Within ten minutes she was back on the empty freeway. She was going too fast, but no-one was around. It was still cool for spring, and people were for the most part still hunkered down in their homes, especially on a blustery weeknight like this one. The radio was playing Elton John's 'Rocket Man'. She could not stand the emotion. She turned it off.

She had that feeling of numbness you got in those split seconds between having an accident and looking down to discover the extent of the injury. Instead of looking into her own mind to examine the wound there, she listened to the dulled roar of the freeway beneath Dent's wheels and watched the shaggy trees by the road shoulder, tall but unlovely, tossing in the wind. The sky was inky now, the treetops only just visible.

She was in the house before the knot in her chest all of a sudden seemed to get heavy, like it had turned into a lump of concrete. A curious pounding sensation began in her head. Abruptly she sat in the armchair, collapsing straight onto the sleeping Macduff, who squealed, squirmed out from beneath her and took off like a bullet into the kitchen. He then miaowed loudly, as if realising there was nothing for him in there. She took a deep breath, which seemed as though it did not reach her lungs, then went into the kitchen and opened a can of cat food. The smell of tuna rose from the can. Cait wanted to gag. She felt her face twist. She became dimly aware that Mac was butting his head against her calves. She put the cat food in his dish and added biscuits. She heard the biscuits shake in the box then clatter into the dish as though these things were happening on another planet, or maybe on a TV in front of her. She got out her phone and rang her mother. It was late in Melbourne but Tania answered immediately, her greeting sounding like she knew why Cait was calling.

'Hi,' Cait said flatly, knowing she sounded sullen, but spoiling for a fight. There was a pause. 'June told me.'

'Are you all right?'

'What the fuck do you think?' Cait spat. She realised her hands were curled into fists. She began to breathe more quickly. It was difficult to think. It was difficult to speak. '*Say* something,' she managed, finally, to hurl at her mother.

'What do you want me to say?'

'*Anything*. Maybe start with why you let me go the past month without knowing.'

'Cait,' her mother said. That was all. But her tone was enough.

Cait let out a dry gasp of a sob. Then another. She squeezed her free hand over her face. The dissociation she'd felt earlier had been better than this. June's going to die, she thought, again and again. No, no, no, no, no. 'Please, God, no,' she whispered aloud. She cried until mucus and tears ran down her forearm. After a while, she realised her mother, too, was weeping. They had not cried together since the early, now largely unmentioned months after her father took off.

'Do you want me to fly over?' Tania said.

'No,' Cait said quickly. The work situation was hard enough without her mother finding out about it.

'All right. I'm on standby, OK? I'll think about coming over in a month or two, when –'

'Yeah, OK,' Cait interrupted. 'Sorry I yelled at you.' More tears leaked out unbidden.

'I'm sorry too. I told myself that you should hear it from June herself, but then I didn't ring you and encourage you to go to see her. I think I was just making excuses. I wasn't sure how you'd react,' she paused. 'I thought ...'

'That I'd flip out.'

'Well, yes.'

'And I did.'

'Well ... Yes.'

'I'm a grown-up, Mum.'

'I know. You grew up very quickly, Cait.' She obviously heard Cait's intake of breath, because she added quickly, 'I know, I know you had to, after Dad and I split up. But June was – well, with June you were always looked after. She was like something sent to us from heaven.' She paused. 'I had tried so many nannies,' she said. 'All experienced, all worthy, all with great references.'

'But I wouldn't have a bar of them,' Cait prompted. She had heard this story before and sought refuge in its repetition.

'You wouldn't let a single one even hold you. You just screwed up your little face until it was as red as your hair and screamed. It was so embarrassing. I was at my wits' end. And then June came. She took one look at you and just caught you up out of your cot without waiting for permission. And it was like a miracle. You kept quiet. And then –'

'I laughed.'

'You laughed! It was just like love at first sight with you and June.'

They were both quiet for a moment.

'And then later, after what happened with Dad ... I know what she means to you, that's all I'm trying to say. And I just thought, I thought, well – I just couldn't bear to be the one who took that away.'

'You're not the one taking it away, Mum,' Cait said. Must she play counsellor yet again? 'Don't get all guilty about this. You didn't give June cancer. Listen, I'm going to bed.'

They hung up, promising they'd talk again soon. Then Cait blew her nose and cleaned herself up. She was watching Mac licking his chops, having annihilated his dinner, when she remembered she hadn't eaten since a bowl of cereal at breakfast. It was now eight-thirty. No wonder she was weeping and falling apart. She got on the phone and ordered pizza.

She sat in the armchair in the living room and waited limply for it to arrive. She didn't turn on the TV or play on her phone. She thought about June. June had looked after her so well. After the divorce, June had stepped back in, this time not as employee but as family friend. In the worst days, she had kept an eye on Tania while Cait was at work, and again had helped out with the housework. She had let Cait flee to her place occasionally to vent, with all the harsh impatience of youth, her frustration at the length of her mother's road to recovery, with all its delays and switchbacks. But June had never expressed judgement herself; maybe through simple loyalty, maybe because she understood Tania better than Cait ever had.

What good could Cait do June in return, now, after all June had done for her? Would June suffer terribly? How could she muster the strength to save Book Fiend without June's help?

How would she live without June, full stop? The unknowns stretched terrifyingly before her. Just hang on, she told herself. Hang on for the decision on the rent. Then think about June. Useless words. She may as well try to hold back the tide with her bare hands.

The pizza arrived. Cait ate half a slice, staring into space, and could not face the rest. She went upstairs to bed, leaving it on the coffee table, where Macduff pounced joyfully upon it.

SIXTEEN

Warwick Randell sorted through his messages, stopping frequently to sip from a jumbo takeaway coffee on his desk. It contained three shots of espresso, nearly half a litre of milk and three teaspoons of sugar, but he downed it like water as he read messages and made notes in a black bonded-leather diary. Nobody watching would have had the impression he was enjoying the beverage, or even tasting it. His whole attention was focused on the work, his thin shoulders hunched over the desk in the manner common to exceptionally tall men. The thick carpeting and brick walls of the office building made the noise of the street outside virtually inaudible.

'Greta,' he called. A woman poked her nose around the door, an expression of friendly inquiry on her face, lost on Randell, who was peering at the message atop the stack. 'Do you remember this one?'

She hastened to the desk to peer more closely at the message. 'Oh yes. Nice girl, that one. She's been in that building a long time, never any trouble. Quite amazing for such a young person. I was surprised to get the call actually, but the hikes have been steep recently, so we're getting all kinds of calls from tenants we don't usually hear from … she sounded very embarrassed –'

'What did you say to her?' He didn't quite cut Greta off, but the tone of his voice suggested he wasn't interested in how the girl had sounded or what kind of tenant she was.

'Well, nothing really. I didn't suggest we'd be able to do it. I just told her it would go to the director.'

'Good. Call her back and say we can't extend, not there. And remind her we've got that relocation service. With any luck she'll take that like the chemist did. We really need movement in that street – I've got a prospective tenant that would make a big splash if they opened there, but they won't wait forever, even for Hay Street.'

'Should I – well, I know we normally have options people can –'

'Those aren't something I'm prepared to keep offering as a general rule, not in that spot. Unless she kicks up a stink and asks about policies, just tell her it's not negotiable. If she can't pay, we'll put in someone who can.'

Greta hovered, looking as though she wanted to say more, but he tossed the memo into the bin and picked up the next, a clear dismissal.

'Greta,' he said when she reached the door, and she looked back hopefully. 'Another coffee, please.'

'Of course. Won't be long,' she said, with perfect courteousness.

Greta clicked the door shut delicately and did not return to her desk, but went straight downstairs to the cafe. This was one phone call she was happy to put off for a while. At least until she got a coffee herself. She placed the order and stood to wait. The atmosphere of the Daily Grind enveloped her: the gurgle of a steam wand plunging into milk, the drone and scent of coffee pouring unceasingly from spouts, the bubble of twenty different conversations and the rustle of newsprint, pages turned idly as people hung about for their takeaways. Greta was usually calmed by the place, her visits a pleasant part of her workdays, but now she stood apart from it all, fretting.

'Hey.' She looked up to see James, one of the agents, right in front of her. She didn't know him that well. He was one of the younger ones. Very cute.

'Oh, hey,' she said. 'Sorry. I didn't see you.'

'Old crow stressing you out?'

'Yeah. Like always.'

He looked surprised at the bitter tone. 'You OK? You look upset.'

'JAMES,' bellowed the barista, and James beckoned Greta over to one of the couches, grabbing his coffee en route. They were secluded there, private in the way somehow only achievable in the middle of a crowded cafe. She sat with him and decided he was safe to confide in.

'I just got told, flat out, to reject this request for a rent extension. To this girl who has always been a perfectly good tenant. The increase has been massive. I wouldn't be surprised if it puts her out of business.'

'Just like that? No wiggle room?'

'Well, there normally would be. We have a policy that people have the right to appeal any rental review and that will receive the attention of the CEO, not just the director of retail leasing. But it's kind of buried in the paperwork and the less financially savvy tenants, the ones without lawyers and stuff, don't generally know about it. It used to be standard that we would tell them about it, no big deal. But Randell just outright told me not to.'

'Right.' James drew out the word, stared at his coffee. He looked oddly troubled. She warmed to him.

'So I thought, maybe I could just tell this girl about the policy. I could just do it quietly, unofficially, or even write her an anonymous letter, or just ring and drop her a hint, or mail her a copy of the relevant bit. There are lots of ways I could do it. That way she would know to ask and we would have to answer her questions. Then she gets a fighting chance at least.'

'Would he know it was you who tipped her off if she did ask for a review? Like, are these policies common knowledge?'

'Sure, I guess there are a few other admin staff who know. And maybe some of the more experienced agents. But someone would have to know her situation to think of telling her. And I think it's just me from the company who knows her.'

'GRETA,' the barista yelled across the room, and Greta sprang up to collect the coffees. When she returned, James looked deep in thought. She sat down again. She was in no hurry to return to the office.

'I think,' James said, 'and I know you don't want to hear this, and I feel shitty for saying it, but if he suspects you've helped her, you'll be out of a job. You know what he's like. And they could easily get someone else. We're always turning away grads. There are so bloody many of them and they're all happy to work for practically nothing – I know they have no experience,' he said as she opened her mouth, 'but that's the way it is right now.'

Greta made a face. 'You're right. I know I can't go behind his back. And I know the market is what it is. I know Randell has a big client wanting in; that's why he's managing that strip himself. Even if she tried to negotiate, the CEO would likely tell Randell to go ahead and chuck her out. But she's always paid the rent. And I liked her on the phone. Hell, I like that shop. You know, that bookshop on Hay Street? It just all feels … bad.'

James patted her shoulder. 'You're right, it's shit, but all you can do is hope that she's got someone else looking out for her who can advise her. You can't save a stranger's business, even if it's a good one. You can't help it that that strip's in demand or that your boss is a prick. Hey, maybe one day you'll have his job, and you can do it better.'

'Yeah,' Greta said, without enthusiasm. 'I better get back. Thanks for the chat.'

'Anytime.'

'Coming?'

'I'm gonna stay here for a bit,' James said. 'Got an issue of my own to nut out.'

'Well, I hope the caffeine helps,' she said, and he smiled. She'd always thought of James as a bit stiff, despite his looks, but he was really a good guy, she reflected. It was nice of him to take an interest in her problems, even when they had nothing to do with him.

SEVENTEEN

Cait took in quite a good haul of second-hand stuff, including a pristine matching Hunger Games set, which flew straight back out the door, and lost herself in the routine of processing the rest. Cobie Strange dropped in with some good crime to exchange, including some Australian stuff – Peter Temple, David Whish-Wilson, Sara Foster – Cait set aside a couple for Max – and another woman brought a very welcome pile of retro Enid Blyton hardcovers, in surprisingly nice condition, which required nothing but a wipe down … and maybe just ten minutes spent browsing the blurbs of stories she'd loved as a kid. Eventually, though, she hit one she remembered June giving her for her eighth birthday, and the panic humming in the back of her mind threatened to take over. She abandoned the nostalgia trip and took the pile to the already groaning kids' shelf. Before she could work out how to fit them in, the phone rang. She turned to see a customer behind her, his mouth already half open in the beginning of a question.

'Sorry,' she said. 'Just let me get that.' She ran to the old cordless handset. 'Good morning, Book Fiend. This is Cait,' she said automatically, and was about to follow this with

'Please hold?' when she recognised the voice of the nice office woman she'd spoken with yesterday about the rent, and stilled.

The woman launched, stammering slightly, into a spiel about how they weren't granting rent extensions anymore on addresses in that part of the CBD, as the waiting list was so competitive. If Cait was having financial trouble, she was welcome to come in and discuss what other properties they might have available that would suit her, as she was a valued long-term tenant and they understood times were tough. She sounded like she was reading from a script. Cait thought about arguing, but the most appalling rush of tears suddenly leapt into her throat. Get off the phone before you cry, her brain said, while her mouth said, 'No, no, thank you, it's OK, I'll figure something out. Thanks,' and hung up.

The man in front of her asked if she had a copy of *Shantaram*. It was by – she interrupted him, as politely as she could. Yes, she knew. It was a popular title. Unfortunately, they rarely had second-hand copies, but she could sell him a new copy if he liked. He declined and left. She stood and looked at the shelves opposite her for several long moments. Maybe it was time for her to leave, too.

'Hello, there, Miss Cait!' said a kindly voice at her elbow. She turned to see Mr Cowper, clutching *Sharpe's Skirmish* by Bernard Cornwell in his twisted fingers.

'Oh, hello, Mr Cowper,' she said, summoning a smile for the old man. 'How are you?'

'Well. I'm well. But I'm going into hospital, soon, for my hip,' he told her.

'Oh, dear,' she said automatically, trying to remember if he had told her about his hip before. He was sure to have done, but sometimes she switched off a bit when Mr Cowper got particularly rambly. 'Will you have to stay long?'

'Well, no. They'll keep me in for about five days,' he said. 'That's if it all goes all right. But I won't be moving around too much for a while after it. That's why I thought I might have to stock up on one of these.' He waved the book, blissfully unaware that he had nearly clocked the woman browsing next to him. 'You know, five days in hospital can feel like five weeks if you haven't got something really good to read.'

'I'm sure. But I thought you'd finished the Sharpes.'

'Not quite. Could you have a look for me, Cait, on your computer, and see if you have the one after this one? *Sharpe's Waterloo*. I've just not been able to find it second-hand, and I would like to have it for this hospital stay.' He showed her his list, which sure enough had a couple of lines not yet crossed off. Cait peered obligingly at it.

'I see. I'm not sure if I actually have that one at the moment. Let me check the computer for you, OK? ... No, I definitely don't have one. Would you like me to see if I can order it in?'

'Oh. Y-yes, I suppose ...' She had already done a quick check of stock at the supplier by the time he got this out.

'It would be twenty dollars, Mr Cowper. Nineteen ninety-nine. It would take about two weeks, maybe less. Would that arrive in time for you?'

'Oh,' he said, blinking owlishly. 'I see. Well ... yes, I think so ...'

'Would you like me to order that for you?' Cait said patiently. 'I could always post it out to you, if it arrives while you're off your feet.'

His expression cleared. 'Oh, yes. Thank you. How much would the post be? And do I need to pay that now?'

She assured him he could pay on arrival, and they could discuss postage then too, but he wasn't ready to leave yet. He had another list. Had Cait read any of these? No, she hadn't.

But she knew that series had many loyal fans, she told him. She helped him find a couple more titles. He extracted a stack of crisp twenties from the immaculate leather wallet he was eventually, with much tugging, able to free from his pocket. She hoped he wasn't carrying that much cash around all the time. She hated to think of this old man getting mugged outside her shop. She flashed back suddenly to the man who had been following her around the other night, pushing the books into the backs of the shelves. How weirdly menacing he'd seemed.

'Are you all right, Miss Cait?' asked Mr Cowper, and she saw he was scrutinising her with some concern. 'You look a bit pale.'

'It's nothing,' she smiled at him. 'I just remembered something. Here's your change. You put that wallet away before you leave, OK? I've had some suspicious types hanging around recently.'

'Oh, dear,' Mr Cowper said, looking innocently appalled. 'What is the world coming to?' He replaced the wallet, his knobbly fingers struggling to get it back in.

After more routine back-and-forth Cait managed to shepherd him out the door, wishing him well for his hospital visit if she did not see him again first. What would happen to Mr Cowper if she lost the shop, and all the others like him? Nobody at the enormous Collins on the town outskirts would bother to learn whether Mr Cowper had finished the Sharpe series. Everyone who worked there looked about fourteen. They'd probably try to start selling them to him again from the beginning. He'd probably let them, too.

It's not your job to look after these people, Cait, her brain said. They wouldn't go through this for you. Shush, she told it. I know that. It's not just about them.

'How was your day?' James said that night on the phone. Was his tone perfunctory, or was she imagining it?

'Fine,' she said. The thought of telling him about today's phone call from Lease Freedom, let alone about her visit with June, made her throat close over. She was already battling to eat. She tried another bite of her toast. 'Yours?' Macduff, who had stopped his galloping headlong around the house now he had reached stately middle age, but who still managed to appear quickly whenever there was food around, sat at her feet, watching hopefully.

'Yeah, fine. Are you eating toast for dinner again?'

'Nah,' she said, trying to chew more quietly, and casting about for something more to say. She was sick of James nagging her to eat properly. 'I had such a cute old lady in this morning.'

'Yeah?' His tone softened.

'I asked her if I could help her and she said, "I need a dictionary. A good one – you know, one with all the rude words in it."' James laughed. 'The two of us spent the next ten minutes looking up all the worst swearwords we could think of.'

'Aw, that is cute. Listen, baby, I might not have time to stop by tomorrow. I have a work thing to deal with.'

'Oh. That's all right. Everything OK?'

'Yeah. I just need to put in a good showing. If you're not too tired, maybe we could do a late dinner on Friday?'

'That's fine. Hey, I'm going to go to bed. I love you.'

'Love you too,' he said, and hung up. He had not sounded loving. He had sounded distracted, and relieved that she hadn't made a fuss about him cancelling. Well, she supposed it was nothing but a taste of her own medicine. Unless it was something else. Or someone else. Oh God, was it someone else?

Don't be stupid, she told herself. You're imagining disasters around every corner now. You'll talk properly on Friday. You'll tell him about June, and about the rent. It'll give you time to make some decisions.

Cait brushed toast crumbs from her lap onto Macduff's head. He began sniffing around. She gave him the last charred fragment and stood up. He jumped ecstatically into the warm spot she had left, his prize clamped in his jaws.

≈≈≈

James had arrived home that day laden with the usual paraphernalia: gym bag redolent of a visit squeezed in on the way home; some files he needed to look over after dinner; the empty Tupperware he had lacked time to wash after lunch, a meal eaten absent-mindedly and one-handedly, the other hand still occupied with typing and clicking as tenants' emails poured in. Emails that had become more frantic of late as business after business hit the skids. He had dumped it all on the floor, to be sorted later. Normally he was tidier. But his mind was troubled, knowing something of what Cait might have been holding back on the phone just now.

James had worked long hours for Lease Freedom, trying to climb another rung of the corporate ladder before yet another crop of graduates came on the scene, an army of white-collar workers produced out of all proportion to the number of jobs Perth was providing. The thought of going and pleading Cait's case to Randell frankly made his arsehole clench. Randell was not his immediate boss, but the executive team was tight. They would probably take a dim view of him interfering in a high-profile portfolio on behalf of his girlfriend. They would just tell him to convince her to move. He could just tell Cait about the appeals policy Greta had mentioned, but as Greta had said,

Cait's chances of coming out on top in such a negotiation were slim to none. He cracked a beer and sat on the couch and contemplated his house. It all showed unmistakeable traces of Cait. His stylish, minimalist fishbowl now sported a little diver figurine, 'to keep Maclary company'. There was even a little diving board hooked over the side. There was loose-leaf tea in his kitchen. Bits of clothing scattered about. And books, of course. She just seemed to trail them along behind her. Like Book Fiend itself, it was all a bit untidy, but the overall effect was undeniably welcoming. Homely. James went and got his laptop and files and looked once again for the perfect property, with the charm and location that would scream, 'Lease Me! Everything Will Be All Right!' He looked on Beaufort, Rokeby, Bay View, Oxford. Albany Highway. Even South Terrace and Market Street in Freo. Nothing looked right. He slept poorly that night and went into the office early. He knew Randell would be there. The man never seemed to sleep. Greta wasn't in yet, but Randell was visible in his office.

EIGHTEEN

'Come in.' Randell sounded testy at being interrupted during what he probably thought of as his quiet time. 'James,' he said, with the air of having laid a hand on the name in his memory banks just in time for it to supply his mouth.

'Morning,' James said, resisting the urge to add, 'sir.'

Randell said nothing, but waited for James to state his business.

'I was wondering whether you might have a moment to speak with me about Book Fiend,' James blurted.

Randell paused, as though racking his brain for where 'Book Fiend' was, which James knew was purely a theatrical move. 'Hay Street?'

James blundered on, further unnerved by Randell's unblinking gaze. 'I was wondering whether you might reconsider the rise. I know the owner. It's not – well, it's not a sustainable increase for her.'

Randell waited a beat that withered James's confidence even further. 'Know the owner, do you?'

'Yesss … ir,' James said, trying his hardest to leave off the sir and not quite succeeding. 'She's my girlfriend.'

'Oh-ho!' Randell said, with the air of having landed a fish that proved even bigger than it had felt on the line. 'Your girlfriend, eh? Well, I'm sorry to hear it. Very sorry indeed.' He did not look sorry at all. 'Now, young James, I'm sorry to have to tell you my hands are tied on this one. Orders from the top, you know. I'm managing the Hay Street strip portfolio myself, you see, because we just have some very exciting things going on there at the moment. Exciting for us and for the city. People love the new vibrancy in that area.'

'People love that shop, too,' James made himself say. 'Listen, it opened in the boom, and you know the crowds aren't what they were. And the spending has changed. If it wasn't for the Amazon factor, she might've coped with the downturn, and if it wasn't for the downturn she might've coped with Amazon. In fact, she seemed to be fine before this issue with the lease.'

Randell sighed and when he spoke again, it was in a skin-crawling man-to-man tone. 'Listen, James. I've got over twenty years of commercial retail property experience. I'm responsible for some of the biggest retail leasing transactions in this state. I've brought Zara to this CBD. I've brought Topshop. I've brought Nespresso and Prada and Miu Miu.' He counted them off on his bony fingers. 'We've got to activate these spaces, and I've got a very exciting new client waiting in the wings whose capacity to pay the rent is not in question. I'm afraid that this little bookstore just doesn't fit the aesthetic I'm going for on this street, and if it's not viable, that can't be a concern of mine. It's survival of the fittest in this climate. I happen to have had a little chat about it with the CEO and he agrees. So, you see ...' he spread his hands as if to indicate helplessness.

James stared at him. He did not feel he could back down. Equally, he did not feel he could argue.

Randell smiled. 'Of course, there's plenty we can do to help your young friend. Please encourage her to contact us. The ink is barely dry on the new lease. If she signed it in error, not realising it was unsustainable, of course we will be very understanding. I am sure we can negotiate a graceful exit for her. We've got plenty of great locations in the suburbs. She just has to say the word and we will find her one.'

James gave it one last shot. 'I don't think she will easily come to a decision to move. She's very attached to that spot. And I understand the fit-out was expensive.'

'That's such a shame,' Randell said, smiling widely. 'I hope she can salvage some of it, or sell it if she decides to close down. Thanks for stopping by, James, I really do appreciate the chat. And close the door on your way out, won't you?'

James forced himself to close it quietly. He walked away, his footsteps noiseless on the soft carpet, resolving never to tell Cait that his one chance to play a real, useful part in her life had done nothing but prove how utterly powerless he really was.

Cait spent Friday in the shop cleaning furiously, her mind in a tailspin. June was dying. Book Fiend was going under. She said these things to herself in an effort to face them. After all, she was going to have to repeat them to James tonight. But then their enormity would overwhelm her with a pain that was almost physical and again, her mind would wrench itself away and lose itself once more in a practical task. It was a long day – she had decided to stay open until ten p.m. for maximum sales – but when she got up from where she had been obsessively scrubbing at a stain on the carpet, she was still surprised to see it was nine forty-five. Time to bring the trolleys in.

Outside on the pavement, a line of people in various stages of intoxication surged ceaselessly past, belched in continuous shoals from the exits of bars and restaurants further down the strip. Crowds had trashed the orderly arrangement of books stacked face-forward in the trolleys, and Cait paused outside to give them a quick tidy before hauling them in. She reached towards the rear of the first tray with both hands, behind the last book in the last row, intending to pull the stack to the front, then push the tops back so they lay with a neat slant, like fallen dominoes. She felt the edges of the last book, a little curly from sitting at the back unsold for too long. Then her fingers encountered an object behind them. Rough and dry, then sticky; Cait recoiled, then stood on tiptoe to peer back there. A cardboard ice-cream cup bearing the logo of a neighbouring store had been secreted there, a paper napkin stuffed into the puddle of melted ice-cream inside. Grimacing, she pulled it out and dropped it into the bin a few metres away on the pavement. She hauled the trolley inside. Its wheels shrieked for oil. She wiped her fingers on the soft, thin fabric of her apron and returned for the second trolley, before which one of the drifters had halted. He swayed slightly as he picked up one of the impulse buys at the front: *I Lick My Cheese and Other Notes*, a collection of humorous notes between the inmates of share houses. As he flicked through it, his companion, perched atop a pair of glittering platforms, looked longingly towards the windows of Prada next door. She plucked at his sleeve. Cait hesitated a moment, wondering if it would be worth staying open a few more minutes to sell one more book. She decided enough was enough.

'Sorry! I'm closing,' she said, in a voice that brooked no argument. The guy put the little paperback down, casually and without reluctance, as if realising that none of it mattered. He turned away, allowing the ponytailed girlfriend to draw him back into the passing stream of people. It swallowed them seamlessly, surging without destination or urgency down the pavement in a ceaseless flow entirely different from the movements of the workers that crowded the street on weekdays. Cait heaved the trolley up the ramp and paused to roll her shoulders before going back for the *Open* sign out on the edge of the pavement. She grabbed it by its grubby metal shoulders and waited for another opening to cross the line of people. She looked back at Book Fiend – the only retailer still open on the strip, a solitary pool of light between Prada and Gucci. Those shops were dark this late, save for LED downlights recessed above their windows, spotlighting the lone handbags on display, glinting off their fine detailing. These disciplined, chillingly uncluttered spaces, gleaming with stateless affluence, made Book Fiend look hopelessly out of place between them. Its interior, designed so carefully to celebrate the cosy and old-fashioned, would probably not just fail to 'spark joy' in Marie Kondo, but would likely give her a conniption. She saw an opening and dragged her sign back across the footpath.

She locked the door behind her, muting the street noise. She went out the back to wash the residual stickiness off her hands before coming back out to count the till. She bagged cash and lobbed it all into the safe. Turning for a final survey as she reached the front door, her eyes fell on the disarranged humour book in the trolley. She patted it back into place, switched off the lights and let herself out. She turned to re-lock the door behind her, and paused for a moment to rest her forehead against the solid polished wood of the doorframe. She let her body sag. She thought about just staying there. Then she jumped a mile when a hand descended on her shoulder. She whipped around in panic, clutching her bag instinctively, then saw it was James.

'Shit! You scared me,' she said. She gave him a huge hug and felt this simple act of connection with another human being drain away a little of her sadness.

'Hey, what's that for?' he asked, grinning down at her. She felt dirty and tired and utterly lucky this patient, lovely person was still turning up here to see her. She kissed him.

'Nothing in particular,' she said when they broke apart, his hands in her hair. 'Just happy you're you.'

'I'm happy you're you too. Look, I got you a present.' And he pulled an object wrapped in white tissue paper from his messenger bag, a manly leather item that probably represented a week's salary for Cait. The busker three doors down launched into Bob Marley's 'Three Little Birds'. Cait tore off the delicate paper on her gift to find a handbag. A dream handbag. A simple bag of baby-soft pale tan leather, with a wide strap held on by big polished loops of silver. She stroked it. It was clearly expensive, certainly more so than any bag she'd ever owned. She looked inside and saw the flat leather nameplate stitched into the silky lining.

'You like it?' he asked, watching her face.

'It's beautiful,' Cait said, giving him another kiss. 'Oh, James, it's gorgeous. I've never had such a beautiful bag. But this must have cost you a fortune! It's not even my birthday! What gives?' And she gave him a playfully reproachful shove. She didn't know whether to be delighted or horrified by such an extravagant gift. This kind of spoiling she could never reciprocate. Their whole relationship involved him giving her things and taking her places she couldn't afford.

He wouldn't do it if he didn't like it, her brain said. He

doesn't love you for your money and he knows you don't expect it. Shut up and take the bag already.

You're just a sucker for a pretty handbag, Cait told her brain. Just look at it!

Cait looked. Her brain was right.

'I just wanted to give you the kind of bag that suits how really, really ridiculously good-looking you are,' James said.

She laughed at the *Zoolander* reference. 'Thank you,' she said, trying to put all the thanks she felt into her voice. 'I love it. It's, like, my dream bag. Here, hold it open for me.' He did so and she upturned her old handbag, a grimy cotton sack, over it, dumping its contents in one mass into the new bag. James looked ever so slightly taken aback at this lack of ceremony. 'I'll sort it out later,' she said. 'For now, I just can't wait to do *this*.' She fought the nightlife once more to reach the street bin, and jubilantly stuffed the old bag inside.

'I'm glad you like it. Turns out it's nerve-racking buying women's handbags. I don't know who found it more exhausting – me, or the lady who sold it to me. Now, should we go find something to eat before everything shuts?'

They set off, hand in hand. It took them a while to find a place whose kitchen was still open, but they finally found a Turkish place they had not yet tried. Cait baulked when she saw she was going to have to sit on a cushion – after a day on her feet, she generally craved comfort and familiarity in a restaurant, not a new experience – but James appeared unfazed. The interior was packed with diners, chatty and expansive on the tail end of excellent meals, if the rich buttery smells in the air were anything to go by. The walls were decorated with pictures whose frames were trimmed with Christmas tinsel, the general cheerful dinginess of which gave every appearance of this decoration being a year-round fixture. A belly dancer was threading her way around the tables, adding to the general mayhem. While James rapidly placed an order for them, to get in before the kitchen shut, Cait carefully placed her fabulous new handbag on its own cushion beside her and put all the bits and pieces in the appropriate pockets. There was a place for everything, even a discreet pocket for keys on the outside. Then she finished. James finished ordering. And she had run out of excuses to put this conversation off.

She tried to think how to begin. The waitress moved away. Cait looked at James and took a deep breath. James looked faintly alarmed at her expression. 'What's –'

'June's got cancer,' Cait blurted out. 'She's dying.' Her face gave a terrible wobble as she said it, and she looked down again, fighting for control.

'Oh, baby.' She could not look at him. 'When did you find out?'

'A couple of days ago.'

'A couple of *days* ago? Cait, why didn't you call me?'

Because that would have made it real, Cait thought, and for the first time understood why June might have taken so long to tell her. 'I don't know,' she said.

James frowned. Then he sighed, obviously figuring this wasn't the time to make a fuss over it. 'What kind of cancer?'

Cait got out the details while around them people talked and screamed with laughter. A swarm of beautifully dressed but crazily overexcited little girls, well past their bedtimes, cavorted about the table next to them. One, aged perhaps five, bumped into Cait, who, overwrought, could not help herself but scowl hideously at the little girl, who beat a hasty retreat to her mother's side, wide-eyed. The silence stretched. Cait wished James would at least come out with the standard 'I'm sorry'. But he seemed not to know what to do. He poured her more wine. 'That sucks,' he finally said. She felt this inadequate.

'A hug is usually an appropriate response when you're lost for ideas,' she told him. She hoped her tone was lighthearted enough to disguise how wretched and angry she suddenly felt. He hugged her. Like any hug that had to be asked for, that also felt inadequate.

'How old is June? Pretty old, right?'

'She's eighty-four,' Cait said, stiffly. 'A *healthy* eighty-four, until now. Eighty-five next year … I would have thrown her a party,' she added, with a sense of desolation.

'Maybe you still can. She might last longer than you think.'

'I don't know. When I went to see her the other night, she looked *sick*. Kind of blasted away. She said she had "a few months". I googled pancreatic cancer and it said only twenty percent of people survive the first year. And I'm assuming that's if they're having treatment. June said she wasn't.'

'Why?'

'She said she was too old and there wasn't any point when the outlook was so poor anyway. I wasn't going to argue with her. There's no arguing with June.' She felt fresh tears threaten and held them back.

'She's probably right. Just because you want her to live forever, doesn't mean she should. Or wants to, even for you.'

It hurt that June didn't want to fight to live just for Cait, as absurd as that sounded even inside her head. James's sensible words and soothing tone all at once made her want to hit him. He should be more upset by this. But why would he be? He hadn't met June yet. Saturdays were often the days he saw his own mother, which had delayed them at first from that sit-down coffee, and more recently, Cait had been too busy to organise it.

Knowledge settled that the loss looming over her was something she could not share with him. For the first time, she understood their essential separateness, as though they were talking through a thick sheet of glass. Was this how all human beings' attempts to communicate, to connect, ended up? With the knowledge they were all completely and unbearably alone?

Before her composure could crack entirely, she rushed on to tell him about the phone call from Greta at Lease Freedom. Then their food arrived. James doled out rice and mains for them both with a practised hand.

'What are you going to do about the shop?'

'Keep going as I am for a bit, I suppose,' Cait said, with a gameness she did not feel. 'Keep working seven days, see mobile clients in the evenings. Just for a while. Just until I work out a way to increase profits.'

'Jesus, Cait. What else would you give up for this shop? Your firstborn son? Your sanity? And you just told me you might only have months left to spend with June.'

'I'm fine,' cried Cait, stung. 'What choice do I have, anyway? I've got some ideas about how to make the business more profitable, I just need a bit of breathing space to make them happen. Anyway, I don't notice you helping. You work there, but you haven't given me a single bit of advice or help apart from telling me who to phone.'

James was silent. Expressions Cait couldn't interpret flitted across his face. Then he spoke. 'Cait. They're right. You can't afford the market rent on that strip anymore. There's nothing you can do. They're not going to let you appeal. I have looked into it. You could take it to the State Administrative Tribunal. But it would cost you a fortune, and you just don't have that kind of money. I don't even have that kind of money.'

'I wouldn't take your money.'

'I know.'

The belly dancer jingled her beautiful navel towards them, then hastily moved away when she caught sight of their faces.

'Look, Cait, you just need to move. There are plenty of nice little strips in the inner-ring suburbs. You might have to modify the shop a bit … lose the second-hand component, maybe. Simplify the fit-out.'

'I thought you understood. I can't just uproot. The store would make even less money somewhere less prominent. And I've spent years building up this customer base. I have relationships with these people.' She recognised her mistake as she said it, and waited for the inevitable retort.

'We've got a relationship too, Cait. At least I thought we did. But it turns out you value just about anything and everything above it. You're banking an awful lot on me just hanging around waiting to see if things magically improve, aren't you?'

'If you've been feeling neglected, I'm sorry. I am, really, sorry.' It sounded unconvincing, but she didn't know what else to say. 'Why didn't you talk to me about this, if this is how you've been feeling?'

'When the fuck would I have had a chance to do that, Cait? When I snatch a weekly dinner with you? When you sneak out of bed in the morning and flee back to work? When I see you looking all strung-out and vulnerable?' She opened her mouth, but he was still talking. 'When you hurry me off the phone? When you keep secret all your latest news? When am I supposed to try to talk to you? Answer me that. I come in at lunchtime, even, but we can't talk then either. I don't have a *flexible* schedule like your precious Sebastian.'

Her 'precious' Sebastian? What the hell did he mean by that? And how did James know Seb was visiting in the afternoons? Had he walked past? But what would he have seen, if so? Nothing, was what. 'What does Seb have to do with anything?'

'Don't give me that. You two are thick as thieves.'

'Seb's just a friend,' she protested, laughing despite her

misery, and her fright at his anger. It was too funny that he would think she was carrying on a torrid affair. She was too tired to shave her armpits or find matching socks. When was she supposed to be shacking up with Seb? Between dings of the counter bell? But she knew a split second too late that laughter had been the worst possible reaction. James looked livid. And would that belly dancer never finish? The music blared overhead, blotting out their raised voices to everyone except, it seemed, the family at the next table. Even the little girls were now staring.

'What do you even want out of your life, Cait? Do you ever want to get married, have kids? How's it all going to work?'

'I hadn't really thought ...' Cait mumbled, hoping to encourage him to lower his voice.

'No, of course not. The future is another country, right? You haven't even bothered to take me to meet June. I've had you round to Mum's. She knows what you mean to me. But you can't even introduce me to your friends.'

'That means nothing.' Cait told herself she was feeling righteous anger, not guilty defensiveness. 'I just haven't had time to introduce you to June. I've been trying to hold my life together, in case you hadn't noticed. I can't just run away from my commitments when things get tough.' She admitted to herself, too late, her own unfairness. She remembered how hard James worked towards financial security for his mother, after his father left them with nothing. How he went round to his mum's just about every weekend to do things for her that it seemed to Cait his mother should be able to do for herself, but that James did not question.

'I don't see you running away from your commitments,' said James with devastating coolness. 'Lucky for you it seems I'm not one of them.'

'What does that mean?'

'It means I'm sick of being at the bottom of your to-do list.'

'James, that's just the way it is right now. You said it yourself; I don't even have the time for both June and the shop the way things are going. You're just going to need to be patient and wait a bit longer for me.' She paused and then added, 'Please.'

The belly dancer finished her set and the music stopped so abruptly that James's next words rang out across the restaurant: 'I can't wait forever.' He quickly dropped his voice. 'I can't wait and keep wondering when you're going to face reality. So let me just simplify your life for you.'

She tried to think of something to say, but he was already rising off the cushion, unfolding his long legs and standing with a grace of movement and a dignity she would never have achieved herself.

'James –'

'Call me when you sort your shit out,' he said. He pulled a couple of notes from his wallet and flung them down on the table with an air so contemptuous she felt actually winded, as though he had thumped her. He walked away without another word, slipping through the tables to the door. He squeezed past the voluptuous belly dancer who was also leaving the room. He did not even glance at her. Or back at Cait.

NINETEEN

Cait got home and fed the cat. Then they both went upstairs and sat on her bed. She and Macduff both looked at the phone in her hand. She half-expected James to ring any minute, for his quick anger to be followed by equally hasty regret. But he didn't. Should she call him? She wrestled with this, and decided not to. Cait wished she had not had to use his money to pay for their uneaten meal. Why had she allowed herself to become comfortable with James taking her out all the time? Well, he had always insisted on it. Why suddenly make a point of it, embarrassing her in public? Especially after she had just told him that a dear friend, virtually a family member, was dying. The word still sounded overly dramatic, unreal, in her head. She tried to be angry, to tell herself James was an arsehole. But he was usually so patient. He must have been really angry to react so extremely. She stroked Mac, then, absently, the soft leather of her new handbag, lying blameless but already tainted on her bed. Guilt enveloped her. She had taken it for granted that James would understand about everything. She had taken him as much for granted as she did June.

Could he be expected to understand what June meant to her? She had never felt the need to spell it out. And he had never seen them together, never witnessed the easy closeness, the laughter that flowed effortlessly between them. If her weekends had been free to spend with him, he would have met June by now. They would be having afternoon teas in the garden as the weather warmed and June's flowerbeds put on their spring show. They would have all gotten to know each other. But it was too late for that now. And she had not realised until now how much she had been counting on him being there for her in the months ahead, which promised to be full of a pain she could barely imagine, but already feared.

He was wrong about Seb too. But she didn't get a chance to convince him of that. She saw again the contempt on James's face, the anger and disgust, as he flung his money on the table. How could anyone who looked at her like that ever go back to loving her? What kind of gesture had that been, chucking money at her like she was a prostitute? She had never been treated so rudely in her life. OK, this wasn't quite true. Plenty of people had been this rude. But no-one she loved. And the scene in the restaurant had been beyond rude. It had been cruel. But James was not a cruel person. He was a good person, she knew it. She had just fucked everything up. Where would she find someone like him again, at her age? She was nearly thirty-four. It had felt like a miracle, someone like James falling for her. Now she knew it was too good to be true. Maybe he never really had loved her, and this had been his excuse to break up with her.

Or maybe he was waiting on an apology. But did he deserve one? And round it went, hour after miserable hour.

Cait woke stiff and cold on top of the covers, hand still cramped around her phone. She checked for a missed call or text. There was none. Dampness from her clutching hand had fogged the screen and she wiped it with the blanket. She lay there for a good fifteen further minutes, trying to convince herself she was happy to rise on another heart-achingly beautiful spring Saturday to go and sell books. And happy to then spend Saturday night going to Max and Dorothy's to sell more.

She worked all day in a daze, trying not to think about James, or what she was going to do about Book Fiend, even as the memory rose repeatedly of James telling her she had to face reality and make a decision. She arrived at Max's worn out from this internal warfare. As she entered, she heard his oven timer go off.

Max, she saw with amusement, had been on Facebook. He shut it down as she entered, though, and got a pasta bake out of the oven. A subtly dressed leafy green salad cut through its richness, a salad that would have looked right at home in one of the fancy restaurants James had introduced her to. She snapped the thought off like a bit of annoying loose thread. She could not bring herself to talk to Max about June. She thanked God that at least she had never mentioned James to Max and didn't have to suffer any well-meant inquiries after him, because she was sure if she heard his name she would burst into tears. She also brushed off inquiries about the end-of-year holiday she was usually planning by this time of year, which she now could not afford. She tried not to meet Max's keen blue eyes, aware that she looked pale and tired, and not wanting to answer questions. Instead she kept up a brittle cheerfulness, distracted Max by praising the silky denseness of the pasta bake and inquiring after his family and grandchildren (all well, as badly behaved as ever). She gave him his books. The first was one Seb had suggested after Cait told him about Max's newfound computer savvy. 'Give him this,' Seb had said, holding out *The Art of Social Media* by Guy Kawasaki. 'He's a smart guy, right? He should learn from the best.' Cait had doubted whether something so in-depth would capture the attention of an aged first-time Facebooker, but seeing Max flip it over instantly and read the blurb, despite not being of the generation to immediately recognise the former Apple evangelist's name, she thought Seb had been right. After all, you were never too old to learn. He bought it, as well as the next Stephanie Plum, a McDermid, Carl Hiaasen's new release, and the Australian crime novels Cait had brought to make up for still not yet having any date on a new Strike.

By the time she got to Dorothy's it was after seven, but Dorothy did not seem at all tired, pulling her enthusiastically inside and forcing on her the chemically scented Diet Coke with lemon, which Dorothy now firmly believed was Cait's drink of choice. The old lady was decked out in a voluminous black trouser suit with low black heels – she had once told Cait she was so used to wearing heels that if she ever put on a pair of flats she felt as though she would fall backwards while she walked. She had accentuated this relatively low-key outfit with the usual perfect beehive and with a double string of enormous red beads that hung around her neck, reaching to her waist, with matching wide bangles on each bony wrist. The effect was somewhat marred by the hairs of the last dog she had groomed that day.

'I like your –' Cait began, gesturing.

'Ooh, thank you, aren't you a lovely girl to have noticed, they're a gift from Charles, he sent them from Barcelona. He's touring there. Did I tell you he was touring? Well, anyway, he was terribly sorry to have missed my birthday, he is such a sweet boy, he never forgets, and I was ninety-three this year, you know, and so he called and told me to expect a package in the mail ...' Dorothy continued in this vein while Cait sat politely, resisting the urge to pull out her phone and check if James had called. She felt rather as if there could be an earthquake, or an alien invasion, while she sat here with Dorothy and they would never find out, ensconced as they were in the timeless land of knick-knacks and faded posters from long-ago concerts. It was an oddly peaceful thought to dwell on while she waited for a suitable opening to produce the books.

Dorothy seemed pleased with Heather Rose's *Museum of Modern Love* and Liane Moriarty's *Truly Madly Guilty*, but was most excited, as Cait herself had been, by the long-awaited *Bridget Jones's Baby*. She and Cait had bonded in their earliest years over a shared predilection for Helen Fielding. Dorothy nestled the new stack, Bridget on top, into the confusion of objects already occupying the coffee table, like a squirrel hiding nuts. She appeared full of boundless energy to talk but Cait, bone-weary and mindful of the night deepening outside Dorothy's net curtains, extricated herself as delicately as she could. She drove through the hills, trying to stay awake by opening the window. Her headlights lit up the forest, and the air revived her slightly. It had been a long time since she'd spent any time in nature. A long time since she'd spent an extended period alone, even. But now, without anyone to listen to or serve, she could no longer avoid her own thoughts.

Her relationship was over. She had to assume it was over. She had to face facts. Her parents had for years turned away from the fact of their own crumbling marriage, and look how that turned out. Cait had never faced the possibility that June would leave her. She hadn't faced the depth of James's frustration. She hadn't faced what was happening in the state's economy, even when its effects crept onto Hay Street and started staring her in the eye. And now she was backed into a corner. She couldn't increase her income by simply working harder and harder. It was getting ridiculous. She remembered mounting staunch defences of this approach to James, and felt embarrassed by how much in denial she must have sounded. She should just shut the bloody shop and be done with it, go and work for someone else. Was running a bookshop really all she'd wanted to do with her life, anyway?

Yes, Cait thought, and abruptly pulled over onto the soft shoulder of the road, hardly knowing what she was doing. Her eyes stung with tiredness. She got out the car. Damp leaves and soft ground cushioned her footsteps. She made her way over to a huge tree stump by the side of the road, lit up by Dent's headlights. It must have been an impressive tree, once. Its rich crimson-brown bark was segmented into thick plates with deep cracks between, like dried-out desert clay. She felt oddly winded all of a sudden, as if a great hand had shot out of the sky and pushed her squarely on the chest. She sat down abruptly on the stump. The only sound she could hear was the wind stirring the trees. The air smelled like damp leaves. This is the first time I've sat outside at night in months, she thought, and felt a sudden rush of soreness up her torso, through her shoulders and her throat. A sob burst out, shocking her with its immediacy, its sudden sound in the dark. This is the sound of my heart breaking, she thought, and she did not care if it sounded dramatic, because there was no-one there to hear it and there never would be. She gave in and cried. And after that first rending sob, the sound she made was muffled by her hands smashed desperately over her face, as though by gripping her own flesh, she could somehow hold herself together. She cried with a steady intensity that swelled her flesh and clogged her throat and nose until she could hardly breathe.

Eventually, she was forced to do an unceremonious bushman's blow onto the leaf litter beside her. The sound brought her back to a consciousness of where she was. She felt the hardness of the stump, the lateness of the hour. She got off the truncated old tree, moving like a hundred-year-old woman, and got back into the car. Her handbag proffered a single crumpled tissue for clean-up, which she took with a prayer of thanks for the former self who left it there. She sat for a long while, breathing through her mouth, waiting for her breaths to quieten. Then she checked her phone. Nothing. Should she call him? No. She drove home, drained by the release of tension that always accompanies the making of a big and difficult decision.

TWENTY

Cait spent the next few days being extra nice to her customers. One woman about her age wanted to know what to get for her nine-year-old nephew. She said he was becoming newly aware of the environment. This was a vast improvement on all the women who never had any clue what their nephews were into, and Cait spent ten minutes with her, rooting through the children's books for a suitable title, both of them reminiscing about the books they had loved as children. *Possum Magic. The Very Hungry Caterpillar.* The Berenstain Bears. Afterwards, she took great care with a display of the six books on the just-announced Man Booker shortlist, and was rewarded with four sales: two to people whose eyes were caught by the display, two to time-poor corporate types who needed thoughtful titles for their next book club and were only too happy to go with what Cait told them to. She gave someone change without purchase, though they clearly did not recognise the magnitude of the favour. She was even polite when a fluffy-haired, vague-looking guy with a voice like Kermit the Frog asked if she sold pencil sharpeners.

'No, you probably want a newsagent,' Cait said.

'Why not? What sort of bookshop are you? Don't you use pencils to write the books?'

Was he joking? Was she getting punk'd? 'Try a newsagent,' she said, again.

'Well, can you tell me where there's a newsagent?'

'Sorry. There was one next door, but it's closed down.'

The feeling of watching herself on some kind of TV show persisted beyond the weird pencil sharpener guy; that sense of unreality that always comes with having made a big choice, but not yet shared it with anyone. She could still, theoretically, revoke it.

She sat by the window, where sunshine was pouring in, to unpack and display an enormous pile of new adult colouring books – the craze was slowing, but soon would come the hordes of desperate Christmas shoppers and they would no doubt still be required. Some of the designs, in intricate black and white waiting to be filled with colour, were very beautiful. She knew from an article in *Books+Publishing* that many of these books were created by professional illustrators who had seized the fleeting opportunity to make a buck from a skill this craze had suddenly, inexplicably placed in demand. This is what people do when they can't make any money doing what they love, Cait told herself. They find another way. They find a new way to pay the bills until the next lucky break comes along, a third option. She had not been able to think of a third option. The thought of setting up somewhere else made her shrivel inside. Book Fiend, custom-crafted shelf by shelf in the heart of the city, was more than a place of business, but a home of sorts, its clientele a family.

Families should not be uprooted. They should be stable, places of refuge. And somehow she could not shake her belief that Book Fiend was more than the sum of its parts, that the magic here could not be replicated. Even the crudest new store fit-out would be prohibitive. She had only just, almost, finished repaying the first loan and her savings had been gutted. To take on further debt without even the guarantee her present cashflow would continue elsewhere was surely madness. No, far better to make a clean break. Implement her decision calmly and efficiently. Focus on a goal: close quickly, gracefully and hopefully debt-free.

She would recoup recent losses by selling off fittings and as much stock as possible. Immediately stop taking in second-hand stock. Make enough to cover the final loan instalments and rental payments, break the newly re-signed lease, hopefully without penalty. Use anything left as a safety net while she looked for a job. Maybe Seb could help with that. Seb had worked a million jobs. He had never struggled. Even in this economic climate, he had found that cafe job quickly and easily. She remembered James saying new cafes were still opening in Perth all the time. Well, good for them.

The thought of working for an employer, after so long making her own decisions, filled Cait with dread. Her jobs before Book Fiend were what had filled her with determination to make it on her own, to implement all the ideas she had despised her bosses for not thinking of. To have control, make something she could be proud of, and without having to abide by anyone else's meaningless rules, their dress codes, their arbitrary decisions. Though ... at least those other retailers weren't struggling like you are, a nasty little voice in her brain piped up. She ignored it. Everything had been different ten years ago. Nobody could have foreseen the ranks of moneyed interlopers now strangling the heart of the city, making everything look shinier and newer and essentially the same. Homogenisation and pasteurisation, on a city scale. Burning off impurities; anything that looked slightly different, or gave off the unmistakeable whiff of the past. Anything unique.

Book Fiend was unique. No-one else combined new and old and collectable stock alike, not only recorded on a searchable database but browseable in a real bricks-and-mortar shopfront. She had done beautifully in this niche before these massive companies decided to move in with their bottomless pockets and their sheer bulk that cut through any obstruction, swallowing up everything in their path like super trawlers crashing through a hardtop ocean; in this case, the black bitumen of Hay Street.

Even now, sitting in her pool of late-afternoon sunshine, she could see through the window a pair of young girls gazing slack-jawed through the neighbouring window at Gucci. No doubt lusting after some completely unaffordable and unnecessary trinket, while just next door lay magic, mystery and unlimited knowledge packaged in that most cheap, friendly and humble of formats: the paperback novel. 'But you don't want that, do you,' she told them aloud. 'You just want a new pair of heels for spring, and you're probably going to put it on Mummy's credit card. Even if you wanted a book, you'd probably order it off Amazon for your Kindle. And then you'd bitch about the price.'

The phone rang and she picked it up. 'Hello, Book Fiend. Cait speaking.'

'Oh, hello,' said a bright female voice. 'It's Julia here, from the library at St Christopher's. We need a copy of Anne Frank's diary –'

'OK, give me a –'

'But not the one with rude bits. Could you have a quick read through the editions you have and send us the clean version?'

Cait politely suggested the woman do a bit of Google searching for what she wanted. She would be happy to order in a specific edition, once St Christopher's knew exactly what it was. She hung up.

'Well, businesses come and go, but it's good to know people will always be idiots,' she said, just as Seb swung in, ratty hair flying, bag thumping to the counter. He carried with him the scent of sunshine and fresh air. There was a goofy, relaxed grin on his face.

'Talking to yourself, Cait?' he asked. 'You're obviously crazy with loneliness since you got rid of me.'

'On the contrary,' she retorted. 'I can finally hear myself think.'

'Well, don't think too loud, will you, or you'll frighten off the clientele. Not that there's much left of it this arvo, by the looks. Why don't you come and get a beer? It's near enough on home time, right?'

'Sure,' she said. 'I've done the tidy. Just give me a few minutes to count the till.'

Knowing talking would delay her, Seb wandered off into the stacks to look through the sci-fi while he waited. Cait shut the doors and started to count the till. Sure enough, the young chinwaggers instantly came to knock on the door, having apparently cottoned on that a dollar stretched further at Book Fiend than it would at Gucci. She mouthed an apology at them, smiling and pointing at the locked doors. She swept the last pile of coins off the counter into an aged plastic coin bag and dropped it in the calico sack, where it joined the others in a jangly thump. She slung the money into the safe.

'Ready,' she called. Seb emerged from the stacks. Now that she could give him her full attention, she noticed how very jaunty his stride was today. 'Why are you in such a good mood, anyway? That was a very big smile on your face when you came in.'

'Just having a good day,' he said, with a simplicity that made her battered heart suddenly ache. 'I'm really liking the work. They sent me on a barista course –' he broke off as they reached the front door. Cait looked where he was looking. Standing outside was James, obviously straight from work. He was wearing the green business shirt she loved him most in, the one that brought out the colour in his eyes.

Their eyes met and her heart soared, then jolted in confusion when a stony expression transformed his face. He was looking at Seb. He looked back at her for one long, agonising moment, then turned on his heel and vanished as quickly as he had appeared.

'James! Wait!' she called, and dropped to her knees to open the bolt on the bottom of the door. Shit! Why did she fumble now? Seb unbolted the top one for her as she scrabbled frantically at the bolt, and when the door finally swung open she flew out, leaving her keys jingling from the keyhole. 'James!' she called again, but he had covered a surprising distance already. She began to run but as she did he lifted a hand in a short, jerky wave, without looking back, an unmistakeable gesture that said, *sayonara*.

TWENTY-ONE

Seb handed Cait her keys. 'I've locked up,' he said. She took them and dropped them in her bag, not bothering with the little side pocket that was their newly designated home. 'What was all that about?'

'Tell you at the pub.'

They set off for the nearest bar, an Irish pub down a laneway fifty metres from Book Fiend. Outside the pub were scarred, dark wood tables arranged outside in a long row on a platform that raised the patrons slightly above the foot traffic passing through the laneway. Seb went to get beers and Cait struggled with an overwhelming sense of hurt and bewilderment. She stared at her hands. They were grubby from the tidy and the counting. The nails were short and ragged. She began to pick at the skin surrounding them and continued until she had ripped off a long and painful strip from beside her right index fingernail. Seb returned with two pints and placed one on the table before her. There was no coaster. She had several large gulps. Coldness settled in her belly. 'Thanks.'

'No problemo,' said Seb. His cheerfulness had abated somewhat after the encounter with James. There was a pause.

Then he asked, with a studied kind of nonchalance, 'So, what's up?'

Neither of them usually inquired much after each other's private lives: Seb probably because Cait had never before had much of one to inquire into, Cait because Seb's girlfriends never seemed serious. Parties at Number Fifty had made her aware that Seb seemed to have no trouble attracting women, but she had no desire to hear the details and Seb did not offer them.

'I think we've broken up,' Cait said into her beer.

'What do you mean, you think?' Seb asked, reasonably. He was not the sort to allow a third, shadowy category between 'together' and 'not'.

Cait wanted to unburden herself, wanted a friend's opinion, even if it was a male opinion. How to begin? She drank deeply of her pint, and when she put it down she saw that most of it had disappeared. Telling him would also necessitate telling him about June. She did not want to. But Seb deserved to know. He had known June, albeit through the intermediaries of Cait and books, for years. So she told him about the diagnosis. And then the prognosis. When she finally looked at Seb, she saw that his eyes were a soft, liquid brown, slightly lighter than his hair. Had she ever really looked at his eyes before? They were full of shock and a concern that made her want to start crying.

'I'm sorry,' he said. He reached out and touched her cheek very lightly with the backs of his fingers, in a way he had never done before. Somehow she found this restrained brush of contact more comforting than James's hug had been when she had told him. Then Seb got up and walked away. He returned a minute later with another pint for her. It was very full, and the head spilled over the rim of the glass when he set it down before her. It cascaded down over the glass and began to soak into the wood.

'I shouldn't. I've got Dent.'

'You can get the train, can't you?'

'Yeah.' She leaned forward and slurped the foam off the top to stop it spilling further.

Then Seb asked, 'So what does June have to do with James and whether or not you broke up?'

The story was the length of the pint and the sunset, and the alcohol began to do its soothing work.

'Sounds like you broke up,' Seb confirmed. Must he sound so cheerful?

'Yeah,' she said miserably, looking at all the wet rings her glasses had made on the table. 'But there's something else.'

'I'll get us another.'

Cait reached into her bag. 'Let me get them,' she said, but Seb was already off. Too dispirited to chase after him and argue, she went back to picking at her nails. A group of tradies in high-vis clattered into the table behind. One banged into her chair and apologised. She summoned her automatic smile and shook her head slightly to indicate forgiveness. Seb returned with the beers, and again she thanked him. And then she told him about Book Fiend.

She didn't dare look at him to see his reaction. She downed the first two thirds of her beer, hardly noticing she was doing it. The warmth of the early evening made it easy to drink. She gazed into her glass, tipping it this way and that to coat the insides with foam from the liquid remaining inside.

'Fuck, Cait. I knew things were tough, but not that tough.'

Cait stayed silent. She wondered if he would blame her for handling things so badly. But he did not seem disgusted, only sad. She felt a moment of vindication that here was someone else who didn't doubt her running of things, who understood precisely what a decision this was, that it was not the practical business matter that James had seemed to think it should be. The reality of it held at bay by the warm glow of beer now wrapping itself softly around her, she spilled her guts to Seb. The long hours, her failure to get an extension, her meltdown on the tree stump. Seb listened patiently. He had another beer. She switched to wine, knowing as she did so that it was probably a mistake. They began to reminisce about the store, its early days, learning to work together.

The pub slowly emptied. The tradies left. Cait's buzz began to fade. She drank more wine, in rebellion. 'Enough about sad things,' she said. 'Tell me about your new job. You said they sent you on a barista course?'

'Yeah. I knew most of it already. I've had cafe jobs before. But I picked up a couple of cool tips. And I finally learned how to draw pictures in the crema. Latte art, they call it.'

'Oh, that's cool!'

'I know.'

'So can you do the squiggle?'

'I can do the squiggle, I can do the flower, I can do the love hearts,' he said, smiling at her. 'It's all window-dressing, obviously. What counts is the taste.'

'Wow. They must love you. And you like it, obviously.'

'I don't mind it. I've always liked cafe work. Cafe vibes are like bookshop vibes. Everyone's mostly cruisy, chatty, there for a nice reason; you get to bond with your regulars. I'd like that place better, though, if I had a bit more control. They could be ordering from a better roaster. And I could jazz up their menu, easily. It's really dated. Turkey and cranberry on Turkish, that kind of thing.'

'Are you still freelancing?'

'Yeah. Just like everything else right now, the industry's not pumping, but I'm getting a reasonable number of new jobs. And I have follow-up work from previous clients. Maintenance, bug-fixing, new features, that kind of thing.'

'Seems a weird combination, hospitality and web design,' Cait said.

Seb appeared to consider this. 'I guess so. I've never thought of it that way. I think of them both as jobs where procedure and precision makes a difference. To do it well, you've got to get it all exactly right for the top result. To make a site for a client, I need to have a feel for what looks good and what works well, but I also need to be methodical about it, and precision in coding is everything. Same thing with making good coffee. It's the importance of detail. It's about what the bean is, how it's blended, how and when and where it's roasted, how and when it's ground. The weight you put behind the tamp, the water temperature, even how you clean the machine.' He counted the details off on his fingers.

Cait was watching him talk with dawning wonder. She had never actually heard Seb speak at this length on anything, save maybe the plots of George R.R. Martin. Cait had always thought of Seb's air of calm, his conspicuous lack of the kinds of fears and worries and insecurities that ate away at everyone else, as evidence of some kind of supreme lack of ambition and passion. But his talk did not fit this picture. And it touched her that he regarded his white-collar professional work and his casual barista job as though they had equal status. It reminded her of the way she loved optimising all the seemingly boring procedural parts of her job, always shaving seconds off the tidy, the counting, the ringing up of sales, the stock processing.

She remembered the forensic zeal Seb had applied and maintained in transforming her sci-fi section, curating its titles and sorting it by micro-genre. She remembered the shock and concern in his eyes when he'd asked about June and about the shop. Had she been selling him short?

'So are you planning to ask the cafe people if you can experiment?' she asked.

'Not a lot of point, not for something short-term. It's good to have some flexibility, so I'm not relying on any one thing for my income, but I have been thinking …' He took a pull on his beer, then said, 'I need to settle down, kind of. Sink my teeth into something big.'

'You don't want to travel more?' Cait knew that before Book Fiend, Seb had backpacked: Europe, South America, and a long stint in South-East Asia.

'Not urgent. I've spent long enough away to know how good a place Perth is to live, even if the economy sucks right now. I've done a lot of travel. I kind of want a totally new challenge, you know.'

'Like what?'

'Dunno,' he said. 'That's the hard part.' He necked the rest of his beer. 'Let me know if you think of anything.'

Cait had drunk too much wine. She excused herself to go to the toilet. In the cubicle, her mind whirled with that sickening feeling that always accompanied the realisation that tipsy had tipped over into drunk. When she got back, walking with care, Seb looked at her tentatively. 'Sorry to bring you back to earth, but do you have a date in mind for the closing?'

'Yes,' Cait said, pulling herself together with an effort. 'It's going to take time for me to sell stock and furniture. But I can't take too long because I've got to keep paying the rent until I'm done. I get the impression they're not going to be upset about me cancelling the lease; I think that's what they wanted all along.' Her voice wobbled. She told herself not to be the drunk girl at the pub. 'I'm thinking stay open over Christmas, make as much money as I can in the lead-up, then finish my clearance when the city's full of Boxing Day shoppers. Then I would close in the New Year. That gives me a few months' breathing space to sort it all out and decide what I'm going to do next.'

'What are you going to do next?' Seb asked.

'Dunno,' Cait said. 'Aren't we the aimless pair?' The drunk-crying-girl-at-the-pub persona inside threatened to break free. Cait fell silent, struggling to suppress it.

'I wish I could do something,' said Seb. 'But it sounds like your mind is made up. And I don't know anything about this stuff. If they dropped the rent back to where it was before, or you could work out a way to make more money, would that help?'

'Both, ideally,' Cait said. 'But for the past couple of years, sales have only crept up in the low single digits. And there's no way they'll drop the rent back to what it was before, or even just to a CPI increase. They want Hay Street all full of super-rich, fancy stores that can pay any fucking rent and all look the fucking same.' She controlled herself, then heaved a sigh. 'Thanks, Seb. It's OK. There's no real solution. Unless, of course, you can organise an angry mob to march on the offices of Lease Freedom and demand they drop the rent. Oh! And then, get the mob to pass a resolution saying they'll all stop buying crap off Amazon and pirating PDFs off the internet.'

'That's in the flying pig order of things for sure.'

'I know. I have to bite the bullet and get moving. I have to tell my clients. Oh God. I have to tell June.' She buried her face in her hands, then wished she hadn't, as her wine-soaked brain spun in her skull.

'She'll be cool,' Seb said philosophically. 'Everything will be cool.'

She lifted her face, with effort, and attempted a smile. It must have looked as ghastly as it felt, because Seb said, 'Let's get you home,' and got up. She got up herself. The world tilted. Fuck. 'Yep, better get the train,' she heard herself say, as if from some distance away.

Right. She had to try to get out of here without embarrassing herself. She tried to walk steadily, but just as they reached the steps to get down off the verandah, she caught a foot on a chair leg poking out from the table next to the top step. She pitched down the steps. She only fell a few, but landed painfully with a calf crushed against a step corner. The other knee banged onto flat concrete. She watched her handbag drop upside down onto the step below. She had, of course, neglected to zip it up, and its contents spilled energetically into the laneway, bouncing across the path of a group of guys who neatly sidestepped her water bottle and purse, glancing at her and at Seb, who was stooping to help. She waved him away and got up, standing still for a moment to regain equilibrium and register the throbbing of her lower right leg while Seb collected the contents of her bag and brought them back. There was an angry black mark on the leather of the handbag. 'Shit,' she said, still standing on the step, clutching the handrail.

Seb gave her that disconcertingly understanding smile again. 'It's OK,' he said. 'No harm done.'

'Just embarrassed myself and wrecked my new handbag,' she said waspishly, climbing down the steps, this time with care.

'Can you, like, clean that?'

'Probably,' she admitted. He took her arm. 'I can make it alone,' she said, when it became apparent he intended to walk her all the way into the station.

'It's cool. I've got plenty of time. There's no way I want you hanging around by yourself at that traino when it's night-time and you're –' he stopped.

'Blotto,' she supplied, and they both laughed.

'Right,' he said, and they walked on. The alcohol coursed through Cait's system, making its full power felt only now that she had stopped drinking. She was finally anaesthetised against all the things that had the power to hurt her. She saw only the yellow glare of lights on grubby corners and crumbling stonework. Felt a mild breeze brush her skin. Heard the faint thump of music from the nearest bar, the laughter of a group of teenagers around the entrance to the traino. It felt good not to think, to spin in time like this. If she could pause it altogether, like Sabrina the Teenage Witch, she might have time to work out what she would do with the rest of her life, now that what she'd already chosen to do had abruptly ended at age thirty-three.

They had to wait fifteen minutes for the next train. Good old Perth. They sat down in the moulded metal chairs. Silence fell. All at once, Cait felt hyper-aware of how the wide seats, with their single shared arm, simultaneously forced them close together and held them apart. Tired and bleary, she was tempted to rest her head on Seb's shoulder, but she had enough sense left to hold back the urge. What had she read somewhere? An urge was a sign of a temporary insanity.

She let her head drift back, instead, onto the cold rear railing of the chair. The after-work crowds were long gone and every noise echoed. A guy in early middle age, with shoulder-length black hair that was either sopping wet or spectacularly oily, shambled past and asked for change, in a blurred voice. They refused, each with practised regret – not enough to encourage further conversation, but enough to avoid confrontation. When the glowing display told them to expect the train in one more minute, Cait said, 'Thanks for taking me out. Sorry to make a spectacle of myself.'

'You didn't,' Seb said. The train pulled in and they got up and gave each other a hug, Cait's chin banging into the front hollow of Seb's shoulder. He was warm beneath his thin T-shirt. She was struck afresh, as she had been all those weeks ago when she'd fired him, by how solid he felt. Cait was again visited by a mad urge to just stay here and let him hold her all night. But she got on the train and sat down. 'Doors closing,' said the cool female voice.

She stashed her bag securely down beside her in the crack between her body and the wall, and shut her eyes. Tomorrow, she told herself. Tomorrow you tell June.

TWENTY-TWO

There was a semitrailer parked on Cait's chest. The semitrailer must have overturned, because it had somehow poured tons of bricks directly into her skull. Its engine still seemed to be running, though. Cait could hear the rumbling. She lay there. Eventually it dawned on her. The semitrailer was purring. Gingerly, Cait stretched out an arm and picked up her phone. She lifted her head slightly to squint at the time and winced as the bricks in her head rolled around. Rather than attempt to rise, she went with the more manageable activity of stroking the semitrailer, which received these attentions with a regal air. It was ten minutes before she could summon the will to move. Mac squawked as she rose in one determined but excruciating movement, dumping him in the warm spot she'd just vacated. She left the bed unmade so he could resettle, and because she didn't think she could manage the exertion of making it. But as she left the room, she heard the soft thump of Mac jumping onto the floor, his bell tinkling as he went in search of a new snoozing ground. Cait herself wanted a new snoozing ground. How much had she drunk last night?

She leaned on the wall of the bathroom for a moment.

The tiles felt cool and solid and comforting. She felt a sick feeling that was not just the hangover but something else: not wanting, for the first time in many years, to go to work and face the day. She had not felt like this since she had worked at Roger David, selling cheap suits to teenagers shepherded in by their mums pre–school ball. It had been years since she'd wanted to skive off this badly. But she went to Book Fiend as she always did, trusting her leaden body to lead her through its familiar routine, and somehow she got through the day. Wondering if James would reappear, which he didn't. Wondering if she should call him. She didn't. Seb dropped in during the afternoon. She knew it was to check that she was OK. She did her best to behave normally and be upbeat, but she cared little whether she fooled him or not. She even let him help with the tidy. Fuck it, she was too tired to argue. And for the first time, she was dreading seeing June.

◄◄◄

Cait found a Silver Chain nurse in June's house, and tried to feel grateful instead of resentful at a stranger invading this space. June was very thin, and the skin around her eyes was yellow. Had it been so yellow last time? But her smile was real and her hug firm and she was on her feet, though she moved with incredible slowness.

The nurse left and Cait insisted June sit down. She made the tea herself, and filled the gaps on the tray with shop-bought biscuits clearly brought in by Silver Chain. June inspected the tray and pronounced it acceptable. She refused to talk about herself. 'I'm being looked after, my girl, don't ask for every detail. Sickness is boring,' was all she said. She was far more interested in discussing the increasingly heated US presidential race between Trump and Clinton, which seemed all-absorbing even for Australians. Cait, still hungover, struggled to follow the thread of June's numerous and unvarnished opinions on the subject. She waited for a suitable pause. Then she told June she was closing Book Fiend.

June had listened to all Cait's problems, big and small, over the years, and she listened in silence now. Cait had by this time had enough practice in talking out loud about closing the shop that the telling was less difficult than she feared, and she got through the tale, the reasoning, and the plans for the next month or two, without falling apart. She had expected to fall apart before June, to receive comfort. But now the moment had come, seeing June's tiny frame and sallow face, she wanted only to spare June distress. She had rather expected June to behave as she normally did. Demand every detail, exhaustively challenge all Cait's reasonings, rail righteously at the injustice of it all, and immediately set to questioning her on possible solutions. But June only watched Cait meditatively, eyes keen, hands clasped with her forefingers steepled into a point, touched to her lips. Cait wondered whether she had imagined the opposite reaction because she had truly expected it or because she had simply craved it, wanted to find the solution over a cuppa and a rousing argument as they always had done. Perhaps June was just too tired. But this matter-of-factness was soothing in its own way. She felt relief. June at least did not appear distressed. This was the best she could hope for, right? The first question, when it came, was rather unexpected.

'Is this still what you wanted for your life, Cait? Or would you have moved on soon anyway, done something new?'

Seb had asked something similar. Cait thought about it, this time more carefully. 'No. I'm not done yet. I mean, yes, of course I wanted to do new things, but I wanted to do them with Book Fiend. Not to fail like everyone else did. I wanted

Book Fiend to be part of the city. To connect with people. I wanted it to grow and I wanted to experiment. Like, I started with the combination of second-hand and new all recorded on the same receiving system, you remember? Now, people thought that was impossible, but it totally worked. And it was new for Perth. Eventually, I wanted to host big author events, because they hardly come here anymore. I thought I'd get involved in the writers festival. Help keep the arts alive here. But somehow I got caught up in just swimming. Just not sinking.'

'You wouldn't be the first.' June looked thoughtful. 'So, the problem is only money?'

'I don't know what you mean by "only" money, but essentially, yes.'

'I see. And what does James think?' It was a relief, too, to talk about James. June frowned as Cait told her what had happened. 'So, our hero turns out a scoundrel,' she said. She sipped her tea, eyes studying Cait over the rim of her cup, awaiting reaction. But Cait was used to June's playful testing of boundaries and did not rise to the bait, partly because she really was unsure of what she thought of this remark, and partly because of the sudden thought that soon there would be no-one on earth who knew how to needle her like this. She felt suddenly breathless. A memory came to her, of a family holiday when she was eight. She'd been running across a car park at full tilt when she'd tripped over something and gone flying, hitting the ground hard. She still remembered the feeling in her chest, a feeling for which she'd had no name, as frightening as it was painful. 'Don't worry,' her mother had said, picking her up. 'You're only winded. You'll be all right.' She felt now like she had then. Asphyxiated with pain. And this time, would she be all right? Cait forced herself to take a long breath. The exhalation was a full-body effort not to cry. She disguised it as a sigh of mock patience. She knew June saw straight through it.

'I don't know, June,' she said, wearily, when she could trust herself to speak. 'James is a good person. I know he loves me. Well, loved me.' Maybe she knew nothing about relationships, and maybe James had given up on her, but she was sure when he'd said he loved her that he had meant it. 'I think it's because he did love me that he was so angry. All he sees is work making me miserable and tired and broke, and I don't think he likes that. I don't think he thinks it's worth it. He's never quite understood about Book Fiend.'

'Maybe,' said June, 'if he really does love you, he doesn't like seeing you love anything else quite so much.'

'Oh, come on!' Cait told her, laughing. 'You can't be jealous of a place. I'm hardly snuggling into bed with it at night.'

'Well, he's certainly allowed to be jealous of Sebastian.' June's tone was suggestive.

'He's got no reason to be jealous of Sebastian.' But Cait supposed that by now she could kind of understand. Seb seemed so secure in himself he felt no need to be conventional in any way, no need to use his skills working a nine-to-five, no desire to wear a suit or look even vaguely professional. She could see how someone like Seb could be deeply challenging to someone like James.

But he had no right to be so possessive. She was allowed to have a job, to have whatever friends she wanted. June was watching her. Cait looked back. 'It's completely ridiculous,' she insisted. June asked a question using only her eyebrows. 'Yes, it *is* ridiculous. Seb's like a brother to me.' Remembering her urge to rest her head on his shoulder at the train station, she wondered if this was strictly true.

'Not your brother, though,' June observed, comfortably. 'Not bad-looking either, I've confirmed from his profile picture. Smart, too. I had a look at his LinkedIn. I reckon you've sold him short.'

'Oh my God!' Cait cried. 'Who let all you old people on the internet! You're all menaces. Stop Face-stalking my friends.'

Then she saw that June, who had already looked worn out when Cait had arrived, was even more so now. She had not even finished her tea. She looked ready to collapse, but her face was alive with – what? Amusement? Excitement, even? Cait could not fathom why June looked so pleased with herself, but it was clear she needed rest, no matter what ideas she was cooking up.

'You've got to get to bed,' she said, getting up.

'S'pose.'

'Let me help.'

'I can get myself off to bed, don't you worry about that. I've perfected the art over decades.'

Cait ignored her caustic tone and frogmarched her into the bedroom, though the authority of her frogmarching was somewhat diminished by the slowness of June's pace. She wondered if June was being perverse and going so slowly just to provoke. But Cait realised when June turned to face her in the bedroom that she was beyond such fakery. Her face looked dreadful, white beneath the yellow. She looked terribly old, and her eyes had momentarily lost their brightness. She swayed and Cait's heart contracted. But June did not fall. She sat heavily on the bed and Cait helped her into a nightie, feeling rather awkward at this reversal of the caring roles of her childhood. She leaned close to help June into bed. Her characteristic smell of rose hand cream had been replaced by something less pleasant. It was not a strong smell, but it was definitely there.

A smell of sickness, a smell Cait associated with hospitals even though June was not in hospital. Perhaps it was the smell of death, Cait thought wildly. Maybe hospitals smelled like that not because of the buildings and the chemicals but because of the misery and death they held. June lay with eyes closed after the exertion, all her banter gone. Cait went back to the living room and fetched June a couple of the books she was currently reading. She saw with a pang that June's bookmark in Annie Proulx's *Barkskins* had barely moved since their last visit. She had only read a few pages in the Foer she had been so excited about and she had apparently not begun the Patchett. She took the books back to June's bedside and left them within reach, next to the glass of water on the bedside table. Thinking June asleep, she bent, intending to give her a soft kiss on the cheek when June said, 'Cait,' making her jump.

'What do you need?'

'Tablet.'

Cait began to sort through the boxes and bottles of pills on the dressing table.

'Not tablets,' said June, with a trace of her usual impatience. 'Computer.'

'Oh,' Cait said, surprised, and returned to the living room to retrieve the tablet. She went to put it on top of the books, but June held out her hands.

'What do you want to do on the computer at this time of night?'

'Never you mind.' When Cait looked doubtful, June said, 'Good Lord, girl, give me my bloody computer. I'm not dead yet.' The old lady's eyes were gleaming once again. With what? Mischief?

'Right,' Cait said. She handed over the tablet and bent again, and this time June accepted the kiss.

'Lock the front door.'

'Will do,' Cait said. She hesitated. 'Love you.'

'Off you go,' said June.

She hugged June goodbye, got back into Dent and turned the key. She let the smile drop from her face. And then, instantly, the radio betrayed her once again. The sound of Billy Joel's 'Lullabye' filled the car. Why did they play this stuff just when she was at her most defenceless? And why was it so much easier to cry in the car than anywhere else? She was howling before he even reached the second verse.

TWENTY-THREE

Cait, her eyes raw and swollen, let herself into the house and checked her phone for a message from James one final time before feeding Macduff, apologising to him for the lateness of his meal. She made herself a cheese sandwich, sat in the living room with it and opened her battered, ancient laptop. First she emailed Lease Freedom, saying she had changed her mind and wanted to break the lease she had only just signed. She tried not to sound too much as though she hated their guts. She glowered at the email before pressing send. That done, she opened Facebook and went to the shop's page. She'd let it lapse since Seb had left. He'd always done most of the Facebooking for her. But the page was still vibrant and attractive. It had plenty of followers, thanks to him. Right. What was the goal? Explain the situation, say goodbye, generate sales. 'Sell' her sale. She needed her customers to buy – whether because of emotion, hype, bargain-hunting instinct, it didn't matter. The eager little white box glowed before her, greyed-out letters asking her what her status was right now. Asking her to commit to a decision that until now had been purely theoretical. Her hands hovered over the keyboard. She looked up. She looked at the bookcase in front of her. She had left the middle shelf empty to accommodate her row of elephants. They stood like little sentinels, trunks lifted before her, stoic and faithful. Right. She could do this. She just needed a cup of tea. To wash down the sandwich.

When she returned with tea, the little cursor was still blinking smugly. She positioned the mouse over the box. *How are you feeling?* It offered a range of emojis to help her express herself. Cursors are not smug, she told herself sternly, and began to type.

> Dear beloved customers,

She did a shift-enter to let her start a new paragraph. She would be damned if the internet took away her right to format like an educated human.

> It is with regret I inform you that Book Fiend is closing down.

Now she had to say why, without sounding like it was all the fault of some evil dickhead in a suit who only cared about money. Well, the dickhead had had no trouble expressing his reasoning. She would just quote him. She rummaged in her handbag, still marked from its tumble down the pub steps, for the letter that had stayed in her bag. She had been reluctant to touch it, as though it were somehow poisonous. She scanned it for inspiration. Then, as Mac slunk in, licking the remains of his dinner off his chops, she began to type.

> I will be negotiating a cancellation of the lease after a recent surge in rent has forced me to join many local retailers who are unable to meet the rents in the area.

> Apparently, these premises are in a highly desirable area now tenanted mainly by competitively

advantaged international brands, seeking
appropriate locations to enter this city's market.

Macduff suddenly gagged at the carpet, then seemed to
recover himself. 'Too right,' she told him, and kept typing.

Apparently, one such brand will believe Book
Fiend's location 'appropriate'. None of us could fail
to agree it is a great spot. With this in mind, I have
decided the business, whose growth has been
minimal in the past year or two, will not remain
sustainable through a relocation. So it is with a
heavy heart I confirm its closure.

Cait took a deep breath. She looked at the elephants. She
reached out and patted the Duffer's head. Then she kept going.

The mobile service will also close and I will contact
these clients individually to discuss final visits. This
week, a clearance sale will begin and continue over
Christmas and the post-Christmas sales. Book
Fiend will close mid-January. Please show your
support in its final months by coming to buy a
book to help me finish up in the strongest possible
position. I will see to it you get some cracking
bargains. Maybe I will finally match some of those
Amazon prices I have heard so much about.

She took a sip of tea. Nearly there, she told herself.

Sale prices will soon be reflected on the website so
you can shop online, but I would urge you to come
and say goodbye in person.

She wanted to cry again. But she had cried herself out in the
car. She took another bite of her sandwich instead. It was cold
and the cheese had gone all rubbery.

Thank you all, particularly my regular and mobile
customers, for your support over the years. I

consider this a community who likes to do things the old-fashioned way, because we find value in a familiar face, a genuine recommendation, an armchair, a lamp and a real book. All these are things I have tried to stay true to and I know that's why you have all stayed loyal. I will miss you all, and Book Fiend, more than I can say.

See you at the sale!

She closed the laptop and sat for a moment. It was getting late, but she felt too worked up to go to bed just yet. She needed something calming and mindless to do. The house, which had once seemed like a haven of solitude, now seemed too empty and quiet. The dust and clutter she had allowed to build up lately didn't help. Maybe if she cleaned, the place would feel more welcoming. The thought of cleaning made Cait remember her soiled handbag.

'How do you get a big black mark off a leather handbag, Mac?' she said aloud.

Macduff gave her a look, as if to say, 'Google it,' and to add emphasis, he backhanded a small metal elephant off the coffee table. It thudded to the floor.

TWENTY-FOUR

If she said, at least to start off with, perhaps twenty percent off everything new and forty percent off everything second-hand, that ought to be an attractive enough deal to get people excited but still retain some margin, perhaps enough to cover her costs in clearing out. And it left wiggle room to go lower if people haggled, which they would. You could be actually bleeding on the ground and they would still haggle, bless 'em. People always seemed to exist in blissful ignorance of their unbelievable good fortune at being able to purchase an original work of art, that had taken anywhere from a year to ten years to write, guaranteed to provide many hours of entertainment and education and insight, for as little as ten or twenty dollars. What painting could you ever buy for that kind of money? You could see a film for the same price, sure, but it would only last two hours. You could buy yourself a Netflix subscription if you wanted art on tap, but its creepy algorithms would end up eroding the independence of your choices, and leave you with no tangible possession at all. A book lasted longer; days or weeks or months, and then you could keep it and lend it to anyone you liked, even resell it.

Yet people seemed to still think books expensive. By contrast, they were happy to pay well above twenty dollars for a manicure that lasted two days then got ruined, or for a can of hair product that would never really give you hair thicker or shinier or curlier than your genetics had decreed, and would end up sitting in your bathroom cabinet for five years. She would never understand it. But she was just procrastinating. Cait turned her reluctant brain to the task at hand. She got out a notebook from her handbag, whose stain had faded to the faintest of marks after she had attacked it with the aid of various household chemicals and a helpful website called wikiHow. She wrote *SALE* in big letters, then *CLOSING DOWN* in smaller letters above it. Resting the end of the pen thoughtfully on her lower lip for a moment, she added at the bottom *Excludes front table and antiques.* She had some valuable stock in antiques. A first-edition *Gone with the Wind* had come in just yesterday. She could always take the antiques home and continue selling them online. And the front table always turned over quickly anyway, consisting as it did of the best of her second-hand stock: the *Shantaram*s, the *Fear and Loathing*s. The latest movie tie-ins, half-price and as-new, after being read once – or not at all – for someone's book club. Turned out a lot of people didn't read their own book club books. She added a 'must end' date to the notice. She could add a border on the computer when she typed it up.

But she didn't get a chance to type it up that morning. It was oddly busy, compared to recent weeks. She found it was lunchtime only well after that hour had passed. There was a pile of deliveries to get through, too, now that the lunch rush had slowed. She had better start cancelling her standing orders and calling suppliers. Perhaps it would be best to send around a bulk email. She should probably have done that before putting it on Facebook. Well, she could do it tonight, and she would still need plenty of stock over Christmas. She wondered, suddenly, if June would make it to Christmas, and instantly banished the thought by getting out her lunch, an apple and a banana, and beginning a to-do list, starting with a note to email suppliers and the smaller publishers she dealt with directly. She finished the banana. Then she started a second list: Things to Do When Unemployed.

1. Cook actual meals.

2. Groom Mac & cut off his dreadlocks.

She had noticed them forming under his fluffy belly. As she ate the apple and contemplated her lists, she gazed out the window, in a watch for James that had become more of a habit than a real hope. Then she was interrupted.

'I'm afraid my child has had a little accident next to your Octonauts table,' the lady said, gripping the tiny offender firmly by the wrist. Thoughts of James vanished.

'I'll take care of it.' Cait turned her attention to the clean-up and then to the boxes, which were piling up, giving the shop a more than passing resemblance to the home of a lonely hoarder. One day, when Duffer got old and infirm and less likely to make a break for the street, she had intended to bring him in and let him spend his dotage in a basket in the shop. She had rather enjoyed the thought of being a crazy old spinster cat lady bookseller. The James interlude – which was really all their relationship was, she told herself – had distracted her from this goal. Thankfully, the position of crazy old spinster cat lady remained forever attainable and open. No harm done. She pulled out a single copy of a book from among the stacks of new releases in the box open at her feet. *Sharpe's Waterloo*, Mr Cowper's special order. That had arrived quickly. He would be pleased.

Wanting to share the good news with him while he still had time to get in – he always came in the moment she rang about a new book – she abandoned the unpacking and took the book to the counter. She pulled her phone out and was surprised to see a pile of notifications from the Facebook app she had almost forgotten was even on the phone – 186 notifications? Surely that was some kind of glitch. Oh well, she could check it later. Cait looked up Mr Cowper's number. She used to keep a separate address book for regulars and ring them on the shop landline, to separate them from her home life, but the boundaries had grown fuzzy for a few, and it had become easier to have their numbers to hand. Mr Cowper was always home and invariably picked up straight after the third ring. She often pictured him hovering over the phone, waiting for what he must consider was the decorous amount of time before picking up. Today was no different. She heard his quavering 'Hello?' after precisely three rings.

'Oh, hello, Mr Cowper, it's Cait. From Book Fiend,' she added after a slight pause, somewhat unnecessarily, because Mr Cowper was already saying, 'Oh, hello there, Miss Cait. And how are you?'

'I'm good, thanks. And you? Not gone into hospital yet?'

'No, no. That's – let me see, that's not until this coming Friday. Ten o'clock. I've got my sister coming to take me in. I don't want to drive, you know. The parking there is just terribly expensive, and if I might be in for five days or even longer, it would be foolish to park the car there all that time, especially since my sister, you know, she lives right around the corner. You know, I've just been looking at –'

'Yes, that sounds like a good idea,' Cait said. 'Mr Cowper, I've got some good news – your Bernard Cornwell has come in. Would you like to come and get it while you're still mobile? Or I could post it out to you.'

'No, no, I'll come and get it. But Cait, I've just been looking at your Facebook page. What's this about closing the shop?'

Good grief, here was another one. Wasn't Facebook supposed to be a young people's platform? 'Yes, I'm sorry I couldn't tell you last time we spoke, Mr Cowper, but the decision's only just been made. I'm sorry you found out like that, but I couldn't ring everyone –'

'Oh yes. Now, we can't all get told individually. But what I wanted to tell you is that there seem to be quite a lot of quite disappointed people. Well, of course they are. I've got to tell you, it's a bit of a shock, and –'

'I know. I know, Mr Cowper. It was a bit of a shock to me to work out that I couldn't keep going after they put the rents up. And I'm really sorry. I hung on as long as I could.'

'I'm sure you did, Miss Cait,' Mr Cowper said. 'You might like to hop on your computer and have a look at all your messages, though. It might cheer you up.'

Cait doubted this. 'I'll see you when you come in for this, anyway,' she said, forcing brightness back into her voice. 'I'm not closed yet. You might even pick up a bargain if you want to wait for another couple of days, until the sale starts.'

'I'm not interested in bargains,' Mr Cowper said. 'No, no, I'll be in directly. You take care, then.'

'OK, then, see you soon,' Cait said.

She had to say goodbye a few more times before she could hang up. The second she did, the phone rang. It was Mags, the Random House rep, who had just read the Facebook post and wanted to convey her own horror, plus that of everyone else she had talked to this morning about it. She indicated this was a fair number of people. Cait told her to tell them all to express their horror by coming in and purchasing a book, and Mags gave an enormous laugh that quickly devolved into a coughing fit. Cait seized the opportunity to tell Mags she had to go – there was a customer standing in front of her, a young Indian guy with a nice face, about her age. He put a second-hand *Zen and the Art of Motorcycle Maintenance* on the counter. Cait smiled at him and checked the price she'd written on the inside. Not a huge discount on the new copies. This one was in good condition and it was a rare treat to get it in second-hand. The guy was getting a good deal. 'That's sixteen,' she said, and the guy got out his wallet. 'Good book,' she said, taking his twenty.

'Yeah, I've read it before,' the guy said. 'But I must have lent it to someone, because I can't find it. I thought I should have one for the shelf. Hey, sorry to hear about the shop closing. I just read it online.'

'Oh,' she said, taken aback. 'Thanks. I'm sorry too. It's just one of those things. I really didn't want to close. But this strip has got pretty fancy; they're kind of squeezing us old shops out. I just can't afford the rent.' She realised she was still holding the guy's change and handed it over.

'Thanks,' he said. 'Yeah, I get it. I've seen all these places opening this end of town. It's soulless, man. They don't appreciate Quality, you know? As this guy would have called it.' He waved the book, and she nodded to show she understood. He smiled. 'This place is Quality, for sure.'

'Thank you,' Cait said, touched. Here was a customer she did not see often enough to remember from the hundreds of others, but who clearly knew her. How many more such hidden regulars were there?

Plenty, as it turned out. The store was definitely busier than usual for a Monday, and no fewer than five more people came through and said sympathetic things to her about the Facebook post that afternoon; people she recognised vaguely at best. She smiled and thanked them all equally sincerely. It eased her heart a bit, to see that others also cared. She was so busy that afternoon she had no chance to check the Facebook page, though from time to time she felt her phone buzzing. It was all she could do to keep serving, put away the boxes of new stock and tidy for closing. She would have to contact suppliers first thing tomorrow instead. It was later than normal by the time she tidied the trolleys, pulled them up the ramps and locked up. The night was warm and she was sweating slightly from all the running around. She closed the windows and brought in her *Open* sign. Today's quote was *We're all so curiously alone, but it's important to keep making signals through the glass.* John Updike originally, later quoted in John Marsden's *So Much to Tell You*.

She locked the doors and went back to the computer to type up the flyer from her handwritten draft. Twenty copies should do. As the printer made regurgitating noises, Cait remembered she had not stopped to check the email in hours. She opened the browser but a tap at the door interrupted. She was looking up, already forming an apologetic smile, when she saw a familiar figure: Seb, peering into the glass. The way he stood there, with his long nose pressed to the window and mane of dreads springing outwards, reminded her ever so slightly of Sideshow Bob, though more benign. And undeniably better-looking. Cait got up off the stool to let him in. 'Hey,' she said, as he squeezed through the partially opened doorway. 'You're looking particularly big-haired tonight.'

'Washed it,' he said. He pulled two beers from his bag and cracked one open before passing it to her. She took it, remembering a time James had brought her beers at work and swiftly squashing the memory. At least if Seb was still willing to have a post-work beer with her, she could not have disgraced herself too much the other night.

'Thanks.'

'Saw your Facebook post. It's going berserk. Heaps of shares.'

'Probably fat cats in fur coats sipping champers,' Cait said gloomily. 'Gloating over how they're going to fill the place with monochromatic cotton dresses. Five hundred a pop.'

'Nah,' he said. 'People are pretty cut. Have a look.'

'I will later. I've got to get these signs up before I head home.'

'Fast worker,' Seb commented, examining one of the flyers.

'Yeah, well, I just want to get it done. Like ripping off a bandaid, you know?'

'I get it. Want a hand?'

'Oh, you don't have to help. You've probably had a big day already, haven't you?' Cait hoped he'd insist. It would be nice to have company.

'Nah. Let's do it.'

They signposted each front window and also slipped the sheets Cait had printed off into the plastic holders she generally used to display book recommendations, and placed these in the gaps on the shelving around the store. The result was somewhat less festive than she hoped, but perhaps she could combine it with some balloons or something. Make it Christmassy. But she'd leave it there for the night. She still had to walk the surrounding streets and stick up a few more flyers. Seb said he'd come along. Cait headed to the computer to pick up the rest of the printouts.

'Oh, crap. I forgot to check the email. Hang on a – woah.' There were not usually more than a handful of emails from customers a day, mostly requests for title searches and follow-ups on outstanding orders. But tonight next to the word *Inbox*, the numeral thirty-four appeared in bold to indicate unread emails.

'What the hell?' she muttered, and felt rather than heard Seb come up to look over her shoulder, wiping his face with his T-shirt. Like her, he'd worked up a sweat clambering around sticking up flyers. He actually smelled kind of good. She hastily banished this thought and opened the first email, from Tara Novak, a name she did not recognise.

> Hi Book Fiend Staff,
>
> I just wanted to say im devastated by the fb post you made last night. Ive been coming to the store to get stuff for my 2 kids basically since they were born and you have this girl working there who always helps me pick a winner. She is part of the reason why my kids ever get off their ipads and read anything. This is basically the only shop I ever go to in that part of town but I always make the effort because it is so worth it and it adds character to that bit of town and there are bugger all bookshops in the whole city. It is easy to just nip in on my lunch break and know i will come back with what i needed. Please don't shut it down. I dont want to have to go drive to the shopping centres on the weekends because the kids will end up wanting all the rest of the crap they see in there. I love this bookshop!!! Please don't shut it down!!!!!!!!! Cheers Tara

Cait smiled, partly at Tara's assumption that behind the 'girl working there' was an employee of some kind of omnipotent company, and partly because the whole email was so genuine, exclamation marks and all. She did make a special effort picking out the kids' stuff – there was so much rubbish around now, Cait considered selecting a good children's book an art – but she didn't realise anyone had noticed.

Next was a short note from a 'Felicity', saying please not to close the store, as their sci-fi selection was second to none and she simply could not do without it. 'Ha!' Seb said.

The next one was a long one.

Hi Cait. I operate Munch Sushi in the city and have been operating for the last 17 years. I just wanted to say a big thank you for writing that post because not a lot of people understand the costs that go into small family businesses like us. A lot of us also have a confidentiality clause that doesn't permit us to talk about rent. My landlord is one always mentioned in the BRW rich list but he doesn't care about businesses like ours. He knows we work 14 hours days and sees how much profit we make by obtaining our financial statements but does nothing when we are in trouble. I have seen so many close around me just because they are new to owning and operating their own business and they close due to the rent. My landlord knows some of us aren't making any profit but they keep increasing the rent because their attitude is 'well if you can't pay then leave and I'll find someone else who can'.

We don't make much but we run the business because we love doing what we do. We keep our prices as low as possible for our customers but we get a lot of backlash from them if we increase anything. The average price of our meals is $10 and it's not sustainable for us to absorb additional costs. Our profit margin is only 8%.

I know a lot of people who work in an office job and decide to open shops and decide to go back to the office job just because it makes more money and less hours. But in any case, I just wanted to say thank you for writing this post.

Regards,

Michiko Itō

'That poor lady,' Cait said. She scrolled through the rest. Most were from people she didn't know by name. One was from Max. She opened it, Seb still reading over her shoulder.

> Cait.
>
> I say this not as an old man dependent on the joy you bring to my life – though this I surely am – but because I know I am surely not the only person who depends on you and your shop. You have something special here. Surely something can be done. I am ready to pay higher prices and I am sure your other mobile clients would be too, but I know it requires more than this. I stand ready to assist. My career is behind me now, but not my business acumen. I hope it would not be overstepping a boundary to offer to take a look at the books.
>
> Max.
>
> p.s. I need more James Ellroy.

'Surly old bugger has a heart after all,' Cait said jokingly, to hide how moved she was. 'If only all these letters translated to dollars in the bank, hey?'

'Yeah,' Seb said. He looked thoughtful.

'OK, let's roll. It's getting late.'

'Cool.' Seb picked up his messenger bag, stuffing the tape and Blu Tack into it. They walked the streets in a big loop, papering up flyers as they went, until they got back to where Dent was parked.

'Thanks, Seb,' Cait said. 'That was really nice of you. You're being awesome about helping with this. It makes me happy, knowing how much you love the shop.'

Seb was silent for a moment. He looked as though he was on the verge of saying something, but apparently decided against it. Then he gave a lopsided smile and said, 'Hey, no problemo.'

'Do you want a lift home?'

'It's OK,' he said. 'The walk will be good. I got some stuff to think about.'

TWENTY-FIVE

Cait drove home, more notifications buzzing periodically from her phone on the passenger seat inside her bag, whose ever-so-faint stain still hovered like a ghost only Cait could see. Max's email threatened the mood of ruthless pragmatism she was striving for. What could she do about Max? Nothing. Without the books it would be weird, her going to see him. Each new book was like a stone thrown between them, sending out ripples of conversation. Stripped of this impetus, what could their relationship become? Cait had always found it easier to connect with people when there was something to hold on to, to focus on. Books performed the same function a glass of wine might for others; a social lubricant. Until James. Somehow their talk had not depended on books, though it was true they had met over one. Such an innocent and hopeful flirtation that had been. She thought again about calling him.

Twilight was falling on her mostly dormant suburb. A neighbour at the end of her driveway was still out in his garden, inspecting the frangipani tree that hung over his immaculate lawn. She had often seen him out raking its fallen flowers off the grass in summer, and wondered at his patience. Now, examining the pale green spears appearing at the tips of its bare skeleton, he looked up as she passed. She waved, and he smiled in return.

Cait fed the Duffer and microwaved soup from a cardboard carton for herself. She settled with it and her laptop in the armchair. She opened the shop's Facebook page and the post she had made the previous night. Macduff came in and sat next to the chair, having finished his food in his usual record time. Cait squinted at the screen. 'Does that say seven *hundred* comments?' she asked the cat. Mac lifted up a back leg, inspected it critically, then began to wash it. Cait began to read some of the comments.

> NONONO. This is the best bookshop in the city. What can we do xxxx

> yet another example of corporate GREED... did u write to the mayor, this should not be happening in our city

> oh hunni I feel your pain I once owned a small business and they just rort you out of existence i eventually went broke and now i have 2 small kids to look after and have been on the dole ever since. hope you don't have kids message me if u want to talk i know others this has happened to as well hang in there!!

The comments went on and on. Most were from people whose names Cait did not recognise. Some of their profile pictures looked familiar but were too small to see properly. The comments were all sad. No-one said good riddance. Some people said things like 'get over it people, this is progress', but were savagely torn down in a storm of replies. It seemed these mild-mannered, lamenting booklovers could turn into merciless hyenas when behind a computer screen. Or when someone threatened their favourite shop. Who knew?

Overwhelmed, Cait was about to stop reading when a profile photo caught her eye, of an immaculately coiffed old lady wearing a startling studded vest and string tie: Dorothy.

Online she called herself Dot, and she had set out her comment as though it were a formal letter.

> Dear Cait,
>
> I am so extremely sorry to hear about this. Is there any way you can continue to see mobile clients? I so look forward to seeing you and I do enjoy our talks so much.

Cait grinned, thinking of their one-sided conversations.

> Please do come to visit when you are in the area, or perhaps I can come to see you somewhere and we can stay in touch. Much love and please let me know if I can be of any assistance. I am good with small business as you know having run them for sixty-five years and would be happy to look with you and see if anything can be done. By the way, have you read Bridget Jones's Baby yet? I thought it quite as good as we'd hoped.
>
> My fondest regards,
>
> Dorothy.

Cait skimmed more comments, clicking into a few of the reply threads, but the sheer number eventually got the better of her. Many pleaded with her not to close the store and promised to pay higher prices without complaint. A few only asked when the sale would be. Some gave just little weeping emojis. Overall, it was an outpouring of goodwill. And as she read, and Macduff continued his ablutions, more comments began to appear at the bottom. The number swelled to 763. Shares were multiplying and more notifications continued to pop up as people liked the page. Her five thousand likes had already climbed to seven. Cait was tempted to respond to some of the nicest comments and even more tempted to correct those containing errors, such as the man who was staunchly insisting that the store had not been open five years, but three at the most ... but the next had already caught Cait's eye, one from a woman, who said that she couldn't stop crying because she felt like she was losing a friend. Cait suddenly felt disgusted, remembering her lonely hours weeping on the tree stump near Dorothy's place, weeping in her armchair, weeping on the freeway in her car. Who were these idiots, crying over a shop whose owner they didn't even know? She was the one losing friends. She shut the laptop with a snap.

'It's lovely that people care. But I don't see any of them volunteering to cover the rent,' she said to Macduff. The cat dropped, rolled and stretched, proffering his freshly cleaned belly for a rub. She obliged. Those dreadlocks definitely needed snipping off. Tomorrow, she told herself.

In a smaller offshoot of the main comments thread on the Facebook post, which by now numbered around eight hundred, an exchange was occurring.

> June Finch: Do you think she's reading this?
>
> Max Butler: Probably not. She's not replying. And she didn't reply to my email.
>
> June Finch: Let's get together and discuss further. Are you mobile?
>
> Max Butler: Somewhat.

June Finch: Likely more so than I. Will send PM
with address.

Max Butler: OK.

A small electronic blip sounded an incoming message. With
a smooth, automatic motion, Seb turned his head from one
screen, filled with a horde of the undead, to glance at another
screen with open chat windows.

June Finch: Sebastian, are you busy?

Seb looked back at his other screen, too late, as the shudders
in his mouse let him know his moment of inattention had
gotten him killed. A zombie was gobbling enthusiastically at
his body. He pressed quit.

⚜

Seb always operated better when he had a clearly defined task.
As opposed to, for example, an emotional problem, where
the parameters were constantly shifting, and the outcomes of
various potential actions were uncharted.

He debated various platforms. For the first task, he was
tempted to play with Google's templates, then briefly considered
Avaaz, but ended up with Change.org. Clean format, well
known, simple interface, good social media sharing widgets.
For the second task, he went with GoFundMe. The childish
design made him cringe, but there was no point designing
a whole new purpose-built website, with the potential bugs
and glitches that would have to be ironed out. This had all the
functionality already built in, and speed was necessary here.

He already had the draft text. June had helped, which was
lucky because writing was not his strong point. And he had
an excellent photo of Cait, albeit one she didn't know he had.
It was taken at Number Fifty's last Christmas party. Sometimes

he couldn't believe she continued to come to his parties. He could see they made her uncomfortable, so he didn't make her come to them all. Only when it seemed she was threatening to vanish completely. In the photo, she was standing a little apart from the group, listening, not talking, as always. The photo told its own story, but there was no need for the story in this circumstance. It made the shot ideal for his purposes. Her being a little apart meant he could easily crop it and turn it into a portrait. Her not talking but listening meant the camera had not captured her face in the awkward moment between facial movements. She just appeared lost in thought, smiling slightly, in the way people did in lieu of actually joining in a conversation happening around them. Slightly side-on, arms crossed at the waist to let her hands cup her elbows. In reality, it would have meant she was between drinks and needed something to do with her hands. But in Seb's cropped version it looked posed. He sat for a moment, gazing at it. She looked wistful. Beautiful. Perfect.

Perfect for this purpose, he reminded himself. That was all he meant. He uploaded the photo and June's text. He messaged June. It was late, but the old lady didn't seem to sleep much. Sure enough, he got a message back almost instantly. June gave him the thumbs-up and promised to get started on her bit in the morning.

He surveyed his work. It all looked good, but perhaps a little bare. Something was missing. He swivelled in his chair, took a sip of coffee and checked his bank account. Yep, he could spare it. He decided to kick things off in style. He hit the button before his logical brain could tell him that this might result in awkward questions down the line. What the hell, the campaign only had one chance. It needed a strong presence, early leadership. If Cait wondered later at the strength of his personal investment, he could always simply tell her that. It seemed the wrong time to tell her anything more complicated.

Right. He needed something to take his mind off all this. And working with these simplistic websites had put him in the mood for a challenge, to code something decent. Even freelance jobs, varied as they were, were getting boring, but he pulled out the file for his newest client and got to work.

TWENTY-SIX

Cait arrived at work the following morning with quite different goals in mind than those of her friends. She stowed her bag and donned her apron. She really wanted the store to look presentable for the sale. She pulled out the ancient vacuum, an accursedly heavy and unwieldy wheeled contraption she called the Dalek. This nickname was born of enmity rather than affection and she suspected the feeling was mutual. The Dalek had a malevolent bent. It had to be dragged viciously towards wherever it was needed and would grab hold of any shelf or corner it could to prevent itself having to come. When it was freed from that anchor it would retaliate – she would swear to it – by pulling out its own power cord, requiring Cait to storm back to the power point to replace the plug. At this point the Dalek would roar complacently back to life, then promptly snag itself on something else, awaiting her to free it again. It was like a manipulative baby, repeatedly throwing food from its high chair in a bid to be let free.

She kept it simple, just targeting the entrance, the biggest dust bunnies and the little snips of paper she and Seb had scattered while cutting and sticking up the sale signage. She

THE LAST BOOKSHOP

counted out the till, pressed play on *The Essential Billy Joel*, positioned the no change sign prominently, cast a critical eye over her front table, opened the windows and unlocked the doors. She put out the trolleys, and the sign, freshly chalked with a new quote: *We read to know we are not alone* – C.S. Lewis. Cait was about to turn around and go back inside when she felt a presence at her elbow.

'Oh, good morning, Mr Cowper! How are you?'

'Oh, well, you know,' he said. 'I'm fine, thank you, Miss Cait, and how are you?'

'Good,' she said. 'Hot!'

'Well, it is at that,' he agreed, following her inside. 'Oh, my.'

He stood for a moment, looking around at the glaring red sale signs, then looked back at her with such a hangdog face, Cait gave him a little squeeze on the arm.

'I know, it's all very horrible,' she said. 'I'm sorry. But let's look on the bright side, you'll get a bargain!'

She led him back to the till to fetch his order from behind the counter, but Mr Cowper would not hear of being given a discount. 'You ordered it especially for me, Miss Cait, and I am more than happy to pay the retail price. I am paying for the service, which, if I may say it, is of a gold standard.'

The old man stood proudly despite his crooked hands and failing hip. He paid cash, fingering the notes respectfully, she taking them in the same manner. She handed back his change, wondering if this would be the last book Mr Cowper would buy from her. He must have seen what she was thinking, because he said, 'Now, I'll be in hospital next week, but if all goes well I'll be back to hunt through your sale, all right? No stone unturned.'

'All right,' Cait smiled at him. 'I hope it all goes well,' she said, impulsively reaching across for a moment, to touch his hand where it rested on the counter.

EMMA YOUNG

He put his free hand over hers for a moment and patted it in a cheer-up, grandfatherly sort of way. 'I'll be out in time to have a rummage, don't you worry.' Then he made a hat-tipping gesture, though he wore no hat, and turned to leave, walking slowly and carefully down the ramp. Cait felt a squeezing at her heart and busied herself by checking the email. There were more letters of condolence, urging her against closing the shop, which, though she appreciated, seemed largely pointless. She felt overwhelmed at the thought of having to reply to them all. But she must at least find time today to reply to, or ring up, Max and Dorothy. Then there were a couple of inquiries of a purely practical nature. Did she have the new Fiona McIntosh book? Yes. Did she have Max Brand westerns? Yes. Did she have any Georgette Heyer? Sorry, not at the moment, but these could be ordered. Billy Joel reached 'Lullabye'. She skipped the track. Today, she could not break down over June. There was, thankfully, still work to be done.

Her first customer was a large man, already sweating profusely despite the relative earliness of the hour, maybe because of his uncomfortable-looking shiny dark-blue suit. He bought a children's book and, when she told him it was nine dollars, paid in change. He was one of those people with the habit of holding out his handful of change on his open palm, making her hunt and peck for the appropriate coins like a chicken foraging for grains. He gave her a gormless, self-deprecating grin as he did it. She found this kind of behaviour not just weird in its babyishness – Help me! I can't count out my own change! – but also somehow demeaning to her. She knew from long observation, though, that such behaviour was too common and too benign to be taken as wilful disparagement. It was more like the part of their brains that considered and calibrated the nuances of social interactions

238

at, say, a dinner party, was somehow switched off when they faced a salesperson. Like they automatically classified a clerk as not really a person, but some kind of machine.

Sometimes in the past she had indulged naughty urges to shock these kinds of people into realising they were dealing with another human as real as they were. As they were playing with their mobile phone instead of looking her in the eye, she would come out with an extraordinary statement. Invent an outrageous fact about the author of the book they were buying, for instance. Like they were really a famous log-chopper, or that they held the Guinness World Record for most days spent wearing a cow costume. Or that this was really the nom de plume of Angelina Jolie, or Prince William. They would glance back at her in a double take, blink at her like owls, awakened from their comfort zone. It was moments like these that made Cait think people should be forced into mandatory retail work experience at high school age, a sort of draft national service, just so they would understand for the rest of their lives that other people did not somehow fundamentally change into a different, lesser-evolved species the moment they stood behind a counter.

But today she couldn't be bothered. She just picked the coins from the man's fat paw and rang them up. Then the man most utterly and unexpectedly redeemed himself. First, he refused a bag and tucked the book under his beefy bicep, beneath which it all but vanished. Then he said, 'Saw your Facebook post. It's a real shame. Neat little shop you got here.'

Cait did a double take of her own, blinked like an awakened owl herself, and beamed at him.

Her faith in humanity was further redeemed by Cobie Strange, who dashed in with neat dark bob flying, delivered a fast but fierce hug, and within ten minutes had rounded up two hundred dollars' worth of brand-new crime novels and slapped down her credit card. Cait told her emerging authors couldn't afford to prop up bookshops to this degree. Cobie's black eyes snapped and she retorted she hadn't treated herself so well in years; and furthermore, emerging authors couldn't afford *not* to prop up bookshops to this degree. Cait found herself returning the hug, tenfold.

There was no-one after Cobie, though. It was not quite the sale rush she had hoped for. Maybe she should spring a few hundred bucks for a little ad in the city paper to reach those oldies not yet on Facebook. Though she was beginning to wonder whether there were any non-Facebookers left in the wild these days. She went to the computer. The social media notifications were still piling up, but she just googled the *Gazette*'s contact details. She emailed them asking for a quote for a small ad in Friday's paper and gave the wording she wanted. It would have been simpler to call, but she'd learned that inevitably if she made a phone call at work a customer would materialise, waving books and a credit card. It was just one of those mysteries, as reliable as the sun rising in the east or bread falling on the buttered side.

Maybe while she was waiting for the ad, she would redo some signs for the weekend. Make them bigger and redder. With some kind of clip art. Bomb blasts, lightning bolts, that kind of thing. Sale explosions! Did clip art still exist? Was it still called that? As she pondered, Seb appeared.

'How ya going?'

'Good,' Cait said, not bothering to sound good. 'You?'

'Good.' He sat on the counter, facing out. Cait did not tell him to get off. No point – the store was empty.

'Want to go get some food? I can watch the till. I'm on a long lunch. Quiet today.'

'Right, so it's not just me,' Cait said, relieved.

'Nah. It's dead. Go grab some food. Would have brought you some, but thought you might like to get out.'

'Thanks,' she said. She was sick of fruit for lunch. It was portable and cheap and required no preparation, but that was about all you could say for it as a complete meal choice. It wouldn't hurt to buy one sandwich. She untied her apron strings at the back and lifted it over her head as she walked round to Seb, still sitting on the counter facing outwards, surveying the store with its forlorn sale signs. She stood between the ragged kneecaps of his jeans and reached up to hook the apron over his neck. He bowed his head so she could reach. The neck strap barely fit over his head and they laughed as it held his dreads over his face, Cousin Itt–style, for a second before it could be tugged down.

'See you in ten,' Cait said.

The streets did seem subdued. They're all probably at the beach, skiving off work, Cait thought. I would be. She bought a chicken salad sandwich from the food court, rejected the tiny, grimy tables in the court and went back outside. She sat on a bench to eat, blinking in the sun, chewing each bite slowly to drag out the break. She walked back equally slowly.

'Anything happen?'

Seb was now sitting on the stool behind the counter, taking care of her Facebook notifications, bless him. 'Nup,' he said. 'Someone wanted the diary of Anne Frank, then when I showed them they said, "No, that's not the one I want, it must be the sequel."' He grinned as Cait laughed.

'Good grief. Seriously?'

'Yep.' Seb unwound his legs from the stool. He lifted the apron off and returned Cait's earlier gesture, replacing it over her head with mock ceremony, as though passing the baton.

'Thanks, Seb. You're a legend for coming. I didn't have any food.'

'I know.' He grinned, and loped out into the sunshine.

I don't know why he bothers, thought Cait. It's not as though he gets amazing company from me, these days. But that easygoing consistency was the nice thing about Seb. One of the nice things, anyway. She had not at all expected this friendship to continue when she fired him, but she now wondered what she would do without him. Then the phone rang. 'Hello, Book Fiend. Cait speaking.'

'Oh! Hello. Is that Cait?'

'Yes, speaking.'

'Oh, hello, Cait. My name's Erica, I'm calling from the *Gazette*, your local paper? You might remember, we did a story on you yonks ago, when you opened.'

'Oh, hi Erica.' The ad, Cait thought. That was quick.

'We've been contacted by a client of yours letting us know that you have decided to shut the shop? I'm doing a story, just about how and why this is happening.'

'Oh,' Cait said blankly, as Erica plunged on, 'We were talking about this in the office and we realised that this is not just the last bookstore in the central CBD but also the last locally owned shop on that end of Hay Street. We thought that deserved a mention, especially since you seem to have a lot of upset customers. I had a look at your Facebook page. It's getting really high traffic. Do you mind if I ask you a few questions for the article?'

'Um,' Cait said, feeling trapped and wanting to buy time, 'I emailed your office this morning about an ad, actually. I'm having a closing down sale. Would that do, just to have the ad in the paper?'

'Of course we would be happy to run an ad for you. I'm

sure our sales team will be in touch about it,' said Erica. 'But that's nothing to do with me. I'm from the editorial team and we think this is a news story. I've got some quotes from your customers, so I can go ahead with a few of the statements from them, plus some words from the Facebook page, a little history of the shop and of retail in the area, some pictures … but I thought you might like to provide a little context, about what's happening, why you're closing, perhaps any challenges in the industry, the retail environment in the city, that kind of thing? Maybe have a picture taken at the shop?'

Cait got the message: I'm writing my story whether you talk to me or not.

'Um,' she said. 'I'm not sure; see, I'm still waiting to hear back about my lease, and I don't want to antagonise the agents in case it ends up costing me, to be honest. Um – and you won't print *that*, what I just said, will you?'

'I *see*,' Erica said. 'I see. Well, it's not a drama. You don't have to give an interview if your landlords might see it in that light. What we'll do is, we'll just go ahead and quote you from your Facebook post. That pretty much explains things, anyway.'

'Oh – I didn't really intend –'

'It was a public post,' Erica said, sounding satisfied now that she had done her due diligence. 'Don't worry, they can't slam you for notifying your customers, and I'll make it clear that I'm quoting from that and not an interview. But you've still got my number, yeah? You never know – we might have room for a follow-up. I've got a good feeling about this story.' Then, apparently realising this was not very tactful, 'Well, not a *good* feeling, you understand, just a feeling that it could have legs. Your clients do seem *very* upset. I think we'll go for a "last woman standing on city's most ritzy street" angle, something like that. Anyway. I'll play with the wording. And you won't mind if I nip down and get a picture of the shop from the outside?

'Well –'

'Just ignore me. It won't look like we've posed you inside. Don't worry about a thing. Well! I'd better get on with it! Thanks so much for your time, Cait! Have a good day.'

Cait was used to managing members of the public on the phone. She knew a steamroll job when she saw it. But she was more used to being the steamroller, not the one flattened. She swigged her water and put it away, wondering who had tipped off Erica. So much for slinking quietly away to lick her wounds in the Centrelink queue. Oh well, what was the harm? She was buggered anyway, financially speaking. What more could Lease Freedom really do to her that hadn't been done already?

She jumped, startled, as a teenager on a mobile phone strode past to exit. She had not seen the girl enter. 'I am literally *so* unorganised,' the girl was saying down the phone, marching out as Cait winced. The girl was not laughing but deadly serious. She sought to impress upon her invisible friend the depths of her disorganisation. Cait wondered what the girl was talking about. Maybe she'd failed to Kondo her socks this week. Cait had been flipping, marvelling, through the Marie Kondo books now flying off the shelves. They seemed to largely concern the art of folding laundry nicely. Their sales figures were proving a close second to bullet journals, an even more ridiculous trend, but one Cait was grateful for as she was for any trend that meant sales.

She spent an interminable Wednesday and Thursday alone in the store, the season's first days over thirty. The air-conditioner begged in its crackly voice for a service, while the fans idled uselessly overhead. Some of her regulars visited to express their dismay at the closure of the store. They kept mentioning the Facebook page, which Cait had stopped reading the comments on. There were just too many, and they made her too emotional. She emailed publishers and reps to let them know of her decision. Replies began to come in, from the reps and also from suppliers she had in most cases never met in person, but had nevertheless known and worked with for years. They were sweet replies, full of concern. They offered her returns, even on stock they didn't normally allow returns on. She knew she should ring her mother and update her, but Tania would only ask for an update on whether she should fly over and say goodbye to June, and Cait couldn't face the conversation. Next week, she told herself. On Thursday night she rang June, who wanted to know if James had called yet. Cait informed her he had not. June refrained from going on about it, which Cait appreciated. They discussed Book Fiend instead. Cait's abundance of wellwishers wasn't necessarily translating into great totals for her sale.

'Enough about me,' Cait said. 'Are they looking after you? I can come tomorrow night if you don't mind it being late.'

'Don't worry about me. I'm right as rain. I'll just waste away here until you can come. We can get a takeaway.'

Cait blinked. She had never witnessed June get takeaway in her life, but perhaps cooking was now beyond her.

TWENTY–SEVEN

Friday dawned warm and slightly humid. Cait got into the shop to find the usual pile of bills and flyers on the ground inside the door, pushed through the brass mail slot. Cait dumped it on the counter and opened the new *Gazette* to check for her ad, then did a double take. Taking up most of page three was a picture of Book Fiend, bathed in morning light, with traffic blurred in front of it in that special trick photographers used. Cait could be seen in the background, through the window, serving a customer. Below, inset into the lower part of the story, was a picture of June. *June?*

Cait read the caption: *Long-time customer June Finch says she will be left high and dry when the shop closes.*

The headline, running above the picture, shouted, LAST WOMAN STANDING.

The tagline below, slightly smaller: LAST INDEPENDENT ON HAY ST BUCKLES UNDER PRESSURE.

Cait sank onto her stool.

BY ERICA BASTIAN. 30 September 2016.

Book Fiend, the CBD's last bookstore and the last independently owned local business in exclusive shopping destination Hay Street, will soon close due to financial pressures.

Owner Caitlyn Copper announced the move via Facebook, citing a surge in rental costs.

She wrote that the premises were in a desirable area now tenanted mainly by multinational retailers, and believed one such brand would snatch up the location as an 'appropriate' one to enter the Perth market.

Ms Copper wrote that business was not strong enough to sustain a relocation.

'I would like to thank you all, particularly my regular customers and my mobile customers, for your support,' she wrote.

It is not just city patrons losing out. For three years, Ms Copper has also run a mobile service for older and sick clients.

Client June Finch, who has terminal pancreatic cancer, said the financial pressure Ms Copper had been under, forcing her to lay off weekend staff and work seven days per week, had not stopped her visiting clients in the evenings.

Ms Finch said the loss of the service would take away the 'one joy' she had left.

'I don't know what I will do without her,' said Ms Finch. 'She has been such a comfort to me and to others who are housebound.'

Ms Finch, despite her delicate condition – Cait snorted *– joined forces with another client to create a fundraiser and online petition to pressure the leasing agency to reconsider the rent increase. At the time of printing, the petition had three thousand signatures and the Facebook page thousands of responses.*

You are kidding me, thought Cait.

Landlord Lease Freedom was contacted for comment, but did not respond by deadline.

Hay Street has seen a steady influx of high-end luxury retailers as Perth CBD's rent prices have cracked the world's top forty. Operating costs have also risen by up to thirty percent, according to a real estate industry insider who preferred not to be named.

He said these pressures had caused the steady exodus of locally owned retailers such as Crabbe's Chemist, Flower Power and the Busy Bee Newsagency from the area.

The changing face of the strip had also increased pressure on retailers to increase spending on bespoke fit-outs.

The bookselling industry itself has faced challenges; a recent report by a leading industry market research firm projected that by the end of this financial year, revenue would have declined at an annualised 10.6 percent over the past five years. It listed causes as lower book prices, tough competition from online retailers and a shift in consumer reading habits towards ebooks. It also said the operating landscape had been influenced by changes in household discretionary income and consumer sentiment, and in IT and telecommunications technology.

It speculated the exit of booksellers from the industry might also be due to a shift in consumer buying habits away from bricks-and-mortar stores.

When the Gazette *put the above to Ms Finch, suggesting it was 'survival of the fittest' on Hay Street, the elderly woman was scathing.*

'Survival of the rich landlords, more like,' she said.

'This shouldn't be about purely money. It should be about creating a city that welcomes everyone and can educate and entertain as well as just sell people things. I just don't know why they can't make allowances to keep some diversity.

'Book Fiend wasn't declining. Before this, Cait was doing a roaring trade, employing a lovely young man, planning a refit and fifth-anniversary party. You mark my words, some fat cat is waiting in the wings for the spot, and that's what made them jack up the prices to turf her out. I would have loved to go to the anniversary party and see the store once more before I die. That's all I want.'

Book Fiend is running a clearance sale, anticipating closure early January. Details in the advertisement, page 25.

Cait did not know whether to laugh or be outraged by June's audacity, her shameless capitalisation on her sickness, her flirting with the truth about Cait's saintliness and success, and her outrageous accusations against the landlord. She hoped to God this would not backfire on her exit negotiations. Still, it had perhaps been a bad move to quote so closely from the Lease Freedom letter on Facebook. Well, she had never dreamed anyone would put it in the bloody newspaper! She wondered if James had seen it.

She turned to the computer and opened the online version of the article. It contained a link to June's online petition. She saw it now had 3,600 signatures where the paper had said three thousand. The petition's photograph was one of her that she had never seen before. There was also a snapshot of the newspaper article, though it had only come out this morning. She saw with a little shock the authors of the petition were listed as not just June Finch but also Max Butler and Sebastian Goldwyer. *Seb*? What were all these crafty bloody old people doing co-opting Seb into their schemes? What on earth did they think they were going to achieve? Just a load of embarrassing publicity. But it at least now made a little more sense how a dying woman and an isolated old man had got the know-how to tempt the media with Facebook campaigns and online petitions. The petition was addressed to both the 'general public' and specifically to Lease Freedom, she saw, her heart sinking. Seb must have remembered the name.

> Hay Street is becoming boring, homogenised and a place only the rich can go. Muscling out local retailers through unsustainable price rises is not in the best interests of our city. You have taken our cinema, convenience store, chemist, record store, florist and newsagent – we will not let you take our bookstore too, the beating heart of the city!

Give me a break, Cait thought. They had no evidence Lease Freedom did all that. And really, the beating heart of the city? Whose line was that? Surely not Seb's. But beneath her internal grumbling, she was touched.

To Lease Freedom, please return the rent to previous levels and lock it in for long enough that Book Fiend can recover and regroup.

To the public, please visit the store, buy books at the recommended retail price, and show your support by liking Book Fiend's Facebook page. To help Cait not only keep the store open but do a refurbish, donate to our GoFundMe campaign.

Cait began to feel once again as though she might be on some kind of comedy sketch show, as though there was a camera waiting in the wings to capture her reaction. She clicked the link to the Facebook page and gaped. The page now had nearly eight thousand likes. The conversation appeared to be rolling. The last post had been only minutes ago. She saw in her notifications that Cobie Strange had written a post urging her own large following to support Book Fiend, tagging Cait's page in. God bless Cobie.

She went back and clicked the link to the GoFundMe. It too had the photograph of her and of the article. Where was that photo from? It had a dim background. Was that Seb's house? Then she was distracted by the donations total, spelled out in big black numerals. Nearly three thousand dollars of donations recorded.

Oh, for goodness' sake. It was probably all donated by June, that mad old woman, she thought, still not knowing whether to feel betrayed or proud. She clicked the bar on the side of the page to break down the donations, and was amazed to see the first: an anonymous donation of one thousand dollars. Who on earth would love the shop so much they would donate a thousand dollars? Or love her, Cait, that much? It must be June. But no, it looked as though both Max and June had contributed shortly afterwards, with a hundred dollars each. She made a mental note to ask them about the mystery donation later. After, that is, she scolded them for what they had done, dragging her name into the spotlight. Why didn't they ask first?

Because, she answered herself, you would have said no.

She saw a hundred-dollar donation from Sylvia Rose, whose junior librarian's salary was not large and who Cait had done little more for recently than send increasingly harried texts and excuses for not catching up. Sylvia had left a single love heart emoji in the message field. Mags had also donated a hundred dollars, writing:

FUCK THEM ALL BABE.

The rest of the donations ranged between five and fifty dollars. She scrolled through some of the messages beside the donations. Twenty dollars had come from a fellow called Michael Reem, who she did not know. There was a message accompanying:

Threw in cost of an ebook ;) Good luck mate!

Another, Peter Derby, gave thirty, and wrote that he would give a little more when he could. The name sounded familiar, but Cait could not quite place it. She kept scrolling. Most people had donated just ten or twenty dollars. They could have come and got a book for that, Cait thought. She of all people knew how twenty bucks could be a lot when you were on the bones of your arse, and she was not by a long shot the only one in Perth who met that description these days.

Some had not left messages at all. But plenty more had. Someone called Sophie wrote:

I've spent so much time here with my friends and now with my baby! It would be a shame if you weren't around anymore.

Alongside a forty-dollar donation, Jay had written:

I heart Book Fiend.

She read more messages, each beside a modest but meaningful pledge of cash. And a glow stole around the edges of her battered heart, like tiny flames playing at the base of a hardwood log.

Book Fiend was the first bookstore I visited when I moved to this city for work. I have since lost my job, but I still shop here. Just for second-hand now :)

Not the biggest contribution, but couldn't go without helping you, Cait!

I love Book Fiend. Best owner, best store, best stuff.

I hope you manage to raise what's needed. We hardly have enough bookstores in WA and this is my favourite.

Best of luck, Cait and Seb. Hope you make it through this. You've been my favourite local bookstore for many years.

Basically my second home. I have to pitch in!

Here you go, guys, not only is this shop great, but I can also see a service to the community. I wish I had the capacity to offer more right now.

Thanks for being there, Book Fiend.

Cait's tear ducts had already begun prickling when she heard a knock. There were people at the door. Shit! It was opening time and all the furniture was still inside. Swallowing hard and blinking, she leapt off the stool and headed to the door. She pulled the bolts, gave a giant sniff and swung the doors outward. 'Sorry!' she said.

'That's all right,' said the man standing there. He was a brush-haired corporate type with a British accent and a nice suit. 'I saw the paper on the bus this morning. I thought, why donate when I can get a book? So I'm just popping in.'

'Oh. Well, thank you very much,' Cait said awkwardly, while trying to work out how she would push the trolley past him, as it was completely blocking the entryway and he was standing on the ramp it needed to go down. Then the man grabbed the other end and pulled. 'Oh – watch your suit.'

'Not at all,' he said, brushing off the dust, and insisted on helping her pull out the other one. Never before had a customer pulled out one of the trolleys for her. As Cait, covered in confusion, locked the wheels, he said, 'I'll just go and have a browse then, will I?' The other woman who had been waiting had already slipped inside.

'Of course – thank you. You mustn't feel obliged to buy – I mean, I had no idea this article was going to –'

'Oh, not at all,' the man said cheerfully, sticking his hands in his pockets and strolling inside. 'I need a new book. And if I can buy it at a good time for you, so much the better. I went online and signed your petition, too. And I posted it on my LinkedIn.'

'Oh, thank you,' Cait said, deciding not to explain it was not really her petition. Especially since it looked as though it was bagging her first sale of the day. Well, not quite the first. The woman who had slipped inside was already frowning at her watch at the counter, with – wait, was that the Dickens collection? Beautiful antiques. And expensive. Cait had been intending to take them home and sell them on eBay if it came to it.

'Good morning,' Cait said, feeling more bemused by the moment.

'Morning,' the woman said. 'Had my eye on these for a while. Saw the paper this morning and thought, well, that's got to be a sign, doesn't it?'

'Well, I guess it is at that!' Cait said, then, though she hated to have to check, added, 'You know these aren't part of the sale?'

'Not a problem.' The woman waved her credit card.

'Well. That's great! It's a beautiful collection. I'm glad it's going to a good home. That'll be two hundred and twenty-five.'

The woman PayPassed and printed her own receipt while Cait separated the collection into four piles, and double-bagged each so they would travel safely.

'Thanks!' the woman said, taking two bags in each hand. She flashed a smile for the first time. It changed her whole face.

Cait smiled back. 'You're welcome,' she said, and turned her attention to the first guy, who had somehow already amassed a decent pile. 'Hi again,' she said to him as he hefted them with a whack onto the counter. 'That's more than "a book".'

'Well, you've got a great range of sci-fi, and I've been meaning to get back into reading anyway,' he said. 'Been watching too much Netflix.'

'Well, this will certainly do it,' she said, ringing them up. He did not at all look the sci-fi type, but he had chosen well: all hard-to-find classics, including John Wyndham's *The Kraken Wakes*, P.D. James's *The Children of Men*, Neal Stephenson's *The Diamond Age* and an old but pristine copy of Arthur C. Clarke's *Rendezvous with Rama*. All up, he spent a hundred and sixty dollars. He paid cash and left with a cheery 'Good luck!'

This was an unusually good start to a Friday. Cait realised the Dickens sale would have left a big, dust-ringed space in

Antiques and the nice Englishman's rapid plunder would have trashed the sci-fi stacks. She was leaving the counter to fix things up when she had to pause to greet another man, then another two women, all dressed for work and striding purposefully inward. Obviously there to buy, not browse, this time of morning. Each told her they had read the paper that morning and thought they would 'just pop in' on their way past. Each picked up not one but two or three books. They clocked up another two hundred dollars in sales between them.

And the stream did not stop there. Cait did sale after sale, the likes of which she had not seen since last Boxing Day. People she had never met, or at least did not remember, greeted her with familiarity and shared their surprise at the news they had seen in the paper or read on their mobile that morning on the train. One had no idea things were so difficult. Another confided that the street was becoming a bit, well, a bit 'samey'. Another said, 'At least books are affordable, right?'

'Right,' Cait agreed. The phone was ringing, but she was forced to put people on hold for longer than usual. Once she forgot altogether and picked up to find the person had eventually hung up. The second time, she picked up thinking it was going to be them ringing back, and wincing at the abuse she was sure to cop. Instead, she was greeted by the sweet and quavering voice of one of her nursing home clients. The old lady had read the paper and was scandalised to find that rents could rise, competition could prevail and that anyone would want to read books on an e-reader, whatever that was. She apparently did not want to buy a book, but just convey her sympathies. She talked so long Cait was forced to cut her off, thanking her profusely for calling and waggling her eyebrows in desperate apology at the three people standing in line in front of her. But even they appeared not to mind. The first in line, an older man, smiled benevolently back.

Cait had no chance to fix the hole in Antiques, or the mess in Sci-fi, or any of the other gaps and upsets that began to appear all around the store like gopher holes. The usual lunch rush mess level was eclipsed well before lunchtime, and it was after three before Cait could pause, sweaty and limp with hunger and thirst. At one stage, she had dashed off to make herself an instant coffee, which now lay cooled and forgotten beside the till. This morning's muesli seemed far away. She'd not brought any food with her and she could not pop out for any, even quickly, with so many customers around. It was as she wilted onto her stool for the first time that Seb bounded in the doorway, looking about as self-satisfied as it was possible for a person to look. Even his hair looked exuberant. Cait saw that he was carrying two paper bags and cardboard coffee cups and her surge of gratitude was so strong she could not bring herself to begin yelling at him immediately, as she had planned.

'*Thank* you,' she said instead, taking the proffered lunch. He sat on the teal velvet armchair near the till and she stayed on the stool, hoping for at least a five-minute break now that the rush seemed to have finally died down. They ate in silence, Seb staring in wonderment at the wrecked shelves.

'What the hell happened in here? Apocalypse?'

'Busy,' Cait said, wolfing her sandwich.

'No shit.'

'Seb, this is amazing,' she said, when she felt she could pause for breath. The greens were crisp, the chicken smoky and the mustard dressing creamy and nutty.

'Thanks. I added this to the menu and it's going bananas. Their sandwiches were really shit before.'

'Shit sandwiches,' Cait said, and they both sniggered.

'They were going to take sandwiches off the menu because they weren't selling and I convinced them to just let me make them. People go to cafes 'cause they're hungry. You can't just sell muffins and biscuits. You need at least one real food option. Good thing they let me experiment. Probably saved their business.'

'Is that your new line of work – business-saving?'

'Yep,' he said comfortably.

Cait took a sip of her coffee, deliberating her attack. Then she was distracted again. 'Oh my God, Seb, this coffee is amazing,' she said. She actually had to take another sip to make sure she had not simply imagined it. Maybe she was just delirious with thirst.

'I know, right? I'm good at this.'

'You are,' Cait agreed, then took a deep breath. She could not yell at Seb for going behind her back. She no longer wanted to. 'Listen, Seb, I'm so grateful to you guys for doing this. The story and the petition and the fundraiser – all of it. I don't even deserve to have such loyal friends, especially since it was me who let things get so bad' – Seb snorted – 'but I don't see what all this can achieve. A business like Lease Freedom won't just back down.' She sensed Seb taking a breath, about to interject, but held up her hand. 'I feel like burying my head in the sand has gone on long enough. I have let you all down –'

'Bollocks,' Seb said.

'– and that's only going to be made worse if I don't arrange properly now for things to be closed off here neatly. Just try to make as much money as I can and go quietly, finish paying off my debt, spend some time with June. If she's got any energy left after her exertions this week, that is.' The thought of June threatened to make her throat close over, but she pushed on. 'If nothing else, though, you've certainly helped me make some cash. I think we might even hit two grand today just in sales.'

Seb whistled softly. 'Nice,' he said. 'But you can't fob us off that easy. We can just see where it goes. There's no harm in a petition that doesn't work. And at this stage the Facebook page has so much traffic on it anyway, someone would just start up another one if I shut it down. The fundraiser's already hit four grand, I checked on the way here. People want to support you, Cait.' She tried to interrupt, but this time it was his turn to stop her. 'It's bullshit, you taking the line that this is all your fault. You read that article. There are bigger forces than just you here. And more people affected. People who love y–' He paused a second, then said, 'who love Book Fiend. They need it for themselves. And I'm sure even if their donations can't turn the tide, they would be happy enough knowing they got to help the owner close down without a pile of debt hanging over her head.' He took a sip of his own coffee and closed his eyes in appreciation. 'Anyway, I'm not having that fight with June,' he said. 'She's one scary lady, even if she is sick. I did the technical stuff, but she was very clear on how she wanted things to play out. So was Max. I think he must have read that Kawasaki book we picked out.'

Cait had forgotten about the social media guide she'd given Max. 'Well, like you say, there's nothing I can do about Max and June,' she said, and then, not wanting to sound churlish, she added, 'How did you even pull this off? How did they team up with you for this crime-fighting trio you've got going on?'

'June found Max and me on Facebook. She messaged us both asking what we thought about doing something. I think she was mad that this could happen without people even taking notice. Anyway, she roped Max and me into coming to her place and we made a plan. I really liked June, by the way.

I wish I'd got the chance to hang out more with her before – you know.'

Cait wondered at the lengths her friends had gone to in order to pull this together. June was a powerhouse, but it was clear even through the pink cheeks and nicely set hair achieved for the newspaper photo that she was very unwell. Cait couldn't believe she had got antisocial Max involved in her schemes. And with Seb, no less – fifty years their junior, working every day and living miles from either of them. None of them even owned cars. 'How did you get to June's?' she asked.

'Max and I caught the train out and then Ubered the rest of the way,' he said, grinning. 'I think it was his first Uber.'

'I'm sure it was,' Cait agreed, grinning herself as she imagined Max's fascination with the economics of ride-sharing. 'Did he quiz the driver?'

'Oh yeah. I think he made the guy a bit nervous. It sounded like he was researching for his own start-up.'

They finished their coffee. It was so good Cait wanted another. But more customers had come in and a couple were now hovering by the main display island with that telltale aimlessness that said they were ready to buy but too polite to interrupt her break.

Seb noticed too, experienced as he was in the shop's rhythms. 'Go talk to your fans,' he said. 'Hope you hit the big two K. Text and tell me.'

'OK.' Cait took his coffee cup and sandwich bag to throw away for him, then hesitated. She looked straight into his eyes. 'Thank you, Seb,' she said, trying to show how much she meant it through her tone.

'Hey, no problemo,' Seb said, and slipped out, pausing to check out the front table for a second. A book had caught his eye. Cait knew it would be the folio hardcover of *A Wizard of Earthsea*. It was stunning, bound in pale green cloth with silver-gold detailing. She made a mental note to put it aside for him as a thankyou. Then he was gone and she was facing – would miracles never cease? – another line of customers. She did hit two grand that day, something that normally occurred just a handful of days a year, usually before Christmas. Driving home, she wondered if she should tell her uncontrollable friends about the apparent effect of their efforts. It would make them even more certain they were doing the right thing, despite her conviction that they were only making this more messy and difficult and emotional than it needed to be. Max was still awaiting a reply to his email. She decided to put off calling him until tomorrow. She still had to make it to June's tonight, and she had decided not to open for late-night shopping. She had already smashed her totals for the day. She had another challenge to meet beforehand, of a totally new sort.

TWENTY-EIGHT

Macduff was waiting for Cait in the kitchen, as though he already sensed there would be action of some sort there. She leaned down and caressed his head, despite protests from her aching back. 'Hello, Duffer.' He watched intently as Cait dumped her shopping bags on the counter and went to the pantry for bakeware and an ancient recipe book, more of her mother's leavings, which she had perused late last night in a fit of what now seemed obviously to have been madness. She turned on the oven with a sense of impending doom and began to unpack the bags. They were full of foodstuffs and potions with inscrutable powers. Polenta. Chocolate chips. Vanilla extract. Not the same, apparently, as vanilla essence.

She looked at Macduff. His disbelieving expression clearly said, 'Are you *baking*?'

'Yes,' she said firmly. 'Biscuits.' Her tone was closer to that in which someone might say 'rabies'. Or 'gastro'. 'There's polenta in them,' she added. 'Does that seem right to you?'

Mac leapt up onto one of the kitchen stools to get a better view. His ginger bulk spilled over the edges on all sides. He watched cautiously, as one might watch a horror-movie madman who appears to have been killed, but may rise again for one last scare. But Cait seemed to get everything in the bowl all right, and she mixed the batter in energetically. She felt a little trickle of sweat move out of her hair and slide down her temple. The oven had already sent the temperature in the kitchen from warm to hot.

'What possessed me to launch my baking career now?'

Mac's face indicated he was taking no responsibility.

'I just wanted to bring something cheerful to June's tonight, you know? I thought flowers would be a downer, somehow. June has baked for me so much over the years. And she tried so hard with the newspaper thing, even though it's not going to work.'

She rolled the dough into balls between her palms, a tablespoon at a time, which the recipe advised would make forty-eight biscuits. She ended up plastered to the wrists in a sticky golden mess. After twenty-four there wasn't all that much batter left. She wasn't going to make it to forty-eight. She debated this with Macduff, casting baleful glances at the treacherous recipe. They finally decided the recipe had surely only meant tablespoons in a loose and carefree sense. Cait grabbed little bits of the leftover batter and squashed them on top of all the biscuits to make bigger and uglier biscuits. By the time she was finished, the sun was going down. She was about to stick the laden trays into the oven when she gasped as though she'd been shot. The Duffer sprang off the stool in alarm and fled into a corner. 'Shit! I forgot the baking powder!' She put the tray down to go and look at the recipe. 'Wait, there isn't any baking powder in this recipe,' she said, picking up the tray again. Didn't all biscuits need baking powder in them? How did they rise without it? Well, that was their problem now. She stuck them in and set the timer for ten minutes and went to have a shower. She reappeared, dressed in fresh shirt and shorts, as the timer went off. She opened the oven door and she and Macduff both stared reverently in at the little golden mounds, mysteriously risen and looking for all the world like correctly baked biscuits. 'It's a Christmas miracle,' Cait said giddily. Mac sniffed in appreciation and began to gather his body in a way that suggested he was preparing to leap into the oven.

'Sorry, Duffer.' She pushed him away. 'Time to feed you, hey?' She filled his bowl, and crumbled half a biscuit on top. She ate the other half. It was good. Macduff's ecstasy over his bowl seemed to indicate that he agreed. He ignored her goodbye.

The light was mellowing to pale gold as she drove towards June's, Tupperware container full of biscuits beside her where the book box usually sat. She thought about the complications that had suddenly appeared in the way of her envisaged quick and neat exit from her life: the sudden uptick in sales and the social media uproar, the unexpected roles of Seb and Max and, above all, June's hitherto unsuspected ability to manipulate the local press. It was all a bit more attention than she was used to.

And a bit unethical, she worried. June was hardly a disinterested party. She was practically Cait's grandmother. If anyone knew that … but they didn't. And it was only the local rag. Hardly *Four Corners*. Anyway, there was no point being cross with June. She was a law unto herself. And she was so ill and Cait had hardly any time left to spend with her. She mustn't waste it squabbling ungratefully about this. After all, June had done it for her, in good faith. She was trying to make sure Cait would be OK after she was gone.

June congratulated her on the biscuits. 'You haven't tasted them yet,' Cait warned. But they were light and lovely, albeit slightly misshapen. June refused Cait's offer to cook her dinner as well, insisting that she had eaten already because Cait had arrived so late. She preferred to gorge herself on tea and biscuits, since Cait had gone to the trouble, she said.

'After all, when was the last time you baked?' she said, giving Cait a little poke.

'Probably when I was nine and you tried that one time to get me interested,' Cait said. She endured some further ribbing, denying that the biscuit recipe had come from a 4 Ingredients book. It felt like old times, or would have, had June not been so conspicuously unwell. Cait suspected June had fibbed about having eaten dinner. She looked very thin and weak, and nibbled on her biscuit appreciatively, but very slowly. Cait once thought she noticed June surreptitiously pressing her fingers to her stomach. Cait made do with a quick sandwich made from some butter and cucumber she found in June's fridge, which was still well stocked. By a Silver Chain volunteer, June said.

Finally, Cait had to broach the subject. 'So, you're famous, June.'

June stopped nibbling and gave her a positively cherubic look. 'Well, you're not one to toot your own horn, are you? How would that nice lady at the paper know what news was afoot, unless I helped her out? It was only polite to assist her with her article, once she'd asked. It was a good one, don't you think? Lots of context.'

'It was,' Cait said. 'Thanks, June. You did a good job. You've brought in a bunch of sales.'

'And donations too, hey?' June replied smugly. 'I don't think you should give up the ghost quite yet. Isn't it astonishing how people will donate to an unknown cause like this nowadays. And all on the computer. We never saw the like in my day.'

Cait refrained from giving her views about the likely outcome of the whole thing, and just told her what sales she had made that day, and about Seb's visit to explain his role.

'Now he is a very nice boy,' June said, maintaining her air of innocence. 'I did like him. I knew he'd be good-looking. Even with that hair. And so sweet. And so good with computers. Nothing going on between you, is there, Cait?'

'June. We've been through this.'

June gave a maddeningly indulgent chuckle. 'All right, no harm in asking. What's become of your fallen prince, then? Has he turned up yet?'

They spent a few minutes badmouthing James and men in general. Cait's heart was not in it, but she could not think of anything cheerful to discuss. No more shop news. No new books being handed over, as June hadn't finished the last lot. June obviously so ill, but skirting around the topic. James gone, and never coming back.

June went off on a tangent about relationships, how different they were from back in her day. Cait still wanted nothing to do with any further conversation that related in any way to the behaviour of James or, God forbid, her father. She picked up the tea tray and went to go and wash up. The kitchen was old-fashioned, a self-contained room with a door that could shut. So she shut it, gaining a moment to drop the facade. Her emotions, held in such stern check, felt taut as wire. She wished she was going to see James after this, to share these burdens with someone. It seemed forever since his arms had held her. A wave of loneliness crashed over her.

She put the biscuits back in the Tupperware and placed it prominently in the pantry. She'd eaten a pile of them, but she suspected June only got through two for her sake. Cait poured out the cold tea and got most of the leaves into the bin, along with the remains of the sandwiches and the crumbs from their saucers. She noticed a faint sour smell, nothing putrid, just as though the bin bag hadn't been emptied in a while. She rinsed the remaining leaves from the teapot and washed their cups. It wasn't as though she really wanted to talk about June's illness, and if her previous couple of visits had been anything to go by, neither did June. But at the same time, it felt surreal to sit in there talking about courtships and newspaper articles and baking when June looked as though she were dying before Cait's very eyes. Cait dried the teapot and the cups and put them away, not wanting June to have to do it tomorrow, and grabbed the bin bag and put it in the green bin outside the kitchen door. She had just put a fresh bag in when she heard a soft cry.

She opened the door to the kitchen and sped down the short length of passage, swerving left into the living room, where June was hunched over, one hand clutched to her abdomen, the other gripping the shining wooden arm of her sofa. June's face looked warped, but her voice was soothing as she said, with a slight gasp, 'I just need to focus on the breath, is what they tell me. It'll pass. Don't worry.'

Cait, feeling at once called to action and completely impotent, crept closer to June's chair and squatted beside her. She put a hand on June's knee, softly, as though touching an injured bird, worried she would somehow worsen the pain.

June looked up at her touch, and the grimace on her face suddenly dropped off, leaving it slack and worn. 'Look at you,' she said in a wisp of a voice. 'It's all right. Just have a bit of pain sometimes, that's all. Comes and goes.' She took her hand from where it had gripped the slender wooden curve of the chair arm and patted Cait's with a semblance of her usual briskness. 'Up you get.'

She did, reluctantly, more out of a decades-old habit of following June's instructions than anything else. 'I'm not sure Silver Chain are managing you as well as they should,' Cait said. Her own voice sounded oddly remote, heard through the fog of her own reeling thoughts. Maybe it was time June went to hospital. Whose job was it to decide? She helped June to bed, as she had done last time. The smell of June's bedroom had further faded from its usual scent of flowers and face potions, and now smelled more strongly of chemicals. The dressing table's usual delicate arrangement of pretty hairbrush and cut-glass jewellery bowls was surrendering to an encroaching army of medical paraphernalia. Foer's *Here I Am* and the Proulx novel on the bedside table were almost inaccessible thanks to the ranks of pill bottles. They seemed impossibly numerous. June took a little tray, with a compartment for each day of the week and an assortment of pills in each. She swallowed the contents of one. At least ten pills.

'How come there's so much medication there? I thought you refused treatment?'

'I refused chemo,' June said. 'This is what they call palliative care. So it's still treatment, it's just not curative. It's more about keeping the symptoms from bothering me too much. Managing the pain.'

'They don't seem to be managing it that well.'

'Can't go without a bit of pain, Cait. I'm relatively comfortable ... all things considered.'

Cait didn't like the sound of 'comfortable'. It didn't sound comforting. It sounded like a death word. 'OK,' she said.

June's eyes were closed. She looked small, like a figurine of an elderly lady rather than a real one. She did not look smiley and pink-cheeked like the old lady in the newspaper photo. She looked deathly ill. But when Cait bent to kiss her, she opened her eyes. She patted the bed in a 'sit-down' gesture and when Cait did, beckoned her close and whispered, 'Look after yourself, my girl, I'm worried about you. You might be losing the plot. You're even baking, now.'

Cait laughed, and the squeezing at her heart eased a little. 'I know,' she said softly back. 'It's definitely a concern.'

'Well, watch out. You could kill someone,' June said. Their eyes met. June patted her hand.

Driving home, Cait recalled this small gesture, and how Mr Cowper and Max had both also recently made similar ones. Her tired brain wandered on. Boys never patted one's hand. James had never done it. Seb certainly hadn't. When did hand-patting age begin? At fifty? Or was it the echo of manners taught by previous generations? Maybe people hugged less back then. Maybe today's hug was yesterday's pat, and once the baby boomers died out, so would hand-patting. It would be a shame, she thought. It was extraordinary, what comfort such a tiny moment of physical contact could give.

TWENTY-NINE

The humidity broke on Saturday as the newsreaders had promised. The Corner Cafe was abuzz with chattering people toting dogs, toddlers and bikes. Warwick Randell sat alone, as ever, inside the cafe, the eye of its storm of activity, rendered almost invisible behind a pile of magazines and newspapers. This was not really a table, being normally just the table to park the morning papers on, but the staff had squeezed him onto it because the place was otherwise full and he had only wanted coffee. Randell's workload at the moment was sufficient to propel him into the office on a Saturday. He had little else to occupy his weekend and his current client portfolio demanded, as he solemnly thought, his full attention. He had been there since dawn and had only come out now to get a break from the computer screen.

He looked across the road. The skinny redhead who owned the bookshop was dragging out those God-awful wooden trolley things that sat outside it all day. Despite her youth, she looked pale and worn, her black outfit faded in the brilliant morning light. The paint was peeling on the facade above her head. He looked back down and something caught his eye.

He tugged out the newspaper halfway through the stack. It was a picture of the same tacky frontage, the same shopgirl. He read the headline and winced with distaste. He read the tagline and his thin lips took on an even more dour twist. He'd known about the story, but hadn't thought they'd go so hard. What was this, the slowest news week in history? How'd they beat this up to be worthy of page three? He took a deliberate mouthful of coffee and began to read. After about thirty seconds, he swore to himself and threw the newspaper down on the table with enough force that a waitress looked over in alarm. He pushed away the cooled dregs of his coffee and stood up, scraping the chair back loudly. He strode from the store, head down, pulling a mobile from his pocket.

≈

Cait, yawning through her morning routine, was only dimly aware of the usual hive of activity at the cafe across the road. She had done her best to tidy yesterday after the rush had finally ended, almost on closing time. But the place still looked ruffled, like a cat with its fur still on end after escaping the attentions of an enthusiastic dog. She would have to hustle today to keep up with the tidying and not let it get on top of her. In an obscure way, being too busy to think was helping keep her mind off June. The thought of going home tonight with only Macduff for company gave her a sick, anxious feeling. To be alone was to face the whole idea of aloneness. So she rang Max, despite the earliness of the hour, and asked if he was free for a visit that evening. She didn't mention his email, figuring they could talk about it in person, and Max did not mention it either. He said tonight would be fine. He would test on her a new dish he'd been experimenting with.

The minute she opened the doors two trendy thirtysomethings entered, offspring restrained in a stroller, giving latte-powered Good Mornings she did her best to return with matching enthusiasm. While they browsed, she embarked on a lap of her crime section to choose some titles for Max. She still had no new Strike. Perhaps one was not coming this year. She made a mental note to google it before she left. She added James Ellroy's crime memoir, *My Dark Places*, which she had ordered specially for Max after his request and which had arrived from the distributor unexpectedly quickly. The couple sidled up with picture books, chick lit and a Tom Clancy.

'Do you have a copy of *Shantaram*?' the dad asked as she rang them up. She went and grabbed a new copy off the shelf for him. 'Oh, thanks. Have you read it?'

'No! But I keep meaning to get around to it,' she admitted.

'It's meant to be life-changing.'

'So I've heard.'

The term 'life-changing' was overused as far as books were concerned, in her opinion, but she was amused by the sudden idea that *Shantaram* was actually as life-changing as people said. Maybe the sun-bronzed backpackers dropping off their tattered copies for exchange were, in fact, the transformed selves of the city dads who bought them new. Maybe this guy was one book away from quitting his job and going bush. Who knew?

The next customer asked if she had 'an updated version of the Bible or, if not that, a modern-day version'.

She dealt with this bemusing query as best she could, then got on with processing the second-hand stuff. As per her gradual shut-down plan, she was no longer accepting these, but one final box remained to be processed. She fanned each book out and sanded their edges, blowing the resulting dust off the counter. She Windexed them all and oiled a stubborn patch of dirt off a cover. The miasma of dust, eucalyptus and Windex, normally soothing, saddened her. She pulled the next pile towards her, a pile of fantasy. She had been particularly pleased with this find: Mervyn Peake's Gormenghast trilogy. Surrealist fantasies hailed in their time as genius, but rarely seen second-hand these days. The matching paperbacks were small and fat, their pages yellow-spotted with age but clean, with vintage illustrations. She had not realised at the time that this windfall would be the last of its kind. Cait picked up the first and fanned the pages. A piece of paper fell out. A list, written by a man from the look of the handwriting, divided into two columns by a free-drawn line.

Pros, the first column read.

Sex is great.

The kids.

Sometimes things are still good.

Great body.

Cait looked at the facing column, headed *Cons.*

Fight basically constantly.

Bitch.

Money.

Feel trapped all the time.

Maybe better for kids if we split up.

Cait lowered her hand with the note still in it to the counter. She hoped the woman who was the subject of this list had not seen it. She didn't know whether to find it funny or be horrified that a guy could reduce a relationship, even one with kids involved, to jotted bullet points. Was this actually how men thought? Had James –

Cait put aside the thought, and also put aside the note, to show Seb. They had once made a point of showing each other the weird or funny notes they found in the processing. Feeling rather grumpy now, she priced the Gormenghasts. Lower than she would have liked, but they had to sell fast. She consoled herself by tying them together with twine and specifying on the sticker that all three had to be bought as a set.

'Hello!' said a woman, materialising before Cait and startling her. This was already more customers than usual for a Saturday morning. The woman was perhaps a couple of years older than Cait and certainly at least twenty grand a year richer. She also had a couple of hours' grooming on Cait. Her smile was insultingly white. She asked for the fitness section, turning her body slightly towards the interior of the store, poised to be led quietly along like a well-bred racehorse. Her spotless white blouse was sheer enough to be sexy and old-fashioned enough to be sweet. She wore skin-tight jeans and below them a pair of nude stilettos of neck-breaking height, held on by two straps so narrow they were barely visible, one around the ankle, the other across ten perfect, nude-painted toes. The effect was devastating, only accentuated by innocent-looking spectacles. Cait led her to the fitness section, agreeing lightly as her customer talked about how difficult it was to find time to get to the gym. Cait pointed out the big sellers. Michelle Bridges, *The 4-Hour Body*, ad nauseam. Instead of picking one, the woman picked them all up and preceded Cait back to the till, blonde ponytail swinging, still talking.

'It's just, I keep reading all these stories online about how *dangerous* it is, you know?' she said, turning to fix a pair of serious blue eyes upon Cait.

Cait started to attention. She had become momentarily distracted by the tiny gold charms affixed to the backs of the soles of the girl's stilettos, so you caught glimpses of them flashing as she walked. They looked like little animal heads or something, the kind with antlers or horns. Cait, who had never even considered wearing stilettos in her life, was battling a sudden but overpowering need to possess those shoes. 'Sorry?' she said.

The girl repeated, 'The sedentary life we are all leading. Just sitting, eight hours a day, you know? Then more when we get home. Sitting, it's the new smoking.' She looked at Cait earnestly.

Cait took a mental inventory of the anti-fatigue matting behind the counter, her own flat rubber soles, the ladders positioned around the store that she was up and down all day, and the lone stool behind the counter, which at the moment featured not her own sedentary bum but a roll of blank price stickers and a dirty cleaning cloth that reeked of eucalyptus oil. She controlled the desire to murder the gazelle and take her shoes as a trophy. She merely said, 'Oh, I totally agree,' and sold her the books. The gazelle vanished in a swirl of ponytail. Cait allowed herself to make a face. Then her mobile rang.

'Hello?' she said, rather more aggressively than usual.

'Oh, hello! Is that Cait?' a perky voice said.

'Yes,' Cait said grudgingly.

'Oh, hello, Cait! It's Erica from the *Gazette*. Hope you don't mind me calling you on the mobile. I got your number from June,' and here Erica paused a moment, obviously waiting for Cait to tell her this was fine.

'That's fine,' Cait said, mentally cursing June all over again. Then she added, with an effort, 'Nice story.'

'Oh, thank you!' said Erica. 'Told you it had legs! It's going gangbusters online. There's been another spike this morning since we boosted our Facebook post. So there's plenty of appetite for a follow-up.'

Cait permitted herself an internal groan.

'I'm still hoping to get comments from Lease Freedom to

EMMA YOUNG

see exactly what's going on. But even if they don't comment, it doesn't matter. It's just going to make them look even worse. However ...' And Cait had an unmistakeable impression, even over the phone, of a crocodile turning its head towards her, lazily fixing her with its unblinking gaze. 'You *will* speak to us this time round, won't you? It's going to need a bit more oomph, a central character, kind of thing. We can't go with someone peripheral, although that old lady was the goods. Amazing she took the trouble, being so sick, hey? No, this time we'll need to really hone in. And with you added to the mix I can say, you know, "owner breaks silence on foreclosure heartbreak", or whatever. What do you think? You haven't had any blowback from the landlord on the first story, have you?'

'No,' admitted Cait, then added, 'Not yet, anyway. And it's not foreclosure; it's a lease, not a mortgage.'

'That's no worries, we can sort the details later, but you've got nothing to lose, really, anyway, right?'

Cait found this statement galling, but there was no denying it was kind of true. Anyhow, Erica focusing on her like this, even over the phone, felt uncomfortably like being caught naked under stadium floodlights.

'OK,' she said, sensing that if she continued to refuse, Erica would stay on the phone combating her objections all day. 'But I have to go. I have customers.'

There indeed were people gathered, clutching their selections.

'No problem!' Erica said. 'I could pop over on your lunchbreak? I'm working this weekend, 'cause we're short-staffed.'

'Don't get lunchbreaks,' Cait said. 'And I have a client to see tonight. Can you come after I close Monday?' The reporter agreed, triumph in her tone, and rang off too speedily for

276

Cait to change her mind. She's like a vampire, Cait thought. I should never have invited her across the threshold.

※

Cait got no sympathy from Max. He was rudely cheerful about the havoc his unlikely team of avengers had created. He kept quizzing her about her 'post reach' and 'audience engagement' on Facebook and repeating his offer to go over her bookkeeping. She could not understand why they all seemed so keen to participate in the grand illusion that all this was somehow going to change things. No matter how tempting it was to address this, however, she knew that she would only be venting to Max, and that it wouldn't be appropriate, especially since he was probably facing his own demons. She knew he would fear that his isolation would only worsen if Cait's visits stopped. She was now thinking, though, that even without a business, she would continue to visit Max, though they might have to find another way to stimulate conversation. Perhaps she could go to the library for him. She wasn't sure she would feel too motivated to go and visit Dorothy out in the sticks, though. And Dorothy, with her dog grooming business, did not seem so vulnerable anyway, thought Cait. Though experience did tell her that people tended to mask their loneliness.

Instinct told her not to try to reassure Max that she wasn't planning to just abandon him. That conversation was best had another time, when things had settled down. Their friendship was predicated on sharing not just food and books but also mutually accepted boundaries. Namely, no talking about feelings. For now, they could just eat Max's homemade parmesan and polenta chips and talk books. Max had loved *The Dry*, calling it 'a cracker'. He was visibly pleased with her wildcard order of the Ellroy memoir as a follow-up to

LA Confidential, despite its grim-sounding subject matter, the murder of Ellroy's own mother. He even relaxed his rules about tech at the table and together they googled to find out whether there would be a Strike book soon, discovering that, while chances seemed remote, a BBC TV series had been commissioned to screen the following year. Which was certainly, as Max said, a decent consolation prize.

THIRTY

The relentless cheeriness of everyone around Cait continued all week. Erica was preening on Monday over the doubling of donations on the GoFundMe site, which was now at more than five thousand dollars. Seb came in on Tuesday and insisted on buying her a celebratory drink after work. On Wednesday night she went to see June, who, although her pain appeared better 'managed' than on the previous visit, was now dealing with monstrous swelling in her legs and could not get out of bed. She had finally consented to be admitted to hospital, on condition Cait bring her a book: the diaries of C.S. Lewis. Cait had ordered it, but she privately thought she might have to read it to June, whose strength was obviously failing. On top of her grief and worry, Cait felt a vague but persistent alarm at the gaps appearing on Book Fiend's shelves, even though the whole point of the sale was to clear stock. It was a general feeling of disorder, of disarray. As though at any moment she would turn, place her elbow somewhere she had previously been accustomed to leaning, and find herself falling, arms wheeling like a cartoon character.

It was not her first vision of herself as a character; Erica had described her as such, Cait remembered, curled on the couch with Macduff on Thursday night. She was trying to retreat mentally into a tattered copy of Madeleine L'Engle's *A Wrinkle in Time*, a childhood favourite, but it was proving difficult to stop her mind going back over everything.

Erica had not been so bad at the interview, though still too probing and rather terrifying in her efficiency. She had looked about the same as she had five years ago, though perhaps a little more tired. Her teeth were still slightly prominent, her hair still shiny, her makeup still perfect. She had brought a photographer along to the interview as well, which she had not mentioned on the phone, so Cait had not been forewarned to wear a less battered work outfit. Thankfully, her hair had been clean. She had tried to put aside her worry about the photo, the story, the whole damn thing, and just be philosophical about it, but she was still terribly conscious it would be coming out tomorrow.

⋘

Cait stopped herself looking at the *Gazette* until she had opened. The morning had the typical, almost unreal perfection of Perth in October, the store full of light, the air touching her skin full of gentle warmth. Perhaps she should do a spring display, Cait thought, a small one on a stand with yellow or reflective books on it that she could move across the store throughout the day so it always sat in a sunbeam. Then she thought, what's the point? She would be better off putting further reductions on the sale stuff that hadn't sold yet, and responding to some of those condolence emails from suppliers.

To delay this depressing prospect, she made a cup of tea and sat down with it and the *Gazette*, which was still folded into thirds as it had been to fit through the mail slot. The mug was one James had bought for her. It featured the quote, *You can never get a cup of tea large enough or a book long enough to suit me*, with a tiny pair of reading glasses on each side that looked like quotation marks. She had thought about getting rid of it, but her love of the mug had won out over the pain of the reminder.

She unfolded the paper and saw that Erica's story was on the front page. The photo covered most of it, this time not a snapshot of the frontage, but a moody profile of Cait in the window of the shop. Her body was turned enough to the side so the twilight caught the red gleam in the dark mass of hair, but enough to the front to see her face. This angle drew attention not to the book held loosely in her hand, but to her gaze through the window, as if she had been distracted from a task by a thought. Cait remembered the cheery banter of the photographer, a different guy to the one she had met at the store's opening. He had kept up a constant prattle of 'turn here, no, too far, turn back, that's right, look up, no, too far, a bit down, chin down, eyes up, hold the book up, no, down, no, up a little more'. She had suffered him as a fool, but now she could see he knew what he was doing. It was a beautiful portrait, pensive, subtly lit, and he had used the window frames and shelving as natural framing devices, blurring the background of bookshelves enough so that it looked more like a pattern, the eye drawn to the central subject alone.

LAST CBD BOOKSHOP OWNER SHARES HEARTBREAK, the headline blared. And underneath, NO PLACE FOR SMALL BUSINESS IN BIG CITY.

BY ERICA BASTIAN. 7 October 2016.

The owner of the city's last bookshop, and last independent retailer on Hay Street, has broken her silence on losing out to big business.

Caitlyn Copper announced to customers recently that Book Fiend would close in the new year after a surge in rental costs made it impossible to keep the boutique store afloat.

Landlord Lease Freedom is understood to be courting luxury retailers looking for high-exposure locations to establish their brands in WA. The process has seen several other independents leave the area and these spaces undergo refits costing hundreds of thousands of dollars. Book Fiend was the 'last man standing'.

Ms Copper told the Gazette *hers was no different to other bricks-and-mortar bookshops finding it tough to sustain growth, or even maintain level profits, in the face of changing technologies and reader habits, but that the rent surge was the final blow.*

She has kept going by extending trading hours, delaying cosmetic works to the shopfront and laying off staff. But the changes were unsustainable, she said.

'This place is my second home,' she said. 'But I am powerless. I can't turn the tide.'

Ms Copper said she could not afford to gamble on a new location without the support of her regular customer base.

These customers have taken to social media to express their sadness at the loss of what one called 'the only reason I still visit that part of the city'. They have waged a campaign to pressure the landlord to drop the rent to previous levels.

One, an elderly woman with terminal cancer, issued a public challenge to Lease Freedom through the pages of this newspaper to grant her dying wish to see the store saved.

Lease Freedom has not responded to requests for comment.

An online fundraiser to allow Ms Copper to stay on and refurbish the store has reached five thousand dollars in just days. To find out more, visit Book Fiend's Facebook page or the Change.org petition or GoFundMe page, both titled 'Saving Book Fiend'.

Book Fiend is presently running a clearance sale, with closure planned for January.

Her phone buzzed with a text from Sylvia, telling her the story in the paper was 'on point' and asking how the sale was going. Cait had just finished typing a reply, thanking Sylvia for her donation and apologising for her recent crap performance at friendship, when the shop phone rang.

'Book Fiend, Cait speaking,' Cait said warily.

'Hi Cait! It's so great to speak with you! It's Laura Priout calling. I'm a producer from *Today Tonight*. How are you?'

Oh, God. 'Good, thanks, and you?'

'I'm great, thanks. Thanks so much for asking! Cait, we've been following your story in the local paper there, and we really think we could help your fight to save Book Fiend reach a wider audience.'

'It's not –' Cait began, but Laura did not pause or brook any of Cait's attempts to back out of the conversation. She countered each objection with an upbeat patter that only barely sheathed her ironclad determination.

It was thus that Cait found herself, the following Monday morning, being attacked by a fresh-faced hummingbird of a makeup artist who danced around her, darting at her with brush after brush while talking with more energy, if possible, than Erica and the formidable Laura combined. Once they had worked out that Cait was not, under any circumstances, going to close for filming – Cait had held her ground here, at least – they had decided to film their interview before opening time and get the rest of their background shots around Cait as she worked. They overrode her objections about the makeup, assuring her it would be necessary to avoid her looking 'washed out', and had taken one look at her black T-shirt and jeans before immediately dispatching a staffer to remedy the situation. The girl returned in record time – she must have persuaded more than one shop to open early that morning – bearing an outfit ostensibly similar to Cait's but inexplicably more flattering. The black jeans hugged Cait's body, as did the small V-neck T-shirt that looked casual but felt expensive. It was bought from one of the same retailers that were edging shops like hers out, Cait saw, when she looked at the label. But she could not help a disloyal thrill as she wriggled into the new gear. It was a long time since she had bought clothes. Memories of early dates with James, celebrated with a couple of new outfits chosen partly to create, partly to celebrate new confidence levels, seemed distant now, though in reality were barely six months ago.

The assistant who had bought her new clothes obviously thought Cait should not cover her nice new duds with a dusty old apron. She took one look at it, attempted to dust it off, failed, then interrogated Cait, who admitted she had a new one stashed away. The girl made Cait bust open the packet and tied the new apron around her waist, far tighter than Cait ever would have worn it. It was somewhat difficult to breathe during the interview proper. This involved the reporter, Pamela, sitting on the armchair near the till while Cait perched on the coffee table beside her. The teal velvet clashed alluringly with Pamela's penetrating blue eyes. These brimmed with such sympathy as she gazed at Cait that she warmed to the woman, rather against her will.

'Don't worry about the cameras,' she said. 'We're just having a chat. Tell me about your beautiful shop.' Cait liked anyone who called her shop beautiful, and found herself describing her bookish childhood, her dream of opening a bookstore, her feeling of flat depression that there just no longer seemed a place for books in the world. She was already feeling weepy by the time Pamela produced a copy of last week's *Gazette*, with its picture of June, and asked if Cait would miss her clients.

Thankfully, the interview did not go for much longer. Pamela managed to simultaneously be delighted to have squeezed a tear out of Cait, and still seem sympathetic and grateful to Cait for 'sharing her story', as she put it.

They allowed her to get on with opening while they got their 'cutaway shots', whatever these were, though she was a bit self-conscious. The cameraman tagged along after her, occasionally asking her to repeat an activity. He seemed most taken with the trolleys, asking her to push them this way and that, filming them going down the ramp from the front, zooming in on Cait pushing the bastards with all her might to get them into position. Be nice if he'd help instead of just watching, Cait thought.

Cait's customers, including a few regulars, were delighted by the circus. Only one or two did not want to be filmed. Others fought, giggling, to be served on camera by Cait, who sweated under both the heavy makeup and the unaccustomed scrutiny. It was then, of course, that Mr Cowper chose to come in.

His new hip supported by a big hospital-issue cane, Mr Cowper made a slow but unerring beeline for Cait. Pamela instantly sensed pathos and made her own beeline for Mr Cowper, who found himself ushered onto the teal armchair, gazed at soulfully and probed with utmost sympathy. Cait, watching from the till, cringed as he proved only too happy to share his memories of the shop, which were so extensive he eventually had to be ushered, again with utmost sympathy, back off the couch. 'Always gets my Cornwells. Every time,' Cait heard him tell the cameraman once more before shuffling with painful slowness to his accustomed corner. She watched him go, to make sure he would not fall over on the way. She had not expected him back on his feet so soon.

She had to admit, *Today Tonight* was a slick operation. They got some more shots of her tidying the shelves, and were out the door by nine a.m., thanking her profusely.

'Will I get to see it before it airs?' she asked Laura.

Laura looked shocked and said, 'Oh my gosh, no, sweetie! But I'm sure you'll love it. This is going to go over a treat. And you have my number if you got any worries, OK?'

This whole thing's a worry, Cait thought. She went off to check that Mr Cowper was still upright. He was, and wanted to tell her all about his new hip, and talk over the thrilling prospect of them both being on TV. She did her best to act excited but was relieved when they were interrupted by a young guy of about twenty in shorts, boots and high-vis.

'I'm looking for a book. My friend told me I had to read it.'

Cait looked at him expectantly.

'The author's name is something like Chemist? I think it was – ah – was it Al? Al Chemist? Something like that.'

Cait stifled a giggle. 'You want *The Alchemist*,' she said. 'Paulo Coelho. Hang on.'

THIRTY-ONE

Warwick Randell swirled his Blanton's and took a sip. It burned sweetly down his throat, ice clinking against crystal. He was still in his suit, reclined on his black leather couch. He had removed his shoes to put his feet on the table. Nothing else cluttered the mirror-like surface of the black tempered glass but an equally sleek black remote control. His thin black socks protected the tabletop from smudges. The carpet had been recently cleaned, and still carried a faint chemical smell.

The nightly news contained unmitigated misery. A young man was missing. His family wept on camera. A young girl, a surfer, had died after being bitten by a shark. Her family wept on camera. A slightly older man had been stabbed in the city in short-term accommodation. He, it seemed, had no family to weep on camera. Police called for witnesses. Another footballer had fallen from grace. Drugs. The media pack chased him from the courtroom. One of the cameramen could be seen, in the background, knocking a young female reporter to the ground in his eagerness to get his shot. The cameraman did not stop but kept running and filming the footballer.

Randell recrossed his bony ankles, to put the other foot on top. He changed the channel. It was time for the bookstore girl to make her debut on *Today Tonight*.

He did not have long to wait. It was the top story. Beads of sweat formed on his glass as he watched.

The interviewer was looking concerned and sympathetic and cooing over that little hovel of a store, coaxing emotion until finally the shopgirl's eyes brightened with tears. She told the same sob-story she had told in the paper. Then they interviewed an old man. Oh God, he walked with a cane. Of course. He loved the hovel and he loved the redhead. Of course. His life would never be complete again without this fucking bookshop. Of course. 'FUCK.' He threw the remote at the television. It hit the frame, bounced off and fell to the floor in two pieces. It made no sound on the carpet. 'Piece of shit.'

After they finished with misty-eyed shots of the girl fondling paperbacks, they ran the statement he had finally instructed the PR girl to feed them. Of course, read out by the sceptical host, it sounded empty and trite. Money-hungry. The whole performance made him sick. It was rubbish. It was complete, utter, dangerous, perfect rubbish and it was forcing his hand.

He drained his glass and replaced it on the wet ring it had left on the coffee table. Warwick Randell did not like coasters. He waited for the cleaner to polish away his water marks each week. He picked up his phone, found a name and pressed the call button.

≪≪

Greta's phone rang. She had been slumped on the couch watching *Breaking Bad*. Tonight bore every sign of being a two-episode night. She was still in her work clothes, an empty pizza box on the floor before her. The scene on-screen was intense and she was already keyed up with suspense, completely carried away from reality. The unexpected blaring vibration of her phone made her jump, with the immediacy of a white-collar worker who carried office tension home each day as reliably as she carried her empty Tupperware. She paused the show.

'Hello?' Injecting positivity into her voice cost the remainder of her evening's energy.

'Greta.' Randell sounded hard and angry. Her stomach twisted. 'Did you see it?'

Greta cursed inwardly. She had known the PR team had provided a response and were expecting the episode to air that night, but she had convinced herself she didn't need to see it.

'Yes,' she lied, keeping up her cheerful, businesslike tone, as though she truly believed in a world in which what happened on *Today Tonight* was not her fault. 'Is there a follow-up action you'd like me to take when I get in tomorrow?' She had been trying to set better boundaries with Randell. She reached for the notepad and pen that lay ready on the arm of the couch and winced when the voice came again, harsh and grating and wiping out her boundaries in one fell swoop.

'This is turning into a nightmare. What possessed Rianna to send through that piece of crap response? It sounded terrible on air.'

'Um, she sent it to you for sign-off, Mr Randell.' There was silence, thick with danger. Greta quaked but went on. 'I brought in the printout?'

Another pause, this time shorter. 'Well, it's too fucking late to fix it now. We need to staunch the bleeding. This site isn't worth the bad PR. We'll wait till it dies down then try again in a year or two. Get onto that bloody Rianna and tell her to put together a statement, will you? Saying ... say my executive assistant was inexperienced and refused an appeal without consulting management. We'll agree to keep the lease at the old rate for, say, two years. The executive assistant has been … let's see … *counselled*. But don't admit error. Call it a "gesture of goodwill". We care deeply about the vibrancy and diversity of the city, add something like that. Get it back to me for sign-off, send it to the station, send it to that fucking local rag, put it on our website. Get on our Facebook and Twitter and start defusing those commenters before the media start quoting them too. Yes?'

Greta took a breath. She thought about telling him to ring Rianna himself, during business hours. She thought about protesting her innocence of the bad judgement about to be publicly assigned to her. Then she thought about how hard-won the title of executive assistant had been. She told herself for the hundredth time how she had planned to build on her successes, keep her head down, negotiate pay rises, squirrel these away and invest them. Pain now meant freedom one day. If not soon, then sooner than many of her peers who were not strategising with such energy. She let the breath out, as quietly as she could.

'No problem,' she said. 'I'll give Rianna a call first thing, when I'm in the office.'

'Now, Greta!'

She caved. 'Right. OK. I'll give her a call now.' She hung up and turned off the TV.

THIRTY-TWO

Social media rewrites final chapter for Book Fiend; Agent bows to pressure, drops rent

By Erica Bastian. 14 October 2016.

The city's premier commercial leasing agency has reversed a rent hike for the last independent retailer on Hay Street following an angry public backlash.

Caitlyn Copper, owner of Book Fiend, which is also the last remaining inner-city general-purpose bookstore, had told customers she would be closing in the face of financial pressures after a thirty percent rent hike proved the 'straw that broke the camel's back'.

Lease Freedom, which manages the city's most prominent properties, previously declined to be interviewed by the Gazette on this issue, but provided a statement on Tuesday confirming it would 'renegotiate' the rent in an unprecedented 'gesture of goodwill'.

'We do not allow feedback received via social media campaigns to dictate our financial decisions,' managing director Warwick Randell said.

In this case, it came to my attention that an executive assistant had refused an appeal by Ms Copper that we would normally have allowed to go through our mediation process. I have counselled the assistant.

'While the increase was considered fair in this increasingly competitive location, as a responsible corporate citizen the firm acknowledges the importance of diversity and character to the city and has policies enabling it to also consider such factors in negotiations.

'We took into account public affection demonstrated for this store, in determining to negotiate a mutually acceptable solution with the affected business owner.'

Mr Randell declined to answer a follow-up question on whether this would cause problems with surrounding retailers.

Lease Freedom was battered by increasingly vicious comments on its social media accounts over recent days after extensive coverage of the issue, first in the Gazette, then on television.

The Gazette understands the company engaged a temporary PR consultant specialising in risk management to help its staff respond to the wave of abuse.

Ms Copper said the news came as a shock.

'I am just incredibly grateful and humbled by the response,' she said.

'I am also extremely thankful to the staff at Lease Freedom for reconsidering my case. I understand it's a difficult business environment for everyone, so I'm just speechless.'

Asked if she had caught up on the social media storm that has resulted from the Save Book Fiend campaign, Ms Copper laughed and replied, 'I don't think I'll ever catch up.'

Ms Copper said the GoFundMe page had raised enough money for her to pay her debts and cover a modest refurbish. Plans to celebrate the store's fifth anniversary are back on for early next year and readers should stay tuned for details of a new venture Ms Copper believes will ensure long-term financial sustainability.

Cait folded the newspaper and stowed it under the counter with the state daily, which had also got in on the action.

'Can't wait to go back to chucking the paper on the table each week without scouring it for a mention of myself,' she said to Seb, who was perched on the counter nursing a tiny takeaway espresso cup. They had both been reading it at the same time, heads together. Outside, the street trees that had stood bare for what had felt like forever were getting their leaves back, courtesy of the spring sunshine, late in arriving though it had been.

'Come off it. You love being famous. You're a new superhero, saving the city from evil corporate wrongdoers. You're Book Girl.'

'Get off the counter. And think me up a new superhero name. That one sucks. Even I don't think Book Girl sounds cool.' Seb slid off the counter. His legs were so long he barely had to point his toes before they touched the ground.

'How's June? Have you told her the news?'

'She's been asleep both times I've been to see her this week. She's on a lot of morphine,' Cait said. Then, wanting to change the subject, 'Hey, I've been thinking about something. I wanted to run it past you, actually, see what you thought.'

'Fire away,' he said, loping across to the armchair and settling into it as though he owned it.

Cait took a deep breath. She looked outside. The plane tree's new leaves stirred in a sudden breeze. 'Change is natural,' she said. 'It's necessary for growth, right? I need to face that. Diversify. Not have all my eggs in one basket. Have income coming in that's not from books. The store needs to bend, not break. But I also want the changes to be on my terms.'

'Like how?'

She took a deep breath. 'Book Fiend Cafe,' she said. 'I'm doing a refurb, right? So I eke out a section – the back, so people have to walk through the shop at the beginning and the end of their visit – and make it the cafe. Hire a barista, do simple lunches: sandwiches, salads, cakes, that kind of thing. I advertise it out the front so people have another reason to come in. If they buy the book first, they can read it while they have lunch. I can put displays in there, or alternatively some condemned stock so people can "read a wreck" while they eat. Then they spend longer, they're all mellow and relaxed when they come out of the cafe.'

'Or jacked up on caffeine.'

'Or jacked up on caffeine. Either way, they're in even more of a spending mood than they arrived in. James told me' – she used the name lightly – 'that food retailers are one of the only sectors of small business doing well in this environment. So if I can't beat them, I can join them. But with one important difference.'

'Such as?'

'No takeaways,' Cait said firmly.

Seb looked astonished. 'What, not even coffee?'

'Especially not coffee. That's the whole point. It was something June said to me, months ago, that made me start realising how obsessed we are with having everything on the go, and how takeaway coffee never used to be a thing. And this entire shop is valued and still here because reading a book is choosing to take your time on something. So, I'm taking back coffee. Have you heard of the slow food movement? Well, no-one's thought of slow coffee yet. If people want to have a coffee here, they can bloody well stop and smell the roses.'

'Bold,' Seb said. 'Risky, but I kinda like it. And it does set you apart.'

'The other thing is merchandise. I read in the last *Books+Publishing* that bookstores are making real money off merchandise: stationery, T-shirts, mugs, stuff that celebrates reading. Nerd goods for nerds. I feel like selling stuff like that would fit in with my values too, that would actually promote reading as a pastime. And get Book Fiend shirts and bags and things made. Capitalise on our new-found fame.'

'All good ideas,' Seb said thoughtfully. 'People do love book cafes. And there hasn't been one in the city since Borders closed.'

'If you count them having plonked a Gloria Jean's inside as a book cafe,' Cait said. 'This would walk all over that.'

'True. But how would you fit a cafe in here? The place is chockas.'

'Not really. Not anymore. Look around. The stock's taken a beating.' This was true. Half the second-hand was empty, the gaps filled with artfully placed Christmas decorations.

'That's a good thing,' Seb said. 'That was mouldy old stuff worth practically nothing. You should have had a clearance ages ago.'

This was true.

'I'll keep the quantity of second-hand stock as it is now, and just keep the rarest and most attractive stuff: the Pratchetts, the Potters, stuff that makes money. I've had this very rude reminder of how valuable this floor space really is. I need to be smarter and stricter about filling it. So ... what do you think, as my consultant?' she asked, jokingly, but Seb did not laugh.

'Not consultant,' he said. 'Partner.' She stared. 'Not financial partner,' he added, 'but make me your cook and barista. You just said you'll need one. I'll make sure my coffee is good enough to sit down for. I know another cafe owner offloading a coffee machine. It's a good one. A good price, too.'

Cait swivelled on her stool, pushing with her fingers on the counter to propel herself. 'What about your other jobs?'

'I can always keep freelancing on the side. And I told you I wanted a challenge. This sounds like one. Setting up and running a cafe, that'd be awesome. And I bet Anthea would do you mates rates for the Book Fiend shirts and things.' Seb's younger sister was a graphic designer. 'We could try the sit-down coffee thing for six months or a year, maybe, and see how it goes. You do have public interest on your side. We can build on your momentum with the publicity and the refurb and the anniversary. Make a big splash opening the cafe. Your mate Erica will lap it up.'

Had Seb changed lately, or was Cait seeing him in a new light? She would have never imagined Seb using a phrase like 'build on your momentum'. And he thought of them, him and Cait, as 'we'. She gazed around, new ideas swirling in her mind.

'Down the back, you said? How much space are we talking?' Seb said.

'Come, and I'll show you.'

᠁

Cait forked out the astronomical coinage demanded by the meter in the hospital car park for a third night running, hoping this time June would be awake, despite the lateness of the hour. June was crabby with pain and drifting in and out of sleep, but she still liked being read to, and Cait had got her the C.S. Lewis diaries as promised.

They covered the period in which Lewis had completed his service in World War I and begun attending Oxford. The twenty-three-year-old had struggled to adapt to life in postwar England, and Mrs Moore, whose exact relationship with her much younger partner had been the cause of so much speculation, had suggested he keep the diary. Despite what seemed a difficult life – of overwork, never-ending chores and constantly threatening poverty – he stuck to the practice. The result was five years of diaries, published as *All My Road Before Me*. The book's title came from a line in one of Lewis's own poems, in which he'd addressed the reader as a stranger, and said that long before they read this, time would have erased the moment of writing; a moment in which his own journey still stretched out ahead.

The diaries were proving a bit unexpected. Social and domestic drudgery had seemed to form the bulk of the Narnia author's daily life, yet the entries were studded with flashes of startling beauty and insight and wit: accounts of his country walks and inspirations, deep reflections sandwiched into accounts of humdrum everyday duties. When Cait thought about it, this was probably a pretty accurate reflection of the way most people's minds leapt chaotically from the sublime to the mundane, her own included. It made for an odd reading experience, but also a frequently amusing one, and June, though she might seem to be asleep, would sometimes show she was listening with a dry chuckle.

Cait entered the cancer block through mammoth glass sliding doors and the now-familiar smell dealt her a backhand. Like shit, or food, or perhaps both mixed together. She rounded a corner and rode up in the elevator, squashed in next to a hulking orderly with an empty bed. He and Cait gazed straight ahead at a ragged poster advertising the presence of a chapel in the block for those relatives who wanted to 'reflect'. Cait exited. The orderly stayed in the lift. She went down the corridor and turned right, then left, then down another very long corridor. Then left at the end, and around another corner. June's room was at the end. The curtain around the bed was pulled back.

June was propped up in the white bed like a little china doll, albeit one whose hair needed a wash and set, and whose cheeks were yellowish and sunken. Cait sat on the bed beside her. June opened her eyes. 'I hear you have some news for me,' she said, managing to sound extremely pleased with herself even in a voice barely above a whisper.

'I do,' Cait said, not bothering to ask how June knew. She probably had a network of spy nurses doing her bidding. 'They called me this week. They've dropped the rent. I've got a two-year reprieve. They said they were making an exception, and did this mean I would stop talking to the media? I said I would, but that I can't control my friends. These old people get ornery.' She looked to check June appreciated her joke.

There were tears in June's eyes. She squeezed Cait's hand, surprisingly hard. The tears slid south and soaked into the pillow. But June was smiling. 'And what will you do now?' she asked.

'Good grief. Can't even give me a chance to bask in my success before you start talking about the future.' But she didn't really mind. Ideas were running, sparkling, through her brain and she was alive with excitement. To have not only the prospect of financial progress but a new project to work on, something to draw a line beneath everything that had happened, to face forward. Soon she would employ a casual and get her weekends back. She could now ring her mother and share not bad news, but good. She would have Seb around again, to share gossip and anecdotes with, to giggle over the weirdos, to speculate on the lists and cards found wedged in the books, to solve problems together. She could, now that it was almost over, admit to herself how lonely it had been. She ran through the details for June and felt her own eyes tearing up.

'Stop it, Cait. We're happy now!'

'I know,' Cait whispered. She leant over and hugged June. It felt comforting, even though June was only able to manage a pat on her back.

'That's it, get comfortable,' June said. 'I want a word.' Cait was happy enough to stay there. She wriggled her legs around so she could lie next to June on the bed. There was plenty of room. She snuggled in and leaned her head on June's shoulder. If she closed her eyes and ignored the smells and the sound of random machines beeping and carts being rolled around in the corridors, she could pretend she was little again, about to be read a bedtime story. But June, being June, had an agenda.

'I want to talk to you about the future. Your personal future, not the shop's,' she said, faintly but firmly. She lifted an arm and stroked Cait's hair, a feather-light touch.

'Must we?' Cait said with disgust, but she stayed where she was, imprinting the feeling of this caress in her mind, trying to create a detailed memory of this moment with June, a memory that would live forever.

'I know you've written this off. I don't blame you for shutting it out a bit while you've had all this to focus on. I know we've never talked much about the personal stuff. And maybe I've held my cards too close to my chest. The habits of a lifetime are hard to break, I know. But I will say this. It's a hard life trying to make it on your own, Cait. Books can forge a connection, but ultimately relationships are had between human beings, and they deserve a chance. That's all I've got to say. Just think about it.'

'OK. I'll think about it,' Cait said.

'Good girl. Now, get through some more of that Lewis diary or I'll be dead before we finish it. See what he cleaned next.'

'Or what he had for dinner.'

'Or who's coming to stay next.'

Cait got the book out from the bedside cabinet and opened it at the bookmark, then sat on the bed again.

Lewis had been prevailed upon to take yet another paying house guest for a few days and felt unable to refuse, even when the few days turned out to be a few weeks. He spoke of frustration at having his and Mrs Moore's privacy, which such guests and other visitors had continually placed out of reach, deferred again; he had, however, been able to get some work in, speaking of reading and enjoying John Milton's play *Comus* and poem 'Lycidas'.

In the next entry, he had been reading *Paradise Lost*, taking pleasure in it, but finding it hard to spot possible 'gobbets'.

'I wonder what he means by gobbets,' Cait said, half to herself as June's eyes were closed.

'It's an extract he might have needed to explain in an exam,' June said, surprisingly. 'To explain its historical significance.'

'Wow, OK,' Cait said. 'Right, we're back to the paying guest.' And she read on through Lewis's droll evocation of his guest: that evening, when he and Mrs Moore asked each other what they thought of her, neither had thought anything at all. Cait looked at June in time to see her smile.

Lewis went on to read even more Milton – tracts on education and, worse, *The Doctrine and Discipline of Divorce*, which sounded indigestible to Cait, but which Lewis described as interesting. Poor Mrs Moore had plenty of extra cooking on her hands because of the guest, who had gone early to bed (a practice she and Lewis applauded, and hoped would continue).

Cait herself smiled at this and glanced again at June. June looked as though she had fallen asleep. Well, the diaries were turning out to be strangely calming. Astonishingly, no nurse had yet interrupted. It was amazing how they always came when you were trying to have a private moment, but if you were in need, you could never find one anywhere. Cait read on a little, softly, to make sure June was really asleep. The paying guest, unfortunately for Lewis and Mrs Moore, discontinued her practice of retiring early.

Cait could feel the rise and fall of June's breath in the bed, the stiff cotton blanket drawn to her chin. The air-conditioning was lifting the tiny hairs on Cait's arm. The room smelled of sickness, coagulated meals, cleaning chemicals. She got out a little of June's rose hand lotion and smoothed a tiny amount, with infinite care, on the cracked backs of the old lady's hands. The familiar smell reached her nose, masking the other smells for a moment, as she had intended, but causing a painful lump to rise into her throat. Cait inched backwards on the bed and rolled off it as slowly and lightly as she could. June did not stir. She was incredibly still. Her chest didn't seem to be rising and falling as before. With coldness stealing over her heart, Cait reached out once more and placed her fingers on the inside of June's wrist.

'Not dead yet,' came a faint voice, making Cait jump.

'For God's sake,' she murmured, and leant forward to kiss the old woman goodnight. The line of pain between June's eyebrows stayed where it was. But there was the ghost of a smile, too.

Cait went back through the halls, floodplains of fluorescent lighting that somehow emphasised, rather than dispelled, the darkness outside. She thought about the tissue paper feel of June's skin, about June's cryptic love advice. About the author of Narnia, who now seemed a real person, who struggled to find space and time to read and write, who bitched about house guests and housework, who worried about what his father would think of his lover. Who worried constantly, just like Cait, about money. Who, despite giving so much to the world, had had to worry like this and who had then died a painful and lonely death.

She thought about the fact that as he was writing, he had indeed, as his poem said, had all that road before him; that time had, as he had foreseen, washed away all those fears and sorrows; and yet his books, full of beauty and hope, had endured.

As she reached the front doors, the fresh, ordinary fragrances of the night air greeted her face like a kiss, delivering her a moment of precious gratitude simply for being young, alive and walking outside.

THIRTY-THREE

Monday was spent in a whirl of removing sale signage and ordering stock to fill the holes on the shelves – though not too much. The more they had, the more they would have to move during refurbishment, as Seb pointed out. He had come by to talk practicalities – renovation costs, timing, whether the place could be ready for a combined birthday party, relaunch and cafe opening early in the new year. They googled and made phone calls, and decided it could. Sweaty and grubby from climbing ladders and ripping off Blu Tack and sticky tape, they high-fived, grinning at each other. Then, without warning, Seb grabbed her and hugged her hard. They both laughed. For a moment, Cait felt light, almost giddy with happiness.

Her phone rang. 'Hello, Book Fiend. Open for business now and forever,' she said.

'Cait?' a voice said. Cait recognised the voice of one of June's nurses, the sweetest one. Annie Evelyn was small and slight, with straight brown hair and round, popping brown eyes like a possum's. Cait liked her. But her tone wiped the smile from Cait's face. The bottom dropped out of her stomach.

'Annie? What's up?'

'Cait, whereabouts are you? At the moment?'

'I'm at work.'

'Have you got someone there with you?'

'Yeah, my ... my business partner's here. Why's that?'

'Cait, I've just got my handover from the morning nurse. There were a few changes in June's condition overnight. She's showing some signs that make us think she might not be with us much longer. If you want to come and spend some time with her, now would be the time, if you can.'

Cait couldn't speak.

'Cait? Are you there?'

'Yes. I mean, OK. See you soon.'

She hung up. Her heart pounded. There was a terrible pulling in her chest. She took a deep breath, but the sensation of airlessness did not abate. She felt a yawing, a pitching, as though she were trying to balance on a boat in a storm, and sat down on her stool so heavily her back jarred. She took another big breath, and another, and another, and heard as though she were an observer the harsh gasping sound she was making, the little moan of her own voice underneath, sounding like a small animal caught in a trap. But she could not stop. She felt a pressure on her back and realised it was Seb's hand. He was saying her name. He sounded worried. He looked into her face. She could not bear to be touched. She wrenched away from him. She needed solitude. She needed darkness. She needed the world to go away for a second so she could think. Her mother was not due to fly in for another day. She had thought they had more time, just a tiny bit more. She was not ready.

But the world did not conveniently fade away. The lights stayed on, pitilessly glaring. The sun remained, beating energetically through the windows. A customer entered and began to browse. Oh God. And Seb was still there, not daring again to touch her, but looking at her. She made a valiant effort to control her breath and stop making the dying animal noise, so as not to attract the notice of the customer. Pressure built in her head. She felt a sudden, almost overpowering urge to pick up a childhood book, as she always did when upset, to go home and curl up in one of her armchairs with Macduff and escape into it. *Anne of Green Gables. Black Beauty. Harriet the Spy. Amy's Eyes.* But there was no escaping this. Anne had lost Matthew. Black Beauty had lost Ginger. Harriet had lost Ole Golly. Amy had lost the Captain. And she would lose June.

She crouched beneath the counter, put her face on her knees, her arms folded back over her head protectively, and burst into something that was not sobbing but a sort of loud, panicky groaning. But at least it was dark down here, folded over. She did not have to see anyone staring at her for making a racket. But Seb was tugging at her arm and she could not slap at him from this position. She let him drag her to her feet and steer her down an empty aisle and out the back. Cait could feel people staring.

The back room was not an inviting space, with its utilitarian white walls and fluoro light. But it was private, a haven. Her head had a weird echoing feeling. Her vision blurred. She could not breathe.

'I'm going to pass out,' she gasped.

Seb removed a pile of books from the one wooden chair she kept back here and forced her onto it.

'Breathe,' he ordered. She could not. She could only gasp in and sob out in a total and horrific lack of control whose very force only scared her more.

Seb squatted in front of her. He put his hands on her knees. 'Look at me,' he said. His brown eyes found hers. 'Deep breath.

In.' She tried. The breath shuddered in. 'Out.' The breath shuddered out. 'Again.' She did it again. She made herself focus on his eyes. They helped. 'Is it June?'

Cait nodded. She took another breath.

'You have to go.' He went into the bathroom and grabbed a wad of tissues, which he gave to her.

'I can't –'

'I'll look after the bloody shop. Just go.'

Cait got up. She had not meant the shop. But, ashamed of her own weakness, she let him think she had. Panic remained coiled somewhere between her chest and her throat. She pressed the whole wad of tissues to her face, ineffectively, and patted jerkily at Seb, aiming for his arm but hitting the area between his chest and shoulder instead. He took her by the shoulders and spun her to face away from him. He untied her apron at the back and lifted it over her head. He gave her a little, gentle push.

They walked together back through the store, Seb hanging the apron around his own neck. They reached the counter. Seb got out her bag and gave it to her. 'I'll call you a cab from here,' he said quietly.

'I can Uber ...' Cait began.

'Don't worry about it. You don't have to worry about money anymore. I'll call you a cab. Go outside and wait.' Cait nodded and started outside. 'Hey,' Sebastian said, still quietly. 'Send my love, OK?'

Cait nodded, swallowing, directing a fearful grimace towards her feet in her effort not to cry as she headed out. She kept looking at the ground, observing all the marks and bumps on the square of pavement beneath her feet. Then she lifted her head to survey the street. She kept her eyes tuned for a cab, but unfocused, attempting to keep her mind blank, not turning again towards the sinkhole that had opened with Annie's words on the phone. She sent her mother a text message, repeating these words, and promising to call her later after she had seen June. She looked at the colours of the passing cars. White. Black. Silver. White again. White again. Black motorbike. She kept at it until a cab appeared in front of her and slowed to a stop. She got in and asked for the hospital. The driver nodded. He had an ancient green tree-shaped air freshener swinging from the rear-view mirror, and Cait kept her eyes on this.

She blew her nose thoroughly, not allowing herself to care what the cab driver thought. She used the last tissue to rub over her entire face, then put the visor down to check the result in the mirror: red and splotchy and swollen, and not helped by the little light that came on beside the mirror. She put the visor back up, shoved the tissues in her bag and got out her purse to be ready to pay the second they pulled up. She focused ferociously on the cars outside. There were a lot of white ones. *It's June*, she heard Annie say again in her mind.

They arrived at the hospital. Cait hated the sight of the place. She paid with her credit card and was already out of the cab when the driver proffered the receipt, which she reached back in to grab. 'Thank you,' she said, without quite managing a smile. The driver nodded, a sympathetic-seeming nod, though maybe she just read that into it because she so badly wanted comfort.

She dashed inside. That smell again. Round the corner. In the lift. Down the hall. Right, left. Long corridor. Left at the end. Next corner. The end room. Curtains round the bed. Drawn, for the first time. Cait stopped. She tried to will herself to place one foot in front of the other, but her body disobeyed, like a horse shying before a jump. Cait was suddenly convinced she had the power to stop time simply by stopping walking. While she hovered here, no harm could befall June. If she did not arrive to say goodbye, June would not die. June would wait.

But then Annie Evelyn poked her head around the curtain so that it appeared to float in midair, before vanishing again. The effect, combined with her possum-like features, would have been comical were it not for the sudden appearance of age on her face, despite Cait's impression that Annie was around her own age. The look on that face scared Cait almost as badly as the thought of what else was happening behind that curtain. Maybe it was bad luck to go in there, she thought wildly. Maybe anyone who stepped beyond the curtain instantly aged. A decade a minute. Maybe when Annie reappeared it would be with white hair and toothless gums. Maybe June was now just a pile of dust on the bed.

She was being irrational. Annie was just tired. She was a shiftworker. Then Cait heard the squeak of sneakers on the rubbery floor and Annie reappeared, hair and teeth intact, herself again. She gave Cait a brief squeeze on the arm that returned Cait to some kind of reality. 'We're keeping her comfortable; she's having a morphine infusion. She's been in and out, but the periods of unconsciousness are getting longer. She might not be able to say much to you. But there have been a few periods of lucidity, so you never know.' Panic flared in Cait. 'I'll get out of your hair.'

Cait opened her mouth to protest. Don't leave us alone, she wanted to say. But Annie was already gone, vanished from the dim room and through the doorway into the rectangle of harsh light that was the corridor.

THIRTY-FOUR

Cait moved unwillingly towards the curtain. She felt a tight, sick feeling in her upper belly. She pulled the curtain back. Some of the fear eased. It was only June, lying there. She was not a pile of dust. She was not terrifyingly aged. There was no grinning skull. Only June, though so altered, such a tiny, faded version of the June she knew.

Cait welcomed a moment of rage that drove away the sick feeling for a moment. What kind of disease was this that could so rapidly vanquish a woman so full of spirit? Cait found she no longer wanted to stay distant from the bed. The chair was not close enough. She did not want to climb on the bed and hurt or disturb June. So she settled for bending over from the waist, awkwardly, and hugging June around the shoulders, as tightly as she dared, though she could not get her arms beneath June without moving her. She nestled her head, facedown, next to June's on the pillow.

'Hello, my girl,' said June, very faintly. Cait doubted she would have heard it had she not been so close.

'Hi,' she whispered. 'How are you?'

'Good,' June whispered. Cait's throat contracted painfully.

She took a long breath, trying not to let it shudder. 'Glad you're here,' June continued, still in that faint monotone. What seemed like an age passed. 'Want to talk.'

'I remembered what you said about James,' Cait whispered. 'I'm –'

'Not James,' June muttered.

'Oh,' Cait whispered, nonplussed. Her back was already hurting from bending in this peculiar position, but she dared not move. Whatever June had to say, she wanted to hear it. June's voice, when it eventually came, was barely audible.

'Lewis.'

'Lewis?'

'Him and … Tolkien.'

'Yeah, they were good friends,' Cait agreed.

'Reading.'

'Yes.'

'Writing … talking.'

June couldn't seem to manage any more. Cait tried to tease out what she meant.

'Yeah, they spent a lot of time talking about books, right? Like us. Though maybe a tad more educated.' Cait laughed at her own joke, but somehow it came out as tears. 'Amazing that Lewis nagged him to finish *The Lord of the Rings*. Just think, if they hadn't kept talking about books, all that time, it might never have happened.'

June gathered breath. 'Between … the wars.'

Between the wars? Was June rambling now? Cait waited. She listened to every little precious breath come in and out. They took a long time. Cait waited twenty minutes, then went and got a coffee, then came back and had time to finish it before June spoke again. Bizarrely, June spoke as though she had not even paused, and this time it was in whole sentences.

'You don't know.'

'Don't know what, June?' Cait bent her head close to June's again.

'The world waiting … for the axe to fall again. Even as a child this feeling …' She stopped. Cait hardly dared breathe. 'The world could end any time.'

'You mean, between the wars?' She willed June to keep talking, to be saying something that made sense.

'I read his books … I could feel those thoughts in his mind. Like mine, back then. I haven't thought about it for a long time, before …' A pause that lengthened into a silence.

'Before what?' Cait prompted.

'Biography. And,' June panted a little. 'Boring bloody diary.'

Cait laughed. Her tears were falling straight onto June's pillow, saturating the fabric. June appeared not to notice, or not to mind.

'He was a housewife. Worried about … money.'

'We all know what that's like,' Cait said.

June opened her eyes. They were watery but they gazed at Cait with sudden focus. 'I thought for a long time it was just stories that mattered … the life wasn't relevant. But … Narnia …'

'He was in such a dark place when he wrote Narnia,' Cait said softly, finally seeing. 'The world was broken, after the war. And he was broken inside too. But what he wrote was so real, it inspired millions of people. And it helped him, too. That such pain could bring such joy, right? I loved learning that too.' Her back was shrieking for release. She had to move. 'June, you're eighty-four and still learning.'

Cait sat down again to ease her spine, and dragged the chair as close to the bed as possible. She did not trouble to wipe her face, just found June's cold hand and held it, as gently as she could, in both of hers to warm it.

June said something inaudible. Cait bent close again.

'What?' she said.

'Nearly ... eighty-five,' June said again, slightly louder. Then she fell asleep.

It seemed a long time between breaths, but they kept coming. Cait rang her mother, who said she had booked the red-eye and would arrive tomorrow. Then she sat for a long time, watching.

About eight o'clock, she went and got a truly disgusting egg salad sandwich from a vending machine. She had just finished half and dumped the other half in the bin and was about to head back to June's room when Seb rang.

'You OK?'

'Yeah. Just waiting.' Cait couldn't think of anything else to say.

'You want me to come by?'

Cait was sorely tempted to make Seb come here and hold her and tell her everything was going to be OK. But she was an adult and there were other things to take care of.

'Seb? Do you still have the spare key to my place?'

'Yep.'

'Would you go and feed Mac for me? He'll be starving by now.'

'No problemo.'

'Thank you so much, Seb. I promise, soon, you can stop looking after me.'

'Cait.' She waited while he paused a long moment, but then all he said was, 'What else are friends for?'

'Thank you,' she said. 'I'd better go. I don't want to miss it if she wakes up.' She hung up and returned to June's room, but June was still unconscious.

She sat there another half-hour before June began to move,

plucking restlessly at the blanket. Cait half rose, wanting to assist in some way, or halt those motions, so distressing in their pointless repetition. She went to the nurses' station and fetched Annie.

'Don't try to stop her doing it,' Annie advised. 'Stroke her hand, talk to her soothingly.'

'Can she hear me?'

'Yes. If you haven't said goodbye, Cait, maybe say it now. Give her permission to go.'

Cait stood and moved closer, once again, to the bed. She stroked June's cold hand until June stilled. Her breathing sounded weird. She would take a few shallow breaths, then Cait could not see her breathing at all. She bent nearer. She felt rather than saw Annie leave the room again. But it was another few minutes before she could bring herself to speak.

'You did so much for our family. And for my mum, when Dad left,' she whispered into June's ear. 'You did so much for me, growing up. Thank you. I'm glad if I was able to do anything for you, even if it was just to find you books.' She paused, searching for the right words. 'I tell people you're like my grandmother so they will find it easy to understand. But that's not really right. You're my best friend. You always have been.' She waited a moment longer, then made up her mind. 'I will be OK. Go, June, if you need to. You have done enough for me. You don't have to stay any longer. I love you.'

She kissed June, very lightly, on the cheek. Then she left the room. She could not bear to stay there a moment longer and not cry, and she did not want June, if she could still hear, to hear that. Alone in the corridor, a few doors down, she sank to a squat on the linoleum and wept, heedless of people walking past. After a while, Annie came and found her there. She led Cait, blind with tears, to a visitors' alcove, a tiny windowless shoebox of a room with a plastic coffee table, a bundle of magazines, a struggling ficus and a water dispenser.

'No, I need to go back,' Cait said.

'Just have a little rest here for ten minutes,' Annie said firmly. She pulled a handful of tissues from a box and in one motion pressed them into Cait's hand, and Cait into a seat. 'We can't have weeping in the corridors. It's bad for business.' She smiled, a sweet, soft smile, and left.

Cait waited. She would just stay here until she calmed down, then she would go back.

⋘

'Cait. June's gone.' The hand was gentle on Cait's shoulder, but the words arrowed straight through her sleep. They jolted her instantly upright in the hard chair, her heart pounding. 'You want to come and see her?'

Cait stumbled with Annie back to June's room. The hospital was silent. Visiting time had long passed.

'You've been here for a long time,' she said to Annie as they walked.

'Stayed back,' Annie said. 'I'm sorry for your loss. What a beautiful lady. She knew her own mind, didn't she?'

'Yes. Thank you,' Cait said. She felt the chasm at her feet open again, but still, she did not fall down it.

She felt none of the aversion she expected to feel at seeing June's body. She just felt an overwhelming wish to hold onto June as long as she could. She bent forward, as she had before, and hugged her. Her throat ached, deeply and severely, promising yet more tears to be shed. Years and years' worth. Annie simply waited, still and silent, until Cait finally made herself turn around.

'Do I need to do anything?'

'Not right now. We'll take her to our morgue. She'll be there for the next day or two, until you can arrange for a funeral director. She's listed you as her next of kin, Cait, so I've got her things here for you.' Annie handed her a bag and Cait looked inside. June's cardigan, her watch and purse and keys. The Lewis diaries. The lettering gleamed gold on the cover. Cait hesitated, wanting to ask something, but not knowing how. Annie seemed to understand. 'You can come back tomorrow if you want to see her again. I put the nurse manager's number in the bag just in case. And the funeral director will get her dressed up nicely, and you can see her again after that, if you want.'

Cait paused another long moment, then stroked June's shoulder, and picked up her hand, and held it for a moment. It felt more like touching a little bird than a person. A little dead bird. Horror threatened.

'Come on,' Annie said. They left the room together. 'Cait, is there someone who can come and pick you up? Or someone there at your house to be with you?'

Cait thought of her home, dark and silent, with only Macduff waiting there. 'No,' she said. She squared her shoulders. 'It's OK, Annie, thank you, but it's fine. I will be fine.'

THIRTY-FIVE

Dear Cait,

By now you know you're both the executor and almost the sole beneficiary of my will. They tell me that's allowed.

Your job as executor is pretty simple. Sell my little old car, and divide whatever you get for it between two charities. A women's refuge and the Red Nose people.

Sell the house, which I'm giving to you. Now, stop your jawing and listen to me. I may be dead, but I'm talking and you're listening.

I know you're sentimental about buildings and places. You're a sweet girl. But you don't want a big old house in the sticks. Though I will say it did offer a lot of quiet time for reading. It was worth bugger-all when my ten-pound-Pom parents bought it in the fifties, but it'll be worth a bit now. If you can, wait until the market recovers a bit.

Sell the house and the contents. Don't keep everything in it. I can't abide hoarders. You can keep a couple of the nicer bits of furniture, the sofas, if you want to spruce up the shop.

You can keep the Royal Albert tea set for old times' sake. And my books, you can keep or sell as you like. You'll know which ones are which.

The rest of it you sell, you hear me? Invest the money wisely, grow yourself a nest egg, and hopefully it'll be a bit of a buffer for you, so you can run that shop for love, not money. The value of some things can't and shouldn't have to be solely about profit, and that is an opinion so old-fashioned that I can see it's high time I dropped off the perch. Nevertheless, I know you agree.

This means you can keep doing what you're doing as long as you want to. I admire you using your brain for something and I might have done the same, had things turned out differently. I always would have liked to be able to go to university. But I have no regrets. I have had a good life, thanks in no small part to you.

But I'm ready to go. I miss my sister and my old budgie. Remember Ginger? And you will miss me, of course, but I want you looking forward, not back. And on that note … choose wisely. Choose someone kind and never cruel. Someone strong enough to stay by your side, and yet willing to let you change – and to change with you. Who you choose is up to you, but I know which one I'd put my money on.

You are probably crying by now. I know I am and that's something. But stop it, now, Cait. Dead is dead. Change is both inevitable and necessary. It's the living who are important. Now get on with it, my girl.

Love,

June.

Cait wiped her eyes with the heels of her hands, looking across the lawn to where the sprinkler was running. She had finally made herself come to the house, conscious that June would have taken a dim view of Cait letting her garden die. The sky was blue. The bougainvillea was flowering. Everything was exactly as it had been. Except there was no June here. Only this letter.

Cait turned off the sprinkler and went inside, where it was cool and dark with all the curtains drawn. She hesitated outside June's bedroom door, then went in. Stillness seemed to have settled like invisible dust over everything, and the air was stale. She sat on the bed and placed her hand on the soft fabric of the bedspread, and she stayed like that for several minutes, breathing in and out, staring unseeing at the bedside table. As her eyes eventually adjusted to the dimness, the objects on it came into focus. The disarray in the bottles and the toiletries, the gaps between them, bore the signs of the hasty pack-up preceding June's move into hospital. The books had remained behind. Idly, out of habit, Cait picked up the top paperback and looked at it. The Lewis biography. An unremarkable photograph. He hadn't been much to look at. A dull, daggy-looking book overall, condition fair at best, with scuffing along the paperback edges. Why had it meant so much? Cait had never been much into author biographies. But she had so vividly imagined the Inklings, the group that talked so inexhaustibly about books, thrilled to think such works had been fostered by these conversations. And she had discovered it alongside June, who had shared her delight just as Lewis and Tolkien had shared theirs. Granted, she and June had not themselves turned out any works of staggering genius as a result, but you had to have people who just read the stuff, right? And who would she share this with now? Max and

Dorothy were all well and good, but they were not June. She had battled, in recent weeks, with the feeling that no-one, no matter how well meaning, really understood.

Except, weirdly enough, Lewis himself. In one of those moments of serendipity that remained the single nicest thing about Book Fiend, someone just last week brought in an unassuming little book, plain and slender: *A Grief Observed*. Cait took it home and read Lewis's account of his reaction to the death of his wife, and here finally heard voiced what she herself could not describe, even to Seb. This horrible consciousness of not only living in grief each day, but of living each day *thinking* about living in grief each day. Well, he had explained it better … explained the absence that was like the sky, stretched over everything. And about the moments of shock, returning again and again, astonishing her with their breathtaking sharpness: June, saying, 'I've got cancer.' Annie waking her in the chair: 'Cait. June's gone.' And about the transformation of a person from a reality into a construction, pieced together from memories that would never be replenished, would only fade: loss piled on loss.

She did, however, have one new thing: this letter, this precious letter, and its instructions, which she would follow. She put the book back down, on top of the unfinished Annie Proulx novel. She took a deep breath in, and patted the bedspread once more. Then she took out her letter, and read it again.

THIRTY-SIX

Warwick Randell finished the dregs of what had been a remarkable coffee. He normally had them tall and very white, with three sugars. But he had been convinced by the barista, a skinny fellow with a massive hairdo, to try a 'long mac', which proved to be a small, dark-brown brew. He had to admit it was good. A shock to the tastebuds, but somehow a pleasant one. Sometimes a change was a good thing. He disentangled himself from the table with difficulty. His legs had been forced to almost wrap around the spindle of the tiny circular table to keep them tidy and stop the young man – barista and waiter all at once – from tripping over them as he threaded his way through this forest of pixie furniture.

But there were a lot of customers, and they seemed undeterred by the cramped accommodations, leaning their heads close over their coffees and sandwiches and biscuits, talking avidly. Two girls were taking selfies together in front of the tea trays and teapots that sat on a high shelf around the perimeter wall by way of decoration, happily oblivious to the traffic jam they were causing before the counter. He headed towards the miniature picket fence, complete with tiny gateway, that separated the cafe from the rest of the store. Before he exited, he nodded a thanks to the barista, who waved good-humouredly and continued his octopus-like operations at the till and coffee machine. Above his head hung a sign: *June's Place*. Beside it another, reading, *We don't do takeaway. Won't you slow, stop ... stay?*

The whole effect was a little too cute for his minimalist tastes, but it certainly looked as though business was booming. He passed the redhead at the bookshop counter. There was a line. She was talking soothingly to a harassed-looking dad type at the front of it. In one hand the man clutched a fat novel, its black cover featuring two white hands holding a red apple.

Randell narrowly avoided running into one of his own employees on the way out. Not wanting his reconnaissance mission sprung, he angled his body in the other direction, but he need not have worried. The young man did not appear to see him. His eyes were fixed on the counter. He had an air of purpose that somehow marked him apart from the rest of the shoppers, who seemed to be wandering in on the spur of the moment with an air of discovery. He looked as though he had already discovered what he wanted and was heading in to get it. Well, he was going to have to wait in line, by the looks.

❦

Smiling a quick apology to the customers waiting at the till for her, Cait walked the man back to the young adult section. 'She'll have read that,' she said, taking the *Twilight* off him and handing him another. 'Try *The School for Good and Evil*. It's flying off the shelves. And it's about the right age group.'

'I'm not sure I want my twelve-year-old reading about any of this stuff,' he said dubiously, scanning the blurb.

'Trust me,' Cait said. 'The horse has bolted. Just be happy she's reading.'

'OK,' said the man, looking relieved to have his problem so summarily disposed of. She brought him back to the counter and sold him the book. The next guy, trendy in jeans and pointy shoes, bought a book about square foot gardening, a term dreamed up by marketers to make gardening in small spaces sound more glamorous. It was working – Christmas and Boxing Day sales had been very strong in Gardening.

The stream of people continued, both coming from the front and from June's. Thanks in large part to Erica Bastian of the *Gazette*, the micro-cafe was proving almost too busy. They were already thinking about hiring an extra person. Cait had just turned to swig some water when she heard a voice she knew.

'Excuse me,' it said. 'I'm looking for a copy of *Getting Back the Love You Lost After You've Been a Total Arsehole.*'

The people in line, scenting drama, stilled into attention. There was a moment of silence as one Cold War Kids track ended and the player prepared the next. Cait dropped her water bottle, which hit the floor with its lid improperly screwed on and promptly began to leak onto her feet. The next track, 'Finally Begin', started to play. Her stomach churned. She didn't know whether the feeling was painful or pleasant. She did remember feeling it before, a long time ago. But on top of it was anger.

'Where have you *been*?' she asked him, trying to speak under her breath, but conscious that people were listening, though trying to look as though they were browsing. 'Look at everything that's happened.' She gestured at the shop, the crowd, the beautifully restored interior. The cavern of books shortened at the back to make room for the cafe. Half the second-hand floor space gone, including the old self-help section and its little couch for two. The place no longer smelled just of 'silverfish and ancient inkiness', but of muffins and single-origin Kenyan, and the fresh inks printed onto totes and mugs and shirts that all said *Book Fiend*. 'You can't just turn up here with a smooth line and –'

'I know. I know. Cait, I'm so sorry. I've been an arsehole, like I said. And I'm sorry to bug you at work. I knew I shouldn't. I just saw how amazing everything looked, and I was going to wait until later, but I just couldn't help myself, I've wanted to talk to you so long and – please, Cait, I want you back. I made such an awful mistake, and I'm so sorry. Will you please just meet with me after work? I could help you tidy, we could go and have a drink, talk about it.'

'June's dead,' blurted out Cait, without having intended to say that at all. Not only were her insides now doing backflips at the way he was looking at her, but pressure was building in her throat and her cheeks were burning. Maybe you'll actually explode, observed her brain, with scientific detachment.

'I know,' James said, looking at her with that heart-melting look of love and understanding. 'Sebastian told me. I rang him at the cafe and asked if he thought you would talk to me. He said he didn't know. He didn't sound too happy to hear from me, but I can understand that.' He forestalled any reaction by continuing in a rush, 'I wasn't there for you. I don't know if I'll ever regret anything more. I was jealous and stupid. It made me crazy. Please, let me be there for you now.'

Another silence. An old lady in line piped up, 'He said he'd help you tidy up. That's a winner in my book, my girl.' A ripple of amusement from those around her. Cait was jolted by the sound of the familiar endearment she had not heard since the cold hospital, months ago, on that terribly lonely night. She looked at the picture of June by the cash register. June was wearing her favourite cardigan, a robin's egg blue.

Cait had obeyed almost all of June's instructions. She had kept the Royal Albert china and the books and jettisoned everything else. Everything except one of the iceberg rosebushes from the end of the row out the front, which she had transplanted into a vast pot and taken home with her. And this cardigan, which still, months later, smelled faintly of rose hand cream. She gripped it around her now. It was a little baggy.

Ultimately, relationships are had between human beings, June had said, lying in that hospital bed. The past months had shown her June was right. Max and Seb had held her together, and the people of the city itself had rallied around her like this was one big country town, albeit one predicted to double in size, somehow, within fifteen years. Cait could not imagine what on earth that would look like, how the city would manage such rapid change. She did not know how she herself would manage. But somehow, in coming face to face with her fears, she had stared them down.

She had watched years of work almost go down the drain. She had adapted, had appeared on TV plastered in stage makeup, had worked herself crazy. She had confronted the death of the person who knew her best. She had confronted the loneliness that yawned beyond and found it only a spectre, without the power to harm her. She who had thought permanence was everything now knew she had no control and no fallbacks. But she had learned and she intended to use that knowledge. However it grew, this was her city too, and she would keep her business alive, boom time or bust, whatever change was required.

A bell rang in her mind. She remembered June's other instruction, in the letter. What was it? Choose someone strong enough to stay by her side, yet willing to change alongside her. There was a choice standing before her, with warm, beautiful hazel eyes that suddenly looked very green. She looked at James. He put out his hand and placed it on hers. It felt warm and human and rather frightening to be touched in this way, by another person, after so long.

She had found a kind of peace and this moment of touch threatened to bring it all crashing down. When James had said he was jealous, he had meant of Seb. Seb, who actually had stayed by her side every step of the way. A friend as vital as June had been, but of a different kind. She had thought James's requests for clarification unreasonable, but now she understood him as someone who chased security and permanence as desperately as she once had, though for his own reasons, and when he could not find it, could not cope, he had veered away instead. Was James saying he could change, could put up with her chaotic and uncertain life in which Seb was now more necessary than ever, yet whose role she had still not clearly articulated, even privately?

Why didn't Seb share all these fears? Seb had supported all her decisions, even as they fluctuated, even the ones that destabilised his own life. He had offered a way for them both to adapt, and had leapt into June's Place despite the huge potential consequences of failure. He was the only person who had not demanded Cait define his role in her life before she defined it for herself. Unbidden, an image swam into her mind, of the bookshelf at Number Fifty: Seb's dusty collection of obsolete technology, the old tapes and video cassettes and CDs.

'It's a reminder,' Seb had told her, in that long-ago conversation.

'Of what?'

'Impermanence.'

James flashed her a hopeful smile, that smile that had weakened her knees since the very first time she saw it. She became conscious of the water soaking into her shoes, of the song's coda beginning.

The line of waiting customers was growing behind James. Then the phone rang. Cait paused, unsure whether she should answer it or let it ring. Then she picked it up, turning away slightly towards the back of the store in the habitual movement that attempted to shield the phone, with her body, from the noise of the shop. She looked over towards the cafe to see Seb watching from behind his own cash register. Their eyes met across the crowded space.

'Hello, Book Fiend,' she said into the phone, and was about to add, 'Please hold?' when the voice on the other end continued.

'Hello, could you please check something for me? I'm looking for a copy of the diaries of C.S. Lewis. I'm not quite sure, but I think it's called –'

Images flashed, of hands held and words read before a hospital bed.

'*All My Road Before Me*,' Cait said. 'Just wait a minute. I think you might be in luck.'

AUTHOR NOTE

This story was inspired by real shops, events and possibilities, but is entirely fictional.

Book Fiend was inspired both by a dream and by elements of Perth CBD's real bookshops, which have had to move locations within the city in recent years for various reasons, though the situation described regarding Lease Freedom is completely invented.

In 2015 (not 2011) Hay Street Dymocks, Perth, announced it was closing, but in real life, they ended up finding a solution to remain open after the public's vocal dismay at the idea of its closure. The city's independent bookshops have also survived and thrived, thanks to their adaptability. This story imagines a scenario in which things went in another direction.

I also took liberties with other dates and locations. For example, it was not 2016 but 2018 that Oxford Street Books closed in Leederville, and Gucci and Prada are on King Street, not Hay.

I must stress that not all commercial landlords in Perth shopping precincts are large faceless corporations; that many leasing agents no doubt care for the city as much as anyone else; and some landlords are local people, vulnerable to the same economic pressures as their tenants, who value the city's social fabric and the role each retailer plays in it.

On p. 222, I have quoted John Updike, who said, 'We're all so curiously alone, but it's important to keep making signals through the glass,' during an interview for the 4 November 1966 edition of *Life* magazine.

ACKNOWLEDGEMENTS

Thanks to my mentor Laurie Steed, Katharine Susannah Prichard Writers' Centre's First Edition Retreat and the Four Centres Emerging Writers Program for teaching me so much at critical times.

To Alan Sheardown, owner of Crow Books in Victoria Park and New Edition Books in Fremantle, for industry insights.

To Bill Campbell, owner of Bill Campbell Books in Fremantle, for allowing his lovely shop to be used in the cover photograph.

To the Fogarty Foundation and Fremantle Press for creating the Fogarty Literary Award, and the Freo Press team: Georgia Richter, Claire Miller and the marketing squad, and my editor, Armelle Davies, who is a true marvel, and made this book fit to publish.

To readers of early drafts including Lencie Wenden and Mum; to the rest of my friends and family and my team at *WAtoday*, for their support, encouragement and assistance.

To the unsuspecting customers, booksellers, readers and social media commenters from whom I filched tales of bookshop life; truth is stranger than fiction.

Most of all, to my husband, Stu. Over the five years taken for this book to go from first draft to published novel, he has engaged with energy and generosity in countless discussions on plot, structure, character and theme, done innumerable read-throughs, consoled and bolstered me after every setback and celebrated every step forward, large and small. Thank you, my darling, from the bottom of my heart (and I hope you're ready to do it all over again).

Finally, to the readers like you, who believe writers are worth paying, and bricks-and-mortar bookshops worth supporting: bless you, for putting your money where your mouth is.

ALSO AVAILABLE

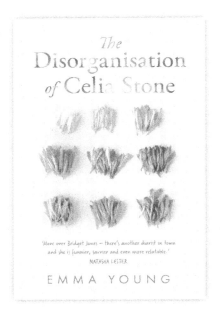

Meet Celia Stone, the ultimate hyper-organised, journal-obsessed thirty-something with a life that is perfectly planned out and running like clockwork. From her promising writing career to her devoted partner and rigorous fitness routine, Celia has it all – and she's right on track with her early retirement plan. But when her husband suggests it's time to start a family, Celia begins to question whether a new addition might just throw off-course everything she's worked so hard to achieve. Follow Celia's diary entries on a year-long journey of self-discovery as she navigates the ups and downs of trying to have it all.

FREMANTLEPRESS.COM.AU

FROM FREMANTLE PRESS

AND ALL GOOD BOOKSTORES

ALSO AVAILABLE

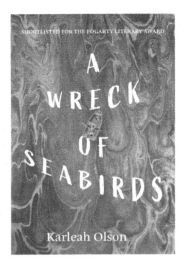

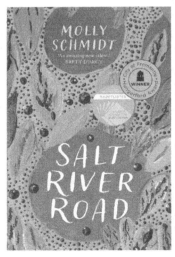

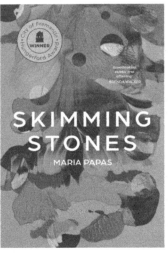

FREMANTLEPRESS.COM.AU

FROM FREMANTLE PRESS

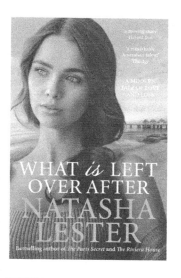

AND ALL GOOD BOOKSTORES

ALSO AVAILABLE

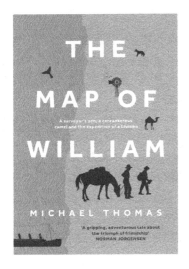

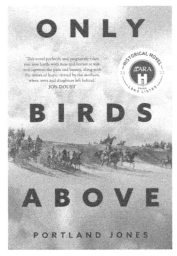

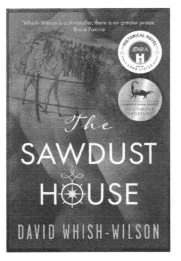

FREMANTLEPRESS.COM.AU